Joy

In A Foreign Land

How a Family Can Stay Together . . .
When Their W o r l d Is Coming Apart

by

JOAN AND RON DENLINGER

JOY IN A FOREIGN LAND

For more information on the Denlingers, visit
www.joyinaforeignland.com

Special thanks to . . .
- *Lois Lantz, a faithful encourager of this book and a praying friend.*
- *Shirley Mast, a friend who helped with editing and book distribution.*
- *Our parents, Joe and Pauline Weaver and Roy and Elverta Denlinger, who always believed in us and help in so many ways.*
- *Our Lord and Savior Jesus Christ, to whom we owe our very lives.*

Some names in this book have been changed
to protect their identity.

Scripture taken from the HOLY BIBLE, NEW INTERNATIONAL VERSION. Copyright (c) 1973, 1978, 1984 International Bible Society. Used by permission of Zondervan Bible Publishers.

Library of Congress Number: 2001099027
International Standard Book Number: 1-930353-44-8

Printed by
Masthof Press
219 Mill Road
Morgantown, PA 19543-9516

DEDICATED

TO

JEREMY RON DENLINGER

———————

MAY YOU BE ENRICHED

BY THE STORY OF YOUR FAMILY.

JEREMIAH 29:11

PROLOGUE

I am suffocating even though the air conditioner is running. Apart from that sound, the room is still. I hate the night. It's too quiet. The silence chokes me. My bedroom, which has always been a haven, is now a prison—a torture chamber.

I lie in my bed beside my son, his faint breath kissing my neck. His tiny body is hot, though his lips and nose are cool. His skin is taut; I know he is dying. My five-year-old son is dying, and what I fear most is the moment he will leave me, when this room will become a tomb.

I stare into his half-closed eyes. I can still see in them his will to survive. He wants me near him. After four days of watching him fight death, I join him in his battle. I perspire with him. My legs throb with pain. My teeth and jaw ache from the tension. My heart pounds. My breathing is heavy as I struggle for air in this stuffy room.

Ryan stiffens and cries out. "Ron," I whisper, awakening my husband who is sleeping on the floor beside the bed. He responds immediately, sees Ryan's misery and stumbles out of the room to alert our friend, Loie, a hospice nurse sleeping in the next room. They arrive back in the room a moment later looking concerned. "Please, Loie, he needs another dose of morphine," I say. She glances at the clock beside our bed and turns to leave to retrieve a suppository from the refrigerator. When she returns, I hold Ryan's weak head in my arms as she inserts the narcotic. "It's okay, baby. This will help," I whisper in his ear, trying to calm him. I wipe my hand across his sweaty brow. He tenses again, terrified. "We need more air," I plead, hearing the panic in my own voice. "Ryan and I can't breathe." Ron leaves the room and returns with a fan. I feel the cool air blow over us.

I try massaging Ryan's legs to settle him. Seeing that his mouth is dry, I creep out of bed to get his toothbrush so I can cleanse his teeth and dry, cracked tongue with cool water. Loie and Ron sit on the end of the bed waiting while I rub Vaseline on my son's delicate lips. Ryan's body stiffens and his pleading dark eyes search for me as I move out of his focus. Lying back down, I place my cheek against his and cradle him in my arms. His body finally begins to relax and I close my eyes indicating to Loie and Ron that they may go. They settle back to their places— Ron on the floor by our bed, Loie on the living room couch. I reach out and hit the play button of the tape deck, which is resting on the nightstand. The lullaby plays again and gently pushes away the silence. The morphine begins to relax Ryan and his breathing becomes less labored. My fear returns as the dark steals in to encapsulate us.

When I awaken, the morning sun is forcing its way through the Venetian blinds, casting a pattern of bars across my bed. We have been held captive in this room for the last four days, endless days that sag into endless nights. I hear someone stirring in the kitchen. The smell of coffee travels down the hall. Now that the night is over and the darkness has retreated, my body relaxes. Daylight brings with it new strength.

My brother Joe enters the room carrying our other son. My newborn smiles at me. Uncomfortable milk-filled breasts remind me it is time to nourish my son, the one who is filled with health and life. I go to the living room to nurse my baby, enjoying the ability and feeling the reward of providing life and food to a child. He gurgles and smiles at me, unaware of the anguish that has invaded our home.

Ron and Loie move about as though each motion is filled with purpose. We keep our thoughts to ourselves. The sound of a guitar strumming and a mellow voice pulls us all back to the bedroom. Joe is singing to Ryan while our daughter Kari sits quietly in the corner listening. We all gather around them. We listen. We cry. It is Sunday.

Joe completes the song and starts reading the twenty-third Psalm. The words are keys which open the doors to our well-guarded emotions, allowing them to spill out. We become vulnerable before God and each other. We pray to God to grant rest to Ryan's body and to have mercy on our son. Ron whispers in Ryan's ear, "It's okay to let go, son! Let the angels take you to Jesus."

The doorbell rings, interrupting these precious moments, causing us to scoop up our emotions and place them again in a protected place within us. Ron's parents arrive, followed shortly by my parents. The house hums with extra activity. Everyone finds some task to perform, stopping occasionally to take his turn to touch and speak to Ryan. I cradle him in my arms, with Ron holding me.

I sit on the bed propped against pillows feeling as if my body is in intense labor. A battle rages within me. I want release for my son for his sake, and yet I don't want him to go. I have given him consent to leave and be with Jesus, and yet I know by the way my body is clutching him that I am also telling him not to leave me. How can a mother ever give permission for her baby to die? No, I can't let him go on this last journey since it means going without me.

Our relatives stare in our direction as Ron holds Ryan and me on the bed. Their presence, which has been a comfort, now feels like an invasion as I realize I have only a few more moments with my son. I whisper to Ron to have everyone leave the room. He gets up and shepherds everyone from the room, closing the door behind them. This final good-bye has to be private, between our son and us. I pull Ryan close to my breast. He no longer responds to pain. His breathing is sparse. Ron prays, committing our son's spirit to God. We play the lullaby tape again. We weep bitterly, our tears falling on his scorched body.

I sense the unseen angels in our quiet room—waiting. Ryan jerks with a long, hard seizure. His eyes open, his mouth gasps for air. Then he is gone. I close his eyes and mouth, and then place his warm body in Ron's arms. He cradles him and tenderly we hug. I am numb.

I walk blindly into the living room to share with the others that Ryan has left. They weep, and then slowly, one by one, they wander back to the bedroom to see for themselves that he indeed is gone. I cover him with a blanket and kiss his cheek. The doctor is on her way to confirm the obvious. I attempt to fill my empty arms with our newborn as I nurse him. My tears will not stop flowing.

We are left to reflect on the meaning of Ryan's precious life. His was an incredibly hard journey, adding to the difficulty of our own. But we had made it—all of us, together.

CHAPTER ONE

I traveled the slippery pavement with a careful gait, my back hunched against March's cold winds. Though cautious because of my present condition, I was eager to return to our cozy apartment following my first visit to the obstetrician's office where I had heard the heartbeat of our first child.

The drab weather couldn't dampen my spirits a bit. Up to this point my pregnancy felt like symptoms of a bad virus. To finally hear the rhythmic beating coming from my slightly bulging stomach was an exhilarating confirmation that I indeed was a mother-to-be!

It was the middle of the afternoon and I still had a few hours before Ron came home from work. Tonight would be another busy evening of leading activities for the youth of our church.

I prepared a cup of steaming herbal tea, took off my wet wraps, curled up in grandmother's crocheted blanket, and settled down in my new rocking chair. The living room was my sanctuary and warm feelings overtook me as I sat rocking. Acknowledging the child within me as a gift from God, I imagined the heavenly Father wrapping His arms around me.

Ron and I adored each other—our two-and-a-half-year marriage was healthy and filled with romance. We both worked and lived in the city of Lancaster, Pennsylvania, a place we found charming and adventurous. We enjoyed strolls around town, visiting coffee shops, and participating in the special events happening in the city.

I had recently cut back my work hours at our local hospital, where I was a registered nurse in the fast-paced intensive care unit. The new schedule allowed me more time to devote to our home. Despite the smaller income, our financial condition remained strong. Ron worked as a full-time salesman. We found ourselves able to live off his income, usually depositing my paychecks into savings in preparation for my upcoming status as a stay-at-home mom.

The floor creaked beneath me as I kept rocking. I finished a mug of tea, but continued to reflect on the great life with which God had blessed me. I thought about the chair on which I was seated, a reminder to me of my thoughtful husband. He bought the rocker for me as a celebration of the positive result on the litmus paper of the home pregnancy test.

The album, playing quietly in the background, had come to the end of its last band. I stopped my rocking long enough to lift the needle off the record. As I did, I noticed a pamphlet lying on the coffee table. My happy thoughts quickly left me, replaced with a sick feeling in my stomach, my heart beginning to race. Confronting me was a photograph of an aborted baby.

We had received the pamphlet from a lady who had recently participated in the National March for Life in Washington, D.C. She spoke to our youth group the previous evening. The large group event, protesting abortion, had made such a profound impression on her that she felt compelled to share with others. Passionately, she urged us to contemplate the statistic of thirteen million babies killed in America since the 1973 Supreme Court decision that legalized abortion.

How could a mother allow that to happen to her baby? I shuddered as these thoughts besieged my mind. *What circumstances could possibly bring her to the point of making such a choice?*

God alone should have the right to take a child. That should be left in His hands! My own hands held my stomach protectively as I rocked harder. *Oh, God, don't let anything take our baby!*

Sleet began pelting the window and I pulled the afghan tightly around me. The living room felt colder. My mind drifted to the story of my mother and the birth of her first child. It took place during the days of the Korean War. I picture her hospital experience as cold, isolated, and sterile. During a snowy December day, as the rest of the world prepared to celebrate Christmas, she delivered a full-term son—born dead! They whisked him away and down a long secluded corridor, without giving Mother even a brief glimpse of him—my oldest brother.

Slipping the ghastly image under a book, pushing it out of my sight, I prayed, "Oh, God, I beg You, if this baby is sick please let him be well enough for me to hold him in my arms and care for him. But if he or she is born healthy, let me never forget *Who* blessed me with this child."

*   *   *

Ron was elated to learn the doctor's good report concerning my pregnancy and that I had heard the baby's heartbeat. My pregnancy became an exciting adventure for both of us with the increasing reality of the new life within me.

Because my brother died of spina bifida, the doctor ordered an ultrasound. The test was negative for any defects. With the first three months behind me, the likelihood of a miscarriage had decreased. Each new step gave us permission to allow our dreams to grow.

I thoroughly loved my nursing career, but the longing to be a mother was even greater. My desire for the role began early in childhood and even until the age of thirteen when I would secretly play with dolls in the attic of my parents' home. I imagined myself being a mom to a whole household of children.

I never thought I had revealed this strong maternal desire to those around me in my adult years. Apparently I had. At a baby shower given by my co-workers, I received a gift that affirmed my passion for motherhood. It was a cross-stitched wall hanging with these words: "There is no higher calling in life than raising the children God has trusted to your care." My co-workers agreed that they knew of no one for whom this saying was more appropriate. I felt honored, especially since I had not yet informed them that my full-time career was going to be in the field of motherhood. I treasured the wall hanging that day, not knowing how much pain this higher calling would later involve. Nor did I have any idea as to how much I would need this daily reminder of my commitment to motherhood.

During shopping trips, Ron and I were quick to notice other babies. As we considered our genetic make-up, we talked about what our child might look like. We imagined, at worst, a chubby little girl, face covered with freckles, bright red hair, and glasses thick as Coke bottles. We laughed as we enjoyed the prospect, but we were sure that whatever our child looked like, we would have no difficulty loving him or her.

Together we bought maternity clothes. We waded through endless lists of names. We went for long walks and bike rides to keep me in shape. We attended childbirth classes. We bought books on child raising and spent hours talking about how we might do as parents and what we desired for this baby.

Although we both had college degrees and valued our education, we believed it would be unwise to make academics the highest goal for our child. We decided that what we wanted most for our little one was that he would be a child possessing strength of character and wisdom. If our child had those things, he or she would also gain the knowledge necessary for success in life.

A few weeks before the due date, with most of the preparations complete, we awaited the big day. Along with his responsibilities as youth pastor at our church, Ron worked full-time for an office supply company. One day, while working in the back stockroom, he received a page from one of his co-workers asking him to come to the sales floor. Near the counter was a group of his coworkers encircling a former employee who had come for a visit to introduce her newborn. Although Ron rarely expressed enthusiasm over babies, he felt excitement for the opportunity to meet this infant. Fatherhood was on his mind!

What Ron did not know was that baby Latricia was born with Down syndrome. As he approached the huddle of excitement and noticed her condition, his heart sank. Latricia's mother asked Ron if he wanted to hold the baby. "Sure," he said, and took her in his arms. Inside he wanted to run from this child. At the very least he felt like saying, "No, I really don't care to have anything to do with this child, thank you!" Until that moment, it had never occurred to him that the baby he cherished inside me could also be handicapped. The thought overwhelmed him. It distressed him because he absolutely knew that he would never be able to handle having a handicapped child. That was a world in which he had no interest.

*   *   *

The sunrise on October 2, 1986, was beautifully stunning. I knew that it was going to be a wonderful day even though

I had been up all night with labor pains. It wouldn't be much longer until we would be heading back to the hospital—only one block away. The day before, I had been admitted to the hospital because my contractions were five minutes apart. I had not progressed after being there eight hours, so, wearing my hospital bracelet, they allowed me to walk home, where I could relax.

Ron had received a few hours of sleep during the night, while I spent the time pacing and crawling around the small living room, intently focused on each painful contraction. By lunchtime, I had decided I couldn't endure the pain any longer. I showered, re-packed my bags, and headed out the door. Because it was daylight, I asked Ron to take me by car. Otherwise, all our neighbors would notice me stopping to pant through my contractions, and I preferred that some surprise would be left for the announcement of the birth.

At the hospital, I experienced those things that are common to every mother who has an uneventful labor and delivery. Kari Jo Denlinger finally arrived at 8:59 p.m. and, from our point of view, the world was much better for it. She was beautiful—a mother's dream. She was perfectly pink, completely healthy, and she was all ours!

Ron took Kari in his arms, bent down and kissed me, and presented me with this very precious bundle. When the delivery room was free of hospital staff, Ron gathered his little family in his arms. He prayed, thanking the Lord for our priceless new gift and for bringing me safely through a painful childbirth. As I put Kari to my breast to attempt to nurse her, Ron called our families and friends to inform them of our wonderful news.

I sat, still shaking from the chill that had overtaken me after the intense delivery. I snuggled Kari closer to me. I wondered if life could possibly get any better than this. I reflected on a warning of our childbirth instructor: "As you leave the door of your home to go to the hospital, look back and remember that life will never be the same again when you return." I smiled and whispered to myself, "Yes, life will never be the same. It will be so much sweeter!"

Ron's Reflections . . .

When God joined Joan and me together as husband and wife, our family was established. But God didn't stop there. He allowed us the privilege of His adding to our family, of our becoming parents, fulfilling dreams that were dear to us. At the same time, God was blessing us not only with a child, but also in ways we couldn't fully appreciate at the time. He was preparing us by helping us understand important truths that would serve our family well.

Issues such as "sanctity of human life" and related topics are often seen as interesting, something to debate, a philosophical curiosity, but something to be quietly placed in the basically irrelevant compartment of "religious" belief. Though impractical and inconsequential in the thinking of many, God made it a priority for us to consider these matters carefully and to understand His perspective on them. It was helpful for the harmony in our marriage to share these beliefs with one another, but there was a more important benefit to both of us holding to these truths.

Jesus described two men who built homes—one on sand, the other on rock. Each worked equally hard. No doubt they both used good materials, but the one house collapsed when heavy rains came because the foundation, the starting place, was insufficient.

When we began our marriage, we concentrated on building a happy life together, the same kind of dream every other couple has for themselves. Though we didn't fully understand what it would take to cause that to be a reality, God was gracious in that He directed us to build on the solid foundation of truth. When we began to build, we weren't thinking about the possibility that heavy rains would come some day. We assumed that ours would be a "they lived happily ever after" kind of story. Life would not be that simple.

We've come to understand that:

A successful family
builds on the
solid foundation of truth.

CHAPTER TWO

He spoke reverently, lowering his ten-year-old voice to suggest maturity. The words of his message started off quietly, growing in intensity as he struggled to explain the main point to his captive audience. He knew criticism would come sharply if he did not finish his sermon on cue.

A hot summer breeze rustled the pages of the song leader's book as he patiently waited his turn to dominate the pulpit area. Bringing the convicting message to completion, the novice preacher hopped down from the step stool. Wiping his brow and feeling quite satisfied, he took his seat. He had delivered another fine speech to his juvenile congregation. The service ended with a carefully chosen hymn from the preacher's brother, followed by a bored sigh from a restless little sister. Her brother had coerced her into another "church service" during the long summer vacation of 1968.

Feeling a message burning within him, Ron knew it had been time to again gather his siblings on the back porch to participate in a public worship service. Whether the sensation was the Lord's conviction or from too much macaroni and cheese the night before was of little consequence. When the call came, he needed to respond.

Ron's passion to speak God's truth continued as he entered into his teen-age years. He eventually led his peers at church in Bible studies and developed an interest in church leadership. A few years out of high school, Ron sensed God leading him to enter Bible college. His minor was pastoral studies, and he assumed he would one day pastor a church. God had taken the amusement of a little boy and directed it toward an ability usable by Him.

When I met Ron, he was already in his junior year of college. My attraction to him was heightened because of his love for the Lord and his intense commitment to the Bible's teachings. He, like myself, had an interest in missions. I was in nursing school at the time and had every intention of using my medical skills in an underprivileged country following graduation. As our relationship grew, we considered the possibility that God was calling us together to do mission work outside the United States.

After his college graduation, Ron began working as the youth minister at his home church, Paradise Mennonite. A year later, following my graduation from nursing school, we were married. Along with our full-time employment, Ron and I continued to serve as youth leaders for another two years. We loved the challenge of encouraging young people to a deeper relationship with Jesus and assisting them in the change this brought to their lives. Despite this rewarding opportunity, our dream for full-time ministry continued to be a strong desire for both of us.

Two years into our marriage, various circumstances brought us in contact with an organization called Rural Home Missionary Association (RHMA). RHMA's purpose is to start new churches and to strengthen already existing churches in small-town America. It seemed as if this ministry would satisfy the combination of interests that Ron had in Bible college. Church planting would be a way to achieve the goal of being directly involved in mission work as well as having the opportunity to use his pastoral training. God was fitting together the pieces of our lives and the picture pleased us.

The summer before Kari was born, we had worked through the application process of joining RHMA. As a result, six weeks after her birth, we scheduled a week of candidate school in Illinois with this mission organization. This would give us an opportunity to closely evaluate the mission and give the board of RHMA an opportunity to interview us. At the end of the week, the personnel committee of RHMA would determine if we were approved to join their mission.

The other piece we had been exploring, in anticipation of being accepted by the mission, was the "where" question of ministry. For various reasons, we both had a strong desire to live and serve in New England. Ron bought a photo tour book of New England. We spent hours poring over it, dreaming of life in that historic and rustic part of the country.

Three months before we were parents, we took a weeklong trip to New England. On Sunday morning, we stopped in a typical eastern Connecticut town, complete with white steepled churches, rural wooded acreage, and friendly folks. We worshiped at a church that RHMA had suggested as a place of possible internship for Ron. Our vacation was everything we had hoped for and more. Again it was clear that God was guiding us.

We were looking forward to many things—anticipating all the joys of raising our daughter and seeing our dreams for ministry unfolding. Living in New England might soon be a reality for us! Filled with hope, we eagerly entered this new stage in our lives.

Our tiny city apartment fit with our ministry plans. Our choice of housing was by design. Because we had no idea where God might lead us, we wanted to stay as movable as possible.

As a result, while our friends were moving into new homes and getting established in Lancaster County, we lived in a rundown, old, smelly apartment in the city. They were driving new cars to work as we contented ourselves with our seven-year-old, brown Ford Granada. It often sat for days at a time as I walked the short distance to the hospital and Ron rode his bike five blocks to the downtown retail store. Having been satisfied for two years in our city home and part-time ministry, we were now anticipating the exciting changes that the birth of our daughter and ministry plans brought.

Kari, at only six weeks old, already grabbed the attention of others. With her dark hair and eyes, peaches-and-cream complexion, slightly upturned nose, and puckered lips, she received more than her usual share of compliments. Even men, whom I assumed never noticed newborns, would comment on how unusually cute she was. Of course it delighted us, but with each week that passed, our beautiful baby grew increasingly irritable. The attention lessened.

Kari did not nurse well. Of course, being a first-time mother, I was quick to blame myself. All the advice I received only confirmed that I was not doing something right. "You need to relax more," the lady from the Le Leche League implored me. My hospital friends encouraged me to "Have a little wine each day to calm you and Kari." I patiently listened to each suggestion, applied what I could, but continued to experience one-and-a-half-hour feedings as I struggled to nourish my daughter.

She was so irritable and was unable to relax even when I cradled her tightly to my breast. The doctor assured me that Kari was gaining weight normally. "Mrs. Denlinger, you just have one fussy baby!" So I continued spending hours each day feeding her, walking her, and swinging her. No matter how productive

I was at keeping her quiet during the day, Kari would begin her ear-piercing screams at four o'clock each evening. Nothing we tried would satisfy her.

Ron arrived home from work each night to a frazzled, uptight, frantic wife. I nearly threw our baby daughter in his arms as I headed out the door for a half-hour walk. As I enjoyed the sights and sounds of the city, my anxiety subsided but guilt settled in. *How could a mother get so frustrated with her baby?* Like a puppy with her tail between her legs, I went back home. Nearing the apartment, I heard Kari's cry, and compassion washed over me. "Oh, Kari, how could I desert you? I know you need me." I opened the door and rescued the screaming child from Ron about the time when he too was ready to storm out the door in utter frustration. Our emotions were becoming less and less synchronized.

Every evening we went about our routine: cook dinner, perform other housework, process the mail, and watch the local news. If we had any remaining time, we played a game together. Being avid game players before Kari was born, we determined to keep this common interest. Through it all, Kari screamed. By eleven o'clock she exhausted herself and would fall into a temporary sleep. Quickly we jumped into bed to get the now usual two hours of sleep before her next round of feeding and screaming began. So it continued through the night—two hours of sleep, two hours of screaming.

After six weeks of this stressful schedule, I was uneasy about our sixteen-hour trek to Illinois for our candidate school. How could I ever handle caring for this baby while attempting to impress this mission organization, let alone survive the trip? I was sure that my fussy baby and my nervousness as a mom would keep us from ever being accepted.

Driving to Illinois seemed impossible because of the amount of time it would take to stop and nurse Kari. We would need at least three days to get there! With our apartment only three blocks from the Lancaster Amtrak station, we opted to take a train. We boarded our sleeper coach early one evening, and by morning the next day we had arrived in Chicago. Kari had slept the whole way and so did we! "God, You are simply amazing!" I exclaimed as we exited the train. Ron was ready to purchase an unlimited pass aboard Amtrak—if such a thing was available. The constant swaying motion of the train was just the thing to settle our daughter.

With the trip completed, we still had a full week to conquer. I knew there would be classes to attend, people to meet, interviews to fulfill, and Kari to care for through it all. Still nervous at how we could make this happen, we entered the door of RHMA headquarters. The brightly lit outer office was furnished with a few well-worn chairs.

From behind a counter, off to the side, the secretary, Jean Miller, greeted us with a smile and a friendly welcome. Then she noticed Kari. Without delay, she came out from behind the counter and enthusiastically threw her arms around us. Snatching Kari from my arms she exclaimed, "Oh, how I love newborns! May I keep her for the week?" I was sure she was an angel from heaven. Except for feeding time and nighttime, we didn't see much of Kari that week.

Before leaving for home, we received our invitation. "Congratulations, Ron and Joan, you have been approved to join RHMA"—Kari included.

There couldn't have been two happier people returning to the Chicago train terminal that day. On the way we learned a song on the radio titled, "It's Amazing What Praising Can Do!"

It was a catchy little tune that we picked up right away and sang at the top of our lungs. We had much to celebrate. Our praise to God came naturally from our hearts.

Ron's Reflections . . .

Early in our dating days, Joan and I realized that we had a common interest in missions. That came to light one day as we sat together in the lounge of the Lancaster General Hospital School of Nursing. I had purchased two copies of My Utmost for His Highest so that we could share in devotional times together. The reading for that day led us to the topic of missionary service. It was then that I learned the reason Joan had begun to study nursing. Through the example and influence of a godly woman in her life when she was eight years old, she became convinced God wanted her to be a missionary nurse. She was now in school preparing to fulfill that call.

A few months prior to that conversation, I had attended Urbana '81, a mission conference for students. Through that event God seemed to be tugging at my heart to consider overseas ministry.

In the end, God had us join a mission organization closer to home, one that would involve more of the skills of the pastorate for which I had been preparing. As for Joan, she seemed to be quite content with the fact that it was a mission organization we were joining. Now that she was a mom, she was happy enough to put her nursing career on hold.

We were indeed thrilled to begin our new venture as career missionaries. God had taken the dreams of my childhood, mixed them with the dreams of my life partner, and allowed those dreams to be fulfilled in ways satisfying to both of us. Little did we know how much each of our preparations would be needed for God's greater work through us. Though ultimately it is God Who directs our paths, we firmly believe that, as part of the process, it is important to consider that:

A successful family
merges the dreams and abilities
of each member into a unified vision.

CHAPTER THREE

Lights twinkled in the city, holly wreaths hung from lampposts, and holiday displays decorated the department store windows. Kari was about to celebrate her first Christmas. This year we were also anticipating my brother's wedding two days after the holiday. These events gave me permission to buy a few dresses for Kari. Together we embarked on an adventure—introducing her to the world of shopping.

Downtown Lancaster's shopping district was six blocks from our home, an invigorating walk for me. The stroller wobbled on the uneven sidewalks. Kari slept, the swaying motion reminding her of a not-so-long-ago train trip.

As we passed other Christmas shoppers along the way, it thrilled me to watch them coo over my adorable, sleeping baby. I smiled at their funny faces peering into the baby carriage. Feeling refreshed and encouraged by these complete strangers, I greeted everyone with Christmas cheer.

Our friends were not always so amiable toward Kari. At two-and-one-half months of age, she had developed a reputation as the adorable-looking baby with very healthy lungs. Because of the latter feature, most knew to keep their distance. Kari was still having many irritable days, evenings filled with intense screaming, and sleepless nights.

I tried to keep our family schedule constant in the midst of this added stress. My reading before Kari's birth convinced me that it was important for couples to maintain their pre-baby routines. I agreed that I didn't want a focus on our child to dominate our home, nor did I want there to be deterioration in our marital relationship.

Because Ron and I had always faithfully attended Sunday morning and Wednesday evening services at church, I determined I would keep this priority, even with a newborn. After two months of this routine, I began to question my devotion. I spent most of the service confined to the nursery, pacing the floor, trying to calm my screaming daughter. The small attic nursery room with its slanted ceiling added to my feelings of isolation. Other mothers provided brief diversions when they would stop in to change their babies' diapers. Otherwise, it was a long time spent alone with Kari. Pictures of happy nursery rhyme characters did little to restrain my growing frustration as I waited until Ron was ready to go home.

Our drive home was quiet, with Ron behind the wheel and my hugging the door. Getting out from time to time would do both of us good—at least that's what my parenting books said. Besides, I loved my church family; seeing their faces weekly reminded me to pray for them. I hoped they were praying for me.

I did not want to give in to defeat so easily. It was too early in my new role of motherhood for that. The other young mothers were successfully maintaining their commitment to church attendance. Their babies, slightly older than Kari, were always so calm and happy. I envied these mothers with little girls who so easily suckled at their breast, whose smiles and cute expressions attracted the attention of those around them. My jealousy would end the day my daughter gurgled and smiled. Then others would want to cuddle her too. I just had to find the key to open the door to successful motherhood and a happy child.

The struggle to keep the normal schedule continued to take its toll. One morning before Christmas, I awoke after receiving only three hours of sleep that night. The house was quiet, giving evidence that Ron had already left for work. I had not been able to cook him breakfast. Kari started crying and I quickly retrieved her from her crib before she awoke the older gentleman living in the apartment above us. I changed her wet diaper and dressed her, but had no energy to change out of my own nightgown. Oh, the life of a stay-at-home mom, I sighed, as I prepared to nurse Kari.

I sat in my disheveled living room, staring at the two large windows in the wall I was facing. A bathroom addition was on the other side of the one—the shade drawn to hide the truth that the window no longer provided a view. All I could see through the other was our concrete porch, the banister and the building across the street. I rocked Kari, desperate to feed her. Again she struggled to nurse. *What's wrong with me, God? Why can't I do this natural act of nursing?*

I started to cry and Kari joined me. *Is this what they call postpartum depression?* I questioned, recalling the term from my classes in nursing school. I've never been depressed in my life! Why am I being plagued with this now? I can't give up. Maybe I'm just not trying hard enough.

In my childhood home, my parents taught us children the value of work, responsibility, and perseverance. I depended on these characteristics to guide me through nursing school since I was not a natural scholar. They also helped me succeed in my career as a registered nurse. In the past, plodding along and working a little harder was my path to achievement. Today, in spite of all my efforts, I felt I was failing miserably as a mother and wife. At twenty-three, maybe I was too young to handle motherhood.

The phone rang, interrupting my thoughts. "Hey, Joan, I have the afternoon off work. Could I come for a visit?" I recognized it as the voice of my older sister and felt some relief as I talked to her. Hanging up the phone, I headed for the shower. I couldn't let her see me like this.

During the past few years, my perspective on Judy had changed. She had become a nurturing friend and was no longer the domineering matriarch as I had viewed her in my youth. She had a happy eleven-month-old boy and seemed well adjusted to motherhood. As I stepped out of my steam bath, I felt new hope. Today I would receive some helpful advice from my sister.

She arrived with our lunch in hand, took one look at me, and instinctively responded to my situation. "Joan, you look terrible! You are going to eat lunch and then go straight to bed. I'll take care of Kari. We'll take a walk, but you need to sleep!" I had to concede. The idea of having four hours of uninterrupted sleep sounded glorious.

As I crawled between my crumpled sheets, however, I again felt defeated. Those women from my church didn't need this type of special attention. I felt like an unfit mother as I cried myself to sleep.

I awoke four hours later to a fatigued sister. "I think Kari needs you. I just can't get her to stop crying!" My sister's inability to comfort my daughter did not thrill me, but it did offer reassurance. Even my competent sister was frustrated with this precious baby.

"Thanks, Lord," I smiled as my sister went out the door. "Perhaps it's not me after all. Maybe I just have an extra fussy baby."

*　　*　　*

Christmas morning dawned. I peered out the bathroom window and looked above the city's clutter. The sky was gray with clouds. It looked as if snow was about to settle on our world. A dusting of snow would be perfect for our festivities.

With Kari still asleep, I rushed to the kitchen to take advantage of a rare opportunity. Mr. Coffee and a waffle maker were waiting for me to use them. I had received them the evening before when Ron and I exchanged gifts. I sang Christmas carols as I worked. Today I had the honor of cooking a fine breakfast for my husband.

The aroma of the coffee awakened Ron, and he made his appearance in the kitchen. We sat enjoying our delicious breakfast and the stillness of the morning. Gradually the slight odor of stale cigarette smoke filtered through the kitchen vent, alerting us that our neighbors were coming to life. Glancing at Ron I smiled. "I'm glad we won't be spending the whole day in this stinky apartment!" We planned to enjoy the day at my parents' home.

Finishing our freshly brewed coffee and blueberry waffles, we sat a moment longer, watching the Advent candle burn slowly. Taking my hand, Ron looked into my eyes and said, "Honey, I am a fortunate man! I love our family and the dreams we have for our daughter and our future. God is so gracious to us. Don't we have a great life?"

Before I had a chance to respond, Kari began to scream, ending our intimate moments. Ron offered to care for her while I cleared the dishes. Wiping the table I prayed, "Oh, gracious Father, can't we have just one day without this awful crying?" Within a few minutes Kari's crying subsided. After ten more minutes of no crying, I quietly tiptoed out of the kitchen to see if everything was okay. There was Kari, lying on her daddy's lap with a sweet look on her face. She was almost smiling. Because of Kari's extreme irritability, she had never smiled at us. Until then, that fact had never crossed my mind, and now here she was, awake and happy. I couldn't believe it. Had God heard my prayers?

The remainder of the day was a true delight. Kari's contentment continued at Grandma's house. The chatter of aunts and uncles did not disturb her. She received a top-of-the-line walker and modeled it for us. She immediately slumped forward and flopped her head onto the tray. We laughed and took pictures of our new compliant tempered baby.

Despite this delightful day, a growing suspicion was threatening to take away my joy. Was something terribly wrong with my daughter? Earlier she had smiled, but according to the growth and development charts she should have been smiling weeks ago. Also, Kari wasn't holding her head like other children her age, making her noticeably different from them.

Why am I plagued with such doubts? I reassured myself. *She received a clean bill of health at her two-month checkup.* Though questions were in my mind at the time of that appointment, the doctor confidently said that Kari was quite healthy except for her extreme colic. I tried to push the negative thoughts away. *Joan, just relax,* I reprimanded myself. *Enjoy your Christmas; Kari is fine!*

Ron's Reflections . . .

It seems naive now and idealistic to think that a couple can keep the same routines after a little one joins the family as that couple had when they were on their own. It should be obvious to just about anyone that a new baby would change many dynamics of family life, especially a baby who screams constantly. And yet Joan was determined to keep things as normal as possible while working hard to squeeze in extra time and care to comfort and pacify our very unhappy little girl.

We've seen families who become so focused on a needy child that all other priorities are pushed aside as though no one or nothing else mattered. And, by contrast, we've watched other families neglect the needs of its weakest members, viewing that member as a burden, often pushing the responsibility for their care onto others whenever possible. I'm so thankful that Joan remained determined to not fall into either trap. We loved each other. We loved our daughter. Somehow we kept holding those values tightly and closely to us, even when it became impossible for many of the old routines to stay intact.

I can't begin to adequately describe the wear and tear on the soul that results when a child cannot be consoled. God has designed a child's cry to be an irritant with good reason. It greatly motivates a parent to immediately address whatever problem or need the child is experiencing. But when the child cannot be comforted after everything is tried and the annoying screams continue, the nerves become frazzled, patience thins, the mind begins to lose its sanity.

Somehow we made it through those trying days. We did so by remembering that our daughter was precious to us. We tried to keep in mind that no matter how miserable and stressed we might be from the screaming, our daughter was even more miserable. And our hearts went out to her. We reminded ourselves that she couldn't help it—it wasn't her fault. If anything we blamed ourselves for being new parents who had not yet become competent in the role. Mostly we just plain remembered that she was our daughter, a daughter who happened to cry a lot. For all those reasons and more, we kept cranking the swing, placed her in the football hold, walked her through the night—whatever calmed her, even if only for a few minutes.

Without compromising too much the priority of meeting the needs of one another as husband and wife, we fleshed out the principle that:

A successful family
bears with the struggles
of its weakest members.

CHAPTER FOUR

Laughter erupted from my crowded kitchen. I entered the room, curious to know what was so funny this time. My relatives gathered around the kitchen table, snacking on treats, obviously enjoying their time spent in our home. Ron hollered across the room when he saw me going to the pantry to refill the dwindling food. "Hey, Joan, only two more hours till midnight. Do you have enough food to see us into the New Year?"

My grandma rocked her great-granddaughter in the living room. Kari was performing her usual evening recital. Her little legs extended beyond Grandma's firm hold and her face was beet red.

"Grandma, let me take her for you so you can eat." I knew the awkward grasp Grandma had on Kari would never soothe her, but she insisted on keeping her. I sat down on the couch, grateful for a little break from my hostessing. I closed my eyes briefly and listened to the chatter coming from the kitchen.

Grandma continued her efforts to quiet my baby, but after a few more minutes she blunted, "Something is wrong with this child!" Seeing everyone coming into the living room to investigate, I jumped up, grabbed Kari from Grandma, and escaped from the room.

In the security of my bedroom, I cradled my chubby three-month-old. "Why can't others love and accept Kari the way I do? Nothing is wrong with my baby. She just needs more time to outgrow her colic!"

With my daily routine becoming increasingly burden-some, after the New Year my mother came to our home a few afternoons a week to give me a break. She began this routine after consulting with her own doctor about her granddaughter's extreme irritability. His only advice to her was to provide me some respite.

During an icy January afternoon, Mother was still there when Ron arrived home from work. I was struggling to nurse Kari but stopped long enough to say hello. He kissed Kari and me and then picked up the evening paper. I focused my attention back on Kari. Suddenly, I noticed her eyes deviate upward in her head. "Mom," I said hesitantly, "do you think Kari can see?"

At first she said nothing, thinking through her response. Then softly she answered, "Joan, I think something does not seem right about Kari. She has no desire to look at things. Maybe you should consider getting her examined by an eye doctor."

Her honest answer cut right through my fearful emotions. "How long have you thought this Mom?" I asked protectively. Ron heard us from the next room and immediately joined our conversation. Soon all of us began sharing observations that we had made over the past two months. Kari's eyes were reactive to light, but she never looked directly at any of us nor had she smiled. She never reached for toys. She never looked at her colorful animal mobile. She never held her head up to glance at someone walking by her.

How can I be so blind to these aberrant responses? I kept my thoughts to myself as Ron and Mom continued talking. How can I deny these signs any longer? I thought I was a com-petent nurse! What is happening to me?

After Mother left, Ron took me in his arms. We cried like frightened children. The suspicion that blindness could be afflicting our daughter was devastating. How could we raise a child that could not see? What would this mean for her life? What would happen to my dreams for her? I envisioned myself picking flowers with her in the spring. I saw her stepping on the school bus on her first day—lunch bucket in hand. I had allowed myself to anticipate the day I would see my daughter bride, radiantly dressed, walking down an aisle into the arms of her husband-to-be.

My vivid dreams were crumbling before me, leaving my mind a blur. Why had I allowed myself to have such dreams? She was only three months old! Thoughts of white-tipped canes, beggars with tin cups, and Kari being sent away to a boarding school for years to learn Braille flooded my mind.

"Oh, God, this can't be true! I know Fanny Crosby and Helen Keller did great things despite their lack of sight, but this is my daughter! She doesn't deserve this! She is innocent. I'm sorry for becoming so frustrated with her screaming, but please don't punish me like this! The problem must be something other than blindness. Maybe she is very nearsighted like her father."

I quieted my inward rampage when I heard Ron's quivering voice praying, as he rocked Kari in his arms. "Lord, if it takes Kari to be blind so that others and myself may see You more clearly, then that will be okay with us."

We prepared for bed without any more conversation, both deep in our own thoughts as we lay beside each other. Hopefully time would allow us better understanding of the evening's events.

Ron didn't sleep well, in contrast to his usual ability. He tossed about, twisting the sheets around him. He wanted to accept God's plans, whatever they might be, but he found it difficult to face this ominous possibility of blindness. Suddenly, he was fully awake, sitting upright in the darkness. It had to be a nightmare, but it wasn't. This was not a dream that he could shake off. He lay back down, knowing the heaviness would remain in the morning.

Early the next day, I looked in the Yellow Pages for the name of a local ophthalmologist. I wanted to prove that our suspicions had no real foundation.

My mother accompanied me to the appointment. We waited in the office, entertaining ourselves by placing Cabbage Patch Doll glasses on Kari. I laughed as I remembered the description that Ron and I had of a little chubby girl with glasses. She looked adorable in the glasses, but I didn't think Kari would need them this early in life.

Mom and I sat quietly as the doctor did his exam. Kari looked so tiny sitting on my lap as he intently peered into her eyes. The doctor dimmed the lights and shown a spot light on a noisy toy in the corner of the room, attempting to attract Kari's visual attention. Instead, she started screaming. He turned the lights on again. "Mrs. Denlinger, I don't see anything wrong with your daughter's eyes, but I do think she is too young for a thorough exam. You could bring her back in three months or, if you would like, I will make an appointment for you at Children's Hospital of Philadelphia (CHOP) to see a pediatric ophthalmologist. They have more techniques to examine younger children."

Glancing at my mother I saw her nod, indicating that I should make an appointment at CHOP. The date was set for three weeks later. I left the office with a mixture of relief and bewilderment. Neither Kari's pediatrician nor this eye doctor seemed too concerned about her. Why did I continue to feel as if something was wrong? Was I a paranoid parent? My mother also seemed concerned. She had raised four children—surely she knew how babies react. Is that why she was pushing for further evaluation?

I saw no change in Kari during the time we waited for the CHOP appointment. I wanted her to focus on my face or toys, but she showed no interest. She only cried or slept.

Two days before our appointment, we visited Ron's parents. I closed myself in a room, needing the privacy that feeding Kari required. She sputtered and coughed on the warm milk. As I watched her, I noticed her arms rhythmically jerking. Her legs became stiff as they had many times before. Her head flexed to the left and her eyes rolled up into her head. I immediately recognized it as a seizure. "Ron, come quickly!" I yelled. Kari continued her seizure as I looked for the phone to call the pediatrician. By the time I reached him, the seizure was over, but Kari continued to cry, showing her irritation. "Mrs. Denlinger, take Kari to the emergency room immediately!" Dr. Tift directed, as we ended our brief conversation.

As we hastily stuffed Kari into her snowsuit, Ron's mother slipped a piece of paper into my hand. She mumbled that it was something she had heard that day from Dr. Warren Wiersbe, a radio Bible teacher. She hoped it would encourage us. I thanked her, shoved the note in my pocket, and kissed her good-bye.

Silently, we drove to Lancaster General Hospital (LGH). Ron concentrated on the road before him. I sat in the back seat, eyes focused on our baby girl. She was now in a deep sleep. We arrived at the emergency room (ER). As I handed Kari over to the nurse who met me, I noticed that my arms were shaking.

The doctor came to us from around a desk and requested a brief history of the evening's events. He then ordered numerous tests. Having worked in this hospital, I was accustomed to the frantic pace of the ER and acquainted with most of the staff.

As familiar as this facility should have been to me, tonight the hospital looked so different. The patient lying on that litter wasn't just any person; it was my daughter. Blood work was no longer routine when the long sharp needle jabbed my baby's soft pink skin. A CAT scan was suddenly more than a simple non-invasive test that takes only a few minutes—it was an overbearing machine swallowing my child's body.

The doctor admitted Kari to the pediatric floor. Because Kari was so young, the nurse chose a room adjacent to her station. I settled Kari into the crib. Seeing the nurses through the window brought me comfort; confidence in my own nursing skills had disappeared. I was a frightened mother, concerned for her baby.

My sister, Judy, was working at the hospital that evening. Her shift was over at 11:00 p.m. She arrived in our room a minute after the nurse had taken Kari to a treatment room across the hall to draw more blood. I rocked myself in the dark room. I appreciated my sister's presence and that she said nothing. I needed the silence so I could stay tuned to the activity across the hall.

I could hear Kari scream. After two hours the staff was still working on her. Her crying was more than I could bear. "They don't know how to calm her!" I looked at my sister with panic in my eyes. "She needs me! What is wrong? What are they doing?" I demanded.

Judy encouraged me to find out. The nurse assured me that they had finally finished the blood work. "Mrs. Denlinger, you may calm your daughter." I picked up Kari and laid her across my arm upside down. She immediately quieted, still gasping for breaths after her traumatic evening. I rocked her until she fell asleep. My sister quietly left the room.

It was 2:00 a.m. when I again laid Kari in her crib. Hours had passed since I had nursed her. I felt miserable. Though I was exhausted, I couldn't sleep.

As I pulled my sweater around me, I saw a piece of paper fall to the floor. It was the note my mother-in-law had given me. "Yard by yard, life is hard; inch by inch, life's a cinch." Salty tears filled my eyes and dripped down my face. "Oh, Lord," I whispered, "remind me not to give in to my fears of the days ahead. I want to trust You for this day. Tonight, You gave me strength and that's enough for now!"

Morning came quickly. The staff neurologist came in to report that he was not qualified to handle Kari's condition. Although all her tests were normal, he felt Kari should be evaluated more thoroughly. He highly recommended that I keep my appointment the following day at CHOP. He discharged her, but we left the hospital still wondering what mystery was hiding within our daughter. Was there a problem or not?

Ron took time off work to take Kari and me to CHOP. I had never been in a children's hospital. The thought of taking my child there frightened me, but we were hoping that finally a medical person would tell us that Kari was fine.

Children's Hospital was impressive. The atrium in the middle of the building was several stories high. A glass elevator lifted us to the third floor, where we found the office of Dr. Schaeffer, an ophthalmologist.

He carefully examined Kari's eyes and then began asking questions. Along with other answers, I told him we had just come from a hospitalization because of seizure activity. At that he immediately stood up and left the room. When he came back he said, "I can no longer evaluate Kari. She needs to be seen first by a pediatric neurologist. I made an appointment with Dr. Packer. He will see you in half an hour on the second floor."

Quietly we packed Kari in her stroller and left his office. "Why are we again being passed on to another physician? Her CAT scan was fine at our local hospital. Why does she need to see a neurologist?"

Less than thirty minutes later, Dr. Packer's secretary informed us that an aide was waiting to escort us to the electroencephalogram (EEG) lab. Although this did not seem strange to us at the time, we later discovered it is almost impossible to schedule appointments and tests such as an EEG on short notice within the same day, let alone within one-half hour of each other.

Kari looked strange attached to all the electrodes from the EEG, but after her head was wrapped in a towel, she looked as if she was just finishing her bath. She stayed awake during the test. The technician was quiet through the entire procedure. After it was completed she said, "Please deliver this report to your doctor now!" I knew that didn't sound encouraging, but I rationalized that this hospital must handle results differently than the one to which I was accustomed. Kari had not had any more visible seizure activity since the night at her grandparents' home, and she seemed less irritable over the past two days. As we returned to Dr. Packer's office, I tried to convince myself that everything was fine. "Ron, did you see Kari smile at me while she was having her EEG done?" He said nothing and continued down the hall.

Dr. Packer was a short, even-tempered, middle-aged man with dark hair and glasses. He introduced himself to us and asked us to sit down. Without examining Kari, he immediately started speaking.

"Mr. and Mrs. Denlinger, I don't want to alarm you, but I would like to admit Kari to the hospital today for further evaluation. Her EEG shows a grave seizure disorder —infantile spasms. Immediate treatment is needed and I need your consent to proceed. After further evaluation, hopefully over the next day or two, I will be able to give you more information."

My mind was numb as we walked out of his office towards the admissions office. After hearing the word "grave," I comprehended nothing else.

Ron's Reflections . . .

I know it seems rather unbelievable that on the evening of realizing that something is seriously wrong with my daughter, I would pray a prayer of acceptance. I find it a little hard to believe myself—my making a pronouncement to God that if this were His plan, it would be okay with us. Did I really understand all of what I was saying? No, I'm sure I didn't. Emotionally I was in shock and not yet fully in touch with the impact of the situation. And declaring I would accept what was unfolding didn't mean it would come easily, as evidenced by the sleeplessness and the living nightmares that followed. In part I was in denial, thinking this was not for real. And later a variety of emotions would overwhelm me—hurt, disappointment, sadness, and anger.

And yet, what I said, to the extent that I understood what was happening, I truly meant. There was a large measure of acceptance that I experienced right from the beginning. I realize that only God can be credited for that fact. And I'm quick to understand that an immediate acceptance isn't the norm, and I am not at all critical of those for whom it takes much time to come to such a place.

As I look back now I can see that God had graciously been preparing me. I had been taught the Biblical truths that He is in control, that He is all-powerful, and that He never stops loving His children. Through the testimonies of other believers, I had been impressed with the thought that God has plans for our lives, and His ways of working them out are mysterious and beyond our understanding.

But perhaps just as important as those truths is the very simple fact that I didn't know where else to turn for help. I think of Jesus and his disciples and of how on one occasion when things got a little uncomfortable and the fan club started to greatly diminish in size, Jesus turned to the faithful twelve and asked them, "You do not want to leave too, do you?"

Simon Peter answered Him, "Lord, to whom shall we go? You have the words of eternal life." (John 6:67, 68 NIV)

All that to say: I wasn't so noble. I wasn't thoroughly convinced that God would make everything turn out okay. I wasn't filled with glorious unquestioning faith. I just didn't feel like I had any other real option but to hang on to the Lord. I've since realized, at least for such a moment, that is enough. Though it may be hard to do, the only thing that works is to allow God to be the one to meet our needs.

**A successful family
holds on to God
in times of trial.**

CHAPTER FIVE

Sitting on the corner of her desk, the professor read the notes from the paper she held in her hand. Her lecture on child development and parental response seemed more appropriate for students majoring in early education.

She shifted nervously, glancing up at the thirty nursing students sitting before her. I smiled in return, feeling sympathy for this lady. It was obvious that none of my fellow students were appreciating this psychology course. I was also having a hard time conceiving how this particular class would help me in my nursing career. Most of our courses focused on the science of medicine.

"Okay, girls," the professor spoke directly to us, "for the last ten minutes of class I would like to illustrate what I spoke on today. I realize that none of you are parents, but you may come in contact with this exact situation some day in your nursing career. This could be helpful." I sat up in my seat, leaning forward on my desk. *Maybe she'll make this class relevant yet,* I thought, giving her my attention.

She continued, "Imagine yourself taking an extended vacation to a destination of your dreams, like Paris. You've worked many years, waiting for the opportunity to take this fabulous trip. The time arrives, and you begin to prepare for this anticipated adventure. With the departure date four weeks away, you visit your local travel agency to collect information about this foreign country. Paging through the brochures, you determine what places you want to visit, what foods you want to eat, what attractions you want to enjoy in this romantic city. You want to know everything about this place, so you can take full advantage of this trip.

"The day arrives and your bags are packed with all the essentials to make this trip the memory of a lifetime. You've booked a direct flight to Paris. As the airplane ascends into the clouds, you recline in your seat, anticipating the exciting days ahead.

"After the long journey, with just minor turbulence, the plane lands and you step out into your dream vacation, only to find the pilot has made a terrible mistake. He has landed the plane in the country of Iceland. Here is where the flight ends. Here is where you must spend your remaining vacation time. There is no turning back and no other flights out. This is not the land of which you dreamed. You know nothing about this part of the world, nor do you want to. In order to survive and experience any satisfaction in this foreign land, you must learn to appreciate and understand the culture or you will be trapped forever."

The story ended and I watched the professor take her seat behind her desk. "This, girls, is how a parent feels when they discover their child is handicapped. It is a whole new world they know nothing of. How can you help them? Write an essay for next week. Class dismissed."

"Joan," Ron shook my shoulder gently, "do we have a social security number for Kari?" I shuffled through the cards in my wallet then focused my attention on the lady in the admitting office. "Here it is," I said, sliding the card across her desk. Ron continued answering the lady's questions and I returned to my thoughts. *Our flight has landed*, I thought. *Our preparation and anticipation of a normal healthy child are gone!*

Ron carried Kari to a room on the third floor. Five other children and their mothers were also occupying the small room. The nurse shoved a lounge chair next to Kari's crib. "This will be your bed, Mom!" Our total space allowance was six by ten feet. A thin, striped curtain separated us from the next patient. I watched the nurse go through her admission routine and wondered if I had conveyed such a mechanical spirit when I worked as a nurse.

I pushed my feelings aside when Dr. Packer walked in. He had a team of residents with him and they began to drill me with questions. Assuming my previous nursing role, I answered as a professional. It did not take long for Dr. Packer to realize that I was trained in the medical field. He too started speaking in that lingo, leaving Ron looking puzzled.

The rest of the day, Kari went through various tests as Ron and I stood by her side, watching. It was late when Ron left the hospital, leaving Kari and me alone. The day had been a nightmare. Someone dimmed the hallway lights. Most of the children in the room were sleeping as I pulled the curtain around Kari's crib and my chair.

My motherly instincts and fears came crashing down on my numbed heart. I cradled Kari in my arms and cried quietly until no more tears came. "Lord, I've done everything during my pregnancy to protect this little child. I never even drank caffeine coffee. Why is something wrong with my child? I'm a nurse, God. I've instructed pregnant women on how to care for themselves and their child. I followed my own instructions. Why is this happening to me?"

Something was wrong with my daughter! My emotions had been anesthetized all day, but now as I discarded my charade as a nurse, the pain was intense. I had deliberately avoided my fear, all day, by focusing on the "nurse role." It was familiar and comfortable to me. I knew if I was going to survive this new and unexpected side of motherhood I needed help to face the pain head on and I needed to be real.

In the morning, I determined to follow through with my decision. I would face the reality of this situation without detaching my emotions. The doctor had started Kari on a seizure medication that sedated her so she awoke looking relaxed. Unlike other mornings, her horrible irritability and shrill scream-ing had disappeared. As I rocked her, surrounded by crying chil-dren and worn-out mothers, joy flooded my soul. She was so content! God had rewarded my attempt to accept this difficult day. I thanked Him for the peaceful change in Kari.

Later that day I experienced another joy of motherhood. The chaos of her hospital room distracted Kari too much for her to concentrate on nursing, so I offered her a bottle for the first time. The nipple was much easier to use. The doctors explained to me that Kari's sucking ability had not fully developed. For the first time, feeding her became a pleasant experience. As I cradled Kari against me, I finally felt the bonding that occurs between baby and mother that usually happens naturally to nursing mothers.

Amidst the storm that was raging around me, God granted me these few moments of peace as I watched Kari enjoy eating. Her big dark eyes blankly gazed toward the direction of my face. She did not focus on my eyes, but I knew that if she had the ability, her desire would be to discover the face that belonged to her mother. At this moment, my daughter showing pleasure in my presence was all I needed.

Later, I attempted to catch a few minutes of much-needed sleep while Kari rested in her crib. I heard a group of people walk into the room but did not open my eyes until I realized they had stopped by Kari's crib. It was another neurologist and a large group of interns. He glanced over the side of Kari's crib. He gently rubbed her legs and then lightly pinched her cheeks. "What a shame! She looks so beautiful!" Then turning his attention to me, he added, "Although externally it doesn't look like anything is wrong, her CAT scan taken last evening shows that Kari's brain is shrunken. We can't give you any hope that she will live to see her first birthday."

No one said another word. As they walked from the room, the neurologist paused briefly, rubbed my shoulder, and then he left. The room was strangely quiet. The other mothers in the room had to have overheard my news. Overwhelmed with and absorbed in their own situations, they ignored it. I was alone with my grief.

I sank into my chair stunned. The doctor had delivered a death sentence to my daughter! My first thought was to pick up Kari and run from this horrible place. I had brought my baby here for a simple eye test! They turned her condition into a terminal illness from which she could not escape. *Oh, God, what are You doing? Today I finally saw my daughter content. She is more beautiful than ever! Now You are taking her from me. Don't do this!*

I reached for the phone to call Ron. When he answered, the words stuck in my throat. At the sound of his familiar, caring voice, I began to cry uncontrollably. How could I tell him? Between sobs, I choked out the doctor's report. Ron said little, but assured me that he would leave work immediately and come to the hospital.

When I hung up the phone, I found my parents standing in the doorway. They had come for a surprise visit. From the expressions on their face, I knew they had just overheard my awful news. What a relief it was to see them and to feel their comforting arms around me. We walked out into the hallway and cried together.

It was unusual for both of my parents to be off work in the middle of the afternoon. God was not allowing me to be deserted in this place. Others were being supplied to travel this foreign land with me.

Ron's Reflections . . .

From my childhood I remember shopping in a clothing store somewhere in downtown Lancaster one Friday night. My dad was buying pants for both my brother and for me. The clerk measured us and found that Laverne and I were about the same size. If I recall correctly, the salesman made such a big deal of that fact that my dad finally explained that Laverne was two years older than I, but he had cystic fibrosis and that was why I had caught up with him in size. The man responded that he knew children who had that problem but that they outgrew it. I was overjoyed at the prospect. I desperately wanted my brother to be healthy.

As we left the store, I excitedly commented to my father about what we had heard. Maybe Laverne would get better. My dad sadly, but very firmly and directly, said that it wasn't true, that the man didn't know what he was talking about. Children don't outgrow cystic fibrosis. They will always be sick with it. My hopes were instantly dashed.

To this day I'm not sure if, at that moment, I was more upset with the man for talking about what he did not know, upset with myself for being so naïve as to believe a stranger would know something we didn't know, or with my dad for being so direct with the truth and taking away my hope.

In any case, I understand now that my father was right in his response. He said nothing to the salesman. He could see that the man's mouth was running because he found himself in an uncomfortable situation. And yet he couldn't allow me to live on some kind of false hope. It is the truth that we need. Denial of the truth is never a long-term solution to our problems.

When my brother was on his deathbed at the National Institute of Health in Bethesda, Maryland, our family was called to see him. One of my friends tried to console me, saying he was sure Laverne would get better. I probably nodded agreement to the statement, but inside I knew it wasn't true. My brother was dying. He knew it. His parents and we, his siblings, knew it.

When my brother shared the last words he had for each of us, we listened. We didn't argue with him saying, "Don't talk that way! You'll be out of here in no time." We didn't try to give him false hope. The blessing of that, even to this day, is knowing he was able to share with us from his heart. And it is knowing we stood with him at the most difficult hours of his life.

There at CHOP, when Joan decided to face the reality of the situation, of not detaching herself emotionally

*from what was happening, of taking the pain head on—
that was a key decision for which I am very proud of her.
It would have been easier to stay in the role of the professional nurse, to be absorbed in procedures, or to become
a scientist in search of the genetic culprit. Each of those
would have been a form of denial—a distraction from facing the pain. I'm glad she chose to be a wounded mom. It
made her real. It allowed her to give the love to Kari that
was needed.*

**A successful family
will face painful loss
rather than deny it.**

Chapter Six

Ron arrived at the hospital shortly after my parents left. His tie hung loosely around his neck. His red eyes told me he had been crying during his hour-and-a-half trip.

The three of us left the room to find a quiet area and privacy. Ron cradled Kari in his arms and kissed her pudgy cheeks. Her dark eyes twinkled, but her gaze focused beyond her daddy's face. I knew she did not comprehend his sorrow. Somehow her devastating prognosis was not as frightening when the three of us were together.

An hour later, a young resident walked into our room and introduced himself. "Mr. and Mrs. Denlinger, the doctor is in a meeting now, but he wanted me to inform you that he had a more experienced radiologist read your daughter's CAT scan. His interpretation of it is that it's normal for a child of Kari's age. We are sorry for this confusion. We plan to do further studies tomorrow. I hope you understand."

Understand? No, but, for the moment, that didn't matter. We were ecstatic! Kari's death sentence was lifted! We wondered how two reports could be so opposite, but we had our daughter back. She was going to live! The abnormal EEG results indicated a "grave" condition, but it was not so serious that she would die before her first birthday.

Before Ron left for home, we bowed our heads over our sleeping daughter and whispered a prayer of gratitude. I walked with Ron to the elevator, hating to see him go. "I'll call you tomorrow when I learn what the 'further studies' are about. No discovery can be worse than the incorrect report we were given today." The elevator door closed between us.

The next morning a nurse walked into the room while I was bathing Kari. "Mrs. Denlinger, you and your husband must learn how to give Kari her daily injection. Why don't we begin the instructions today?" She pulled out an orange and a syringe with a long, fat needle.

The medication that Kari received came in the form of a thick gel. It was administered by being injected deep into her leg muscle through a hypodermic needle. This steroid, ACTH, was commonly used as the first treatment of infantile spasms, the seizure disorder diagnosed on her EEG. She received the injection each morning and, although I did not like her having to go through this, the medication seemed to be working. Kari was no longer having seizures, at least none that we could see. She was much more content and eating well.

I had not been aware that ACTH was going to be continued long-term or that I was going to have to give it at home. It didn't matter. The thought of Kari being home again was incentive enough to be willing to give this injection to my daughter.

The nurse carefully demonstrated the drawing up of the practice saline into the syringe, skillfully injecting it into the orange. She then handed me the bottle, syringe, and orange. Without hesitation, I repeated the entire procedure exactly and handed them back to her. When she showed amazement at my mastering this activity after only one attempt, I felt compelled to inform her that I had been an intensive-care nurse before Kari was born. Giving an injection was second nature to me, but I was having a tough time with the thought of giving it to my own baby.

After learning that I, too, was a nurse, she walked out of the room and returned with the ACTH. "Today you are going to give Kari her injection." I sighed. Why did I tell her? The nurse held Kari firmly while I rubbed her plump thigh with alcohol and cautiously injected the thick needle deep into her muscle. Kari screamed. I cried. The nurse assured both of us that we had done a great job.

Later that morning, a team of geneticists walked into the room. They explained that they were being consulted to do "further studies." Surrounding Kari's bed, they examined every inch of her body and took measurements. With an ultraviolet light, they looked for birthmarks. They questioned me about every detail of my pregnancy and Kari's birth.

Following this thorough examination, I went to meet with the genetic counselor. I spent the next two hours answering more questions, especially about our family medical history. Our ethnic background was of particular interest. Because Ron and I were raised in a Mennonite community, the geneticist was concentrating his efforts on several conditions known among our ethnic group. The doctor seemed hopeful that he could diagnose Kari's condition and proceed with the proper treatment. She would receive the "work-up," his term for blood and urine tests, for these genetic possibilities. Ron and I also needed to have DNA testing completed. I left his office feeling drained.

When I returned to Kari, her arms were covered with Band-Aids; more blood had been drawn while I was out. She was sleeping with tears still on her face, her gown and sheets disheveled. I gently picked her up and rocked her. She woke for a few moments, but her warm body soon went limp as she nestled her head into my neck and went back to sleep.

My distressing thoughts would not allow my exhausted body to relax. The doctors seemed so excited to learn that both my husband and I were Mennonite. For the first time they were expressing hope in discovering a diagnosis for Kari. I squirmed uncomfortably in my chair. Were they blaming me for the sickness in my daughter?

I had married the wrong person. It was because of our union that this little girl had to suffer. Why did God unite Ron and me together if He knew that our child would not be healthy? I loved Ron, but now I also felt selfish. My happy marriage was the reason my daughter is suffering.

Ron appeared in the doorway. I had forgotten what time it was and had never called him. The day had been busy. Emotionally, I was a wreck. He bent down to hug me, but I resisted him. Any other time, I would have been overjoyed to see him, but horrible thoughts and questions were dominating me. I had been wrong for loving him.

He followed my cue and backed away. Instead, he handed me a newspaper and quietly said, "Joan, there is something in here for you." I opened it to the section he had marked and found a segment devoted to Valentine messages. I had forgotten it was Valentine's Day. A message highlighted in yellow read, "Joan and Kari, it's easy to see that you're both very special and perfect to me! Your husband and dad."

I closed the paper and began to cry. Ron had written that, knowing something was less than perfect with Kari. We hugged each other and shared a Valentine kiss. I knew that even if Kari's problem was genetic, Ron was right. Kari was perfect. God had not made a mistake by bringing Ron and me together. All the doubts I experienced earlier that day mysteriously vanished at that moment. This was God's perfect plan for us. He knew we would need the ample love we had for each other to provide a secure and loving home for Kari.

"Ron, today they told me Kari may have a genetic condition, and they also confirmed that she is cortically blind. She can't see, Ron, but I do believe that God created her perfect in His eyes. That is the way I always want to see her." I continued, my confidence rising, "She hasn't developed since the day she was born. I loved her then, and no diagnosis, no matter how devastating, will change my opinion of her. She needs us to stick together as a family and I know we will."

Ron's Reflections . . .

What a traumatic experience it was to have that CAT scan misread. We've told that story to many and their response is usually one of horror and anger that doctors would so callously pronounce such a sentence on our child without knowing for sure that it is true. Friends have regarded it as some kind of malpractice and expressed their feeling that doctors like that should be put in their place. I understand their sentiments. At the same time, I've thanked God over and over again for that incident. Here's why.

In a very short time we went from believing we had a normal child, to hearing our daughter's condition was quite serious. Things were spiraling downward fast. Everything kept being taken away from us. We had nothing left, at least that was what we thought.

And then came the news that Kari would not die within a year. Whatever it was she was facing was not immediately fatal. We realized that we still had Kari. Gratitude for that washed over me.

My thoughts went back to the day she was born. There in the delivery room I was asked what I've often considered to be one of the stupidest questions ever asked of me: "Would you like to hold your daughter?" Would I like to hold my daughter? What kind of question was that? Of course I wanted to hold my daughter! It was an unbelievable wonder to be able to hold a little baby and know that I was now a father!

That evening at CHOP, after receiving a brighter picture, it was as though my daughter came into my life once more. I picked her up and held her. I remembered how privileged I was to have her and to be able to love her.

That false diagnosis (with its subsequent retraction) impacted me in other ways. I realized how much I had been assuming that all would go well, that our daughter would be normal. I almost expected it in the sense that it was owed me, that one should be surprised when something goes wrong. My eyes began to be opened. The more time I spent in CHOP, the more suffering I saw. I can picture one little boy walking the halls, pulling along his IV pole. The lack of hair on his head made me realize the solution flowing into his veins was chemotherapy. The more I began to see all the things that can go wrong, the more I realized how surprised and grateful we should be when a little baby is born without any maladies.

A doctor's diagnosis changes nothing. It merely expresses what he believes the situation to be. When we were told Kari would die in less than a year, the words didn't make it so. When it was told us that she would now live, there was no sudden rush of health into her body. The diagnoses changed nothing, and yet they changed everything for me. I went from seeing nothing for which to be thankful, to being grateful. I would always need that perspective.

A successful family
focuses on
evidences of God's goodness.

CHAPTER SEVEN

I stopped and looked out the window to the street below. Yellow cabs hurried about in their pursuit of business. People rushed along the sidewalk with an obvious destination in mind on this Friday evening. I turned away and continued my stroll down the hospital corridor. *What a unique world behind these walls,* I mused. *After only five days in this place, I have already forgotten my life outside this building. I hope I'm ready to face the rest of the world.*

The doctor had just informed me that Kari could go home tomorrow. Although the results of the genetic tests would take weeks to complete, she was doing well on her new medication. He felt confident that I could continue her injection. It would be good to be home again.

Saturday morning, the nurse checked Kari's vital signs. She put the tiny blood pressure cuff on her arm and quietly listened. She repeated the procedure. By the third time, I became concerned. Turning to me, she finally spoke. "I must call the doctor. Kari's blood pressure is very high."

He arrived, studying Kari's chart, and then took the blood pressure himself. "I'm sorry, Mrs. Denlinger, but it looks like Kari has developed hypertension, a side effect of the ACTH. I need to start her on blood pressure medication right away. We need to lower that blood pressure. She'll have to stay here in the hospital a couple more days." Sadly, I looked around the room.

I wanted what was best for Kari, but having to stay in this crowded city hospital room was more than I thought I could handle.

I gave a half-hearted smile to Justin's mother who had heard the conversation. "Join the club," she calmly said to me as the doctor walked out the door. Justin had already been here three weeks. He was ten years old and severely handicapped. He was in much pain from a recent surgery and cried every time he was moved. His mom sang to him and rubbed his legs, constantly reassuring him she would not leave him alone. Although he couldn't talk or see, I observed a tender bond between the two of them. Justin always knew when his mother had left the room. He would wake up and cry until she came back. One day she told me that she had been in the hospital over twenty times with him. She knew the technique of surviving hospital life, a skill I benefited from a few times that week. Her calmness and confidence in caring for her son, despite his many needs, impressed me.

Priscilla's mother sneered as she spoke. "This is a miserable club to be part of." I smiled politely but said nothing. I had not talked with her much all week. She always seemed distant and bothered by the other children in the room. She saw Priscilla a few hours each day, but spent most of the visit on the phone, talking to her friends about how lousy the hospital was. She seemed angry much of the time and frequently expressed her frustrations to Priscilla. Her six-year-old girl had spina bifida and had just undergone her fourth surgery.

The other children in the room were also older than Kari, with various disabilities. As I looked around, a terrifying thought struck me. *Will my daughter be like these children?* Kari was still a baby who was easy to handle. She was attractive and lovable, especially now that she did not cry all the time. *What is this club they are talking about? I can't imagine Kari ever having contracted muscles like Justin. Her plump little body is normal. Why am I even thinking this way about the future?*

"Hi, honey," Ron popped his head in the door. He had spent the night in the parents' lounge, expecting to take Kari and me home today. After I told him the change in plans, he suggested we leave Kari in the care of the nurses and take a walk around the city. I had not been away from her all week.

Outside the cold air and sunshine on my face felt refreshing. We walked in silence, listening to the sounds of the city and enjoying the scent of steaming soft pretzels and greasy cheese steaks from the sidewalk vendors. Before long, my nose was frozen. We stepped inside a warm cafe to eat lunch.

At our little table, Ron brought up a subject that we had avoided for weeks. "Joan, what are we going to do about our plans to move to Connecticut?" We were only a few months away from our projected moving date. I knew much planning needed to occur before that could happen. Because RHMA was a faith mission, we church planters needed to obtain our own financial support. Our original goal was to speak at various churches in hopes of raising money for our mission work.

Kari's hospitalization had changed my focus. I was hesitant to even think about moving from the security of my present world, unsettled as it was, to a world of even more uncertainties. Living by faith financially was not something I wanted to consider at this point. Could it really be that God would still be calling us to move into church planting?

"Ron," I questioned, "why would God give us a desire for something that we may not be able to fulfill? There is such a need for missionaries and we are willing to serve. Why does it seem like He is preventing us from going?"

"I don't know, Joan," Ron answered, "but I do know that we need to trust Him one day at a time. I learned this week that our church has already pledged forty percent of our full-time support, and we haven't even given our presentation to the congregation. They are behind us, honey."

I couldn't deny the support of our church family. All week we had been receiving cards and phone calls from them, telling us that they were praying for our family. One of the church elders and his wife were coming that evening to take us out to dinner. This man had a passion for missions, and I knew he would encourage us not to give up hope.

I placed my crumpled napkin on the table and looked Ron in the eye. "I know, I'm not to worry about tomorrow, for today has enough problems of its own. Pray for me that I can trust God for today," I pleaded.

Ron took my hand and said, "Let's keep ourselves open to the possibility of God using us in missionary service."

Kari's discharge from the hospital was delightful. I couldn't wait to get home. We opened the door to a squeaky clean apartment. Groceries filled the cupboards and overflowed onto the counter. My mother, aunt, and grandmother had devoted their time and energy to making our homecoming pleasant. Oh, the little city apartment never looked and smelled so good. Home Sweet Home!

I immediately set up a mini-medical center in our kitchen. Kari came home on four medications, three of which were to counter the side effects of the steroid. I made a chart to help me remember the amount and times for each of them, and I organized the supplies for her daily injection. She also needed her blood pressure taken four times a day. Along with the normal infant care, I had to be extra careful to keep Kari's environment germ free since ACTH suppressed the immune system.

Despite our round-the-clock meticulous care, Kari was sick within days of her homecoming. The ACTH accumulating in her body was causing more negative reactions. Her appetite, which had increased in the hospital, was now decreasing to the point that I needed to work all day to feed her eight ounces of formula. She developed severe diarrhea, irritability, and insomnia. Her breathing was rapid and her temperature climbed.

After only a few minutes of examination, our pediatrician sent her to the local emergency room. Kari's admitting diagnosis was pneumonia and severe intestinal flu. While I answered the questions of the admitting physician, Ron called our pastor to have him pray for our daughter. Kari was fighting for her life, and only after four days of battle did she start to improve.

Our friends from church celebrated with us as they saw their prayers for our daughter being answered. One couple especially encouraged Ron and me. Mel and Joyce Eby were the parents of two special needs children. Their oldest son had been a part of our youth group and died when he was only sixteen. Jerry's response to life was powerful. He was a teen who was not afraid to face his impending death. He was not ashamed to voice his need for God, even among his peers. I knew Jerry only a short time, but his joy was contagious.

That day in the hospital room, the Ebys brought advice, encouragement, and hope. They informed us our parental rights to know about all the medical tests and decisions concerning Kari. There would be times when we would need to be her advocate—to express the needs of our daughter. They assured me that I shouldn't feel guilty about requesting to be present during Kari's tests.

Listening to their sound advice, I felt relieved. It wasn't that I didn't trust the experts—up to this point we had no complaints about the competency of either hospital. I just wanted to be an informed parent.

After Mel and Joyce left, we were given our first opportunity to practice advocacy. Because of Kari's difficulty swallowing, I had requested that I be the only one who feed her. Over the past few months I had become quite adept at holding her neck and head appropriately so she would not choke. The nursing staff also allowed me to give Kari her medications since they too were difficult for Kari to swallow.

A frazzled nurse entered the room. I did not recognize her as one of Kari's regular nurses. She studied Kari's care plan, then quickly took her vital signs. She did not speak to Ron or me but hurriedly went about changing the IV bag and preparing medications. Before I had a chance to interrupt, she shoved the medication down Kari's throat. By the time I reached Kari's crib, the nurse had left. Kari gagged, sputtered on the liquid draining down her bronchial tube, and then turned blue. I quickly grabbed her, turned her upside down and pounded on her back until some of the medication drained out. She again gasped for air, coughing violently. After ten more minutes, her sweaty body went limp with exhaustion.

Ron left the room to find the nurse. "Excuse me," he spoke firmly, "but you have just put my daughter in a compromising position. She has been choking for the past ten minutes because of the careless way you gave Kari her medication. I hope this does not happen again! I do not wish to have to speak with your supervisor." She mumbled an apology combined with an excuse about things being busy on the floor that evening.

The same nurse returned to the room later that evening after Ron had left. "Mrs. Denlinger, I'm sorry about what happened tonight. I never had a baby like Kari. I am new here. Will you show me how you feed her?" I was very grateful for my husband's protection of our daughter. His willingness to be the assertive one allowed me to focus on being a mom. Staying in the hospital alone left me physically and emotionally drained. I did not need the added stress of dealing with inadequate care for my daughter.

Following Kari's discharge at Lancaster General, we were to take her directly to Philadelphia's children's hospital. Overnight, the city of Lancaster had received eighteen inches of snow. When Ron left our apartment, few streets were cleared of the deep snow. He worked over an hour, shoveling and plowing his way through the alley to reach the hospital, a half-block away. Kari and I patiently waited for him, her discharge process completed. We had two hours to make our appointment at CHOP.

As I packed Kari in the car, I looked around at the mountainous snowdrifts, wondering how we were going to make it to Philadelphia in this mess. Both Ron and I had been anticipating this trip. Kari was going to have a repeat EEG to determine if the ACTH was clearing her seizure disorder. Since we weren't seeing any more seizures, we hoped for a change in her EEG. Perhaps it would show that her brain-wave pattern was returning to normal instead of the previous highly abnormal pattern that interfered with her development. We also hoped to receive a report on the genetic tests that were completed. Despite the snow, we were determined to make our appointment in Philadelphia.

After forty-five minutes of pushing our way through city streets, we reached a main highway. The traveling was slick and tedious. Every so often we had to stop so Ron could push someone out of a ditch or snow drift, allowing us to pass. I prayed while he pushed. Somehow we never got stuck.

As we approached Philadelphia, we encountered less snow. By the time we reached the city limits there were only a few inches on the ground. We reached the hospital three hours after leaving LGH and one hour late for our scheduled engagement.

Seeing our fear that we had missed our neurology appointment, the secretary quickly assured us that they too were running behind schedule. Ron slept in the waiting room and I fed Kari. After an hour, the secretary called to us. "Mr. and Mrs. Denlinger, do you mind bringing Kari back tomorrow for her EEG? Our technician lives outside the city and she said there are six inches of snow out her way."

Ron calmly walked to the desk and in an even tone explained, "We have just traveled four hours through eighteen inches of snow to bring our daughter to this hospital. Can it really be true that in a children's hospital of this size there is only one person with the ability to administer an EEG and she is stuck in only six inches of snow?" Within ten minutes Kari was being prepped for her EEG.

Upon completion of the test, Dr. Packer explained to us that Kari's EEG continued to show the devastating abnormal brain-wave pattern. He wanted to continue her ACTH therapy a little longer. The fact that she was not having seizures encouraged him. He went on to say that none of the extensive blood and urine tests, which included the genetic screens, were abnormal. He encouraged us to enroll Kari in an infant stimulation program in our local community to bolster her lagging developmental skills.

We left the hospital with new hope that maybe God was testing us. Perhaps nothing was seriously wrong with Kari. She just needed more time to develop. Keeping her on ACTH longer would cause her brain-wave pattern to return to normal we hoped. She truly could live a normal life. I clung tightly to my hopes. I focused on enrolling Kari in the best infant stimulation class possible and resolved to be diligent with her therapy at home.

Now I understood why God was taking us through this! Kari was going to be a miracle child who broke all odds. Even though born with a devastating EEG and blindness, she would overcome. She would be a shining example of how God can do anything. I had new hope and energy.

I looked over at my husband as we crept along in the snow returning to Lancaster. "Ron, let's talk again about our plans for moving to Connecticut. I think God wants us to move forward with our desire for ministry."

Ron's Reflections . . .

If we were looking for an out from missionary service, we were given the perfect excuse. But we weren't looking for an out. We had the opposite problem of wondering how in the world all the pieces of our dream could come about with these new developments.

I was hesitant to bring up the subject with Joan. I wasn't sure how she would respond. I certainly couldn't expect her to be overly enthusiastic. When we made the big decision to become missionaries, it was back when life was simple. Would she rethink the whole thing? It would have been understandable had she done so. But Joan responded in faith.

I believe that faith isn't a passive thing. Although God was providing in many ways for us, we also knew that we wouldn't get to the mission field if we didn't talk about what needed to be done, if we didn't make plans or start to implement those plans. I also understand that faith isn't guilty of manipulating circumstances. It certainly doesn't take shortcuts or compromise in any way.

If I have a choice, of course, I'd rather that things come to me than my having to go after them. I'd rather that my daughter would always get the best possible health care without our feeling as though we have to oversee the work of others. I'm not fond of those times when I need to call the complaint department in order to insist that our daughter's needs are addressed. But sometimes that is exactly what is needed. The same was true as we sought to advance the kingdom of God, to fulfill the dreams we had of serving the Lord.

**A successful family
pushes forward
to fulfill its dreams.**

CHAPTER EIGHT

Fred Martin, the pastor of Paradise Mennonite Church, was Ron's role model. Pastor Fred's enthusiasm for Jesus was contagious, motivating Ron to have the same love for ministry. The people of the church gave encouragement to Ron, graciously allowing him to serve in a broad range of ministries.

Ron led a Bible study at Paradise. Although I accompanied him to each meeting, most of the time I found myself outside the room with Kari. It was difficult trying to keep her quiet. The longer she was on ACTH, the more irritable she became. As I walked the hallway, I could still hear the discussion through the open door. As they studied the Book of Philippians, Ron highlighted the theme: "Rejoicing in the Lord in spite of circumstances."

I knew I needed to hear this truth from God's Word. My daughter's medical issues dominated each hour of my day. Kari's complex routine allowed me little time to be involved in other interests or hobbies. I was weary from lack of sleep, but the greatest threat to my happiness was my anxious thoughts of Kari's future.

Ron's messages challenged me to find joy even in the daily grind of my life. I received encouragement from my friends at the church while I was there, but I needed more. I needed a joy that came from within me, one that could sustain me throughout the week. God's Word told me that His joy was possible in the midst of my trials. This message had not yet connected with my heart. I longed for this joy to be a genuine reality in my life.

Four weeks into Ron's Bible study, Kari was again admitted to our local hospital with pneumonia. At only five months of age, her tiny lungs struggled for air as the virus raged within her. I stayed by her side, watching and praying that her life would be spared. The doctor said time would tell.

I sang to her, talked to her, and assured her that she was not alone. The croup tent covered her body with a light mist and the oxygen flowed into the plastic cave to aid her breathing. I placed my head in the tent beside hers to cry. The mist joined the tears on my face. The nurses were silent while caring for her. What is there to say when a little child suffers?

The fourth morning of Kari's hospital stay, the doctor aroused me from my vigil by her bed. Relief was written in the lines of his face. Kari had improved and was breathing easier. I called Ron with the great news and he alerted our friends and relatives.

My parents arrived at the hospital that evening and asked if they could stay with Kari so Ron and I could have dinner together. Kari continued to breathe effortlessly, so I felt at ease about leaving her. We celebrated Kari's improved health by going out for a steak dinner.

We ordered our food and sipped soda while we waited. It was good to be alone with my husband and to talk. "Ron, Sara stopped in to visit Kari yesterday. She is a good friend, but something was different this time. It was as if she didn't know what to say. Ron, I saw fear in her eyes. She could barely look at Kari. It was very awkward. I felt bad for her, so we walked down to the sunroom. We talked about her new house."

I stopped talking when the waitress brought our rolls. "Did you talk about Kari?" Ron questioned when we were alone again.

"No, not really. You know, after she left, I realized that I haven't been afraid at all this week. The fear in her eyes surprised me. It seems God is giving me the strength to handle this, but He isn't necessarily giving that strength to others. I felt like I needed to comfort her."

Our meal arrived and we focused briefly on our food. "Honey," Ron looked up from his plate and continued, "last night I was thinking about Kari and how I would give anything to have her healed. I wish it could be me instead of her. This is the toughest thing I ever faced. Our dream for ministry, our possessions, everything seemed pale in light of her struggle for life."

"Even the things we argue about seem petty," I interrupted, smiling.

"Joan, we must stick together through this. I think we can if we don't give up. I have had an incredible calmness this week that I know is from the Lord. Our strength does have to come from Him."

I finished eating and sat back in my chair. Tables filled with people surrounded us. Country western songs blared from an overhead speaker. A singer mourned his lost love. I sighed. "The problems of mankind are so varied, aren't they, Ron? But the pain is felt in the same place. I think I am experiencing this week what you have been talking about in your Bible study. God has come along beside me in my pain. He is giving me joy and a greater sense of His power." I smiled, "He is going to sustain us, Ron, no matter what happens!"

Ron laid down his fork and looked at me with his dark shining eyes. "Joan, I understand more than ever when Job said about God, 'My ears had heard of you, but now my eyes have seen you!' Jesus is revealing Himself to us."

We sat in awe in the crowded restaurant, feeling the presence of the Lord around us. The singer crooned on, but we didn't hear him. We were on holy ground. We left there, knowing that God had given us a glimpse of Himself. Would our understanding of God be strong enough to sustain us through the days ahead?

*   *   *

By late spring our family started to feel as if we were experiencing a normal schedule. On a beautiful warm Sunday morning I awoke refreshed. Kari was up only twice that night. She had completed her ACTH therapy. The roundness of her face, caused by the nasty steroid treatment, was subsiding. I dressed her in a pink frilly dress then prepared myself for church. It was a few weeks since I had been there. I looked forward to showing off my newly contented baby.

Our church had gone through a baby boom the year Kari was born. Most of the babies were girls. I entered the church nursery, sporting a "proud mama" smile. I laid Kari in the middle of the floor while I removed my coat. Immediately, her little friends surrounded her, crawling over her. It pleased me that Kari was able to be among these children without screaming. She seemed genuinely happy to be there. What progress that was for her!

I listened to the conversation of the mothers around me, waiting to share my delightful news regarding Kari's progress.

The mom by the door was speaking to another, "Krissy has been crawling non-stop. She's into everything!"

"Ashley is pulling herself up along the couch. It won't be long before she is walking," Marie replied.

From behind the changing table Joanne looked up, "Marie, do you have an idea how to cure diaper rash? I feel so sad for Beth. She is really suffering with it."

"Look here, Wanda, I want to show you Danae's recent picture. Isn't her smile adorable?" Two other women by the coat rack chatted happily. From every purse emerged a picture of an adorable child as the ladies compared baby pictures.

My heart ached to interrupt: "Kari attempted to kick her legs and made cooing sounds this week." But I was silent. It seemed so trivial when I compared it to the comments just shared. It was so obvious that Kari was different. The initial attention that our family received when Kari was first hospitalized was gone. Now I was outside their circle. As they continued to chatter on about their children's achievements, I felt invisible. It seemed I was alone in my joys and in my grief.

I left the room taking Kari with me. Did she scare them? Had I failed by not joining their conversation? I squelched the thoughts and joined Ron for the worship service.

After church I walked directly to the car and avoided stopping at the nursery. Kari wanted to eat, but that could wait until we got home. The earlier experience in the nursery still troubled me.

"Joan!" I turned toward Sandy's familiar voice. She continued talking when I smiled at her. "I want to tell you that I am happy to see you and Kari here today. How is she doing?"

Her concern brought tears to my eyes. I shared with her the news of Kari's progress. I could tell my face radiated with joy as I spoke. As we talked, she lowered her voice and stepped closer. "I'm sorry about what happened in the nursery. I saw how no one was talking to you. Joan, I think no one knew what to say. I know this sounds awful," she hesitated. "After you left, someone said that if she had a child like Kari," she paused again "she would wish she would just die!"

I stepped back, horrified. How could any mother feel that way? Kari was flesh of my flesh; she was the child God had entrusted to my care. I knew well the work and patience it took to care for her. It didn't matter; she was my daughter! I wanted the best for her like any mother would. I loved Kari! She needed my love even more because of her weakness and vulnerability.

Couldn't that mother see my joy as I cared for Kari? Could she not see my pride? Did Kari only look like a burden to live with, a huge interruption to a normal life, a waste of time and energy? "No!" I wanted to scream. Tears stung my eyes. Am I the only one who sees any value in her life? Kari was a child created in the image of God Himself! I was extremely grateful to Him for his precious gift to ME!

I hurriedly thanked Sandy for talking to me as I opened the car door to put Kari inside. Protectively, I placed her in her car seat. I wanted to escape and go to the haven of our home.

*   *   *

Our final visit to Dr. Packer's office began like all others. We anticipated facts that would provide more information about Kari's illness. Maybe the genetic tests had led to a diagnosis so we could start the appropriate treatment. In a few weeks we would be moving to Connecticut. During this visit, we hoped to receive encouraging news for the future.

The crowded neurology waiting room overflowed with children of various ages and conditions. One mother was trying to keep her year-old daughter from crawling over a nearby infant. When I struck up a conversation with her, I learned that her baby also had seizures as an infant. Now she was doing well and was just here for a routine checkup. My heart began to soar as I imagined Kari crawling in six months.

I had been researching carefully at the local medical library. I knew that infantile spasms was a seizure disorder that usually accompanied severe mental and physical disabilities, but not in every case. Girls were more likely to avoid the severe disabilities.

The nurse, interrupting my hopeful thoughts, called Kari's name. The three of us entered Dr. Packer's cozy office. He asked us questions concerning Kari's health. I answered as positively as I could. He then started to review all her recent test reports. Everything was normal. The geneticist had not been able to locate any defect but wanted to do one more urine test on Kari before we left. My excitement rose as I waited for his glorious words that everything would be fine. Then the bomb dropped.

"Mr. and Mrs. Denlinger, I've tried to prepare you for this news over the past few months. Your daughter is severely mentally and physically retarded. Since we have not been able to find any abnormal test results except for her atypical EEG, we cannot determine a diagnosis. Her lack of development indicates that her prognosis does not look hopeful." His voice was gentle but firm. "She probably will never walk, talk, sit, see, or understand more than maybe a few basic sentences. I doubt that she will even be able to crawl or hold her head up without support. Her life expectancy is about ten years. You need to start preparing for your future."

I could hear no more. His voice became distant, his head a silhouette against the blinding sunlight that was streaming through his oversized window. The room was unbearably hot. Through my fog, I heard Ron ask a question. They were discussing the name of a neurologist to whom Dr. Packer was referring Kari once we settled in Connecticut. He would transfer her records there.

Dr. Packer ushered Kari and me into a very small room to wait until she would give a urine specimen. Ron hugged me before leaving to settle a billing problem. I sat alone in total silence, shocked and furious. There were pictures, drawn by children, hanging all over the wall. I wanted to rip down every one of them.

I hated the thought that Kari would never be able to litter my refrigerator with her own special artwork. I hated seeing my daughter's blank stare, knowing she would never see any of those bright colors. She would never see my face! What was the purpose of all those grueling tests, medications, and hospitalizations over the past six months if my child was just going to be a "vegetable" all of her life? Why did the doctor raise my hopes by suggesting this one more urine test, when we all knew it would be normal like the others? Why were we waiting in this claustrophobic room? I wanted out of this hospital!

My thoughts on the drive home raced on mercilessly to me. I once had so much hope. Where was it now? I sat in the back seat with Kari, withdrawn in my own bitter world. Ron said nothing. The city traffic was heavy and noisy, and he concentrated on maneuvering the car in and out of the congested streets. In the midst of my turmoil, I heard a whisper. "My hope is in the Lord Who gave Himself for me."

Where did these words come from? They were only vaguely familiar. The words grew louder, becoming a melody that pushed away my despair. "My hope is in the Lord Who gave Himself for me!"

Was God speaking to me? Was He making His presence known to me, even in my pit of bitterness? Cringing from His gentle correction, I started to cry. "Yes, Lord, now I see what You are trying to teach me! All these months I thought I had trusted You. Now You are showing me how much I was still trusting in medication, doctors, tests, therapy, a potential diagnosis—anything except trusting in You alone."

This must be what God was trying to show me all along! My joy couldn't depend on my circumstances; it had to come from Him. My greatest hope was in Jesus Christ Himself! He was asking me to trust Him for everything in my life.

How could I not trust in Him? How dare I not depend on the One Who set the world in place? Certainly He was capable of handling my daughter's life.

No, I didn't know what the future held, but I had to believe Jesus cared for me. Because of His love, He died for me. I knew He would give me hope for the difficult days ahead. Now, could I trust God enough to show me how Kari's blindness and disabilities could benefit her life and others?

Ron's Reflections . . .

When Dr. Packer leveled with us and spelled out the condition of our daughter and her future, it was hard to take. It was almost as though we were back in his office the day he first told us that Kari's condition was "grave." In a way this day was worse because, back then, medicine hadn't yet had a chance to give its best shot. But now, after months of effort, the verdict was the same. Any hope we had in medicine and doctors had run dry.

When all the other props are gone, when others can't seem to find a way to encourage us, we are left with the realization that the answer is found in God—either that or there is no answer, no meaning or purpose in life. It is then that we are forced to face the true meaning of life. And God, in His love and mercy, is willing to bring us to this point for our own good.

As long as there is another medication to try, we don't need to trust in the Lord. As long as we see some way to put the pieces together in a meaningful fashion, then we don't have to put our hope in the Lord.

Some of our richest times were when the bottom had fallen out, and all that the world offered to us was as nothing, when even dear, caring friends had no idea how to encourage us. It was then that we realized that God was enough, even more than what we would have ever imagined. The "trick" is to remember that God is our only real hope ever, at any time. All other ground is sinking sand.

We all need hope, real hope, substantial stuff that will prove itself sufficient for the most difficult days. The question is where will we seek to find it.

A successful family
finds hope
in knowing and trusting God.

CHAPTER NINE

The warm sun's rays flooded through the large window of our little cottage in the woods, chasing away the dampness of the morning. I rocked Kari as she sucked contentedly. I loved our surroundings. After only one month, rural Connecticut felt like home.

Our house nestled among others in this munchkin village, an old Methodist summer camp meeting. It was a fascinating experience, living in this unique community on top of one of Connecticut's rolling hills. Half of the one hundred homes, including ours, had insulation for the winter. "Snowbirds" occupied the other cottages and would migrate to Florida for the winter.

Kari was the object of adoration by the senior residents of this community. Her disabilities gave them all the more reason to spoil her. During our walks around the shaded grounds, someone always stopped to talk and fuss over my now contented baby.

Kari was thriving in her new home. She was healthy and eating better. Along with controlling her seizures, her new medication also acted as a sedative. She was actually sleeping through the night! Her new adopted grandmas appreciated her calm demeanor, almost as much as her mommy did!

Ron was at church today. He served as an assistant pastor at Scotland Christian Fellowship. RHMA recommended this church to Ron. He would do intern work here before starting another church nearby.

Kari finished her bottle and I placed her in her infant seat. We were expecting a morning visitor, a physical therapist, who worked for the state of Connecticut. Nervously, I straightened the pillows on the couch. I wanted everything to be in order before she arrived. We had to make a good impression during this evaluation so we could receive the free services that Connecticut offered to special needs children.

I brushed back my hair as I heard Diane knock. Her friendly demeanor instantly put me at ease. She had beautiful dark hair and eyes. She spoke softly and wore a type of clothing and jewelry that made her appear to be of Native American descent. After we settled in the family room, Diane began asking questions about our family, focusing on Kari. Her facial expressions conveyed genuine interest in my answers. Before I knew it, an hour of conversation had passed. She then asked to hold Kari.

I watched her calmly move Kari through various exercises, making notations on a paper as she worked. How professional Diane seemed! My face reddened. I had just shared my intimate feelings and emotions with this stranger. Feelings I had never even shared with my friends. Oddly enough, she seemed to understand everything I said. My honest confessions had not offended her.

"Joan, I believe Kari is a very good candidate for our early intervention program. Today, let me explain the range of motion exercises you can do with her until our official program begins." With that, Diane showed me how to gently work Kari's muscles. Diane became my trusted guide over the next six months through the world of caring for a disabled child, a realm that often overwhelmed me. I couldn't have asked for a better teacher and friend.

*   *   *

I flung the door open to Diane's smiling face. "Good morning," she spoke cheerfully. "I think it is time we provide support for Kari so she can sit up."

Kari, at almost a year old, was very normal-looking lying in her stroller, but she continued to have no head control or back support. Out in public, people thinking she was three to six months old, would comment what a perfect "Gerber" baby I had. I enjoyed the attention she received from them and never bothered to correct their misconceptions of her. This type of impression Kari left with people was about to change.

Out of the trunk of her car, Diane pulled an odd contraption and placed it in Kari's stroller. It was ugly! The wooden padded mold had various straps and buckles and head support—all designed to hold Kari in a sitting position. She tightened the straps over Kari's shoulders, making her sit perfectly. Feeling pleased that she had provided Kari with adequate seating equipment, Diane went home.

I stood and stared in disbelief at my daughter, swallowed up by this uncomfortable looking chair. It was more than I could bear. I turned away from her in distress. I collapsed my head against the wall, crying. "Oh, God, no! This is something handicapped children use. What is my attractive daughter doing in a seat like this?"

I vowed I would never take her out in public in this hideous chair. People would no longer be able to see my Kari. They would see only this equipment that amplified her disabilities. They would turn away from her as I did. "I can't let my little girl face this rejection!" She did have some severe disabilities, but I wanted others to be able to look past them. I wanted them to focus on her strengths, not on her weaknesses. They'd never see the real Kari when she was in this horrid chair!

I remembered what Kari's new neurologist had told us a few weeks before. Dr. Russman at Newington Children's Hospital was honest with us, providing more straightforward facts about Kari's situation. He wanted to prepare us for the future. He said she would need a wheelchair. Her seizure activity will continue to be hard to control throughout her life, and her extensive care may require her being placed in an institution. Joan-the-registered-nurse calmly nodded as he spoke. Joan-the-mother heard nothing.

How could I accept such statements about a child that I loved dearly? None of the things Dr. Russman described were close to what we were experiencing, so I disregarded his advice. Didn't he see how well Kari was doing? Almost a year old, she was healthier and stronger than ever. She was improving. After months of showing her how to roll to her side through patterning exercises, Kari had done it. Naturally, Ron and I focused on the encouraging progress.

There was more good news. One Sunday evening during a church service, Kari got our full attention. A young man shared that he had left a life of drugs and alcohol when he came to know Jesus as His Savior. As he spoke, Kari started to giggle. She had never done this—even her smiles were rare. Stunned, Ron and I watched her as her whole body shook with joy. Ron could barely contain himself until the young man finished talking. He jumped from his seat and announced to the congregation that Kari was laughing for the very first time. The entire congregation burst into applause.

I sat there, holding my giggling baby, enjoying the celebration going on around us. *Dear Jesus, look at this child You have created,* I thought as the clapping subsided. *Somehow her heart understands the joy of a life set free from sin.* I pulled her close to me as other thoughts crept into my mind. *Kari will never willfully disobey You, Lord. She will never deny Your existence. She will never pay the consequences of a bad choice. She'll never be bitter, jealous, or have hatred or the selfish emotions that I struggle with. She is innocent, but needs You to save her from this world that is so corrupted by sin. God, You are protecting her mind from understanding how vile life can be. Maybe within her inner being she is more in tune to Your wisdom than I will ever be with my functioning mind. My selfishness interferes with a pure relationship with You.*

*   *   *

I awakened early, eager to begin my morning project. I gathered the supplies needed to decorate the cake I baked the evening before. Today was Kari's first birthday and nothing would interfere with our celebration. Three hours later I emerged from the kitchen, hands aching from squeezing the decorating bag, but satisfied with the iced lamb that had emerged.

The gifts lay arranged on the living room floor. Kari sat contentedly in the beanbag, waiting for attention. Her eyesight was still deficient, showing no signs of improvement in her vision over the past few months; therefore, we chose gifts for her that we hoped would capture her attention in other ways. There was a yellow record player, complete with 45s of Big Bird singing his ABCs and other wonderful songs.

Ron added wood to the fire then curled beside Kari on the floor. "Joan," he said, "do you remember how the doctor misread Kari's CAT scan and told us she wouldn't live to see her first birthday?" I nodded and he continued, "I never want to take for granted how precious her life is and that we have the opportunity to know her."

Later we packed her in her stroller and hiked through our little quiet village and down the hill to the mailbox. The dry leaves crunched under our feet as I sang to Kari. Daddy took videos of our little adventure, to record this special day for years to come.

The trip to the mailbox was rewarding. Kari received forty cards and gifts. One exceptional card from Grandma Weaver told Kari what an important role she had filled her first year of life. Grandma explained that whenever she held Kari, she felt the joy she had missed because she hadn't been able to hold her own very special firstborn child.

*   *   *

The same season of Kari's first birthday, Ron sought a location in need of a new church. Usually groundwork for a church plant involves much survey work by the church planter to locate a town that would be a potential area for such a work. God helped shortcut Ron's process through a connection with a family who were members at the Christian Fellowship Church in Scotland.

The Calderwood family had been praying for years that God would raise up a new church in their home town of

Lebanon, Connecticut. While waiting for an answer to their prayers, they attended the church in Scotland, thirteen miles from their home. It seemed God was putting together Ron's desire to be involved in church planting and the Calderwoods' vision of a new church in their town. We prayed and talked about this possibility.

Lebanon was a picture perfect New England town complete with town green, historic buildings, and cemetery stones dating to pre-Revolutionary War days. Although the community had several mainline churches, the Congregational Church in the center of town being an especially beautiful building, the timing seemed good for the planting of a new church. God was preparing Lebanon for our ministry.

The Calderwoods met weekly with us to share a meal, pray, and strategize about how this new work would begin. We also began a Bible study from the Gospel of John. Another family of six joined us in our mission. Individuals seeking fellowship also gradually became part of the group.

As we approached the fall of 1988, we realized that we had enough committed families attending the weekly Bible Study to begin Sunday morning worship services. We would hold our first morning service in September at the Lebanon Elementary School. Our dream of ministry blessed by God and the birth of the new Lebanon Bible Church was becoming reality.

Ron and I believed that it would be helpful to our ministry to become part of this town. That meant moving from our home in the camp meeting village. We would put down roots in Lebanon by purchasing land on which to build a home.

We bought a three-acre grassy field not far from the center of town. Then we began the hard work of preparing the site for the delivery of our modular home in September, the same month in which we were planning to begin formal worship services.

Ron worked diligently removing rocks from a section of the wall that beautifully marked the front boundary of our property. He developed a great appreciation for the early settlers who had probably built the wall by hand as they cleared their land to farm.

He also acted as general contractor for this building project. The excavator pushed dirt around our piece of land creating a hole in the ground. Days later concrete was poured into the forms that framed the basement walls. After it dried, the foundation was prepared for our modular home. We dug a well that produced an abundant supply of fresh water. Friends from the church in Scotland and from the developing church in Lebanon donated many hours in their areas of construction expertise.

On the eve of our proposed house delivery, we received a call from the manufacturer. They had made a mistake in scheduling so it would be a few weeks before our house could be delivered to our property. As a way of apologizing for their error, they provided us with a consolation meal at a fancy restaurant.

Our disappointment faded away as we reflected on God's goodness to us. We trusted that He had orchestrated this for a purpose only He knew. An evening of fine dining would be a wonderful reprieve from the past few months of preparations for the church and home.

Because of my physical condition, I hadn't been much help to Ron over the past few months on the land preparations. Along with a new church and a new home, I was also expecting our second child during the busy month of September.

Ron and I sat enjoying each other over the glow of a candlelight dinner. Our conversation was carefree as we talked about our new home. We laughed at a couple next to us who were trying to keep their two-year-old from destroying their dinner completely. It was fun being together without having to fuss with Kari, who was with a sitter. We acted like we were teenagers, falling in love again.

As we left the restaurant, we stopped in front of two fun-house mirrors and giggled some more as I stood in front of the "short and fat" mirror and inspected my magnified waistline. Ron weakly flexed his muscles in the "tall and skinny" mirror. We felt pity for this child soon to be born as we considered his pathetically silly parents.

We had lived in Connecticut for over a year now, and it seemed as though God had paved a successful road for us. Ron's career was progressing beautifully. The money we had saved from my nursing career became a handsome down payment on our first home, and now we were on the verge of expanding our family to welcome another member.

Kari had been in and out of Newington Children's Hospital over the past year for various illnesses and tests. After each discharge, she was a little stronger. We were more confident that soon she would be through her vulnerable baby stage and therefore requiring less medical care. During this time we also continued to have her tested for various genetic and metabolic diseases but all the results were normal.

During one of those appointments with Dr. Russman, I asked about having more children. Dr. Russman leaned back in his chair, arms behind his head. "Mrs. Denlinger," he replied confidently, "if you were my wife, I would not hesitate at all to have more children. This condition of Kari's appears to be a fluke of nature that I'm sure will not be repeated!"

This news was promising, so soon after that assurance from our neurologist, I became pregnant. Despite the long, hot summer of 1988, my pregnancy was uncomplicated. All my prenatal tests were normal and our hopes were high.

Surely God was blessing us because we had not cursed or doubted Him through our difficult trials. We felt we had passed His test of our faith. Others recognized how well we had accepted Kari's situation. Even Diane had asked us to visit parents with newborn disabled children because she was impressed with how well Ron and I managed our circumstances. We were confident that God would give us the privilege of having a healthy child.

We would raise this child to have the strong moral and spiritual characteristics that we had often talked about as being important in the training of children. Before Kari's birth, we had discussions along those lines, and now we again resumed those conversations. We talked about how easy it would be to teach this child to be sensitive to others because of his or her sister's disabilities.

Perhaps we would have a son who could follow the footsteps of his father into ministry. We could teach him the importance of defending the cause of the weak in our society. Many from our church were praying for us to have a son who would someday be strong and able to help me in caring for and lifting Kari as she got older.

If the baby were a girl, she would be compassionate, knowing how to connect with Kari as only a sister can. They could share a bedroom, clothing, and smiles. Maybe some of the dreams we had for Kari could now be fulfilled through another baby girl.

September 9, 1988, I awoke to a warm muggy morning like many mornings over the past few months. My due date was two days past. I rolled my awkward body out of bed and showered, washing away the sweat of my restless night. The cool water felt good on my aching muscles. As I dressed, I heard Ron rescuing Kari from her crib. She had been crying for someone's attention. Ron responded to her. He was a good father. He met Kari's needs with compassion and gentleness, never complaining that she had so little to give back to him. I hoped it would be soon that I could provide him with a child that he could play with, wrestle with, teach, and pass on all the admirable qualities that he himself displayed.

I said good-bye to my little family after breakfast and drove to the obstetrician's office. During my exam, the doctor stripped my membranes, a technique that often encourages an overdue labor to begin. Within the short distance of the ride back home I noticed that the procedure had been effective. The contractions soon were regular, though still very tolerable. I contained my excitement when I walked in the door, calmly telling Ron to go to work and I would call when I thought I needed to go to the hospital.

I packed Kari in her carriage and set out to walk around the hilly campground in hopes of encouraging my contractions even more. The sweat dripping off my brow and the long pauses during each contraction drew the attention of some of my neighbors. They took turns walking with me. The campground was humming with excitement. "Their" baby was soon to be born.

The snowbirds had hoped this moment would come before it was time for them to return to Florida. They desired to share in the joy of this birth. Two weeks earlier, these women had surprised me with a baby shower that included lace tablecloths, Victorian teacups, and a variety of hand-knitted baby clothing. Everyone was cheering for us.

Ron arrived home from the church around five o'clock to find me in active labor. I packed Kari's bags and delivered her to friends in the campground. Ron ate dinner while I showered and cleaned the house. Then we left for the local hospital, arriving in the emergency room about 8:00 p.m. The secretary told us to go directly to the maternity floor.

As we got off the elevator and entered the unit, we faced a dark hallway and a deserted nurse's desk. All five of the birthing rooms were vacant. I started to panic. Where was everyone? Ron found a phone and called the main lobby to inform them that no one was here to assist us. Soon a nurse and doctor burst through the door, apologizing for their absence. They flipped on the lights and the nurse busied herself by preparing me for the birth.

Dr. Larmane was a short, stocky man with a calm personality and catlike smile. He chatted with Ron about world events and offered him coffee and a sandwich. Glancing at me, the doctor saw the panic in my eyes and realized he should direct his attention to the fetal monitor and me. Everything seemed normal and according to schedule—no concern showed on his face.

Dr. Larmane believed in "natural" childbirth. The thought of providing me with some "unnatural" pain relief did not cross his mind. The only sedatives I received were his relaxed voice and Ron's reassuring face, both of which were telling me, with each contraction, that I was doing a great job. I still would have preferred a shot of Demerol!

The pain was unbearable. As the baby progressed down the birth canal face forward, it pressed its head into the nerves in my back. With this back labor I had no relief between contractions. The awkward position not only caused pain, it slowed progress. But no one seemed in a hurry since I was the only labor patient in the town of Willimantic, Connecticut, that night.

After four more grueling hours, Ryan Keith Denlinger entered the world at 12:31 a.m., September 10, 1988. Ron shouted, "I have a son," over the cry of our newborn. I was proud. I had made it through this horrible delivery and God had given us a baby boy. All felt right with our world on this special night! As Ron worked his way through the long phone list of friends and relatives, I snuggled my newborn son and reflected on God's goodness in answering our prayers.

Ron's Reflections . . .

Life seems to come to us in seasons. There are the seasons of planting, even sowing in tears. There are seasons in which we wait, wondering if anything will happen to our dreams. And then there is the season in which God seems to give us so many gifts, showering them upon us in large quantities. We experienced such a season in Connecticut. The thing to do at such a time is to enjoy it, to be happy, to sing songs of praise.

No season is pure in the sense that everything that happens is typical of the season. That was true of this period in our lives. Not every moment was a happy one. There were setbacks and disappointments. But overall it was a time of healing for us, a respite from recent, difficult months. At the same time, it is true that previous seasons of trial were not completely dark and dreary.

Even then, God gave us good gifts. There was always something for which to be thankful.

When things are going well, I'm tempted to guard my emotions, to keep myself from enjoying life, telling myself that it probably won't last, that another trial is just around the corner. With a handicapped child with a prognosis that is less than encouraging, there is reason to be cautious, to brace oneself for difficult days ahead.

While it may seem prudent to approach life that way, it isn't really a good way to live. It is based on the thought that God is out to get us, as though with each happy day He is only setting us up for disappointment. Instead, we should remember that God gives us good things to enjoy. Every good and perfect gift comes from above. He loves us. He is gracious to us.

In a fallen world, the truly happy times may seem to be rather few and far between. But when they do come, take advantage of them.

**A successful family
reflects on God's provisions
and enjoys them.**

Chapter Ten

We scurried about the large auditorium like squirrels preparing for winter. It was September 25, 1988, a beautiful crisp fall morning in New England. Our little group was preparing for our first Sunday morning service. Each of us was busy with a specific job, intent on converting the school gymnasium into a place suitable for worship.

Earlier we extended invitations to many neighbors and friends in town. For the community, we had an informational flyer inserted in the local paper. On it a picture of our family was prominent with a brief introduction of us and a description of our plans for the new church.

We wanted to reach the general population of the area with this information for two reasons. We hoped to spark interest in some who were looking for a church. We also realized that in this small New England community it would be best to be out in the open and try to head off any misinformation or suspicion about who we were and what we were doing. With these and other preparations behind us, we eagerly awaited the response.

Ed Calderwood pulled chairs from underneath the stage, unfolded them, and carefully lined them in rows. For the size of our group, the use of the stage was out of the question. Instead, we placed a small lectern on the floor before the platform. The chairs began to take the form of a semi-circle, all facing the pulpit.

In many ways, Ed was a typical New Englander, probably more so than most who lived in Connecticut. His accent, quiet way, and mannerisms revealed that his roots were from a place farther north in Vermont, one of the pure New England states. Though not very verbal, Ed was a man of spiritual conviction and a key support to my husband in this new ministry venture. He felt most comfortable quietly serving behind the scenes.

As we worked, Ed had a way of keeping the atmosphere lighthearted and cheery. He spotted anyone who was taking things too seriously and failing to enjoy this special day. At one point, I became frazzled, not being able to locate some of my teaching tools. He approached me, whispering something in my ear as though he had a thoughtful point to make. Instead, what he told me was one of his tidbits of dry humor. He stood back with a sly grin on his face, waiting for me to catch his wit. It worked. I relaxed, and back to work we went.

Off to the side Tom was busily setting up a sound system. An electronics expert, Tom focused on this contribution he was making. Dressed in a suit and tie, he appeared to be a little out of his comfort zone. I was accustomed to seeing him in one of the service uniforms he wore the other six days of the week. A perfectionist, he labored with diligence and precision. As a single dad and a young believer, Tom never lacked enthusiasm for his daughters or for the way God was at work in his life. When he saw me watching him, he stopped long enough to say, "Isn't this exciting? God is really going to do something great here today!"

Back by the entrance to our "sanctuary," the Harrises worked on setting up a literature table. Beside the guest book and neatly printed bulletins was the offering box.

Carlton, a carpenter by trade, had crafted it in the shape of a church. He decided to keep the project a secret until today and proudly presented it while we admired his work.

Our group had decided that we would not pass the traditional offering plate. We didn't want people to feel pressured to give. We reasoned that if God wanted this church to succeed, He could do it without coercion from us.

Carlton's wife Renee offered to be the church's treasurer. She was a bubbly, talkative woman with unlimited energy. The only one matching her animation was her one-year-old son. At the moment, she was chasing down young Jonathan who saw our meeting place as a huge playground. Renee was trying desperately to calm him for the service.

Paula Calderwood worked with Tom in testing out the sound system as she practiced her special music. She appeared serene, yet had her nervous smile that told me it would be good to pray for her. I went behind the large stage curtain and whispered a prayer for her and for the hour ahead.

Ron and I had arrived early so I could set up my primary Sunday School class and nurse Ryan before the others came. Now as I helped with the last-minute preparations, the teen-age girls were cooing over my handsome little newborn and fussing with Kari's thick, wavy hair. Seeing my children occupied, I stole over to Ron's side and slipped my hand in his. My squeeze was a reassuring signal that I thought he was doing a professional job of greeting the people arriving.

Some of the folks we knew from the weekly Bible Study, and we were glad to see each one. I smiled when the Dickinson family came through the set of glass double doors with their four children in tow. Each one was dressed handsomely, clothed with attitudes prepared to worship. They filled the front row.

Quietly, others that were unfamiliar arrived. They had seen the flyer and had enough of a pioneer spirit to try out this new church. Their presence added much to our excitement.

By the time the service began, forty-two people had gathered for the occasion. I gathered the children and led them in singing and a Bible story while the adults met for coffee and Bible study. Then we joined for the worship time as Ron led us and presented his well-prepared sermon. I proudly joined him at the back of the auditorium following the service to greet the people as they left. They seemed truly sincere in their compliments of the day.

This was our first experience in starting a church and the event left us with mixed emotions. Both of us had always attended well-established churches with an attendance of at least one hundred people. Because of the smallness of our new congregation, I had the odd feeling that I was a little girl "playing house." I hoped that just as those days grew into my being a real mom with real children, so one day this "playing church" would feel like a real house of worship. On our drive home that afternoon, Ron shared that the service brought back feelings similar to his back porch preaching days. At any moment, he expected to hear his little sister's bored sigh.

Our first Sunday service was an exciting adventure. I felt great joy within me as we ministered to people that day. Only occasionally did a nagging thought interrupt the celebration I experienced. I tried hard to keep the dark fear suppressed in a far corner of my mind, for my desire was to give my full attention to these precious people. The last thing I wanted was for anyone to sense a concern I had over my son—I prayed it was unfounded.

Ryan was a chubby, dark haired, dark eyed little boy. At only two weeks of age, his little round face and squinty eyes had earned him the nickname of "little China boy." Like many newborns, he attracted attention with his adorable looks, gas-induced smiles, and his cute wiggles. One of his movements, however, had frightened me since the day I brought him home from the hospital.

Mother had come from Pennsylvania when I arrived home from the hospital to assist me. She kept active with Kari and doing household chores, so I usually sat alone while nursing Ryan. During these quiet times, I noticed his one leg jerk while he suckled at my breast. Jerking movements were something I was familiar with because of Kari's severe seizure disorder. What I witnessed disturbed me. I didn't want to believe my suspicions, so I said nothing.

The last evening of my mother's visit, she was relaxing with me in our living room when Ryan awoke. In his charming newborn style, he requested his dinner. I started to nurse him; within a few minutes, Ryan's leg began to jump as it had many times before. I concentrated on feeding my son but I could sense Mom's gaze fixed on Ryan's leg. Panic rose within me. The fearful secret was bursting out. With Mom's stare burning the veil that concealed my heart, I knew I needed to address the obvious.

"Mom, do you think this kicking is normal?" I tried desperately to show no real concern. I only wanted to test her thoughts. Mom said nothing, but I knew by the expression on her face that she too was concerned. Like me, she was afraid to verbalize it. We turned our conversation elsewhere, changing the subject, hoping it would go away.

The day after Mom went home, Ryan had his one-week checkup. The nurse quickly did her routine assessment while Ryan lay quietly with a wide-eyed stare. Weight, head circumference, reflexes, skin color all were normal for his age. "Mrs. Denlinger, you have a beautiful, healthy little boy!" she said cheerfully as she washed her hands.

As she made her exit to find the doctor, I interrupted her. "Oh, just one question before you leave," I said casually. "Ryan has been displaying some occasional rhythmic movements of his left leg when I nurse him. Is this anything to be concerned about?"

"Mrs. Denlinger," she responded with a patronizing tone, "don't be paranoid. Just because Kari has seizures doesn't indicate that Ryan will. Jerking movements are very normal for a newborn. Your son looks wonderful. Relax and enjoy him!"

I still felt humiliated when Dr. Conrad came in. Evidently, the nurse told him nothing of my concerns. Neither did I.

I left the office convinced that I had been foolish for thinking such negative thoughts concerning my son's health. Even though I possessed an RN license and a mother's intuition, occasionally I lacked confidence. My life revolved around nurturing and caring for my kids, and I did not want to neglect something important.

Driving home, I thought about how fulfilled I was in my mothering role even though it allowed little time for other interests. Between Kari's disabilities and my newborn, I felt as if I had infant twins.

At home, the wall hanging carefully positioned above the changing table reminded me, "There is no higher calling in life than raising the children God entrusted to your care." I quickly changed the children's diapers and smiled. Yes, Lord, what a good feeling it is knowing I'm doing exactly what You want me to do at this time in my life. When the children are older, then I will return to my nursing career.

That evening, Ron relaxed at home with his family. He was relieved at not having other commitments, even though it was the week leading up to our first church service. He sat holding Kari while watching the news, as I nursed Ryan. Again, Ryan's leg began to jerk and my dreadful fear crept out where I could not suppress it any longer.

"Ron, could you look at Ryan for a second?" I asked cautiously during a commercial.

Ron watched Ryan intently. "What is he doing?" I quickly spilled the whole story, including the reassurance of the nurse that everything was fine. The commercials ended and we both resumed staring at the TV, but I sensed Ron's attention was no longer on the news.

"How about we just watch him for a few days?" I said when Ron flicked off the TV. I thought it best to speak first, before Ron had a chance. I knew from the expression on his face that his concerns were the same as my own. I didn't want him to verbalize them, needing to keep our emotions in check for the week ahead of us.

Ron was focused on the preparations that needed to be done for our opening Sunday as Lebanon Bible Church. I remained at home and very attentive to Ryan's activity, but I did not witness any more jerking episodes for days.

Then Wednesday night Ryan awoke at two o'clock to eat. I shuffled through the dark bedroom to his crib and sat on the rocking chair with the lights off to avoid disturbing Ron. Ryan latched on as usual and sucked vigorously. Subtly, the twitching began in his leg then suddenly his whole body shook, his head repeatedly striking my chest. He cried out, unable to control the unwelcome wrenching of his body. During brief respites, he desperately searched for my nipple but each time his face hurled into a different direction than he intended. Frustrated, he screamed until the jerking subsided. I sat sobbing as he finished his nighttime snack. The ordeal did not waken my soundly sleeping husband.

I crawled back into bed after Ryan settled in his. As I lay there, with the truth staring me in the face, my fears finally overtook me. I knew I could no longer deny that something was wrong.

Thursday morning I awoke to Ron placing Ryan beside me. Four hours had passed and he was ready to eat again. As I began to nurse, he again repeated the nighttime incident. This time it was more forceful. Ron couldn't help seeing. I called Dr. Conrad's office immediately and described the body jerking episodes to the nurse. In her most professional voice she responded, "Mrs. Denlinger, I still don't think anything is wrong with Ryan. Our schedule is full all day, but if you insist on an appointment, bring him in at the end of our hours—at eight tonight." I insisted!

In contrast to the last visit, I entered the office feeling empowered with my husband beside me. If there was anyone who wanted to deny that my son was having seizures it was I. Stronger than my denial was my love for Ryan. I knew something was not right!

On our arrival, Dr. Conrad listened to our story and then told us to sit in his office while he finished up his paperwork in another room. If Ryan did anything unusual, we were to call him.

Ryan lay awake squeezing my fingers in his tiny hands. He looked adorable in his little bear suit. After thirty minutes of waiting and our watching Ryan's every move, Dr. Conrad reappeared. He suggested I nurse Ryan, since that is when I had usually observed these episodes. Despite feeling very uncomfortable nursing my son in front of him, I followed through, determined to do whatever it took to get that skeptical look off the doctor's face.

Ryan nursed quietly as he often did. Satisfied, Dr. Conrad dismissed us and turned to leave the room. Undaunted, Ron firmly addressed his back. "Dr. Conrad, Ryan has had several episodes of rhythmic jerking. It does not look normal to us." Dr. Conrad spun around as though he heard it for the first time. "Did you say 'rhythmic' jerking?"

"Yes, Dr. Conrad, that is what we've been saying!" We again shared our story in detail.

I heard a hint of urgency in his voice as he continued. "You should contact Dr. Russman tomorrow. Better yet, let me call him and I'll get back to you as soon as I can!"

We left the office feeling somewhat rewarded that at least Ryan was getting attention, although we were unsure of what that would mean.

The phone rang at seven the next morning. "Mrs. Denlinger, this is Dr. Russman. I understand you've been having some problems with your son. Could you have him here at Newington today? I have him scheduled for an EEG."

Late Friday afternoon, Ron and I crammed into a small quiet EEG room. We waited and watched the technician connect the electrodes to our son's small head.

"Lord, are You here? Do you see what we are going through?" My mind was racing as Ryan lay sedated on the table. The technician completed her preparatory work, then she turned on the switch. Reading an EEG print out was not one of my specialties, but I could see immediately there were no hyper arrhythmic spikes that would diagnose the devastating infantile spasm disorder.

Ron searched my face for any clue what the multiple rows of scribble on the sheet of paper indicated. I gave him two thumbs up at one point and saw the stress lines in his face ease. The technician turned off the machine and informed us that it was too late in the day for the complete reading of the EEG report.

After looking briefly at the EEG script, Dr. Russman was hesitant to make any definite interpretation, though he did confirm my observation of no recorded infantile spasm spikes. He said he would see us Monday morning with the complete results.

We left the hospital relieved, but the nagging questions continued. Were we paranoid parents? What were those episodes that so clearly looked like seizures? We told no one of our trip to the hospital or the warning flags that we had seen. This weekend we needed to purposely lay aside all our fears, to focus on our first church service just two days away.

*   *   *

Two weeks passed and Ryan showed no more seizure activity. We hoped we were wrong in our evaluation of his previous episodes. We wanted life to return to a more relaxed schedule as we anticipated the winter ahead.

Ron's Reflections . . .

Shortly before we moved to Connecticut we were at a family picnic—one of those fun Weaver gatherings. It was there that we received one of our greatest encouragements for our moving out into ministry in spite of our having a handicapped child.

Uncle Dale told Joan and me how happy he was to hear that we were going forward with our plans to go out into missionary service. He shared it so emphatically that we knew he felt strongly about what he was communicating. He added that, through his work in the medical field, he had seen several families who had a child with a disability who focused all their attention and energy on that child. I don't recall what he specifically said about the consequences of that, but I remember him saying that the outcome wasn't positive. He acknowledged that it seems right to put all one's focus into a needy child, but he encouraged us not to isolate ourselves but to serve others as well as our precious daughter.

And so, there we were in Connecticut, beginning services in a new church under the shadow of something being wrong with our second child. We moved forward, not out of denial, not trying to avoid the problem. We remained concerned for our baby boy, but we tried not to allow that to paralyze us or keep us from the work to which God had called us. And God rewarded us. We found then and since that there was much wisdom in Uncle Dale's advice.

A successful family
occupies itself
with the work of serving others.

CHAPTER ELEVEN

The New England October air turned brisk. Trees were already barren and deer gleaned the harvested fields for remaining corn. The autumn celebration days ended on the town green. Men cleared the area of booths and flooded the large grassy field, creating a skating rink for the cold winter months.

I also was eager for a new season. Kari and Ryan were both healthy, and I desired to integrate them into our ministry work. Ron and I made plans to make pastoral visits and neighborhood contacts, and Kari and Ryan traveled with us. The church people adored them, and our neighbors opened their doors to us willingly when they saw Ron and me, each laden with a baby.

I never worried about receiving help with my children when we met for our church services. Even when hosting meals, I became very efficient in handing off Kari and Ryan to our guests while I prepared dinner. I enjoyed teaching our friends how to feed Kari and they in return felt honored to help her. Ryan's chubby grins were attention getting, and it was never a problem finding someone to feed and rock him.

Our dream of ministry was unfolding and I felt rewarded. The insecurity that I had felt about leaving my hospital job to become a full-time mother and missionary no longer troubled me. Helping my husband succeed in his career and working along side him fulfilled me. Ron and I made an effective team as we ministered, counseled, and worked through many issues concerning church planting. We were discovering the strengths and weaknesses of our different personalities and were using them to benefit our work.

The common struggle of overcoming daily life with a handicapped daughter was deepening our appreciation of one another, instead of pulling us apart—what we often observed among other marriages in families with disabled children. It appeared more common for a family to be torn apart because of the added stress of the child's care than to be strengthened. We hoped this wouldn't be true of us some day. After all, right now we had much to be looking forward to—helping a new healthy church grow and raising our son.

We lay in bed one Sunday evening following another busy day. Ron held me gently, my face against his muscular chest. The children were sleeping for the night. "You know, Joan?" Ron reflected. "I think Ryan's life is much like mine. Soon after my brother Laverne was diagnosed with cystic fibrosis (CF), the doctor told my parents that he thought I had it also. Only after numerous CF tests were negative did they finally conclude that I was okay. That was a difficult time for my parents. Now I wonder if we are going through that same experience." I leaned back into my pillow and thought about what he said. Certainly he was right.

Even after weeks of no seizures, we both had continued nagging doubts about Ryan's health. Could this be God's way of testing our character—checking to see if we would trust Him? Ryan will be just fine!

I sat up in bed and impulsively started to tickle Ron. "Oh, no! This kid is going to be just like you, honey!" I laughed, eyes twinkling with mischief. "My job will be to keep him from getting too stuffy! Ryan needs just a little bit of his mom's fun-loving personality."

I laid down again and let my mind drift to Ron's state-ment as he picked up a book to read. Was this a test of God? Even more significant, was I passing the test? I hoped so.

Despite the nagging fears, outwardly I still displayed a very happy, warm appearance. I was always ready for a good party and to be in on the latest joke. Our new friends at the church quickly discovered that I was an easy target to tease and I loved it. In this sense, I was a typical youngest sibling. Although during my childhood my brothers and sister and I rarely fought, I, as the youngest, did get my share of being tormented, but I loved their attention. Now too as an adult, I still enjoyed being the brunt of many jokes.

Ron, on the other hand, provided me with a view of the more sane and serious side of life. He was always philosophiz-ing about anything from the meaning of life to why people act the way they do. With my sense of humor, I kept him from get-ting too buried in an introspective thoughtful world. He taught me to be sensitive and responsive to the pain in the people around us, even those who hid it well. We complemented each other well, and I realized our different traits were a huge advantage toward providing a healthy home for our children.

Ryan would need to know that joy and laughter can coin-cide with the suffering that his sister daily displayed. Our hope was that Ryan would grow up having a tender heart towards those who are underdogs in this world and experience the happiness that trusting God can bring even in troubling circumstances.

That week I had finished reading the book *Power of the Powerless* by Christopher deVinck. Raised in a home with a sibling much like Kari, Mr. DeVinck beautifully describes the value of his brother's life. The book inspired me as I reflected on the ways this wordless, helpless brother affected Christopher's life. The author himself displayed wonderful Christ-like character as he allowed this very weak sibling to teach him wisdom for life—wisdom that is almost impossible to learn except through suffering. I desired that kind of insight for Ryan.

Ron and I drifted off to sleep on a pillow of peace. God was with us and had His best in store for us.

A few minutes later a loud cry from Kari wakened me. I lowered her crib rail just in time to see her dispose her evening bottle all over the sheets. She was burning with fever and struggling to breathe. The coziness of my sentimental dreams ended with the reality of the night growing cold around me.

Kari had another upper respiratory virus complete with croup, fever, and an upset stomach. The remainder of the night, I sat in the bathroom with Kari, shower running, trying to humidify and loosen her constricted bronchial tubes. Ron came in at 6:00 a.m. to relieve me so I could go pacify our screaming, starving infant. Groping my way to Ryan's room, I picked him up and he quieted to my touch. He knew breakfast was on its way.

As I started to nurse, Ryan's leg began to twitch like a cat's tail. Soon the jerking was so hard he could not suck. He was victim to this uncontrollable force. His head thrashed into my chest. I hugged his convulsing body and cried out for Ron to come. He witnessed the distressing scene and immediately left to call Dr. Russman. The neurologist asked us to bring Ryan right away to the children's hospital—an hour's drive from our home.

"Ron, do you mind taking him?" I asked wearily. "I really need to get some rest. Maybe he just has the flu like Kari, and fever induced his seizure." As they drove off, I envisioned Dr. Russman examining Ryan. Maybe he would do a blood test or two, ask a few questions of Ron, and send them on their way with a diagnosis of influenza. Exhausted from being awake all night, Kari slept soundly in her crib, so I crawled into my own bed, feeling somewhat guilty that we had to disturb a pediatric neurologist for a simple thing like a cold.

The phone must have rung several times before waking me. Ron sounded a bit annoyed that it took me so long to answer it. His voice was urgent, "Joan, Ryan is being admitted. Come right away! I'll explain everything when you get here!"

Click. The dial tone droned on. Was this a bad dream? Did I hear him correctly? What did he want me to do? My body started shivering as the fog started to clear. I placed the phone back on the nightstand and ran to check on Kari. She was sleeping peacefully. With Ron and Ryan gone, the house was quiet.

Ryan's been admitted? My legs felt like Jell-O beneath me, and my body shook as I tried to pull on my clothing. I collapsed in bed, tempted to release all my panic in a puddle of tears. *No, Joan, pull yourself together. Ryan needs you!* I forced my mind to focus on my task ahead and my body to move into action.

I grabbed the phone again and dialed a familiar number. "Hello, Wallis'," the feminine voice sang into my ear.

"Hi, Sylvia, this is Joan. Hey, Ron needed to take Ryan to Newington and he has been admitted. Could you drive me over there?" Sylvia had become my best friend since living in Connecticut. She was warm, compassionate, and always available when I needed her. Sylvia and her daughter arrived within fifteen minutes.

Our drive to Hartford was quiet. The remaining dry autumn leaves carelessly danced upon the highway as we hurried toward the hospital. The sun, high in the sky, warmed the four of us as our little girls slept in the back seat snug in their car seats.

My mind was numb except for a small voice that started out as a whisper. "Find rest, O my soul, in God alone. My hope comes from Him!" I recognized it as a well-memorized Bible verse that I had clung to during the early days of Kari's illness.

Flashes of that experience in Children's Hospital of Philadelphia flooded my mind. "No, God! This can't be happening again!" I started to cry. Sylvia, with a merciful touch, reached over and held my hand and wept along. The more my tears flowed, the more insistent the whisper became. "Find rest, O my soul."

We arrived at the hospital and searched for Ryan's room. We found it across from the nurses' desk. Before I entered the room I glanced at the nametag by the door. My heart froze within me. *No, that's wrong! It's Kari that is always in the hospital, not my beautiful son!*

I entered the room and saw Ryan resting in a metal en-closed crib with a nurse hovering over him. Before I had a chance to absorb the rest of my surroundings, Ron greeted me and started reporting on the morning's events.

Ryan had another jerking episode in front of Dr. Russman and the nurse was now preparing him for a three-hour video EEG monitoring test. Sylvia hugged us both and offered to keep Kari as long as I needed, then quietly left the room with the girls.

The orderly arrived to transport Ryan to the Neurology lab where they would begin the EEG. I nursed Ryan while they continued to monitor him on video. He looked like something from a science fiction movie with the electrode wires protruding from his head. Ryan had many seizures during the test; there-fore, they followed the EEG with a CAT scan of his brain. Before allowing Ryan to rest, the doctor drew five vials of blood from his tiny veins.

That evening, Ryan lay exhausted from the day's events. Still under the effects of the sedative given for the CAT scan, he hadn't awakened for his evening feed. Hungry, tired, and uncomfortable from my not nursing him, I stood by his bedside watching his tiny chest rise and fall as he slept.

The only light permeating the room was from the fading sunset. Ron had gone home. The crib next to Ryan's was unoccupied and the nurses were busy with other patients. I was grateful to be alone. As I collapsed in the chair, a sensation overcame me—the feeling of despair. I knew I should resist, but I had no desire to fight its determined grip on my heart.

"No, God, I cannot handle another handicapped child." I felt a heavy cloud closing in on me.

"Please get me out of here. I don't want anyone telling me anything else bad about my child!" The room darkened as the sun slipped below the horizon.

"God, is there no one else for You to harass?" The demon Bitterness was winning. It clenched its ugly fingers around my neck.

"Haven't I praised You enough during my daughter's afflictions? Have I not satisfied You?"

My heart pounded and I struggled to breathe.

"Why do You torture me in this way? Why are You taking it out on my children?"

I sobbed angrily into my pillow, determined to win this ugly battle, resolved to prove my point before the Almighty. The blackness moved in and the cloud was now suffocating me. In desperation I cried out, "God, I'm so sorry. I'm so scared. I can't push You away. I need You now more than ever, even though I don't understand. I can't do this on my own. Give me Your strength!"

Silently the cloud of depression slipped away. Fresh air filled my lungs as I inhaled deep long breaths. The room seemed larger when I opened my eyes, and feelings of relief overcame me, comforting my distressed spirit.

"Find rest, O my soul, in God alone. My hope comes from Him." I whispered it silently into the darkness to chase away any lingering forces of evil desiring to defeat me.

*   *   *

I spent the next five days at Ryan's bedside while more tests were completed: a spinal tap, eye examination, magnetic resonance imaging of his brain, and numerous blood tests. The doctor started Ryan on Phenobarbital for the seizure activity.

Before leaving town on Friday, Dr. Russman discharged Ryan, but we needed to wait until the following Monday for the results of his tests. Patience—a virtue needed, we were learning, when dealing with undiagnosed symptoms.

The weekend was upon us, which meant preparing for another busy Sunday. Still afraid to let anyone know that our son was having seizures, we went through the entire Sunday without sharing our hospital experience with anyone.

Ron's message that morning was on perseverance. He also asked me to sing the little song we had learned so long ago, "It's Amazing What Praising Can Do!" Our duet was harmonious, but our hearts were heavy. We realized that even as we led in worship, God was teaching us much more than we could ever share with others.

After the weekend, we met with Dr. Russman to receive the results of Ryan's five-day hospital stay. I was hopeful as our family entered the doctor's office. Over the weekend, the Phenobarbital had done its job of eliminating Ryan's seizures, and he acted and looked like a normal infant again. He smiled more than Kari ever did at that age, his neck and trunk muscles were firm, and he nursed well with only occasional irritability.

"Ron and Joan, have a seat!" He addressed us as though we were close friends. We certainly had been through much with him over the past year. He continued in a very nervous, dry voice, his gaze avoiding direct contact with us. "I want to be straight with you. One of Ryan's blood tests was a bit elevated. It's called lactic acid. I do believe it could be related to a genetic, metabolic condition. What I'm saying is, I believe the seizures you are witnessing in Ryan is a disorder that is a forerunner to the infantile spasms in your daughter. I believe Ryan and Kari are afflicted with a similar condition." He leaned forward in his chair and quietly continued, "I'm sorry."

He mumbled more about both children requiring further testing. Ron and I both nodded our heads without saying anything or showing any emotion. The conversation ended and I slipped from the room while Ron gathered the children.

Alone in the corridor, I collapsed against the wall in tears, the doctor's words penetrating my suffering heart. I whispered into the cold hard wall, "Not my son! This can't be true!"

Ron approached me from behind to comfort me. I pushed away his embrace and spoke directly, "I want to leave this place now! I hate this hospital." My thoughts continued as we hastily walked towards the main door. I hated Dr. Russman. I hated blood tests and EEGs. I hated seizures. I hated what God was allowing! He was betraying me. Our drive home remained silent as I allowed my hatred to rise within me. My tears had stopped.

Entering the house, I mechanically went about the routine of caring for my children without words or emotion. I avoided Ron; consequently, he left. The children were content in their distant worlds, so I was able to desert them downstairs and close myself in behind my bedroom door.

I threw myself into my bed, burying my head in the pillow. After sobbing for some time, I felt my heart melting and my spirit opening to the acceptance of whatever lay ahead for my children and me. As I rose from the bed, I looked in the bedroom mirror. A weak, pitiful woman stared back at me.

"God, I'm sorry! I know I'm so frail, but I just don't understand. I know You are in charge here. Forgive me for my hatred. Thank You for the children You have blessed me with, but I desperately need You to help me get through the rest of today!"

I went downstairs and prepared Kari's dinner. Ron came through the kitchen door a few hours later. His face was sad and his shoulders were slumped. He did not respond to me and went to pick up Kari who was crying. "I'm sorry, honey, for pushing you away," I said as he brushed past me. "I know we need each other right now."

He hugged me without saying anything. I knew I had hurt him deeply by closing my spirit to him. He needed me and I, him, even more if we were going to hold our lives together despite this devastating news about our children. We prepared Kari and Ryan for bed in silence.

When I had shut Ron out earlier, he had gone to our friends from church. Visiting the Calderwoods, he poured out our story to them. After the kids were sleeping, late into the evening, one by one, our church friends appeared at our door with food, hugs, tears, and even laughter to encourage us. At midnight my mother and my brother and his family arrived for a visit. God provided me with the arms that I needed to get through that day and night.

Ron's Reflections . . .

We've always been part of a Christian community. We've never been alone in that regard. God consistently surrounded us with care through the love of others. Time and again there has been someone available to listen when we've needed to talk. When Joan needed a ride to the hospital that day, Sylvia dropped everything else and made herself available.

We can't really comprehend what it must be like to be completely and chronically alone. The only feelings along those lines come when we refuse the comfort of God and others, when we choose to give in to the bitterness of our experience and shut out everything else.

Why we didn't inform our church of Ryan's hospitalization, I don't know. I suspect it was because we wanted to hang on to the hope that it was all a bad dream. If people were to be informed, then they would put their arms around us. If they extended sympathy to us, then the tragedy would feel all too real. We weren't quite ready for that.

A long time ago we realized that no one fully knows the pain of another person. Sometimes others don't have a clue. The folks of Lebanon Bible Church couldn't see that behind our praises were broken hearts. But after we revealed it to them, they were there for us.

"What should the church be doing to help families with a disabled child?" We've been asked the question on different occasions. Sometimes it seems that behind the query is the assumption the church is consistently inadequate. That hasn't been our experience, at least not when we've pushed aside the curtain hiding our pain. At those times the response has consistently been good. If anything, we've probably been too slow in letting others know how they can help. We tend to focus on the truth that "each one should carry his own load," and we should. But we're not always as good at remembering that when our load becomes too heavy we are to "carry each other's burdens."

"Find rest, O my soul, in God alone. My hope comes from Him." It is true that we find our needs met in God alone. At the same time, God uses dear people to deliver His provisions to us.

A successful family
accepts the help and comfort of others
as part of God's provision in times of need.

Chapter Twelve

"Silent Night" drifted softly from the lips of the angels surrounding the manger as the baby Jesus lay quietly in the hay. Ryan played the part earnestly as if he understood the role of the Holy child—a perfect, sinless baby who came from Heaven for the salvation of mankind. Would Ryan ever grasp the significance of this Holy Celebration? I shifted in my seat as the Christmas pageant continued on the stage of our church auditorium. Kari, disguised in a woolly sheep outfit, traveled in her stroller, escorted by a lowly shepherd toward the place where Jesus lay. I watched them proudly, feeling honored that the people of our new church granted positions for my children in the first Christmas pageant of Lebanon Bible Church.

Three months after the birth of the new church, this successful event was a reward for the energy Ron had poured into this new work. The desire not to fail in this ministry venture and the commitment to serve God faithfully drove Ron to devote endless hours to this task. This also allowed him little time to focus on our situation at home—life with two severely disabled children.

I, on the other hand, absorbed myself in the responsibility of caring for Ryan and Kari. It was an exhausting job, but my love for them and my desire to understand all I could about the care of raising handicapped children motivated me each day. Conquering this new world was important for my survival as their mother.

It took considerable physical and emotional energy for me to endure endless hours of children crying, maintain feeding and medication schedules, and implement therapy programs while receiving a maximum of three hours of sleep at night. This schedule blinded me from seeing needs beyond the care of my children, especially those of my husband. I was hesitant to have too much of an interest in the new church work, because I feared it would become a deterrent to my focus at home.

One week before the contractors delivered our modular home to our well-prepared foundation, I suggested to Ron that perhaps we should have the house directed to Pennsylvania instead, and then move back there. Instinctively I knew that I couldn't continue the round-the-clock care of Kari and Ryan without help of extended family.

Ron accepted the comment like dynamite receiving a spark. "Joan, you must be kidding! Are you crazy? Do you have no understanding of the work I have done on our land or my dream to pastor a church?" My cheeks reddened and I vowed never again to speak about the issue. I was ashamed to have even considered giving in to defeat, being too willing to let go of our dreams. The decision I made that day to recoil rather than confront the stress of our lives initiated the building of a wall within our marriage bond.

*   *   *

Kari started attending an infant stimulation class three mornings a week shortly after Ryan's birth. Frequently I would also attend to learn the exercises the therapists instituted with Kari. I loved the times spent in the busy classroom, and I enjoyed learning to know the teachers who loved and cared for my daughter. They were not awkward around Kari or afraid to involve themselves in her life. With her thick dark hair, dark eyes, pleasant smile and attitude, Kari attracted the staff. Acceptance and love were abundant in that room and I felt at home there.

Even though Kari's progress seemed very minimal, we all worked hard to bring her to her optimal level of functioning. Beginning with head control, then hands-to-face coordination, to body rolling, cup sipping, eye acuity, and weight bearing, everyone resolved that this two-year-old was going to complete their state required goals before she moved on to a preschool level. I worked right along beside them, surrounding myself with these people and the families of Kari's classmates, because we were in the same world, facing similar struggles. We related to each other automatically.

My surroundings at church, among neighbors, friends, and relatives, were threatening. It was difficult to face the reality of normal development in healthy children.

The world around me focused on moving ahead at lightning speed—raising kids to their full potential and encouraging them to be as good as their peers, if not better. School systems encouraged children to be active and involved members of society. Parents searched for the best training philosophies and education for their children. Even within the church, there were advocates pushing for more education, involvement, and recognition of our children, so that they would succeed and not look like strangers in our post-Christianized world. The minuscule accomplishments of my daughter were tiny steps when compared to the fast pace of our society. Kari was squeezed out of participation in a system designed for "successful" children.

I felt jealous of other parents whose children measured up to the world's standards. Parents who didn't appreciate the abilities of their healthy children angered me, and others who talked incessantly of their child's accomplishments intimidated me. I flip-flopped between feeling like a failure for not having a child that was succeeding and then bouncing to another extreme— a state of anger and determination. I wanted this world to accept my daughter, yet I knew they would only if she succeeded. So I threw myself all the more into her world. I had to draw her out and find her potential! During this process, I lost God's perspective and my joy.

I enrolled Ryan, at three months of age, in an infant stimulation program. I had more hope for his development, because he didn't have the devastating infantile spasms that continued to bombard Kari's brain. Because of his young age, a therapist named Amy came to our home to work with Ryan.

Amy was a dedicated, loving person who fell in love with Ryan and our family. Ryan was always alert and ready for Amy's attention, but he set the boundaries. When she pushed those limits, he fought back, determined to control his environment. She loved his feisty attitude and became a good match for him. She nicknamed him "Handsome" and treated him as His Royal Highness. Kari with her mellow do-whatever-you-want attitude received the nickname "Princess." I don't believe Amy remembered their given names as these pet names overruled. Amy received my full attention because she was my guide through this foreign land that had captured me.

Ron was rarely a part of the children's therapy lessons, and I did very little to communicate to him what I was learning about their care. I assumed that his intense ministry schedule was his way of telling me that the needs of our children overwhelmed him. He seemed focused on what he could control. I did not have the energy or desire to keep up with his schedule.

We silently consented to be alone in each of our assignments, afraid to be vulnerable and ask for the nurturing we both needed so desperately.

*   *   *

Christmas season brought with it a break from the therapy and school routine. We planned on traveling Christmas Day to Lancaster, Pennsylvania, for a week's vacation. The time there would be busy, celebrating holiday parties and getting re-acquainted with friends and family, many of whom had not met Ryan. The church's pageant was over, so I was eager to spend a quiet Christmas Eve at home together as a family before our trip.

A week before Christmas we had moved into our new home. Although delivered at least a month earlier, it took a number of weeks until we could complete the requirements to get our certificate of occupancy. When we moved in, the electric company still had not connected us to their power. The temperature dropped in the single digits that week, so Ron rigged up a wood stove that kept us warm, and a friend loaned us a generator that produced enough electricity to take a hot shower in the morning and cook our dinner in the evening.

The day before Christmas, I packed Kari and Ryan into their car seats and drove the ten miles to the nearest grocery store. Once there, I settled them both in their special chairs inside a shopping cart and pushed past crowds of people who smiled at my charming arrangement. Their seats occupied the entire cart and left little room for food.

It seemed much hassle for just the few items that I needed, but I wanted this holiday dinner to be special, containing Ron's favorites: shrimp cocktail and steak smothered in mushrooms and onions. Through this meal, I wanted to show Ron that I loved him and hoped things would be better soon. I knew we were drifting apart emotionally over the past few months but was unsure of how it happened.

When I arrived home, I was relieved to see that Ron was not there so that I could surprise him with this special meal. I quickly fed the kids, gave them their seizure medication, and settled them in their cribs.

Before I exited their room, I paused at the door. A warm sensation overcame me. I allowed the feeling to cuddle me for a few moments before I rushed back to my dinner preparations. I was a blessed woman. I had a new house that I loved, I was on top of my kids' health situation at the moment, and Ron and I were providing a warm, cozy home for them to grow. I also had a husband who, despite our recent decline in communication, really did love me.

For a moment, I felt the joy I had had before Ryan's birth, and I realized that the worry and stress of his life had been robbing me of this emotion that once was so abundant. I wanted that happiness back. Tonight's celebration, I determined, would be the start of our family communication again.

Enough reflecting, I dashed into the spare bedroom closet, dug out the few Christmas decorations I had strategically hid during the chaos of our recent move, and carefully placed them around the house.

Suddenly, Ron came bursting through the front door with a grin on his face. As he flicked on a wall switch, light filled the living room. He picked me up and swung me around the room laughing. He had persuaded the electric company to connect us to their power in time for Christmas.

The evening dinner was a delightful success. Warmed by our electric heat and Christmas candles glowing from all darkened corners, the atmosphere was just perfect. A newly-fallen snow covered the New England landscape outside our dining room window. I had prepared the food with great care and it smelled and looked delicious on our decorated table.

Handel's "Messiah" played in the background as we settled the children in their seats. They both sat quietly, tuned into the activity, aware that something special was happening. Kari's eyes darted about, trying to focus on our celebration. Ryan seemed content to allow us a few moments of eating enjoyment since his tummy was full. We bowed our heads in prayer as Ron thanked God for sending His Son and for giving us this special Christmas season.

Our evening was peaceful and the affection felt that night would certainly nourish us for the months ahead. God in His great wisdom was showing us what love could look like when we gave to each other selflessly, just as He had sacrificially given His Son as a baby.

Unfortunately, the dismal days of January overshadowed the memories of our Christmas Eve dinner. Dr. Russman arranged an appointment for our children to see a doctor in New York City who specialized in metabolic, genetic diseases. The slight elevation in Ryan's blood lactic acid level indicated to the neurologist that he might be getting closer to discovering the disease that afflicted our children. Dr. Russman noted that if the diagnosis could be made, he could treat the root problem and not just the symptoms. The hope that something more could be done to help our children develop made everyone excited: Dr. Russman, the kids' therapist, our family physician, but most of all Ron and me.

On a bleak, bitter cold January day, we drove two and a half hours to the immense Upper Manhattan hospital. The sky was gray, the ground was frozen, and cinder-covered snow piles lined the city streets. As we entered Columbia Presbyterian Hospital, we encountered large and echoing hallways. Ron and I, each laden down with a child, diaper bag, and medical records that Dr. Russman sent along with us, searched for the Department of Metabolics.

Dr. DeVivo was ready for us when we finally arrived at his door. The oversized office immediately created an eerie sense within me; the room looked as if it may have once housed a tuberculosis sanitarium. Even though the room had large stained-glass windows, the skyscrapers outside prevented them from displaying their full beauty as they were blocked from much of the sun. The floor was old tile, stained by years of abuse. The olive green walls looked as though they had been around long enough to tell many pathetic stories of suffering.

Chills went up my spine as I wondered what might await us here. Dr. DeVivo started to speak from behind his large clumsy mahogany desk. It was obvious by his dull mannerisms that his specialty was research and not in building patient rapport, but that was okay. We weren't here to have a friendly feel-good chat. We wanted to get down to business.

Our family intrigued him—this family with two children two years apart and supposedly afflicted with a similar condition. The lack of any real clues to their problem added to his challenge. He seemed determined to conquer their disorder and be the first to treat them and give them more quality of life.

After a few minutes of explanation of his intentions, he took Kari and Ryan individually into a side room only big enough for an exam table. He worked silently just beyond our vision, taking a full hour to complete his exams before reappearing.

With a sweep of his arm he invited us to sit. He then began explaining in technical terms the metabolic trail he would be taking to search for this mysterious disease. He gave us the name of a condition that he was hoping his further testing would reveal. Ron and I intently scratched out on paper, in phonetic spelling where needed, every word he said.

He wanted to admit Kari soon for the tests he needed to perform to test his theory, promising it would be only a two-day stay. In the meantime, he wanted to submit all of her records to a nationwide computer database system with the National Organization for Rare Diseases (NORD). Through this network, her symptoms could be compared with others whose condition had similar characteristics. Before we left, a hospitalization was scheduled for two weeks. We went home to wait.

During our waiting time, Ryan became increasingly irritable. At six months of age, he no longer took pleasure in nursing. He screamed incessantly night and day. Finally, in desperation, I quit nursing and switched him to formula.

The change was helpful but temporary as he soon returned to a constant state of misery. He cried whenever awake, which seemed a majority of the day and night. Most of the time, rocking him did nothing more than cause further irritation. I went about my household chores to the sound of his shrill cry. He would eventually exhaust himself, sleeping only long enough to recharge him for another two-hour round of screaming. "Oh, God," I wept one morning, "I'm so exhausted. What is it that You are trying to teach me?" God seemed silent. I couldn't remember hearing Him since Christmas.

The winter days were long. I felt like a caged animal in my house. Ron spent hours in his office, meeting with people or preparing Bible studies and sermons. During his break times, he would chop wood for the stove and do other jobs around our new home, taking great pleasure in each of these tasks.

Daily I received encouraging cards and letters from friends in Lancaster—the word having reached them about Ryan's symptoms. They shared their love and concern for our family with promises to keep praying for us. I sat on the couch each day after the mailman came, devouring every word on each card and looking up every Scripture reference enclosed. I appreciated their support, but I still felt very alone and exhausted in my daily routine.

Kari experienced many types of seizures, but she now began to have a large increase in a form of grand-mal seizure. With no warning, her body would convulse violently for several seconds before she would collapse in sleep. This occurred many times throughout the day, despite a recent increase in her medication.

One morning, I awoke from another night of catnaps. Between Kari's seizures and Ryan's extreme irritability, there was little time left to sleep. I needed to find a motivating project to energize me for the day. I decided to try my luck at playing photographer.

I had given up taking Kari to a professional photographer when she was an infant. The ability it took to get her positioned so she wouldn't look abnormal and the patience needed to wait until her eyes were open and focused ahead went far beyond any normal photographer's call of duty and sitting fee. At best, the outcome was very different from the perfectly posed, adorable children's prints decorating the walls of his studio.

My last appointment was a complete disaster. I left the studio in tears, determined that I would never put Kari or myself through that again.

The only good print we had of Kari was her year-old picture. Ryan, at six months, still had no picture of himself. So today, I thought I would set up my own studio in the basement and chase away the winter blues with this industrious project.

First, Kari needed a haircut. I packed them both in the car and headed to the first available hair salon. Kari sat quietly on my lap as the hairdresser snipped away her thick wavy curls, creating a cute bob. She finished, I paid her, and then placed Kari's cap back on and hurried home.

When I removed the cap, I gasped in horror. She looked awful! Her short hair stuck to the side of her head and her bangs sprayed out like a rooster. At that moment her body convulsed in a seizure.

"Oh, God, she looks so handicapped! I've never seen her look so pathetic!" I moaned. For a brief moment I saw her as one of the institutionalized handicapped children in the home where I had worked during nursing school. Even the smell of that depressing place came to mind and made me nauseous.

This was to be my special day? I had destroyed my daughter with an obnoxious haircut—I, who took great pride in keeping Kari dressed and groomed beautifully, wanting to remove any further chances of her being rejected by the "normal" world.

I scooped her up and placed her in a hot soapy tub and shampooed her hair, then dressed her in a frilly blue frock. I stood back and gazed at her, my precious princess having returned to me.

Ron helped set up his photography equipment and focused the camera. Then we both spent the next four hours doing physical, mental, and emotional gymnastics to get both children to cooperate with my agenda. The hard work was well worth it. They both smiled beautifully. Our reward was pictures that remain my favorite to this day.

Two days after the photo extravaganza, we had Kari admitted to Columbia Presbyterian Hospital for her prearranged diagnostic work-up. The large hospital intimidated me—not nearly as child-friendly as Newington in its appearance. Kari and I chose to stay close to her room. Kari's first test was a simple muscle tissue biopsy. She was to have general anesthesia, but even at that the whole procedure was to take no more than one hour.

As I sat in the holding area cuddling her flaccid thin body, I thought how fragile her life was and how dependent I had become on God for His daily strength. As we waited, Ron prayed, asking God to send His angels to guard our baby during her surgery. Soon a nurse, dressed in her operating room garb, arrived to take Kari away, reassuring us as she left, "Don't worry, Dad and Mom. She'll be fine!"

Eight hours later Kari emerged from the recovery room with us by her side—exhausted, famished, but finally feeling relief. While under anesthesia on the operating table, Kari had begun to suffer a seizure. The doctor called us in to be with her in the recovery room when her seizure would not stop. After five hours of potent intravenous seizure medications, frequent suctioning of her lungs, and administration of oxygen, her convulsing body finally relaxed. The experience terrified us. We attributed her survival to angels who rescued her from another life-threatening encounter. The incident required her to stay an extra day in the hospital until the completion of all the tests. We went home, not knowing any more, as it would take weeks for all the results to be formulated.

An abundant number of distressing ingredients for creating a family crisis were present as we awaited a hopeful diagnosis for our children. We had endured days and nights of seizures, rigid feeding and medication schedules in two severely disabled irritable kids, dreary winter weather, and the pressure of a new ministry. We were exhausted. The dam was about to break.

Ron's Reflections . . .

Within a few months' time we experienced the birth of a new baby, church, and house. Labor was involved in bringing each into existence. Much attention and energy was required to give appropriate ongoing care to each. We had been eagerly looking forward to the addition of each of them in our lives. We knew it would be a busy time, but we had braced ourselves for that, or so we thought.

If Ryan had been a normal infant with typical needs, in the context of the other things going on in our lives at that time, we would have been a couple of tired parents. But to say we were tired under these circumstances would be a gross understatement. We were exhausted.

I don't remember us ever sitting down for a lengthy conversation about the stresses of our lives, of thinking through what we could cut out in order to reduce the busyness of our schedules. For one, I don't remember us sitting down all that much, at least not to relax. We sat to feed a child, to study, to discuss a church matter. And there was nothing to talk about as far as reducing the workload.

I had a church to care for. That was why I was in New England. It was my work, the means of providing for my family. I couldn't stop planting the church and hope to survive, any more than a factory worker could stop punching the clock and yet expect the paychecks to keep coming. Joan couldn't stop caring for household duties. Dirt, dishes, and laundry didn't stop accumulating just because we had more important things to do. These things demanded our attention as well. And then there were the children—most consuming of all. We loved them and did whatever we could to meet their many needs. All of this to say, none of our work was optional. There was no luxury overtime to cut.

We worked hard, caught a few hours sleep here and there between feeding and settling children, and awakened to work some more. And that was okay. We were willing to do it. The problem was we were moving at a pace we couldn't sustain, without any breaks in sight. But I'm not sure what other option we had. Our working hard was the loving thing to do.

**A successful family
works willingly,
even to the point of exhaustion,
in caring for its members.**

CHAPTER THIRTEEN

Our car sliced through the black night as it raced along the winding, dark country roads. Afraid to look at the speedometer, I prayed, "Oh, God, please get us to the hospital safely." Ron drove, focusing on making every turn as smoothly as he could under the threatening circumstances. I held my thrashing daughter's body gingerly in my arms to protect her from further harm. This merciless seizure had started thirty minutes before, and by now her face was blue. "Father, please don't take my baby's life!" I prayed desperately, looking into the ominous sky.

The sight of the well-lit emergency entrance brought relief to my anguish. I rushed Kari through the automatic doors into the quiet emergency room. Within seconds of seeing my terrified look and blue seizing baby, the staff grabbed Kari from me and huddled around her bed with the doctor in charge shouting orders. Minutes after starting the intravenous dosage of Valium her muscles went limp and she lay like a rag doll. An oxygen mask filled her air-deprived lungs and her blue complexion changed to pale.

The doctor turned to me for information. The words stuck in my throat and all I could do was cry. My weary body quivered. I turned around to see Ron coming through the emergency doors. I collapsed in a chair to gather my emotions as he explained to the doctor that Kari had been sick since leaving the New York Hospital a week earlier. She was up every night with fever, vomiting, diarrhea, and a respiratory infection. Now, at midnight, she topped off her week with this finale.

"Ron," I said as we traveled home with our sedated child, "yesterday's mail included a card that read, 'Life's hardest task is to accept what we cannot understand, and we can do even that if we are sure enough of God's love.' Just when I think I have accepted Kari's condition, I have to go through a week like this. I wonder if God really does care!"

"Joan," he said softly, "we have no other real choice but to know that God is good and He loves us. He does care for us, and Kari. If we deny this, our emotions will destroy us." I knew he was right, but lately my physical exhaustion prevented me from really appreciating God's personal connection with me. I mumbled a response back to my husband. "I know people are praying for us. I guess I need to rest in that."

Four days later, we were back in the local hospital. Kari had been spiking high fevers and had difficulty breathing. The doctor admitted her to the pediatric floor with viral pneumonia. I sat by her crib and agonized in prayer over her fragile body. Intravenous fluids were delivering antibiotics to her infected lungs and an oxygen tent covered her body as she struggled for each breath. "Oh, God, here I am again! Please help my baby! I know I have been questioning Your goodness lately, but please don't punish my skepticism by taking it out on Kari! Hear our cry for help."

Four days into the hospitalization, Kari started to improve. A nurse allowed me to cuddle Kari outside her oxygen tent that evening. She and I were both enjoying our time together rocking when the phone rang.

Ron was on the other end. All week he had been juggling caring for Ryan and working out of his office, trying to keep from falling too far behind in his work. This evening he was to be leading a Bible Study, so his call surprised me. "Joan," his voice hinted with fear, "I'm down here in the hospital lobby with Ryan. He is having terrible seizures like he has never had. What should I do?"

I hung up the phone and immediately dialed Dr. Russman at the Children's Hospital. He was at home but returned my call within minutes. He told me to bring Ryan immediately to Newington Children's Hospital and he would meet us there.

I hated leaving Kari, but I knew Ron would not feel comfortable admitting Ryan and answering the endless questions. We made a quick decision that Ron would take Ryan and me to Newington, and he would later return to stay with Kari.

I sat in the back seat with Ryan as we drove along the deserted expressway. I watched his body racked with yet another new type of seizure, but my exhaustion prevented me from even crying.

"Ron, what do you think the people of our church think of us?" I asked, aware that our family situation was again pulling him from the church work.

"One thing I know, Joan, they care very much for us. Why don't we talk about something else?" He suggested we fill the hour-long drive with taking turns praising God for things we can be thankful for.

I was glad at the moment I was in the back seat, because I didn't want him to see my eyes rolling toward the back of my head. *What's there to be thankful for?* I thought. He started with a simple list and soon I joined him with a few of my own. As we pulled into the parking lot of Newington Children's Hospital with Ryan still seizing, a duet in perfect harmony came softly and naturally from our lips. "Lord, listen to Your children praying, send us love, send us power, send us grace!"

Two years almost to the day after Kari's initial EEG showed the devastating infantile spasms disorder, Ryan's brain presented the same dreadful EEG recording. Dr. Russman immediately started him on the potent steroid therapy (ACTH) in hopes of arresting the horrible abnormal electrical impulses in his brain.

Kari was eventually discharged from the local hospital, and my mother again came to our Connecticut home to care for her while I stayed with Ryan in Hartford. I hated having our family split, and after five days of staying with Ryan alone, I was eager to be with Ron and Kari.

My patience was running low; I wanted to be home. Ryan was improving and I believed I could handle his medical care at home. I had been through the whole ACTH daily injection routine before and was capable of performing the nursing care that accompanied it, so I pleasantly begged Dr. Russman to discharge Ryan.

He granted my wish and we went home. With our family again living under one roof, Ron seemed relieved to have me undertake the care of both children again. He worked fervently trying to catch up on his work.

His men's accountability group was flourishing and Ron seemed highly motivated by the level of interest in it. He hosted the meetings in our home every week and I provided refreshments. Apart from the moments while delivering coffee and doughnuts, I was not allowed access to their meetings. Although I was happy that my husband found support through this group, I noticed he seemed tense. I realized that I had not been available to listen to his feelings; we were all experiencing stress.

Despite the daily injection of ACTH, Ryan's seizures continued to attack his increasingly chubby body. The steroid made him very hungry. He was constantly crying for food. When his stomach was satisfied, his screaming continued out of fear from the controlling spasms. Dr. Russman wanted me to double the dose of ACTH, and reluctantly I did. I hated this toxic drug; it caused horrible reactions in Ryan's body. Besides the increase in weight, it also raised his blood pressure, requiring medication to keep it in a tolerable range. ACTH made him very irritable and suppressed his immune system making him extremely vulnerable to all viruses.

For three weeks, Ryan awakened every hour around the clock, screaming in misery. I mechanically cared for the needs of my kids. I felt my body and mind shutting down from exhaustion. I couldn't focus my attention on anything that I once enjoyed. It was as though a thick blanket of fog smothered my every activity. Emotionally, I no longer responded to the children's cries for help; they did not even evoke pity within me. I avoided Ron. His happiness in his work made me jealous.

One morning, still in my pajamas, I was preparing Ryan's injection. Both children quietly sat in their seats, seemingly oblivious to the world that I was experiencing. Over the past few months they had been so sick that I only had time to care for their physical needs. I had slacked off doing their therapy, which was to keep them in tune with their present environment. Their eyes stared blankly into space.

Though I had so little energy to face it, I could not avoid the suffering that was showing itself in full color in our home. A somber tune from the "Fiddler on the Roof" album was playing in the background—its doleful music the perfect backdrop for my feelings. I looked at both my children sitting there and angrily cried out, "God, this is not what I had in mind when I had children. These kids should be running around here, pulling pans from my perfectly organized cupboards, spilling milk on the floor, and making irritating noise. I should be exhausted from their play, not their pain! Would it spoil some vast eternal plan for my children to be normal?" I received no answer from above.

I called Dr. Russman to inform him of Ryan's twenty-thirty-a-day clusters of seizures each lasting ten to fifteen minutes. The ACTH was destroying his body and I refused to have him increase it again; besides, it was doing nothing for his seizures. The neurologist's only answer was to admit him to the hospital again. Ryan and I spent another full week in the hospital while the doctor attempted to calm his seizure activity and wean him off the destructive steroid.

I ate Easter dinner alone in the hospital cafeteria. Ron said he would come later in the day with Kari, after the service. I felt distant from my church family. It wasn't that they didn't care for me, the opposite was true. But I had no energy left to devote to my church family after caring for the incredible needs of my children.

Now again today, I sat on this Holy day feeling guilty that I was not with these people I loved and not available to support Ron. My son suffered terribly and I couldn't leave him; he was helpless and sick. Nurses and doctors could provide the medical care he needed, but the love Ryan needed to survive this world had to come from his family. He searched for me with his dark, scared eyes when disturbed and then relaxed on hearing my voice and touch. I was the one stable, secure thing in his dark, frightening world. He was a human being just like me who needed love, security, and a place of belonging. My arms provided all three.

Over the past few months I struggled with how God could use our family in church planting ministry when our family needs incapacitated me. I had not been voicing my concerns to Ron, but today as I again agonized over this thought, I knew I couldn't keep it quiet much longer.

When Ron arrived that evening, we took turns sharing with each other about our day. I gave the update on Ryan and what the doctor was now trying to control his seizures. Then Ron went into detail about the events and happenings at the church. We each spoke fully about our area of expertise, but it was obvious by our body language that neither one of us had the emotion or energy to empathize with each other to provide the encouragement that we so desperately needed.

The lack of concern we had for one another frightened me, but I did not know how to address it. Instead, I hesitantly asked, "Ron, does the question ever cross your mind how we can keep up this crazy lifestyle?" When he did not immediately respond, I continued on about how I sensed our family was suffering from the kids' constant needs and hospitalizations.

After I exhausted my supply of pent-up feelings, Ron answered cautiously. "I admit, Joan, something must change. We cannot go on like this. I need your support as my wife and in the ministry. I'm starting to have panic attacks, and I'm not sleeping at night."

My heart sank. Ron so seldom shared his feelings with me and I cringed, knowing he was suffering silently.

He continued. "I don't know how to accomplish all that I need to do in my work and provide for the needs of my family. There are days I feel paralyzed from moving forward. Joan, I feel on the verge of a nervous breakdown."

This was the first time in months we were vulnerable before one another, laying out all our thoughts and emotions.

At this point, I had courage to be frank and share my desire to move back to Lancaster to be closer to extended family. "Ron, I need help, and I can't constantly be calling my mother away from her work to help us."

Ron nodded his head as though he heard my plea, but waited several moments before responding. "Joan, I have no energy to even process such a drastic solution, but I will pray." I bowed my head with him as Ron began to ask God to show us how we could be responsible for all that He was asking of us.

After Ron left for the night, I prayed my own prayer. "God, reveal Yourself to us soon!" I spoke with urgency as I prepared my cot for another night of restless sleep.

Before the sun even arose, I was awakened for the sixth time that night. This time it was not Ryan waking me, but the voice of Dr. Russman. I sat up quickly and straightened my sweatshirt, rubbing my eyes, and brushing back my hair. *What is he doing here at this ungodly hour?* I thought to myself as I tried to orient myself on my rumpled cot.

When Dr. Russman pulled up a chair indicating he wanted to talk to me, I really got nervous. It was his usual practice on morning rounds to assess Ryan's situation and then address me. When he ignored Ryan, I assumed something must be terribly wrong.

"Joan, I need to talk to you if that's okay." By now he was staring intently at me, leaning forward in his seat. Trying to carry on a respectable conversation looking the way I did, did not thrill me. I had a total of three hours of sleep and my mind was foggy, but I nodded agreement, for it appeared that the doctor meant business.

He continued. "First, I want to give you the results of the tests that Dr. DeVivo in New York has been working on. It doesn't look promising. He can't find anything abnormal. Therefore, we don't have any answers as to how to help your kids. We can't come up with a diagnosis. We can only treat their devastating symptoms.

"Secondly, I know this is no news to you, but your family has been through hell, and I can't give you any hope that the future is going to be brighter.

"The last thing I want to say is personal. I couldn't get you guys off my mind last night, and I want to offer a suggestion that I want you to talk to your husband about. Joan, you are going to need help on an ongoing basis! Kari and Ryan will be increasingly difficult to care for. I don't know if your husband's parish will allow this, but I think you guys need to move closer to extended family. I want to help you in any way I can. Think about this and we'll talk more later."

I sat dazed, unable to utter even a word before he left the room. Did I hear him correctly? Did he say last night he thought all this? Could God have orchestrated our talk and Dr. Russman's thoughts in the same evening? Was God using Dr. Russman to speak to us? I quickly got dressed and tended to Ryan, who was now crying. He was going to have another EEG conducted today with sedation. I had already decided that since he would be sleeping most of the day, I would go home and relieve Ron of Kari and complete a few other neglected chores.

Ron was glad to have me home if even for just a few hours. I hadn't yet relayed Dr. Russman's advice to him. Knowing it was a very fragile subject, I hoped that he would initiate continuing the discussion from the night before.

"Joan," Ron said quietly during our lunch, "I talked to Trevor Baird this morning." Trevor was the director of the RHMA organization, so I braced myself for what was coming. "He said he would encourage us to do whatever is best for our family. He will be supportive of any decision we make, but I don't know, Joan—I don't think we can move. What would I do in Lancaster? Ministry is what I want to do. I love it here! What about our new home? Life just has to get better!"

I listened to him agonize and then relayed Dr. Russman's suggestion earlier in the day. Ron said nothing at that point, but the subject was not dropped. I could tell he needed time to process the idea.

Later that week, I brought Ryan home. Life did not get better. In fact, Ryan and Kari continued their burdensome schedules even out of the hospital. After two more weeks of sick children, uncontrollable seizures, no sleep, buckets of tears, and hours of talk between us and consulting others, the choice was clear. Ron made the decision to end our ministry in Connecticut and move closer to extended family. We were exhausted and the more we had resisted the inevitable, the harder life was for us.

God provided for us, as we trusted Him for the details of our move and acknowledged that it was His will for us. Within a week of the news hitting Lancaster that we were moving back, Ron received two job offers. A field director from RHMA was willing to move into our home and continue the church planting work we had started. We arranged with the church to lease our home to them. My parents encouraged us to move in with them until we could find housing in Lancaster. The most important confirmation to us that God was leading in our move was our church family's affirmation that we needed to take care of our children first. It was a tearful good-bye on that final Sunday, but we all knew it was for the best.

It was heart-wrenching leaving behind our friends, our new home, and dreams, but God was making it clear that this was His choice. The last thing I picked up as I left my kitchen on the day of our move was a card stuck to my refrigerator. It read, "See, I have refined you, . . . I have tested you in the furnace of affliction. I do this. I do this, for my own sake. Isaiah 48:10." We closed the door to our home and left Connecticut feeling as though our God was burning our dreams in His furnace.

Ron's Reflections . . .

Needing to leave Connecticut added to my deep pain. Had there been a way for us to stay in Lebanon we would have done so. Dreams for healthy children had disappeared. Now dreams of church planting in New England had drawn to a close as well.

What does one do with God and His promises when so much of what one desires has shattered? Did God love us? Did He care? If so, why didn't He change things? Was it love that allowed our children to suffer? Was it love that ended my calling? Why didn't he change our circumstances? Why hadn't He intervened in the development of my children? Why hadn't He contained the electrical currents in their brains, preventing the devastating storms that constantly interfered with their learning?

A few years before our children were born a book was written, entitled When Bad Things Happen to Good People. *It, like many other books before it, wrestled with the problem of suffering. Many accepted its conclusion that God loves mankind but is limited in preventing bad things from occurring. Our study of the Bible taught us otherwise.*

In God's Word we found a God Who is all-powerful, Who not only knows about each sparrow that falls and the number of hairs on every head, but even ultimately takes responsibility for the number of our days and the plans He has for us. We were amazed to find that God went so far as to say, "Who gave man his mouth? Who makes him deaf or mute? Who gives him sight or makes him blind? Is it not I, the Lord?"

One day I came across a few verses from the Psalms that helped me immensely. In typical Hebraic fashion, David shares with us two truths about God. "One thing God has spoken, two things have I heard: that you, O God, are strong, and that you, O Lord, are loving." (Psalm 61:11,12)

If God is not love, then what is there to conclude but that He is cruel? If God is not strong, then what assurance did I have that He could bring about any purpose or meaning to my life? Though I could not reconcile these qualities in God of which David spoke, I knew that both must somehow be true. And confidence in a God who was both strong and loving would carry us through those days and many more dark days ahead.

A successful family
chooses to believe that God loves them
even in the midst of shattered dreams.

CHAPTER FOURTEEN

I wiped the sweat from my brow to keep it from dripping into my eyes as I pushed the clumsy mower up and down the steep terrain that was our yard. Although the grass was long and thick and the July sun scorching hot, I radiated with delight.

The change from Connecticut to Pennsylvania had not improved the physical condition of my children, but it certainly had revitalized my innermost being. Extended family surrounded and encouraged me faithfully. My mother, who lived only two miles from our country home, came frequently to aid me in the twenty-four-hour care of Kari and Ryan.

The house we rented sat on the bank of the Pequea Creek in the heart of Pennsylvania's Dutch Country. From the porch that encircled our house, we could see Amish farms sprinkled throughout the plush green rolling hills that surrounded our home. Sightseeing tourists envied our picturesque setting.

Not long after we arrived, the news had spread among the Amish community about our "special" family. The Amish are known to be generous, a reputation they soon demonstrated for us. Within the first week of our arrival, many of our neighboring Amish women came to visit. Several children trailed each mother as they hiked up the hill to our home. They came to deliver the excess produce from their abundant gardens, fresh baked breads, pies, and homemade soups. I exchanged a friendly conversation with the mother while the children sat quietly, watching my children. We sipped ice tea and talked about the weather, but before she left she requested the "story" of Kari and Ryan to pass along to her neighbors.

*   *   *

Kari and Ryan sat on the porch above me as I worked diligently at manicuring our little plot of ground, hoping to keep it as well groomed as that of our caring neighbors. The kids were enjoying the sensations of the outdoor atmosphere, hearing and feeling the warm breeze rustling through the large maple tree shading our house. I cherished the time working in the yard.

Growing up on a farm had given me a great appreciation for the open air and hard work. I loved caring for my children, but I needed a break from their demanding routine. Seeing tangible accomplishments in my yard work was satisfying and rewarding.

The progress within Kari and Ryan was slow. Their physical and intellectual abilities still functioned at a three-month-old level, despite their true ages. After arriving in Lancaster, Dr. Clancy, a neurologist at Children's Hospital of Philadelphia (CHOP), followed their medical needs.

Although they were siblings suffering from the same undiagnosed genetic condition, Dr. Clancy referred to them as yin and yang. Their personality differences were that significant. Ryan continued to be very high strung and Kari was quiet and mellow.

As we settled back into the community in which Ron and I were raised, all was not positive. It wasn't long before whispers of our "tragic family" rumored beyond our circle of influence. It discouraged me to learn that others viewed our children as hopeless, time-consuming, and wasted lives before they took the time to know them. What these strangers were missing or choosing to overlook was that Ron and I loved these two little people. In return, Kari and Ryan had an extraordinary way of communicating their love for us and for life. A few, who took the time to get to know them, saw it too.

Lois Woolston was one of those persons. I first met Lois before ever having children. I had the opportunity to orient her to the Lancaster hospital unit in which we were employed. Because of her quiet mannerisms and reserved emotions, my co-workers and I titled her the "mystery woman." Lois was competent in her nursing skills, but I knew very little else about her. Our conversations had only to do with our employment.

After we moved to Connecticut, she made one visit to our family that was a pleasant surprise. She wanted to see what church planting involved and meet our children.

It was because of that visit and her correspondence by mail that I learned to know a more sensitive side of Loie—our nickname for her. She was a single woman with a deep concern for spiritual things. Her interest in our children revealed her exceptionally caring and giving spirit. When she learned our reason for moving back to Pennsylvania was our need for more assistance with the care of our children, she responded. She visited on a weekly basis and became a student of Kari and Ryan. She watched them and me closely as I performed the routine of their care.

One day, after weeks of observation, Loie asked to finish feeding Kari. Confident that she could complete the meticulous process, Loie placed the pureed spoonful in Kari's mouth. Kari, aware that the change of hands had happened, curled her tongue, spewed the food back at Loie, and kicked the feeding bowl out of her hand. She had properly initiated Loie into the world of caring for disabled children. Loie determined to rise to the challenge of getting to know the character of these two children who were trapped in debilitated bodies. It was not an easy task because their ways of communicating were so different from any other child. Ryan gave her an even bigger challenge as he was doing for me as well. His ways of declaring his needs were not so amiable.

Not even a year old yet, Ryan had the same stubborn strong will of his mother. On the outside, both of us appeared lovable and warm, but inwardly we had a persistent determination to never give up, especially when the going was tough. It was that will to fight that had caused Ryan to survive his first year of life. Like Kari, he also was diagnosed as cortically blind; his brain was not responding to the message his eyes received. Therefore, in his confused dark world he would fight us, the ones who wanted to show him love and acceptance. He would scream and demand to be left alone in his own quiet space where he could feel in control.

I, with just as much determination, kept insisting that he be part of all our family events. I wanted to introduce him to the sights, sounds, smells, and movements around him. I refused to isolate him by abandoning him to a sterile, quiet world.

My efforts eventually paid off at Ryan's first birthday party. His pre-school cousins, aunts, uncles, and grandparents surrounded him. Children squealing, party horns tooting, relatives hugging and squeezing his chubby body, laughter and conversation engulfed him. Amidst the activity, his eyes twinkled and he smiled to let us all know he loved us and approved the love we were pouring on him. Ryan's normally rigid body relaxed as he enjoyed his party. He had much to battle in life.

Nothing was more rewarding to me than to teach him that there was much in the world around him that was not his enemy.

The mystery disease that attacked the very core of our children's lives had symptoms that were relentless. Seizures were the first indication that this disease would prohibit their chance to function as normal children, but as both of them continued to grow, it was also evident that other afflictions would make life a struggle for them.

Because the condition originated in their brain, it did not send proper signals to the muscles; therefore, their responses were inappropriate and unproductive. Kari was flaccid as a Raggedy Ann doll; in contrast, Ryan's muscle tone was very rigid.

It happened to be Ryan's first birthday when we had both children examined at a cerebral palsy (CP) clinic at A.I. Dupont Children's Hospital in Delaware by an orthopedic doctor, Dr. Freeman Miller. This was their first exam of this nature. Dr. Miller's prognosis for our children's future was not a happy one. With a compassionate expression, he explained to Ron and me the difficulties Ryan and Kari would face as they grew older because of the CP. We nodded understandingly as we were already seeing his predictions to be true in a significant area— a feeding problem with Ryan.

We told Dr. Miller about Ryan losing his ability to suck and swallow correctly without choking. The CP also affected his tongue muscle, and he could not conquer the very natural phenomenon of eating. Dr. Miller referred Ryan to a feeding specialist who explained to us that Ryan would eventually need a gastrostomy tube (GT) inserted through his abdominal wall so we could feed him directly into his stomach.

We learned many new and discouraging reports during that initial visit to Dupont, but Dr. Clancy's prediction a year earlier that seizures still would be the most difficult thing to manage did hold true.

A month after Ryan's birthday, our family retreated to a cabin in northern Pennsylvania for a three-day vacation. Ron wanted time away from his stress-filled job, and I desired time off household responsibilities to be with my husband. We assumed the refreshment and calmness that the mountain atmosphere offered would be good for all of us.

Within minutes of arriving at our destination, Ryan noticed the change of surroundings and routine and dealt with it like he did all change—he screamed non-stop for the first two days. He had difficulty fitting something new into his very private world.

When he finally realized that his caretakers had remained the same and it was only the house that was different, Ryan calmed on our final vacation night. We all relaxed, hoping for a good night's sleep, only to be awakened at two in the morning by Kari, who was having a horrible bed-shaking seizure. A half hour later and with several administrations of her seizure medication, she showed no sign of quitting the violent contractions. We had to get her to a hospital—but where? Unfortunately, it was nothing we had researched before coming. Now this serene setting had become a nightmare with no help or phone. Ron woke a neighboring farmer who gave directions to the closest hospital—thirty miles away.

Over dark mountainous roads we went, winding through seemingly ghost towns nestled quietly along our way. Ahead in the beam of our headlight we saw two eyes flashing back at us. Ron swerved, narrowly missing a head-on collision with the deer. I hung on tightly to Kari's thrashing body in the back of the van. I was grateful that it was dark so I could not see her body turning blue. I knew we didn't have much time.

Ron shouted back to me that he saw a sign for a hospital up ahead. As he pulled into the emergency entrance, our hearts sank. The lights were off. A sign on the door said, "Closed!"

"Joan, just get her inside that building," Ron hollered. I burst through the front doors with my convulsing blue child. Immediately a nurse met me. She took one look at Kari and frantically paged the doctor. He arrived, grabbed Kari from me, and started an intravenous line while the nurse connected her to oxygen. I stood in the corner, watching, as other nurses arrived to assist.

A nurse's aid pulled me aside and whispered, "Mrs. Denlinger, you are very fortunate that a doctor is here in the hospital tonight. We have only twenty-four beds and it is extremely rare for any doctor to be in-house overnight. Our emergency room is only open 8:00 a.m. to 5:00 p.m. Monday through Friday." I smiled at her weakly, not sure if I should be relieved or worried.

The doctor turned to me and asked if this had ever happened before. In my brief history report of Kari's medical condition, I mentioned a neurologist at Children's Hospital of Philadelphia was following her. His expression brightened and he asked what neurologist she saw. Amazingly, he had just completed his training at CHOP and was very familiar with the physicians there. He promptly placed a call to Dr. Clancy, Kari's neurologist, and received the information on how to treat her.

Within two hours, we were heading home to the cabin with our sleeping little girl. The sun was barely peeking above the horizon, but life was returning to the same quiet villages we had passed a short time ago.

"Ron," I whispered, "it wasn't coincidence that a doctor was there tonight. In this little out-of-the-way town, God providentially placed him there to save our daughter. It wasn't Kari's time to leave us. God gave her life once again."

We parked our van in the grassy lot beside the cabin. As I opened the van door, the fresh scent of the pine trees embraced us, as if to beckon: "Come here and relax!" The sky was clear, but a thick fog still covered the floor of the forest. I took a deep breath, desiring for this beautiful scenery to be impressed on my mind.

The time soon came for us to pack the van and say good-bye. That day we traveled home from our vacation—weary from our attempt to relax.

Ron returned to life in the fast lane of business, and I continued my vigilant care of the kids with their unpredictable medical needs. Our marriage existed, but we failed to know how to energize each other. Life was hard and filled with burdens. We were blind to the ways we could fulfill each other's needs.

We celebrated a New Year, 1990, hoping for a healthier year for our children. It soon became evident that this year would be no different, as uncontrollable seizures continued to plague both Kari and Ryan. It was not unusual for me to witness eighty to one hundred seizures a day between the two of them. In mid-January, I made an appointment with a new neurologist at A.I. Dupont. Dr. Marks took great interest in our children and wanted them admitted to the hospital immediately so he could start them on new medication, monitor medication blood levels, and continue testing for an underlying diagnosis.

Room 233 A and B housed the Denlinger kids for eight days. To make myself available for both, I placed my cot in the middle of the room in my new home away from home. Not knowing which child to care for when both were suffering tore me apart.

Wednesday, the first day of admission, was a busy one. Along with the start of a new medication, each child was scheduled for a different procedure at the same time. The doctor wanted Kari in the operating room for a tissue biopsy and Ryan was to have a magnetic resonance imaging (MRI) scan of his brain. I needed to decide whom to follow. Because Kari's previous surgery experience was so traumatic, I chose to stay with her and let Ryan go alone for his test.

I sat in the surgical waiting room, trying to focus on the passage of Scripture before me. Other parents in the small room either stared at the blaring TV in the corner or paced back and forth, sipping the free coffee available from the small kitchenette adjacent to the waiting area. A crackling voice across the hospital paging system interrupted the tension in the room. "Would the mother of Ryan Denlinger please report to the medical imaging area promptly?" Never having been paged before, I paused, allowing the fact to sink in that this was not a good sign. I quickly gathered my things.

I took the steps to the ground floor, hoping to avoid the congestion at the elevator. I ran along the corridor till I located the sign pointing me in the direction of the MRI testing area. When I burst through the doors, the first thing I saw was the big red crash cart shoved alongside the table Ryan was resting on. I had been involved in enough "code blue" crises in my nursing career, so after a quick assessment of the scene, I needed no explanation to realize what had happened. Ryan had stopped breathing because of the heavy sedation, and a team had just resuscitated him.

When I neared the MRI table, the doctor stepped aside, permitting me to see my little boy. The nurse quickly provided a rocking chair for me close to the bed and said that I may hold Ryan. His oxygen mask covered his face, but he fluttered open his eyes when I picked him up. As I sat rocking Ryan's quivering body, I wondered how much more this little boy could take. He relaxed in my arms, as I silently prayed for strength for him and myself.

The remaining hospitalization went more smoothly. Both children responded to their new medication. By the time they were discharged, their seizures were under control again for the time being.

The remaining last months of winter were quiet ones, but by early spring Ryan's seizures were out of control again. Throughout the spring and summer of 1990, I traveled with him in and out of the hospital. Kari's daily routine also was demanding, and she seemed prone to pick up every virus that passed through our community. As the summer came to a close, the children's health slowly improved and I looked forward to starting them in new "special needs" preschool programs.

Ron's Reflections . . .

Ryan didn't enjoy a lot of stimulation. Rather than be around people who couldn't resist pinching his chubby cheeks or wanting to hold him, he constantly communicated that he was happiest in a dark, quiet room far away from anything and anybody. As much as we wanted the little guy to be happy, we couldn't grant him that wish. Instead, we increased the stimulation, stretching him, helping him to tolerate more and more.

We took our children just about everywhere that we went. We didn't shelter them from the world and neither did we hide them from society. We love our children. They are important members of our family and as such remain with us as much as possible.

Are there limits to how much such children can relate to their world? Of course there are. Their disabilities make it so. They can't communicate with us in ways that we ourselves would long for. They certainly can't interact with others as children normally do. We couldn't place them in a typical preschool program, expecting them to have the same experience in the world that others their age would have. Therefore, we sent them to the "special needs" preschool program.

In light of who Ryan was, it was a great achievement for Ryan at the birthday party Joan mentioned—when he had all his very noisy cousins surround him. It is true that he didn't blow out the candles or pin any tail on a donkey (at least not without our help). But we were so impressed that he didn't go into overload and scream the whole time, as he previously would have done. We were so proud that he was able to fit in—in his own little way.

**A successful family
helps each member
discover his or her place in the world.**

Chapter Fifteen

I looked out on the drying cornfield and watched the fog lazily rising from the golden creek. The sun was peeking above the horizon, casting a brilliant, honey colored hue on the earth below my bedroom window. I could see the Amish farmer gather his milk-laden cows in the meadow behind our house and encourage them towards the barn. He had already started his workday. The rhythmic banging of his generator had awakened me. I stretched and sat straight up in bed, breathing in the sweet honeysuckle scent that drifted through the screened window.

"Put your hope in God, for I will praise Him, my Savior and my God." I whispered the Psalm 42 verse into the cool autumn air permeating my bedroom. I had written the verse on a small card and taped it to my dresser mirror to daily remind me that my hope for living had to come from Jesus.

Ron was showering, preparing for his day at the office. Kari lay whimpering in her bed, but I hesitated before retrieving her, since I was enjoying the calm of the morning. "Good morning, Lord," I whispered my thoughts aloud as though He was sitting on the end of my bed. I felt so close to Him lately. The bitterness and disappointment of having two severely disabled children that I felt so sharply in Connecticut now seemed like a distant memory. With the help of friends and family and my renewed energy, God was showing me how these two precious children were all part of His plan for my life.

"God, You are refining and testing me to see if I will totally rely on You just as my children are totally dependent on my husband and me for their needs. My greatest loss, not having healthy children, can become my greatest gain if I allow You to change me. God, I want You to continue working in my life. I promise to believe in You no matter what circumstances You take me through. Help me to be a comfort to others who are discouraged in life. I love You so much; You give me joy for living!" I finished my prayer and tossed back the covers.

Ron emerged from the bathroom, silent and focused on his day ahead. "Good morning, honey! Kari and Ryan slept all night, and I feel great this morning!" I spoke cheerfully, trying to cut through the fog that clouded our relationship. "How about I make a cooked breakfast this morning?" He nodded but said nothing as he knotted his tie.

We ate breakfast in silence except for a few basic courtesies. I kissed him good-bye and watched his car disappear over the hill. His job took him into the city and the stresses of the corporate world. I wondered if it was hard for him to be part of two extreme worlds each day. Our life in the rural, quiet Amish country had soothed my soul, but was it only a constant reminder to Ron of the world we left behind in rural Connecticut?

As I fed Ryan his morning bottle, I could not get Ron off my mind. His deep sadness was intensifying and affecting our relationship. Our only conversation lately involved my babbling about the kids and experiences at their therapy programs, or Ron talking about the stress of his job—which I knew he didn't like. I tried to listen and be a part of the pain he was feeling and praised him for the way he supported our family and the great employee he was, but I could tell his passion was gone. I couldn't seem to encourage him in any way.

Ron became more easily angered over issues that previously we had been able to talk through. He was often tired and didn't enjoy my positive spin on life that he once had cherished. At times when he held the children, his body language showed he was in a distant world. He no longer talked and played with them as he used to. I feared that his sadness eventually would become a bitter root entangling him, from which he would never escape.

A glance at the clock reminded me that I needed to lay aside my meditating and start packing the kids into the van for the fifteen-mile drive to their school. Kari giggled as we drove past the clopping sound of an Amish buggy. Ryan looked perplexed as the brisk air, coming through the window, whipped the cap off his head. With neither of them responding to my chatter and singing, my thoughts migrated back to my husband.

During the past year in Lancaster, Ron continued to pursue possible ministry opportunities available locally, but each endeavor ended with the door closing in his face. I could see now how each experience had resulted in greater bitterness that choked him. His final attempt at receiving full-time work in a church had occurred the last week of the summer.

A pastoral search committee requested an interview with Ron. The church had recently lost their pastor because of his overwhelming family commitments. He had one handicapped son, and the pastor had become burdened with the financial and emotional stress this child placed on his family. During the interview, it was obvious to me that the folks on the committee were skeptical of Ron's ability to perform the role of pastor and provide for two disabled children. As we drove out of the church parking lot following that experience, Ron decided that God was making it clear He did not want him in pastoral work. His hope died within him.

I arrived at the therapy center, and Kari and Ryan's program totally absorbed my attention for the next few hours. That night after dinner, Ron left me alone to clean the kitchen and prepare the kids for bed. Since his final rejection of possible ministry work, he frequently sat on the porch late into the evening—self-absorbed, ignoring me, and saying he needed time to think.

His miserable job was adding insult to his already injured heart. The paychecks barely covered the expenses of our family, and the savings we brought back from Connecticut had dwindled to nothing. He felt he was an inadequate financial provider. Even worse, he was unable to provide for a greater need—health for his children. Seizures continued to control Kari and Ryan's fragile bodies, interfering with any hope of them ever having normal minds.

Questions of the meaning of life besieged his mind. Why was God putting him on a shelf? Why had God turned a callous heart to his desires and wants? Why was God overlooking the many needs of his family? Like the shadowy night around him, darkness consumed Ron's bitter soul.

I lay in bed, waiting for him to come in from his refuge on the porch. My heart ached for him, but I didn't know how to reach him. He did not want me to share his pain, neither did he want to understand nor participate in my joy. His wounded heart did not appreciate the fulfillment and hope inside me. Jesus continued to give me hope for living and strength for each day, but I could not force this satisfying relationship on my husband. He was suffering and all I could do was to plead with God that He would soften my husband's hardening heart.

"Oh, God, please help my husband. He has been so faithful to You all his life! He allows me to stay at home to care for my kids while he works at a job he hates. He loves me and proved that devotion by moving here and leaving a ministry he loved. He has followed You and trusted You in all Your directions. He would do anything to take away Kari and Ryan's pain and suffering. God, why does he have to struggle with all these trials? Haven't You humbled him enough through his job change, financial difficulties, and children who don't respond to him? Please release him of his prison of pain! Lord, I know You hear me. Help us both overcome these circumstances and not be destroyed by them."

Ron entered the darkened room and collapsed on the sheets. I felt his body tighten from the strain and agony of his soul. I reached over to caress him and massage his tense muscles, but he made no response to my touch or attempts at comforting him. He drifted off to sleep to avoid any further inward torment.

Feeling rejected, I cried softly into my pillow, then prayed that the events of this coming weekend would somehow ease his pain by helping him put his dreams behind him.

*   *   *

I hurriedly placed the dinner dishes in the dishwasher as Ron changed the kids into their pajamas. It was Friday evening and we were expecting a visit from the new director of RHMA and his family. We had not yet met this man, but already we had a very skeptical feeling about his leadership.

Since leaving our church-plant, we had requested numerous times to resign from the mission. We saw no hope of ever being able to be involved in the work of church planting with our increasingly needy family situation. No opportunities within already-established ministries in Lancaster worked out. It seemed best that our dreams were put to rest. RHMA kept delaying our resignation process.

Finally, the director conveyed that he would not accept it and the mission board placed us on an "associate status list." This "hanging on" had become quite an irritant to us. Why couldn't RHMA see we would be of no use to them again? Why were they leaving us dangling?

"Joan," Ron said brusquely as we rushed through the housecleaning while we waited for Ron Klassen and his family to arrive, "I have every intention in making this director see first hand what life is like for us! When he sees our kids and how disabled they are and how much support you need, he will be forced to understand our situation. He can't leave without accepting my resignation!"

A car pulled in the driveway. Within minutes of their entering our home, we clearly saw that this family was a special one. Despite hours of traveling, they radiated phenomenal warmth and sensitivity. We talked and laughed for hours, getting to know one another at a deeper level. Their children were drawn to Kari and Ryan. In a short time, this family had become tender shepherds to hurting sheep.

By the time Ron Klassen started to speak about his purpose for coming, our spirits were open and our guard lowered. He spoke in a deep, steady tone. "Ron and Joan, I can see the needs of your children certainly are a great challenge to your being involved in ministry. At the same time I believe that God delights in our attempts to find ways to overcome obstacles in our desire to serve Him."

My husband shifted in his seat, I could see he was cautious about what was coming next. Mr. Klassen continued, "As I was driving across Pennsylvania I had a thought. I realize it may sound crazy. I have no idea how something like this would work, but what if you or the mission were able to find a nanny to help with your children so that you may return to church-planting ministry?"

Ron and I looked at each other and immediately knew what the other was thinking.

Ron's Reflections . . .

Our little house on School Lane Road was in a picture perfect setting, with the kind of view that is enviable to the many tourists that come through that part of Pennsylvania. What serenity, to be able to live among peace-loving people who enjoyed such wonderful simplicity. Anyone who might have gone by, seeing me on that porch, would have thought I was privileged to bask in such tranquility.

Joan knew the truth, that inside me a storm was raging, with the result that I was sinking deeper and deeper into depression. She didn't always know what to do about it. There were a couple things she did that helped a lot. She prayed for me and she didn't cater to my pity parties. Each was important.

Hebrews 12:15 says we are to "see to it that no one misses the grace of God and that no bitter root grows up to cause trouble and defile many." My bitterness caused not only me to be in agony, my family suffered as well. Joan didn't feel encouragement from me. My children didn't receive the affection that I could offer. I was a miserable thing to live with.

Common enemies outside the family, those things against which we had struggled together in the past, generally tended to pull us together. As big as those foes might loom before us, the more dangerous ones are those that creep in and take root in a small way at first. They too must be identified, with war waged against them. My growing bitterness was one such evil that needed to be eradicated.

**A successful family
recognizes and overcomes the enemies
that threaten to destroy it from within.**

CHAPTER SIXTEEN

Heavy rains pelted the cobblestone streets of Boston with the dark October skies indicating the torrential downpour would continue. The 1990 bicycle marathon was canceled. Rather than seeing the city from the seat of a bike, Loie sat on a living room chair, solemnly looking out her friend's apartment window.

She had been looking forward to this special time with her friend on this long weekend away from her hospital work. Her eight-hour trip had passed quickly with the anticipation of the biking event. Now, not only was there no bicycle adventure, there was also little interaction with her friend who was now sleeping in the next room, exhausted from having been up all night fighting a nasty virus. Nothing seemed to be going as planned.

Loie's anxious thoughts surprised her. It was not primarily the disappointment about the weekend that created her bewilderment, but a nagging idea that had grown in intensity and now was as consuming as her friend's virus. The notion began to take shape the previous evening while traveling through Connecticut. The last time she was in that state, we were in the midst of our church-planting venture. That trip to New England was more exciting than this one was turning out to be. During her visit with us in our ministry, she witnessed our passion for that work.

Loie replayed the idea: "Ron and Joan had to leave a church-planting ministry because they were too overwhelmed with the care of their children. I should offer to dedicate myself to helping Joan with the kids. I could move with them, and Ron could be involved in church-planting again." Loie sat in the quiet room, contemplating the idea.

She stood, stretched, and paced around the room. "This plan is ludicrous! The Denlingers haven't expressed any intention in going back into church planting, but maybe this is what God would want me to do for them. They really did seem to enjoy being involved in mission work."

Her friend stirred in the next room but did not awaken. "I can't help the Denlingers. I have my heart set on being a missionary nurse in an African orphanage. I want to impact many lives, not just one family."

The pelting rain against the window drew her focus back to her surroundings. She gathered up dirty cups scattered around the apartment and took them to the kitchen. "I must put this absurd thought out of my mind," she reasoned to herself. "I think Ron and Joan were meeting with Ron Klassen last evening to inform him of their resignation from the mission. Why should this idea harass me when THEY aren't even thinking of any such thing?"

She glanced at the clock and saw it was already noon, but her friend showed no signs of desiring to eat. Loie picked up her Bible; reading would be a distraction to her thoughts.

She felt compelled to read the book of Ruth. The story instantly intrigued her. Ruth, a widow, left her homeland and father's house to travel with her widowed mother-in-law to a land that was foreign to Ruth because of her love and commitment to this one lonely woman.

Loie hesitated at one particular verse. Ruth was passionately persuading her mother-in-law to allow her to move with her, "Where you go I will go, and where you stay I will stay. Your people will be my people and your God my God."

Loie looked up from her Bible. There it was! A woman who committed herself to one family and God blessed her for it. Was God Himself confirming to her that she should be willing to commit to one family?

Would the Denlingers think of moving back into church planting? Would they consider having me with them? Why would I want to leave my secure nursing job to go somewhere else and start again? She shuddered at the thought of uprooting and leaving friends and her familiar surroundings.

Before she closed her Bible, she again read the words in front of her. "Will you go?" She dropped to her knees and cried out to God. "Lord, I will go if it is where You are calling me."

She opened her eyes and anxiously looked around the room. Her friend hadn't seen her. "I must be crazy, I am not telling a soul about this!"

*   *   *

Ron and I sat quietly at our Sunday dinner table. The Klassens had left earlier in the morning. The past twenty-four hours had been a whirlwind filled with fun, laughter, and a fascinating proposal. The idea of having a nanny, by which we could again have the opportunity to move into ministry, had never crossed our minds.

As soon as Ron Klassen had spoken the idea, Loie immediately came to my mind. Last night, even into the wee hours of the morning, the concept was increasingly thrilling to us the longer we spoke of it. Ron agreed with me that he too thought Loie would be the perfect person to fill that role. She was terrific with the kids, she had become a trusted friend of mine, and she really did seem to enjoy spending time with our family. Ron's eyes had glimmered with hope as we tossed around reasons why the whole scenario might be feasible.

Now, just a few hours later, we sat solemnly as we allowed the reality of the situation to penetrate our practical minds. "What right do we have to ask Loie to leave her secure world to help us fill our dreams? Why do we even think she would consider this? Where would we go? Would we be able to raise financial support again? If we could, how would Loie be supported? Why do we even think God wants to use us back in ministry? Hasn't He already made it clear that He was finished with us? If we were to be in ministry, why didn't He show us a way to remain in Connecticut? Why does God keep raising our hopes only to have them shattered?

I quietly cleared the table and started to wash the dishes while Ron pulled Kari from her chair. She had fallen asleep at the table. He curled her floppy body around his as they settled onto the couch for a Sunday afternoon snooze. Ryan was already sleeping in his crib. The morning's commotion at church had exhausted him.

I halfheartedly slopped the dishcloth across a plate and looked out the kitchen window over the barren cornfield. The Amish children were taking turns riding their new cream-colored pony down in the meadow. They seemed so carefree and happy on this autumn day. Oh, how I remembered those days!

Flashbacks of my childhood appeared in full color in my mind. Sunday afternoons were filled with delightful bike

riding adventures or tunnel building in the dusty hayloft of
our big mysterious barn. Hikes to the "haunted" house with my
brothers send goose bumps throughout my tired body even now.
Choosing teams for a game of baseball or football with the
neighborhood gang always was a challenge and fun.

But my most vivid, heartwarming memory was riding
horseback, trotting Patches, my oversized pony, through miles
of barren fields in the fall and winter months. The cold air stung
my face and reddened my cheeks and ears, my hair tossing in the
air with each bounce. Patches exhaled steamy air through his
velvety nostrils and snorted with joy. Alone with my horse,
I spent hours dreaming I was a fair maiden living in a castle in a
faraway land.

The squeak of the glass I was washing brought me back
to my humble abode. Far from a fair maiden, my twenty-seven-
year-old body felt the years of hard knocks I had been through,
but as of yet, Cinderella had not emerged. Living in my sixth
home in six years of marriage often left me feeling unsettled,
longing for stability. I loved my two severely handicapped children dearly, but their constant needs zapped my energy. Their
condition had drastically changed the dreams I had for our
family, and their daily suffering reminded me that my life was
far from any fantasy.

Being the mother of children who would never succeed
in life was neither prestigious nor was it enviable. Living with a
husband who desired a ministry career that dangled beyond his
reach was painful. Financial stress hung over our heads each
month as we attempted to make his paycheck cover all the bills,
including large medical charges.

A card caught my eye as I glanced toward the window
again. It was another Bible verse that I had placed there this week

to encourage me in my daily grind and to keep my focus on the things that are not visible in this world. "God understands and knows me. He is the Lord who exercises kindness, justice, and righteousness." (Jeremiah 9:24)

"Okay, Lord," I said aloud, "I know You know me. Help me to understand You, Your ways, Your plans, and Your timing. I know You desire good things for me and You know my needs. I'm really struggling to understand the difficulties of my life."

I picked up another dirty dish as my tears fell into my dishwater. "Lord, I need faith—faith like the great men and women of the Bible. You are faithful and You do delight in taking care of me. I need Your unfailing love and compassion. I'm so sorry for my lack of trust. My soul is being decayed by worry. I'm ugly inside and out. Strengthen me today!"

Ryan's crying upstairs alerted me that it was time to begin his feeding regimen. For the next hour, I busied myself with his care, but all the while the desire to talk to Loie continued to nag at me.

I entered the living room where Ron was busy clapping on Kari's back to loosen the phlegm that had congested her lungs during her short nap. "Ron, I think we should bounce the nanny idea off Loie. If she doesn't show interest, at least then we'll know."

He smiled, "It's up to you; you know her best."

It would be at least four days till I would see Loie again, so when Monday morning arrived I simply put the idea out of my mind and continued with my workday. Transporting Kari and Ryan to their schools and working with the therapists encompassed most of my time and energy.

As the week continued with all of its pressures and commitments, I lost all hope that the nanny idea of Mr. Klassen's would ever come into fruition. It was too large a task to ask Loie to consider.

The colorful leaves on the autumn trees posed a brilliant contrast to the gray sky of the dreary afternoon. It was Thursday afternoon and I knew Loie would be arriving soon for our weekly time together. I wrapped a sweater snugly around me as I walked to the mailbox to retrieve the day's mail. My soul felt more like the gray sky than the colorful leaves. Since rejecting the nanny idea, Ron and I had no hope of ever being in full-time church work again. During my prayer time this morning, I received no assurance that God was hearing me.

I flipped through the letters as I scuffled back to the house. One envelope with a familiar logo caught my eye. I hurriedly ripped it open. It read, "Dear Ron and Joan, Just wanted to let you know that the board of RHMA and myself are intently praying for you that you will consider the 'nanny plan.' I trust that you are continuing to make this a matter of prayer with us. Warmly, Ron Klassen."

My heart fluttered within me as I bounded up the remaining steps to the porch. I went inside and threw the rest of the mail on the desk and dropped onto the sofa, still clutching the letter to my chest. I carefully read the letter again as tears started to stream down my face. "God, what am I to think? Loie will be here in any minute, do You really want me to ask her?"

There was a knock at the door, and Loie peeked her head around the door. "Hello, is anyone home?" I dried my tears and went to greet her. Her long, dark hair covered my face as I hugged her. She walked over to the kids in their wheelchairs and gave them each a kiss. Ryan hollered in response and instantly she released him from his harness and held him closely. I watched the interaction and knew in my heart that she was the one who would be my choice for a nanny to my children.

She sat rocking Ryan as I nervously poured us each a cup of tea. We chatted briefly about her trip to Boston, but Loie knew me well enough to know something was heavy on my heart. "Joan, is everything okay?"

"Loie," I began very hesitantly, "this is really bizarre, but I need to talk to you about something. I'm afraid to say it, but I just have to get it off my chest! Last weekend when Ron Klassen was here, he made a suggestion."

Loie interrupted me before I finished. "Joan, I know what you are going to say. God has been speaking to me, but I want to hear you say it."

Without further delay, I continued to explain Mr. Klassen's suggestion, convinced that Loie couldn't possibly know what I was about to share. Loie's eyes filled with tears as I spoke. When I finished, she related her experience in Boston.

We sat silent, afraid to move. God's leading seemed unmistakable. He had revealed his plan to both of us completely separate from one another. His invisible presence filled my little living room, giving us peace and assurance that He would continue to go before us and chart the course we were to take.

Loie stayed through the evening so we could share our story with Ron. He listened with amazement. We sat huddled on the living room floor, shaking with excitement, believing this was clearly from the Lord. Ron's eyes sparkled with hope again. The part of his heart that had died was now coming to life.

None of us knew how all the details would work out, but tonight that didn't matter. We were content to trust God for those. We held hands and took turns praying, the kids lying on the floor in the middle of our tiny circle. The five of us would proceed together in this adventure.

We decided to pray about the plan for a few months before seeking the opinions of others. We did not want to be hasty in any of our decisions, and the timing of this change seemed a major issue.

That week, Ron and I signed a year's lease on what would be our seventh rented home. Our little country house on the hill had fifteen steps to get to the first floor—too many for carrying two children and wheelchairs. Our new ranch-style home was seven miles closer to the city to which Ron and I both continued to travel on a regular basis.

Ron was also in the midst of being trained for a new position within his company, and he had agreed to remain in the position for at least a year. This new job involved a lot more stress, but he needed to take on the extra responsibility with its larger salary to keep his family from slipping beneath the rising financial flood.

Eventually we did begin to share our plan with friends and relatives, receiving great encouragement from them to follow the path that God was leading us. RHMA began their search to locate a town in which a new church-plant was needed. To serve under RHMA, we would again need to raise financial support from individuals and churches as we had done before going to Connecticut. This time, as we began our deputation process of speaking at various churches explaining the vision we had for our work, we had Loie join us.

Our audiences were very receptive to our message as the three of us dressed in Biblical costumes. Loie impersonated Ruth because of her willingness to leave behind her home and move with us and assist our family. I acted the part of Jonah, not only because of our similar names, but also because I was apprehensive about all the changes this would require in my life. I was tempted to run in another direction, as did the prophet in the scripture.

I liked my comfortable surroundings and support of my family members. I was not convinced that I had the energy it took to start another church. The dark, lonely days of Connecticut continued to plague my mind. I was afraid I would fail again at combining mothering disabled children and supporting a husband in his ministry.

Ron played the part of Moses, a man asked to lead a nation. Although Ron was not being asked to sacrifice as much, he was cautious about the idea of moving forward and again attempting to bring something new into existence. The question of finances also loomed large on his mind. Would God provide for all his family needs?

Throughout the following year, each of us took our turn at being fearful about this immense move, but the "Boston story" continued to reassure us that God was the one who ordained this challenging adventure. We pressed forward despite our fears.

One thing each of us learned: When God puts a desire and plan in our hearts, He does not intend to let it go. His timing was perfect. The skills Ron learned over the next year as a sales representative prepared him for the even bigger responsibility of presenting the need for a new evangelical church in the town to which we would eventually move.

We received amazing support from our church family and relatives. Not only did they give their encouragement and blessing to the five of us in our venture, but they also gave financially to help us get started. Through RHMA, we learned of an area in which a few believers already had strong interest in beginning a new church. God made sure that it was within driving distance of the Delaware hospital where I took the children on a regular basis.

Loie also planned for the new change in her life. Before we moved, she had inquired about part-time nursing employment in the region where we were going and had a new job by the time we moved.

The hardest thing to let go of was the help of my mother. She had been very faithful in supporting me while we lived in Lancaster. Kari and Ryan had grown to love and trust her, and she thoroughly enjoyed caring for them. They had filled a special place in her heart that had been empty many years since losing her own handicapped child. Letting them go beyond her daily reach was very difficult for her and for me.

The last day of November 1991, with all our earthly belongings crammed into the largest U-haul truck available, the five of us headed down the road of faith. We were ready to embrace an adventurous journey—led by God.

Ron's Reflections . . .

What more could one ask for in terms of clear direction from God? A director coming up with an idea, our immediately knowing who would best fill that bill, that individual having the same idea cross her mind and choose to be willing—all within one weekend. We may as well have encountered a burning bush and heard the Lord's voice booming from within it.

Even with these undeniably amazing "coincidences"

before us, and having an awesome provision unexpectedly presented to us, we struggled to believe that God could pull it all off. We had felt beaten down too much for too long. We had become convinced that God was not going to use us in church planting. Lots of thoughts and emotions needed to be turned around before we could say yes. That is only reasonable, isn't it?

God was calling us to believe Him, to step out in faith, even though we didn't feel very confident, even though we could cite plenty of reasons why things couldn't come together, not the least of which was that our children remained disabled. One by one the excuses I threw toward heaven seemed inadequate in comparison to the infinite power of our heavenly father. And so we said yes and pressed on, with our fears hanging on as best they could.

A successful family
perseveres
in spite of doubt.

CHAPTER SEVENTEEN

They flew in their typical Canadian "V" formation with grace and style, each following the lead of the goose in front of them. The crisp January air motivated them toward their warmer destination. I watched the flock flying over the lake that lay in clear view below my bedroom window. This incredible phenomenon of nature, a group united together to accomplish the same goal, fascinated me. Each fowl was capable of surviving on its own for a time, but, for the benefit of the whole, hung together for strength as they advanced. They aided one another in their trek toward their destination.

"God, let this new baby church fly with just as much harmony and clear direction under Your leadership," I whispered into the quietness of the morning. Closing my Bible, I sat at my little desk a moment longer, relishing my time alone in my bedroom cove. As I gazed out over the huge reservoir before me, my thoughts drifted back to the events of the past month.

Our relocation to a little town called Red Hill went smoothly—a small group of enthusiastic Christians greeted us and helped us unpack. The home we moved to was unusual in its size and layout. Four bedrooms gave us ample space to have Loie live with us. Her bedroom and bath were conveniently located together at the other end of the house. Because of the house's deteriorating condition, the monthly rent was affordable for us. Soap and water did much to make the sprawling house a home.

The folks who helped us unpack were enthusiastic about seeing an evangelical church started in their community. Two months earlier, they began meeting Sunday mornings for worship but were eager for more consistent pastoral leadership. Ron was more than ready to fill that role.

We had little time to adjust to our new surroundings before the Advent season was upon us—a very busy month for anyone in the work of ministry. Ron plunged into the duties of his new position, thrilled to be a part of a new church ministry again. Along with preparing sermons related to the Christmas season, he spent time with people already coming to the church and attempted to get a feel for the administrative responsibilities needed for this work.

The Sunday before Christmas, we hosted a pageant and an open house in our large home for the folks attending the new church. Our living room featured a fifteen-foot stone fireplace and hardwood floor space that provided seating room for sixty adults and children. The stairway to the second floor had a fifteen-foot-long by four-foot-wide platform that served as a stage for the Christmas play.

Two days before the holiday, Ron organized an evening of caroling on the streets of Red Hill as means of sharing the spirit of the holiday with the town. On Christmas Eve, ninety-one people crammed into our little rented basement church facility for a holy candlelight service, which concluded our series of Christmas ministry events.

Later that night, Ron and I excitedly talked about the successful service—how the church was growing so quickly and it seemed that God was adding His blessing. Ron glowed with enthusiasm as he talked on about the new ministry he was enjoying so much.

Between our excitement and my preparations for fifteen people coming the next day for Christmas dinner, we got little sleep that night.

The only cloud that cast a shadow over the active month of December was the task of nursing Kari through a nasty influenza virus. I couldn't have accomplished all the ministry tasks without Loie's tireless support.

With the New Year now upon us, Ron was focusing on what he was seeing to be the enormous task ahead of him—uniting this core group of families under a common vision, one that would be in line with the leading of Jesus Christ. Everyone had ideas and desires of what the new church would accomplish, each one good in its own way.

Bringing the group together to a common goal and purpose proved to be a challenging job. Some days I saw him struggling with questions. What was God's desire here? Why had He chosen me to lead such an ambitious group? Together we prayed for God's help, and I encouraged Ron to keep devoted to the task God had given him.

I knew that God had given Ron the abilities needed to evaluate the progress our small church was making, and then give vision and direction to this mixed group of people. He was working with very talented and passionate people and he wanted to help foster their individuality even while uniting them as a church. He was concerned that he not fail them, nor did he want to fall short of God's desire for the church.

God was the one allowing him a second chance in this kind of work that Ron loved. Because he did not want to disappoint Him nor did he want to be a failure, he worked seven days a week. Loie's faithful service relieved him of helping me with the children.

Ryan crying in the next room reminded me that the routine of the day needed to begin. The first task was getting my children ready for school.

Shortly after arriving in Red Hill, I explored the therapy school options for Kari and Ryan. The program I chose for them was situated close to our new home and they were in their first week of attendance. In just two short hours, the van would arrive to pick them up and transport them to the school. I had much to do to get them ready on time.

*   *   *

The phone rang just as I was ready to deliver a meal to a family whose mother was in the hospital. I carefully placed my box of homemade food next to the door and grabbed the phone. "Mrs. Denlinger, could you come pick up Ryan here at school? He is having terrible seizures. We think you should get him to a doctor." Before hanging up, I reassured the school nurse that I would be right there.

I stuffed the car keys in my pocket, called Ron from his office, and asked him to deliver my food while I went for Ryan. Once in the solitude of my car, I began to cry.

Throughout the four weeks in their new school, Kari and Ryan had managed to stay healthy. With February's chilly weather, I expected them to have colds, but out-of-control epilepsy was not what I wanted to deal with. The recent increase of his seizure medication seemed to be making little difference.

I quickly dried my tears as I arrived at school. Ryan was lying on a cot in a quiet room. His body was rigid and he made no response to my voice. He struggled for air between each rhythmic body contraction. I scooped him up and rushed to the car. Ron met me at the door of our home. He had already contacted Loie to see if she could be home in time to meet Kari when she came home from school. He took over the wheel as we drove to A.I. Dupont Hospital, an hour and a half away.

The emergency physician took one look at Ryan and immediately started an intravenous line. After several doses of Valium, Ryan finally stopped seizing and fell asleep.

His neurologist arrived. "Mr. and Mrs. Denlinger, I want to admit Ryan. We must find something that will better control Ryan's seizures. We cannot have him doing tricks like this again." Ryan remained in a Valium-induced sleeping state for the rest of the evening as I prepared myself mentally for another stay in the hospital. Ron needed to leave but reassured me that he would bring me fresh clothes the next day.

Five days into the hospitalization, one of Ryan's new seizure medications caused his respiratory muscles to relax so much that his airway collapsed. It was Saturday night and I was holding him when he started gasping for air, his whole body crying out for help. The roommate's mother pushed the bell for the nurse and within minutes an entire emergency team was working to reestablish his breathing.

I stood shaking in the corner of the room, watching the action before me. "Oh, God, I would rather die than watch my son struggle for air! Please don't take him; I love him so much," I cried silently.

Within thirty minutes, the doctors informed me that they had stabilized Ryan's condition and he was breathing well. His big dark eyes looked wearily in my direction as I picked up his weak body and cradled him tightly to me. His lips were pink and medicine flowed through his intravenous line to keep him breathing freely. A few minutes later he was asleep.

"Lord," I whispered as I rocked, "I see myself in Ryan. When I'm struggling with my own pain or sin, I know You are there for me just as I am for Ryan. Thank You for going before me and dying on the cross so I never have to face eternal death."

The hall lights grew dim, reminding me it was late. I needed to call Ron and Loie to inform them of Ryan's traumatic experience earlier in the evening. Loie was at home taking care of Kari. Ron was in his office preparing tomorrow morning's message.

*   *   *

"Ron, listen to this!" I spoke enthusiastically as we sped along the interstate coming home from a week-long RHMA Conference. The April sun beat down on my open Bible. "'I will open the eyes that are blind, and release captives from prison and those who sit in darkness. I am the LORD!'"

I finished reading the Isaiah passage. "Won't it be thrilling to see that happen in Kari and Ryan?" He smiled and nodded as he concentrated on the traffic around us. He was happy to see me so relaxed; the conference was a much-needed break for both of us. Loie had offered to stay at home with both kids so we could enjoy the time without them. Trying to keep their feeding, bathing, medicating, diapering, and therapy schedule intact would have been too overwhelming for all of us with a 900-mile-trip.

Loie was such a godsend. We were becoming very close friends and confidants. I was eager to see her and the kids after spending a week away from the routine of their care.

The church-planting conference was special. We were introduced to Warren Wiersbe. His was the quotation I had treasured since Kari's first hospital admission: "Yard by yard life is hard, inch by inch life's a cinch." Dr. Wiersbe spoke at the main sessions and was a wonderful encouragement to our thirsty, tired souls.

I scratched a few lines in my journal before I threw it in a bag with my Bible. "Jesus, You are showing me lessons in life that others may not see. My children possess a mystery and sweetness. I want to see in them what You see! Have You made them blind so my eyes would be open to Your desires? Have You made them mute so I would speak for them and show the world what holy joy is—joy that does not come from temporary pleasures in life?" We continued down the highway, back to our busy life in Red Hill, not knowing the roadblocks we would face.

*   *   *

The door slammed behind us as Ron kicked a rock up against our brick house. "Why didn't you tell me you were worried about these things? You never talk to me anymore!" He threw the words into my tear-stained face. Although we had taken our heated argument outside beyond the earshot of Loie, she was well aware of the growing tension between us.

Our discussion began when I described the "tip of the iceberg" fears I was having concerning a problem at the church. By now a huge mountain of anxiety revealed itself.

"How am I supposed to know or understand you, if you are only telling your feelings to Loie?" I cringed under the truth of Ron's words.

The helpful insights we had received at our conference a month earlier regarding communication with our spouse, now seemed distant and confusing to my stressed mind and emotions.

The church was continuing to grow and, with it, Ron's added responsibilities. I was happy for his success, but along with growth came a tremendous influx of spiritually needy people.

The straw that broke the camel's back came the Sunday before. A gentleman visited our service and, in conversation with him afterward, Ron found out that he was a minister from Baltimore who had heard about our church. This should have been a red flag since our new church was not well known. In his customary hospitable way, Ron invited him home for Sunday dinner.

The second red flag appeared when he declined having lunch with us. He instead waited in our driveway till we were finished eating. I was sufficiently suspicious of this man that I decided to remove my children from whatever might unfold. I asked Loie to help me carry them upstairs. I was glad I did. Although they communicated nothing orally, Kari and Ryan seemed perceptive in their spirit and often reacted negatively when conflict was present. We settled the kids in bed for a nap. Loie offered to stay with them while I went downstairs to be a moral support to Ron.

When the man came into our house, he began with theological small talk. I wondered what his real purpose was for the visit. As the afternoon wore on it became evident that our visitor held to heretical teachings. To these, Ron remained calm as he responded with Biblical instruction. After another hour of conversation, our visitor was completely frustrated in his inability to convince Ron. There was rising intensity in the man's voice. His final obnoxious attempt to change Ron's mind was to threaten to destroy our ministry. I stayed on the couch, silently praying for this evil man, with his curses, to leave. Ron, realizing the man wasn't getting the point that he had long overextended his welcome, escorted him to the door and with a firm hand and a good push, threw him out of our house.

When Loie heard the man's car pull out of the driveway, she reappeared. "What was going on down here? Kari has been convulsing with seizures ever since that man came. She has now finally stopped!"

In that instant, I knew that although my daughter's mind and body were disabled, something within her was not. It was as though she sensed an evil presence had been in our home. To see what my children were being exposed to frightened me.

This attack came from outside our congregation. Although it was a disturbing circumstance, the situations that caused increasing dread in me were disgruntled people within the church.

Some people's ideas of ministry were not being developed as they had hoped. As a result, they verbally attacked Ron's vision for the church. I knew that every leader experiences criticism, but seeing my husband mistrusted by some of those he was serving dismayed me. These were the same people I daily rubbed shoulders with and loved. I felt powerless to change the situation, so I said nothing to Ron. Instead, I expressed my fears and frustrations to Loie over bowls of ice cream late in the evening while Ron was out at meetings.

I knew the conflicts at church troubled Ron so I didn't want to bother him with my own anxiety. I didn't want him to think that I was afraid. On this spring day when I couldn't contain my apprehension anymore, Loie persuaded me to talk to my husband.

As Ron and I aired our frustrations, a sober question began to form in each of us. "Was life returning to the unmanageable pace we experienced in Connecticut?"

*   *   *

"Dear Journal, it's June of 1992 and I'm sitting in a hospital room again—the fourth time this year! Ryan is having surgery tomorrow. He needs his hip muscles and right shoulder muscle lengthened so he can move his joints again. He is in much pain now, and his surgery will result in more pain until he recuperates.

"Lord, will my son ever be relieved of pain? The suffering of a child is unbearable! How can I avoid this? Can I hide? Can I turn my face away? Will I ever see an end to all this pain? Ryan fights this horrible war with pain. His eyes question me, 'Why don't you help me?' If only I could.

"I'm so jealous tonight of Ryan's roommate. The child smiles and responds to his parents' attention. Forgive me, Holy Father! Give me the eyes and heart that You have so I can see beyond the suffering of this little boy who reflects Your character.

"Separated again from our family, Ryan and I are confined to a sterile hospital environment battling questions in life that have no answers. I look forward to Ryan's discharge from this place filled with suffering children. At least at home my attention is pulled in many directions and I can avoid these questions that slap me in the face every time I'm restricted to these hospital walls.

"I too feel completely estranged from my husband's world of ministry. The growing emotional distance I sense from him is so evident when we are apart. At least when I'm home, there is some appearance of a normal relationship."

*   *   *

The fulfillment of my desire to be at home was short-lived. Within six weeks of Ryan's discharge, he and I were back at Wilmington's Dupont Children's Hospital.

The phone rang, startling me. As I straightened my drooping neck, my stiff muscles reacted, sending shooting pain down my back. Ryan lay quiet in my lap. His intravenous line draped over my legs and the humidified oxygen mask dangled to one side of his face. We must have drifted off to sleep while I rocked him. The phone rang for the third time as I reached for it, my hand accidentally knocking off a suction catheter lying on the bedside table.

"Hello, honey, this is Ron. How is Ryan doing?" I quickly glanced at the clock, realizing I had been sleeping for half an hour. The hospital room was dark and the IV continued its droning tap while delivering fluids into the dehydrated veins of my son.

"We got back from the gastrointestinal lab a while ago," I responded in a fatigued voice. "Ron, the doctor was unsuccessful again in getting the G-tube in Ryan's intestine. It looks like he's heading for major surgery." We exchanged a few more pieces of information, then Ron assured me he would come to visit after services on Sunday.

I said good-bye, cutting off the only outside contact I had in two days.

I had brought Ryan to Dupont two weeks earlier with pneumonia and weight loss. His breathing had improved, but he continued to vomit profusely and was aspirating much of the regurgitated feeding into his lungs. Medication and various other techniques were unsuccessful in getting his food into his intestine where it could be digested and provide nourishment to him. Our only solution left was a surgical procedure to tie the stomach closed at the esophagus so his G-tube feeding would only have one direction to go—down.

My only comfort to spending more time in this prison was that it provided an air-conditioned room during the sweltering days of August 1992. I had been glued to Ryan's bedside twenty-four hours a day, his wrenching body needing constant assistance and comfort. I had exhausted every lullaby and nursery rhyme I knew and resorted to repetitious melodies to calm his rigid muscles. His fingers grasped my thumb and he held tight to the one stable source he knew. He cried in fear when I pried my hand away for just a few minutes.

"I love you, Ryan." I kissed his cool forehead, tasting the salty sweat beading on his brow. "We're going to get you better, buddy. Mommy is here and I won't leave you!" I whispered reassuring words as I settled him back in his steel caged crib and wound the music box to let the soft melody soothe his spirit.

I stretched my sleeping muscles and arranged the sheets on my cot. "Oh, God, I'm so lonely. I know You are my constant companion, but right now I need arms to hold me up and a listening ear. You say You are collecting all my tears, but does anyone else see the pain I'm in?" I walked out into the hallway towards the soda machine.

Loie arranged her home-health nursing job to be available to help care for Kari while I was away. She was working hard at keeping Kari healthy and bringing her for weekly visits to Ryan and me, so I knew I shouldn't disturb her with a phone call from a lonely friend.

Ron was in the tangled organizational web of administering our church's first Vacation Bible School for children. Our church had recently purchased a facility. Although renovations were in full swing, it would not be ready to house the weeklong adventure. Somehow the cramped quarters of the rented basement would have to do.

Ron's attention was needed in many areas to keep everything running smoothly. The extra activity within the church revealed stressed and frayed emotions of the ones who were giving their all to the life of our church. Ron spent time consoling those who were feeling burned out. He also continued the hour-and-a-half trips every third day to the hospital.

The thought of what Ron was experiencing pulled an aching muscle in my soul. I knew how much he depended on my emotional support when he was in the midst of making decisions that were not always popular. I listened on the phone as he would tell me the struggles of his heart. We always ended our talks with prayer, acknowledging before God that we were weak, but He was strong. We committed our stresses to Him. Even so, here I was confined in the hospital during a rather stressful time at the church, not fully available for Ron's needs.

I sipped my soda and prayed as I strolled back to Ryan's room. "God, I know by Ron's voice he is stressed out. His son is seriously sick, his daughter is severely disabled, and I'm here having no extra energy to give to him. Lord, we are trying to do what You have called us to do. Please give us courage to not withdraw from one another. Please give us supernatural strength to go on!"

As I entered Ryan's room, the verse that I read earlier in the morning crossed my mind. "God looks down from heaven . . . to see if there are any who understand or any who seek Him." I grasped the railing of Ryan's crib and looked down into his cherub face and whispered, "I'm sorry, Lord. I know I'm in the pit of depression. Look at me and find a woman who desires to do Your will. Refresh me with Your Living Water!"

Ryan did recover from his major abdominal surgery. On his fourth birthday a few weeks later, we celebrated his ability to be fed again. His slender body slowly filled out and he appeared healthy. We rejoiced that our family was able to be together again after the disruption of the long hospitalization during the month of August.

*   *   *

Autumn brought with it a demanding church schedule and hibernating viruses waiting to attack my children's weakened immune systems. Ron did his best to keep on top of the ministry. I took aggressive action to keep the kids' environment as germ-free as possible and away from those who were obviously sick. Our desire was to prevent our work, church, and kids from causing further stress in our home.

Despite our efforts, we both felt like we were losing ground in each of our areas of responsibility. Five families within the church were facing major crises and Ron was called upon to minister to their intense needs. He loved these people. To see them struggling through difficult situations added to his own tension. Ron and I spent sleepless hours many nights, crying out to God to give us wisdom and courage to know how to help in their time of trouble.

On the home front, Kari and Ryan continued to have frequent seizures and constant colds. Shortly before Thanksgiving, I realized Kari was losing her battle with her most recent infection. I drove her to Dupont where the doctor immediately admitted her. He placed her on oxygen and ordered pulmonary treatments every two to four hours. An intravenous (IV) line was started and slowly dripped antibiotics into her vein, as we waited to see if she would improve.

Three days later, on Thanksgiving Eve, I threw myself a major pity party. The respiratory therapist had just completed another pulmonary treatment where he flushed out Kari's lungs with deep suctioning. The energy it took to help Kari through this horrific procedure had used up all my emotional reserves.

I was alone with no shoulder to cry on and felt abandoned. I knew I was missing another exciting event in the life of our church—a Thanksgiving Eve Service. Ron was there now, leading the service and directing the people's thoughts towards thanksgiving and praise to God for His abundant care in their lives.

Anger rose within me and I allowed it to take full control of my thoughts. How could I be thankful? Suffering children and anxiety-ridden parents surrounded me. Who could explain suffering? Even while Ron preaches, his daughter lies in a hospital bed, gray and dusky, as a thirsty suction catheter relieves her lungs of the thick, infected secretions. She vomits and gasps for air as she struggles to breathe. *No six-year-old should ever have to face this much suffering!* I justified my angry thoughts. Her body is weak and hot from fever. *No, God, I refuse to be thankful on a night like this!*

For two hours I hardened my heart, tossing and turning on my miserable cot. My thoughts rambled; my body ached and allowed me no sleep. I refused to pray, and I had little strength to help my daughter when she cried out. I was the perfect picture of an ungrateful, ugly, angry spirit who had cut off contact with God.

It was a dark and lonely choice I made that night until I gave in and yielded my anger to the One who created me, and I acknowledged before God that I desperately needed Him and His forgiveness. He filled me completely with inward joy.

That night I realized that all those who suffer ultimately have two options—to receive suffering as though it is a curse from the pit of hell or to accept it as a gift from the hand of heaven, a gift that builds character and makes us more like Jesus. The choice we make determines the outlook of our lives.

Thanksgiving Day on the pediatric floor was somber and quiet. Working on a holiday did not thrill the staff. We parents sat by the bedsides of our children—mindful of the festivities we were missing. The children lay bored in their beds, saddened by sickness, pain, and loneliness.

Amidst this atmosphere of hopelessness, I felt contentment and peace. Despite serving time again in my prison called Dupont, watching Kari suffer with another case of pneumonia, God was coming alongside of me.

The abundant joy that my heavenly Father showered on me the night before overflowed to my daughter and those around me. Kari started to improve, so I walked the halls pushing her wheelchair and IV pole and chatted with other discouraged parents. God knew I needed an extra dose of strength that day, for I was about to face a different type of hospital experience.

Before Kari was discharged the Sunday after Thanksgiving, she got a new roommate, someone she knew quite well. Her brother Ryan was admitted to the same semi-private room.

Ron brought him in with high fever and projectile vomiting (something that was supposedly impossible because of his August surgery) and uncontrollable seizures. Despite large doses of IV antibiotics, he continued to have dangerously high fevers and severe vomiting. His liver enzymes were highly elevated. The doctor gave us several possible reasons why this may be happening, but none of the further testing confirmed any diagnosis. Ryan's symptoms totally perplexed the doctor. He was running out of options in treating Ryan.

Would we lose our son? The ominous question rose in our minds. Ron stayed at the hospital with me as we watched and waited to see if Ryan could again fight an unknown destructive invader. His pathetic cry and big dark sunken eyes elicited the sympathies of the nurses too. His was a little life that never spoke an audible word. Yet he communicated volumes to those who knew and loved him by his very presence. Ryan's teachers from school called daily to inquire of him. Our church family prayed for strength for Ron and me and health for Ryan.

One day a hospital volunteer dropped off a card at Ryan's bedside; enclosed was a scripture quote from Philippians 3:10. It said, "That I may know Him and the power of His resurrection and the fellowship of His suffering." I bowed my head over Ryan's feverish body and prayed, "God, thank You that You are not abandoning Ryan or me during this horrible suffering. I know You share my pain."

Just when Ron and I thought we couldn't bear Ryan's agony any longer, he started to improve. His liver enzymes miraculously dropped to more normal levels, his vomiting ceased, and his fever disappeared. No medical explanation could be given, but God convinced us that He was not finished with Ryan or us. The night before Ryan's discharge, I paraphrased the beautiful Psalm 66: 10-12 passage in my journal to fit my family's experience of the past few weeks.

"For You, O God, tested us; You refined us like silver. You brought us into prison (the hospital) and laid burdens on our back (bad lab results and illness). You let men ride over our heads (worry consumed us), we went through fire and water (Kari and

Ryan being hospitalized back to back), but You brought us to a place of abundance (our children are going home)!"

*   *   *

It was Advent season again. Our family had survived a challenging first year of ministry in Red Hill and another grueling year with the health of our kids.

Ron and I quietly talked at the dining room table, two candles from the Advent wreath granting us our only light. Kari and Ryan lay on opposite ends of the couch, their gurgled breathing providing us our only background noise. Both of them had been sick all day with fever and congestion.

During the past week, two sets of parents we knew lost children through unexpected death. The one child attended school with our son Ryan. His name was also Ryan. When the word went over the school's phone chain that Ryan died, it was assumed that it was our son. The second couple was serving as missionaries in Haiti and their newborn died an accidental death. Our thoughts were drawn in compassion towards their incredible pain.

"Ron," I said softly, "what do you think God is preparing us for?"

He stared into the candlelight a few moments before answering. Then as though he had received wisdom from heaven, Ron responded, "He is preparing us for Jesus' return to earth." His dark brown eyes pierced my heart as he continued, "Joan, we are privileged to know firsthand the suffering of Christ. We are constantly aware of the destruction that sin is causing in this world. We never lose perspective of eternity, our hope lies there and not in some superficial happiness here on the earth."

Ron looked out a window into the dark night then continued. "Christ is coming again to rid the world of this horrible evil, pain, and suffering, and to claim His kingdom forever."

I said no more; I knew his words were true. I extinguished the candles as I rose from my chair and walked over to the couch where my children lay unaware of how difficult this world could be. They just innocently put their trust in us. Ron joined me as I picked them up to prepare them for bed.

I prayed over Kari and Ryan as I rapped on their backs to loosen the congested mucous from their lungs. "Oh, God, in Your compassion hold our family together so that we can be overcomers in the life You have given us until You return. I want the same innocent trust in You as my children have in me."

Ron's Reflections . . .

God called us to be in ministry. He also called us to care for our very needy children. We've found that it is difficult to do both and be a close family. During this period of our lives especially, the needs of each were so great, the cries so strong, that Joan and I felt pulled in different directions.

When Joan and I experience things together, it is relatively easy to understand one another, to have a good idea of what the other is feeling, and to know what it takes to encourage one another. But when the bulk of our time is spent in two worlds so different, each with their own set of challenges and struggles, being in sync with one another doesn't come so easily. What does come easily is misunderstanding and conflict.

When the pressures of life are bearing down on us, we are in great need of mutual love, care and compassion. At the same time, the greater the stress, the more focused we become on our own problems and we often fail to put the concerns and interests of others before our own. The result is isolation.

The goal and the essence of marriage is oneness. Every marriage is either on a path of increasing oneness and therefore knowing intimacy, or it is on a path of painful isolation. Joan and I know each path pretty well. We've spent enough time on each. There is no doubt as to where we want to be. The question is: How do we stay on the right path? The answer is: sacrificial love.

Conventional wisdom says that when we're under stress and overwhelmed, I need to take more time for me, to pamper myself, to meet my needs. The truth is that when we're under stress, we benefit far more by meeting the needs of one another.

When Joan and I were preparing to be married, Pastor Fred insisted that we remember two verses of Scripture: Ephesians 4:2, "Be completely humble and gentle; be patient, bearing with one another in love," and Philippians 2:4, "Each of you should look not only to your own interests, but also to the interests of others." This is great advice for any relationship at any time. It is especially so for a family under stress.

**A successful family
maintains intimacy in times of stress.**

Chapter Eighteen

A refreshing breeze blew through the newly budded trees. I looked over our backyard, watching the branches lazily swaying in the wind. "God certainly has placed me in a beautiful location," I mused. Before turning my attention back to the kids, I took one last breath, savoring the sweet fragrance of the balmy spring day.

"Let's get on the road, Loie!" I shouted excitedly. I slammed the van door, causing Kari and Ryan, who were buckled in their wheelchairs, to jump in their seats. Before slipping behind the steering wheel, I gave the old vehicle a good luck pat for our long trip. The engine sputtered to life when I turned the key—it would be a great day!

Loie and I had completed the children's morning care—baths, breakfast, therapy, medication—and now we had them packed in the van along with their supplies for the day. Loie was not on call as a home-health nurse this weekend, so earlier in the morning I had suggested we diverge from the normal Saturday schedule to do something fun. Ron's plans for the day could not be so easily changed. Meetings and sermon preparation consumed most of his Saturday schedule, so it would only be the four of us making the trip.

Our destination was the Philadelphia Zoo. I knew Kari and Ryan would enjoy the outdoors. Although neither could see, I would have fun describing the animals' activities to them.

Attempting a spur-of-the-moment trip was not my usual habit, but, since having Loie around, I was becoming more impulsive. Going anywhere with two kids in wheelchairs was always an adventure, but Loie and I decided we were up to the challenge this morning.

Ryan continued to have difficulty digesting food. His tummy revolted frequently, increasing his chance of aspiration and making life generally miserable. Since December he had managed to avoid pneumonia and other life-threatening complications, so today we would also celebrate a hospital-free 1993.

Loie and I chatted freely as we drove down the turnpike. I enjoyed her companionship and the stimulating conversation we usually created. I glanced in the rearview mirror and saw the kids were taking advantage of the long drive by falling asleep.

After exiting the freeway, I maneuvered the van through the congested streets, then found a handicapped parking space in the zoo's parking lot. The sun was warm overhead so we threw our jackets in the van, leaving behind any extra baggage that would encumber us.

We patiently waited our turn in the long line at the crowded admission gate. The sign above the cashier caught my attention, "Wow! Loie, check out those prices! The zoo isn't exactly cheap!" I hesitated before moving ahead in line as I calculated whether my minister's budget could handle this frivolous expense. My conservative mindset didn't prevail after considering the active schedule I had kept over the past year-and-a-half. I needed this vacation day! In an attempt to save a few dollars, I informed the cashier that both my children were severally disabled and blind, and then boldly asked if they could have a discount.

She glared at me as though she had heard that line before, and then responded with the full admission price. I reluctantly paid my entrance fee and shoved the kids beyond the gate. Shrugging my shoulders, I mumbled to Loie, "Oh, well, I won't let her callous response spoil my day."

We wove our way through the reptile section, passing the alligators and giggling at the gigantic turtles, which were enjoying a mating session in the sun. "Well, Loie, I'm glad I don't have to explain everything I see to the kids. There are some advantages to their blindness." I winked at her as we continued down the path.

Loie pushed Kari, who was attentive to the different sounds and smells around her. Occasionally when the commotion was too much for Kari, she'd throw her head forward and rub her eyes and then peek upward with a smile when she felt secure. I escorted Ryan alongside the tiger cages as he kept his little head pushed backward into his headrest with his eyes fixed upward towards me—his tour guide. His eyes sparkled and he held his hands up in excitement. Occasionally as we strolled, I mentioned to Loie that something smelled bad. After I repeated this for the fourth time, Loie turned to me somewhat annoyed with needing to state the obvious, "Joan, we are in a zoo!"

With my olfactory nerve continuing to react, I quietly continued along until Ryan became irritable, indicating he needed a break from his chair. As I began to unbuckle him from his seat, I realized that my senses had not been deceiving me. Ryan was saturated from the back of his neck to the bottom of his toes. It oozed from his chair and dripped down to the gravel path. I stood frozen in panic. I caught a glimpse of Loie's horrified expression and I broke into laughter. What else could I do in this embarrassing situation? Quickly the four of us headed to the nearest rest-room, with Loie and me in hysterics.

When we arrived, I discovered the bathroom was not equipped with paper towels, and the few baby wipes I had were dried out. "Loie, it looks like toilet paper will be our only tool for the job!" I chuckled.

Loie poured the rest of her soda in the sink and began dumping cups full of soapy water on the soiled chair. Ryan lay contentedly on the infant changing table, relieved of his uncomfortable predicament. Women coming in on our scene politely stepped around us as we finished our task. Exhausted from cleaning and laughing, we exited the bathroom, my son clad only in a diaper.

Loie offered to retrieve clothing from the van for Ryan, so I sat down in the grass with him, his wheelchair drying in the sun. Kari sat beside me in her chair, making melancholy noises to those who would listen. I watched the hordes of people walking past, intent on conquering the zoo. All at once I felt conspicuous as I sat alone with my two severely disabled children, one of whom was exposing his feeding tube.

People smiled at me graciously as they tried to make sense of the situation, but I could tell they felt sorry for me. Pity was not what I wanted to elicit from these people. I should have been used to it by now. I saw it often enough. Just a week earlier, Ron and I had been out for a walk, pushing the kids near a construction site. One of the workers said to another while pointing to our family, "Look at those pathetic people!" Now, as I sat waiting, I felt the same silent judgment hurled at me.

Pathetic or deprived were not adjectives that I would use to describe my family. Instead, I felt we were very rich. God was promising our family an inheritance waiting in heaven. We may not appear advantaged in this world, and in many ways that is right. On the other hand, it is because of the weakness in my children that I consider myself blessed.

Kari and Ryan's limitations forced me to look beyond what this culture esteems as valuable. I know that this present reality is not all there is to life. The more God withholds from my children and me, the better prepared we are for His heavenly kingdom.

Having disabled children may appear tragic to these people at the zoo. Some days it feels that way to me too. But Kari and Ryan are never a burden to me. Their suffering is only distressing to me when I view it from my vantage point. When I allow God to show me His design for my life and theirs, then I receive wisdom and peace that I otherwise never would know. Kari and Ryan are not weights that burden me down, but wings that elevate, allowing me to soar above the rat race of this world.

I was not to be pitied, but how could I tell the people who were passing me, viewing this rather odd "exhibit" and thinking how unfortunate I must be. "Oh, Ryan," I muttered as I shifted him in my arms, "we human animals are so fascinating. I'm learning more about myself than about zoo creatures today! Does it really matter if people think we are strange?"

I smiled as Loie approached, hurriedly pushing her way through the crowds with an adult sweatshirt in her hand. Waving it frantically in my direction she hollered, "This is all I could find, Joan! Will you be embarrassed if Ryan wears it?"

I shook my head no and got ready to get back to the fun of our day.

*   *   *

As we traveled home from the zoo to the Upper Perkiomen Valley, I sensed anxiety creeping into my mind like dark rain clouds invading a picnic, pushing away the sunny day. The tension was becoming all too familiar, but not a welcomed visitor. I looked down at my whitened knuckles as I gripped the steering wheel. "Why, God? Why am I troubled in this way? Why can't I be released from this horrible feeling?"

The children slept behind me, and Loie sat daydreaming out the window. I drove in silence, not allowing her to be privy to my dreadful thoughts. I pulled the van into the driveway and Ron appeared at the house door when he heard us arrive. He greeted us both, then hugged me. I bristled at his touch, feeling guilty for my chilly response. I realized that the day at the zoo was more than a break from my routine. It was also a reprieve from this nebulous feeling.

That evening I busied myself with getting the children prepared for bed and tried to ignore the tension between my husband and me. He went back to his office to complete the final details of his sermon, and I relaxed with a steaming cup of herbal tea.

"We've been through worse times than this. Why is our marriage strained now?" I questioned as I reflected on the nine years of our married life. Since the time of Kari's birth we knew of the disturbing statistic that more than eighty percent of marriages with a disabled child end in divorce. We both had determined not to become part of that number and I thought we were on the right track.

I slowly ascended the steps towards my bedroom, realizing that Ron would not be coming home soon. As I lay in bed, I continued rehashing in my mind, *Where have we gone wrong?* Over the past year Ron and I had persevered month after month to set aside at least one evening for each other while Loie provided respite for us. Even during the lengthy hospitalizations and the uncertain outcome of our children's lives, Ron and I found creative ways to meet the other's emotional needs. We had refused to allow the devastating illness of our children to disintegrate our love for each other.

Despite our efforts, something was still causing us to remain in our separate worlds. The strain we were dealing with now had nothing to do with the demands of our children's health, but this fact was not obvious to me or to those around me.

*   *   *

I sat crying softly, my tear-stained face buried into my drawn-up knees. Ron was on the phone informing my mother that we would not be attending the family picnic. He hung up the phone. A crisis was upon us and he had begun to take drastic action to fix it.

Turning to me he said, "Joan, I'm calling a counselor today! We need help! You and I can't talk without our conversation ending in an argument. I don't know what is going wrong, but we need to figure it out soon or there is not going to be much left to this marriage!"

We arrived at the counseling office, having driven there in silence. Besides being confused by how our breakfast conversation could spiral downward so quickly into mayhem, I was also upset about missing time with my extended family.

Sun streamed through one small window as we were ushered into the counselor's office. She offered Ron and me the seats that faced her organized desk as she finished writing a few notes from her last session. I sat with my legs crossed and my arms protectively hugging my heart as I surveyed the wall hangings and bookshelves. The walls were painted a pale blue, leaving me with a cold feeling about this place.

The blond-haired, middle-aged woman laid down her pen and looked up smiling. "Hello, Ron and Joan! It's so good to meet you. I've heard a lot about your new church in Red Hill." The reference to my husband being a pastor caused me to squirm. I was hoping to avoid that connection. She continued speaking, her professional voice bringing my mind in focus as she laid before us the common problems she frequently encountered among married couples. Her calm, nonchalant demeanor slowly disarmed my emotional defensiveness and soon I found myself connecting with many of the thoughts she was expressing.

As I started to talk, my evaluations of our marriage surprised even myself. Avoiding eye contact with Ron, I expressed to the counselor that emotionally I felt as though I was bonded to two partners—ministry and Ron. He worked eighty hours a week away from home, but even when he was home, he talked incessantly about ministry-related issues. I shared in Ron's passion for leading the church, for I too loved the people. Many times I acted as his sounding board for things that he was dealing with. But because of Ron's intensity for his work, I thought I needed to feel it with him or he would lose interest in me. He was on call twenty-four hours a day, seven days a week, never taking a day away from his work.

However, after two years of this hectic schedule, I had come to feel more and more competition from what appeared to be his first love—the ministry. Sometimes in my jealousy I had even concluded that Ron used his busy ministry schedule to avoid the fact that his children could not give him the gratification that parents desire. I saw him throwing himself into a work that had more tangible rewards.

Ron watched me intently as I spoke and he remained quiet. The counselor summarized our time together and cautioned us in problem areas of our marriage relationship. She then prayed and expressed appreciation to us for coming—an important step in resolving our pain. Before leaving she reminded us that our problems were not too big for God to handle. I walked outside feeling encouraged that she saw hope for our marriage.

I opened the car door and smiled over the roof at Ron before getting in. He had not yet commented on what I had revealed within the session, instead he started the car and drove toward home. Just when Ron's silence convinced me that he would never talk to me again, he pulled the car into an ice-cream parlor and offered me a treat.

As we sat licking our cones, he leaned over and looked into my eyes. "Joan, I never want you to think that ministry means more to me than you and the kids. I am sorry for not seeing your needs. The counselor is right. I have been working so hard to succeed at this work and to meet my own expectations that I'm failing to see what you need and what God wants. I love you, honey, and I am not going to hurt you like this anymore. Things will change."

His words sent shivers down my neck, for I knew he was speaking the conviction of his heart and that he would keep his promise. The changes occurred slowly. He committed to taking a day a week away from ministry to fulfill his commitments to his home. I could see it was a struggle for him to let his mind rest from work on his day off, but he continued to persevere. He was doing his part at repairing our badly injured marriage and it softened my hardened heart.

What I could not see during this time was my part in this healing process that kept me from experiencing complete joy.

*   *   *

I quickly finished pushing the final medication through Ryan's gastrostomy tube, prayed a hasty goodnight prayer by his bedside, and kissed his chubby cheek before turning off the light.

"Ryan's finished. Now I just have to calm Kari before I go back out there." I quietly rehearsed my nightly ritual as I continued to rush through the children's bedtime care. Ron was counseling our guests in the living room, a couple who was having a crisis marital problem. Ron had asked me to join him in the session. They had arrived late so our kids would be in bed, allowing us uninterrupted time to counsel with them.

When I entered Kari's room, a sickening feeling entered my stomach. I immediately saw why she had been crying. She had vomited all over her bed and it was matted in her hair and soaking her sheets and blankets. Her body was warm, and I could hear the rasping breath sounds coming from her lungs as they reacted to the aspirated fluid.

"Oh, no, Kari, why did you have to do this now? I don't have time for this! Your daddy needs me!" My spirit was anything but gentle and compassionate as I rushed Kari through a soapy warm bath and shampoo. "God, why can't I ever be involved in a ministry-related task without my kids interfering? What are these people going to think of me?"

I quickly dressed her in clean pajamas, still determined to return to the living room. Kari's breathing continued to be very coarse. I couldn't ignore that symptom, knowing if I didn't start a respiratory treatment soon, she would be in trouble.

I pounded on Kari's back, attempting to loosen the thick phlegm in her congested lungs while the aerosol mask blew the misty medication into her face. Finally she produced a series of weak coughs. I listened to her lungs through my stethoscope—"Clear enough," I whispered. Kari closed her eyes in exhaustion as I placed her on her side to sleep.

I was racing around Kari's room, clearing away the dirty linen, when I heard Ryan crying from his bedroom. "Oh, no, not him again!" I moaned. "I must get out to the living room. I know Ron needs me!"

I entered the next room and discovered that in my haste I had forgotten to unclamp the tubing that was allowing Ryan's formula feeding to flow into his stomach tube. It was now flowing out a side port onto his bed and Ryan was reacting to his soggy pajamas and sheets. It had been an hour since I had excused myself from our guests. This latest disaster made it clear that I was not going to be able to return before they left.

I collapsed against Ryan's bedroom wall and cried out to God. "Father, You have given me these two precious children who need so much care, but You have also made it abundantly clear that we were to go back into ministry. I don't see how I can possibly do it, Lord. This is my constant battle; I can never be an effective pastor's wife. My children are always demanding my time and often seem to be a hindrance to my caring for other people. Ron can never count on me. I'm constantly failing at fulfilling my role as mother and pastor's wife!"

That night when Ron crawled into bed, I kept my back toward him. Tears were burning my eyes, but I stubbornly restrained my body from sobbing. I felt like a failure, but I couldn't let him see my weakness. I could not be that vulnerable.

We didn't pray together as we usually did. Instead he turned out the light and said goodnight into the dark.

*   *   *

A month later, on a Sunday night, I sat shaking on my bed. Ron had not yet returned from the church. I clutched my arms around myself in a hug and cried out the words from my open Bible. "Fear and trembling have beset me, horror has overwhelmed me." Tears blurred my eye. "Oh, that I had the wings of a dove! I would fly away and be at rest. I would flee far away and stay in the desert, I would hurry to my place of shelter, far from the tempest and storm. If an enemy were insulting me, I could endure it . . . But it is a man like yourself, my companion, my friend . . ." (Psalm 55:5-8, 12-13)

At that very moment I wanted to run far from this place and never return. Today my suspicions were confirmed. I truly was a failure as a pastor's wife—this letter said so. It was from a very distraught woman whom I had apparently offended by a comment I had made. Now she was responding in a biting, angry tone, attacking me, aiming at my Achilles heel of insecurity. Her letter ended with words I had come to fear were true: "You are the worst pastor's wife I have ever had!"

The letter lay on my bed, burning a hole into my already weakened heart. "Lord, I never meant to offend her! How can I ever live up to the expectations of all these people? You never told me it was going to be so hard. I never thought Christian people would respond this way! How can I ever walk back into that church again? Who is going to attack me next? Why does Ron allow me to be put in this horrible position? Why doesn't he defend me? Can't he see how it is destroying me?"

By the time Ron arrived home I had expressed all my fear to God, but I still appreciated my husband's arms around me after he read the letter. I could feel his pain for me as he spoke, trying to reassure me of his love and confidence in me as his wife.

We went to bed, but I lay awake long into the night, testing Ron's words against my unbelieving heart. Is there any way I was pleasing him? I didn't look like any other pastors' wives that I knew. They all seem to have such a vibrant role in the life of their church. I could barely teach Sunday School three weeks in a row without having to cancel because one of my children was sick. I finally sank into a restless sleep.

*   *   *

He slammed his fist into the edge of the sofa, causing me to jump in fear. We were steering towards another head-on conflict, our marriage on a collision course. Ron cried out, "Why can't I make you happy? All I want to do is to make you happy! What is it that you want me to do? Should we leave the ministry?"

The argument began when I told him that I couldn't handle being the parent of two severely handicapped children and minister's wife of a growing, active church. God was asking too much in moving me to this town where I did not feel fulfilled. Loneliness and defeat were my constant companions.

The pain in Ron's eyes and frustration in his voice jolted me to look candidly at what I was saying and see the agony I was putting my husband through. I attacked the very core of his life, and he responded defensively to my hopelessness. Underneath all my passionate arguments, I knew none of what I was saying created my unhappiness. Neither Ron nor the church caused the turmoil within me, but both were easier to blame for the pain inside me. It was too painful to face the truth of my heart.

"No, Ron, you are not responsible for my happiness or my unhappiness. Only I can be accountable for that. You are responsible to do what God is calling you to do. I don't want you to be anything except a pastor." I spoke quietly as though I was convincing myself of these truths. I sensed that the Spirit of God was confronting my heart and I was treading on holy ground. The Creator of the universe was again trying to show me that the pressures I had placed on myself were created by me only. Neither Ron, the church people, nor God Himself were to blame for my formulating the impossible job description that I had written.

God never intended for me to bear the problems of my family, the church, and the world—that was His job. I did not please God by trying to accomplish more than what He was asking me to do in caring for my children. All that He wanted from me was my undivided trust and adoration of Him. God did not love me for the work I could perform. He loved me because I was His child. He never intended for me to carry such an unbearable load. My job now was to release the expectations I had for my life and believe that God's plan for me included peace and fulfillment beyond what I could ever imagine.

This first step of trust needed to begin in my own marriage. I had always refused to believe Ron when he told me I was doing a good job as a pastor's wife. I had been convinced he was just trying to be nice and make the best of being married to a failure. My drive to do more, to be successful, to gain recognition clouded my husband's gracious gift of love to me.

My problem was that I feared people and I cared too much what they thought of my reputation. I was looking for significance beyond my role as a mother. I was succumbing to the popular opinion that caring for "hopeless" human life is energy ultimately wasted.

Searching for importance outside the work that God had already given me to do had almost cost me my marriage and inner joy. Trusting God and finding contentment in the position where He had placed me did not come naturally or easily, but it was the only safe and secure place to be.

*   *   *

A month later Ryan lay struggling for life in the hospital bed. He looked at me with longing eyes, desperate for all the love and assistance that I could give. This two-week hospital stay was like many others that our family labored through. The possibility of our child's death lingered on our minds. Miles separated Ron and me from physical contact with each other, and the continuing work of the ministry competed with Ron's devotion to our family.

But unlike many hospitalizations, I was filled with peace and strength for I was convinced that we were fulfilling the responsibilities God had given us. In return, God opened His vast storehouse of blessings and delivered His best to us as we continued to trust His plan for our marriage and life.

Ron's Reflections . . .

As a family with two handicapped children, we've often appeared an unusual sight. People try not to stare, but sometimes their curiosity overcomes them, causing them to neglect basic manners. I'll never forget the day our family had a teenager with us from another ethnic background. We were walking through K-Mart. Joan pushed Kari in her wheelchair while I pushed Ryan, and the boy with us pushed the shopping cart. Almost without exception people turned their attention toward us. The puzzled expressions on their faces said it all. "I can't figure this one out. What kind of family is this?"

Most of us are concerned with what people think of us. Sometimes, as in the day at K-Mart, Joan and I are able to mostly laugh off what others think of us. Occasionally we are even able to wear it as a badge of honor. "We know who we are. We know what God has called us to. The children God gave us are by His choice. This is our family and it doesn't matter how odd we look to you or to anyone else. This is God's design. If you have a problem with that, take it up with Him." Such thoughts are a strong fortress against potential attacks.

We become fearful and apprehensive about what people think of us when we bear, or at least think we bear, some responsibility for circumstances. For example, in the ministry when things aren't going well, I can easily fall into the trap of thinking, "If I just work a little harder, smarter or longer, I'll be able to make everything better. With more effort I can be the super-pastor everyone seems to want."

The truth is that I am a finite being. I have many gifts, but I have even more limitations. There are many things which are beyond my control. When I forget that, I get into trouble.

One awful consequence of giving in to fear of what people thought of me was that I neglected my family in my attempts to please the church. Joan was very patient with me as I began to face what I was doing and worked to change. Taking a day off from ministry was a way for me to demonstrate my belief that God is in control. Gradually I began to relax as that truth sank in. It also took a long time to get out of the subconscious habit of watching the congregation's opinion polls, a key cause of my anxiety.

The expectations others have of us, even the thoughts of our spouses, are not necessarily right. They can expect more of us than what is reasonable. This too can create anxiety.

Shock is the best way to describe my response when Joan told me one day that it wasn't my job to make her happy. I truly thought it was. Aren't husbands to make their wives happy? I now believe the answer is no. My job is to do what is right and to love my wife, realizing that I am finite and cannot meet all her needs. Only God can do that. I now realize this applies to all relationships.

Now when people are critical of us, it still hurts, but we try to remember to take it to God. We ask Him what He thinks and are open to change where needed, but basically we move forward the best we can. We allow God's love to cast out all fear, including the fear of what people think of us.

**A successful family
overcomes fear of people
and their criticism.**

CHAPTER NINETEEN

Mickey Mouse and friends danced on stage as the young audience responded with giggles and hand clapping. As the show ended, swarms of children pushed towards the front to get one touch from the big Mouse himself. They turned away sadly when Mickey quickly exited before the mob of children attacked him.

Kari and Ryan sat wide-eyed and quiet in their wheelchairs, patiently waiting their turn to leave the large colorful auditorium. I watched my children stare blankly into the air, knowing they had no understanding of how entertaining the show had been, but their smiles indicated that at least they enjoyed hearing the other children's laughter.

The room was almost empty when, out of the corner of my eye, I spied him sneaking up behind my kids and slipping a sheet of paper onto their laps. His big white paw fluffed their hair and his whiskers tickled their faces as he gave them each a big rodent hug. He said nothing and disappeared as quickly as he came. Cheerfully scribbled on the paper were all the personal signatures of the Walt Disney characters who had just performed for us. Ron and I smiled at each other as we witnessed again the royal treatment our family was receiving here at Magic Kingdom.

The Sunshine Foundation gave our children the five-day trip to Disney World—all expenses paid. The organization fulfills dreams of chronically or terminally ill children, and they chose our family to receive this generous gift.

Although we were extremely grateful, we were very hesitant to accept the trip. I knew it meant traveling by airplane with two severely disabled children, one of whom had not been able to keep food in his stomach. Vomiting had become a way of life for Ryan over the past few months.

With the charitable offer too good to pass up, we took a step of faith and began preparing for the trip, including the careful packing of necessary medical supplies. Our journey would become a treasured memory for our family.

When our plane was at cruising altitude on September 10, 1993, the pilot informed the passengers that a very special boy was on the plane celebrating his fifth birthday. Ryan's eyes twinkled with joy as the stewardess came to sing "Happy Birthday" to him and squeeze his rosy cheeks. He loved the attention and proudly displayed his "I'm 5 today" pin on his chest. For Ryan, there would be no greater badge of honor for him on this earth. He had made it this many years, with each day a battle for life.

God rewarded our small step of faith. He granted Ryan's stomach a five-day reprieve from its revolt—the entire time in Florida the children didn't have any symptom of illness. Mommy, on the other hand, suffered every morning from a familiar sickness in the pit of her stomach.

The week before our flight to Florida, I had the nagging suspicion confirmed by my obstetrician—I was two months pregnant. Following my internal exam, Dr. Hoff asked Ron and I to sit in his office. Eager for Dr. Hoff's results, we listened to the soft music playing overhead in the bright cheery room. While I waited, I allowed my thoughts to drift back over the past few years, compiling my many prayers and emotions concerning this very moment.

How long it had been since I first agonized over the desire to have another child? Suffering constantly surrounded me during the day. I had no healthy child to divert my attention. Was I wrong in my desire to have a child whom I could teach— a healthy child who would be able to fully respond to my love and conversation? One who could play, get into trouble, be disciplined, and grow to be a responsible adult. Someone who would help to carry through many generations the values and morals that God was teaching my husband and me.

In the middle of the night, this prayer was constantly on my lips. "Dear God, I am grateful for what You continue to teach me through the lives of Kari and Ryan. I love them dearly! I see how Your gift of children to me enhanced my spiritual growth. There was no other way to teach me how priceless human life is had it not been for these two children. I have accepted them as good gifts from You, children that you have entrusted to my care during their time spent here on earth. I am privileged to be a caretaker of Your special children!

"Oh, God, I promise to dedicate a third child to your service if You grant me a healthy child. I will raise him to follow Your heart. I will be diligent to train him to know Your character and wisdom. You have opened the wombs of many barren women in the Bible, and I know You can control the genetic weaving for my husband and me to have a healthy child. You Yourself have said, 'Is My arm too short?' I know that You can do anything You desire."

Before the Lord in prayer, I had confidence that He would grant me my heart's desire, but when I looked away from my Creator to the community around me, turmoil reigned within me. "What will people think of me? Am I absolutely crazy to think of bringing another child into this world who could suffer like

Kari and Ryan? How would I ever handle a third child? I can barely survive life with two! What about all the children in the world who would dream of living in a loving family as ours? Why would I risk producing a less-than-normal child when adoption may be an option?"

The longing in my heart for another child continued. Our family was not complete, and I knew God was preparing both Ron and me for an addition. Could we trust Him enough to take this huge step of faith, accepting the child God would give us?

We considered adopting, but each situation that might have led in that direction ended with a closed door. The suggestion from our neurologist to use donor sperm for in vitro fertilization to lessen the possibility of producing another child with a genetic defect did not fit with our walk of faith.

The question still remained: Would we be willing to accept another handicapped child if we pursued God's natural design for procreating children?

During one of those times that I agonized over this issue, I met a man through Kari's school who shared his philosophy with me. He said, "No person should have children unless they are willing to accept a disabled child." His opinion encouraged me greatly that day. It was another reminder to me that God is the one Who knits together children according to His design. He also offers the needed strength to those caring for his precious, weak, vulnerable little babies. We made the decision. Ron and I did our part; it was up to God to take care of the rest.

*   *   *

The creak of the office door brought my mind back to the present situation. "Mr. and Mrs. Denlinger, I see here on your chart that you have two handicapped children." Dr. Hoff continued in his most professional voice, staring at us over his half glasses. "I'm suggesting that we run further genetic tests on you and your children so we can attempt to diagnose their condition. If we could know more and have the ability to test the fetal tissue, then perhaps you would want to exercise the option of terminating this pregnancy."

The matter of fact tone and the cold words caused me to bristle. Taking a deep breath, I responded, "Dr. Hoff, we will be happy to have further tests completed on ourselves and our children for diagnostic purposes. I will visit any specialist you would like me to see, but I will not be aborting this baby!"

He removed his glasses and rubbed his chin as he looked at us thoughtfully. Speaking gently and with obvious compassion, he continued. "I will see you through the next seven months. You are off to a great start, Mrs. Denlinger. Everything looks fine!"

On our way home, Ron and I had decided to wait until after our trip to Florida to tell Loie of our good news.

*   *   *

Loie greeted us enthusiastically when we entered the house after returning from our adventure at Disney World. She hugged the kids and told them how much she missed them. We talked excitedly about our enjoyable trip, saving the best news for last.

My eyes twinkled with anticipation as I waited until I had her attention. "Guess what, Loie? I'm pregnant!"

She hesitated, grinning ear to ear. Not to be out done, she shot back. "I knew it! You're glowing from more than just the Florida sun. Congratulations, guys!"

*   *   *

A few months later, I as lay on the padded table, staring up at the ceiling, the classical music station provided soothing music through the intercom while I waited in the examination room. Dr. Hoff intently moved the ultrasonic stethoscope over my slightly bulging stomach. He was not promising me that he could hear the heartbeat at fourteen weeks' gestation, but it was worth a try.

Unexpectedly, Handel's "Hallelujah Chorus" came resounding into the room, reverberating off the walls at the exact time the stethoscope picked up a healthy rapid heartbeat. Tears flowed out of my eyes down into my ears, as I realized this "coincidence" was a reassurance from God that He had this tiny life in His hand.

"Well, Mrs. Denlinger, it sounds like a strong healthy heartbeat to me!" Dr. Hoff smiled at me as he extended his hand to help me sit up. "You are past the first trimester and everything still looks good!"

As I drove home, I realized I had not shared the news of my pregnancy with anyone other than Loie, even though I was confident that God was allowing Ron and me the blessing of another child. I wouldn't be able to conceal the fact much longer, as I was entering my fourth month of pregnancy. Still I was hesitant, doubtful that others would share the joy that I was experiencing.

My reluctance in revealing our decision to have a third child after the birth of our first two severely disabled children did have some validity. When it became obvious that I was pregnant, there were several people who stared in disbelief. Their expressions communicated that they thought we were out of our minds.

It saddened me to know that they felt this way, for it was a time of celebration for us. My confidence did not lie in myself but on God, the Creator of our fetus. I still had no guarantee of this child's quality of life, but this I did know: God was in control and would give us His best. Ron and I loved Kari and Ryan and we were convinced we had enough love for one more.

When Ron shared in our Sunday morning service that I was pregnant, applause and shouts of praise rose from our congregation. They continued to give us their encouragement and support throughout the remainder of my pregnancy, overpowering any unfavorable responses.

*   *   *

Ron paced in the back of the auditorium, stopping occasionally to listen by his office door. He did not want to miss the phone ringing. An elder was preaching the Sunday morning message and was soon concluding his sermon. Ron was doubting his decision to leave me this morning; he was of no use at the church. I, however, had insisted and assured him that if my labor pains became closer, I would call him. He planned to greet people after the service, wrap up a few administration details at his office, and then make his escape for home.

At home, I timed contractions as Kari and Ryan rested in their chairs. I had completed their baths and dressed them. Loie would come soon to care for them as I headed for the hospital. My bags were packed and I was at peace.

It had been an uneventful pregnancy, but I was eager to meet the little person who had taken up residence in my overcrowded abdomen. I wondered if there had ever been a child who had received so much prayer before he or she had even taken the first breath. Today, as I worked through increasingly stronger contractions, I knew my church family was petitioning the Lord on behalf of the baby and myself.

Finally Ron and Loie arrived home and found me timing contractions only five minutes apart. Ron immediately packed my bags in the car and was ready to rush me out the door in good father-to-be fashion.

I was not as determined to go. I did not want to spend any extra time at the hospital, so I persuaded him to escort me outside on this beautiful April day to take a walk. Loie settled the kids for their naps while we were gone, and then the three of us gathered for a time of prayer. At last, I gave permission to my increasingly anxious husband to take me to the hospital.

Jeremy Ron Denlinger entered this world quietly on April 24, 1994, without any complications. He looked perfectly healthy with his red hair sprouting over the top of his head. His eyes were extremely alert as he looked about the delivery room quietly, observing his brand new world.

This tiny baby boy had no idea of the dreams and hopes that we had for him. As he lay cuddled in my arms, Ron gave thanks to the Lord for the safe delivery of another Denlinger son.

When the staff left me alone in the room to nurse my newborn, I felt tension rising in me. Was he healthy enough to suckle at my breast? Jeremy did not allow me to question him much longer. He immediately latched on and nursed as though this was an extremely natural thing for him to do. Tears of joy streamed down my face as I looked up to see if Ron was witnessing this true miracle. "Oh, Ron, look at him, he has an appetite just like you!"

That night as I relaxed to sleep, I felt perfectly satisfied with the newest member of our family. He was so beautiful and showed signs of real hope.

At two in the morning I awoke in a sweat. My heart was racing and panic tore through my body. "No, God, Jeremy can't be handicapped! Please let him live a normal healthy life. He is so vulnerable, so delightful. He just can't suffer from the same undiagnosed illness as Kari and Ryan!" My fear rose menacingly within me and crowded out any joy that had still remained from my delivery a few hours earlier. I tossed and turned until I couldn't stand it any longer and I paged the nurse.

"Could you please bring my son to me?" I stated into the intercom, hearing the trembling in my own voice. "But, Mrs. Denlinger, he is sleeping. Are you sure you want us to wake him?"

I insisted and soon heard her wheeling the bassinet down the quiet hallway. As I picked up my securely wrapped infant, he stretched and pushed his tiny foot out of the swaddling blanket. "Five toes, that's good!" I whispered as I squeezed it and tucked it under the blue cover again. He blinked open his dark blue eyes and yawned contentedly in my arms. He did not hesitate to nurse, even though it was my idea, and competently suckled with great enjoyment. I felt my body relax with the warmth and security of this little guy in my arms.

"Nothing can be wrong with him; I never had a child nurse as vigorously as he." My pleasant thoughts soothed me back to sleep, only to be awakened an hour later by a distraught nurse who was sure I had smothered my newborn when she found me cuddled next to him in the hospital bed.

Ron arrived late in the morning bearing a proud father grin, chocolate cigars, and a beautiful bouquet of flowers. He was so happy with his new baby son and tenderly unwrapped Jeremy's blanket to count each toe and finger. He rubbed his nose and fuzzy beard up against Jeremy's soft face and grinned as the baby scrunched his wrinkled brow. Ron pinched his puffy cheeks and spoke fondly to him and then cuddled him in his awkward muscular arms, handling him like a little football. I watched the father-son interaction and felt so fortunate to have such a wonderful husband. The days of tension and arguments seemed far away.

As we talked, I vulnerably shared the intense fear I experienced during the night concerning our son's health. "Ron, how could I have been in so much peace about this baby throughout my pregnancy, and now that he is here and doing well I am so afraid? Will he be like Kari and Ryan? Honey, did we make the right decision?"

Ron sat down on the bed, laying Jeremy beside me. "I had nightmares of my own last night," he confessed. "Joan, I so badly want Jeremy to be a healthy child, especially now that I've actually met him. God has to hear our prayers!

We both began to watch our baby closely as he lay sleeping. Was he doing any abnormal twitching? Why did he have two cowlicks on his head? Was not this the same pattern that Kari and Ryan both had? Was this a genetic indication that he was following their same course? Our restlessness invaded the joy that had filled us the evening before.

A stack of mail lay on the bedside table and Ron reached over and opened the top one. He pulled out a homemade card, designed and decorated with various baby items and colors. It was from a young girl in our church. Ron read it silently and then handed it to me as tears filled his eyes. She had written: "Dear Mrs. Denlinger, Congratulations on your new baby! He is so lucky to live in a beautiful family like yours. I hope he's healthy and I'll be praying for him. But I know that even if he isn't healthy, the Lord will give you the strength and grace to handle him. Love, Patrice."

The precious message reminded us of the hope we had always relied on in the past. The innocence of this nine-year-old girl confronted us with the fact that our doubts and fears were causing us to take our eyes off Jesus—the One who supplied our only hope.

As Ron drove home from the hospital later in the afternoon, God impressed on his heart a scripture passage he had been studying over the past few days. It was the story of John the Baptist who had given his life passionately to prepare people for the ministry of Jesus Christ here on earth. While sitting in a prison cell waiting for his execution, John began to experience great doubt of whether this Jesus was indeed the Son of God. From his dungeon of doubt, he sent a message to Jesus requesting more assurance. How could a great prophet like John the Baptist ever question that God had called him to do the work that he had done? He had, after all, baptized God's Son! The answer was because he was human just like us.

Jesus' response to this fearful, doubting man comforted Ron. Jesus did not rebuke John or ignore him. He did not give a long lecture about how awful it was for John to doubt Him. Instead He began to praise John for being the greatest prophet that ever lived. Jesus then sent a message back to John, informing him of all the miracles He was performing and reassuring him that his life work was not in vain, but was now fully complete.

How we needed to be reminded in our time of extreme doubt that God was not condemning us. Instead He reminded us of the strength and guidance He had granted to us in the past. Now He wanted us to trust Him for our little boy's future. We had a significant foundation for taking the step of faith we did when trying to conceive him. It was not a blind leap into the dark, but a step that required greater vision than actual sight.

God was increasing our ability to see beyond what is visible to man and causing us to trust in Him.

*   *   *

We introduced Jeremy to his siblings when we arrived home from the hospital. As Ron, Jeremy, and I pulled in the driveway, the school van drove in behind us. I jumped out to greet my big kids being lowered off the wheelchair lift and together our family entered our home. We celebrated the homecoming of Jeremy by taking videos of our three children. Nothing could bring me greater joy—God had brought us together and I was complete.

Ron's Reflections . . .

As I think of our stepping out in faith and allowing God to give us a third child if He would choose to do so, a saying comes to mind: "Nothing ventured, nothing gained." That isn't a phrase found in Scripture, but the idea comes through in several places.

Jesus tells the story of a man who went on a long journey and as he did so entrusted his money to three servants. The first two put their money to work and doubled it. The man commended them highly for it. The third servant buried the money in the ground where it would be safe and gave it back to the master upon his return. The man scolded that servant, saying that he should have at least left it with the bankers so that it could have gained some interest.

Jesus seems to be saying that risk-taking investments are not just a good idea—they are essential to living a life pleasing to him. There is something very wrong with playing it safe all the time. To do so would communicate that we can't trust God to do significant things with our lives, that the gifts He has given us aren't worth growing.

When our little family moved to Connecticut, it was a scary venture for us. When we followed the call to Red Hill—that was an even bigger risk. And bringing a third child into the world with the genes we had to work with—that seemed like a giant step. But God blessed us richly every time. How poor we would be if we hadn't made those investments!

**A successful family
takes risks.**

CHAPTER TWENTY

The sun's rays glimmering through the shade trees cast dancing shadows on the path before us. A chipmunk scampered up a tree to make his escape before we reached the spot where he was playing. Ron and I hiked silently through the woods, hand and hand, enjoying the placidity surrounding us and the rare time spent alone.

Our family and Loie were taking our final vacation together. Loie was engaged to be married and had moved into her own apartment before Jeremy's birth. She continued to help me whenever I needed her support, often arranging her daily work schedule so she could spend lunch with me. She had recently started to work with a local hospice care agency. Our luncheon conversations often contained stories from her emotionally demanding job. When I suggested she accompany our family on one last camping trip before her marriage, she jumped at the opportunity.

We were in the middle of a hot and humid July, so we headed north to the Pocono Mountains and pitched our tent at a cool, shady campground. Kari and Loie shared a pup tent; Ron, Ryan, Jeremy, and I shared another. My first night under the stars was similar to my nightly stint at home. Ryan coughed and vomited all night, allowing me only several catnaps. I attempted to care for and comfort him without waking Ron or Jeremy, who at three months was sleeping through the night.

In the morning, I placed Ryan in his wheelchair and watched him relax. The serene look on his face as he gazed up into the pine trees surrounding our campsite caused me to forget my horrendous night. On my way to the water faucet, I whispered in his ear, "What do you see up there Ryan? Angels?" He turned his face towards me and sighed as I kissed his pale cheek.

After the griddle was cleaned, Jeremy nursed, and the kids fed and dressed, Loie suggested Ron and I take a short romantic hike alone before the next round of meals and medications needed to be started.

Ron jumped at the opportunity and grabbed my hand as we started off for the woods. Not far into our walk I began to share my thoughts with my husband. "You know what, Ron?" I spoke softly so as not to disturb the peaceful setting surrounding us. "I really feel like God has been incredibly good to us! I know many people looking at our family would not have that as their first thought. In fact, I wouldn't have believed it either if God had allowed me a peek into the future on our wedding day."

He stopped and looked down at me, tenderly tipping my face up towards his for a kiss. "Yeah, Joan, and isn't it amazing that we are still together and madly in love with each other?" I smiled at his attempt to make sure this walk stayed romantic.

He was right! It seemed like the past few months we truly were connecting and not arguing as much. Both of us were attempting to put into practice the wise advice of our counselor a year earlier. As a result, we were experiencing a lot more intimacy in our marriage.

We hiked for another half-hour till we reached a steep, rocky incline. Ron assisted me up the hill and we stopped to rest and enjoy nature. I broke the silence, "One day we will be able to take hikes with our son. I feel so honored to be trusted with a child I will need to teach and train and play with. God did not have to give us a healthy son when He blessed us with Jeremy."

Ron nodded his head in agreement as he bit into an apple. Our agonizing over whether Jeremy was affected with the same disabilities as his siblings ended only two weeks earlier when our doctor finally convinced us that he was healthy.

Ron continued to give me his listening ear as I spoke. "Sometimes I wonder what God has in store for us in the future. Do you think we are going to make it? With caring for our three babies, helping out in the ministry, and running a household, some days I don't even think I'm going to make it through the day, let alone years down the road!"

"Well, honey," Ron responded after a long pause, "I can't promise you it's going to be easy. I wish I could provide a better answer, but I do know we will need to trust God. What is that little saying you have printed by your kitchen sink? Inch by inch life's a cinch, but yard by yard life is hard. How about we enjoy our time together now and leave the rest of our life to solve for another day!"

I picked up his clue that this was not the time for heavy philosophy. I grabbed the apple out of his hand and darted down the path. "If you catch me, I might even let you steal another kiss!" I teased.

We ran cheerfully back to the campsite then suggested that we all go to the pool. Despite the obstacles that abound for bringing handicapped children and a baby to a swimming pool, somehow we were able to overcome and enjoy the water. All it took was a little creativity. Each of us cradled a child and cautiously lowered them in the warm water of the baby pool.

As we laughed in the sun that day, we were unaware of the clouds rolling in and the storm about to descend on us.

*   *   *

One week after our little escapade to the Poconos, I sat rocking in the living room nursing Jeremy. He smiled at me as he ate. It was such a joy feeding him and watching him grow. Today he was celebrating his three-month birthday. Ron was spending the weekend in New England with the youth group on a mission trip, so my mom had offered to take Kari while Ron was away.

My sons and I had just returned home from the Sunday morning service. It was a different experience for me. Usually I sat in the front with my children and pastor husband, rarely getting a chance to greet people in the back after the service. This morning I sat in the back, alone with my sleeping newborn and Ryan beside me in his wheelchair. He had been having so much difficulty with breathing; I wasn't sure he would be able to stay throughout the service. For two months he had chronic pneumonia. His lungs were no longer recognizing the aspirated tube feeding as foreign material, and they were accepting it without resistance. He was constantly experiencing shortness of breath and gurgling sounds came from his lungs. Despite frequent pulmonary treatments, including suctioning, his lungs continued to fill up with fluid.

I watched Ryan with great delight as he sat quietly in the back row throughout the morning. He even enjoyed all the attention he received as people filed past him after the service. Being in the back, right by the aisle, he caught the attention of everyone who came by. He intently looked in the direction of each person as they rubbed his buzzed hair, as though he was saying to them, "Thank you for noticing me. I won't forget you." All of his actions had intrigued me this morning because they were out of character. Now as I sat watching him lying on the couch, I saw something else that I had not seen before. I was terrified.

While he lay before me, his feeding pump droned on, forcing the formula into his stomach. Fear filled Ryan's eyes as the feeding refluxed into his lungs. His garbled breathing caused him to foam at the mouth. None of his medications were doing anything to prevent this devastating reaction.

"God, can You hear me? My son is suffering incredibly and nothing is working anymore! The doctors have tried everything! He is drowning in his own secretions. Why is he suffering like this? Is Ryan preparing to die? I saw his face this morning at church. He knows something that I don't. Why does he now look at me with those terrified eyes as though I don't understand? Is he trying to tell me something?

"Oh, God, my heart rejoices with my baby son, but it is being crushed with grief for my oldest son. How much emotion can one heart withstand? Tell me, God, is Ryan going to see his tenth birthday? Or even his sixth? Will he never even lose a tooth? Will he ever be free of this horrible suffering? Please, God, don't turn a deaf ear to me. I'm so afraid! I'm so alone and feel so hopeless to help him anymore. Do You know what it is like to watch Your son die before Your eyes?"

I knew the answer to that—of course God knew, but I needed desperately to voice it so I could release all my fears. I focused my attention back to Ryan, turning the dreaded feeding pump off and suctioning the thick white secretions from the depths of his bronchial tubes. He coughed, arched his back, and screamed in protest.

Finishing this task that I had grown to despise, I watched him relax in my arms as I put the breathing mask over his face to fill his lungs with air again. His stomach was bloated with just the two ounces of formula the pump had forced him to take. He looked like a child in a country of famine. "Ryan, honey, you just have to eat!" He whimpered in complaint and pressed his head into my chest. He took deep, rapid breaths as I began to sing the song I had written for him during a long ago hospitalization. It was my hope that he would sense my love for him as he heard the soft melody.

Oh, Ryan, all I want you to know with your eyes, with
    your ears and your soul is that I love you so.

May your eyes see the light that shines from my face
    when I hold you tight.

May your eyes always speak the desire for life and love
    until they close to sleep.

Oh, Ryan, all I want you to know with your eyes, with
    your ears and your soul is that I love you so.

May you hear the words that I sing to you.
May your ears always know my voice.

Listen, my child, to the sweet sounds of your family
    around you.

Oh, Ryan, all I want you to know with your eyes, with
    your ears and your soul is that I love you so.

*May you always feel in your soul the compassion that
    flows out of me.*
*And may you always be the little boy God created you to
    be.*

*There may be a time when you see or hear or feel no
    more.*
*The things that bound you will be gone, but my love for
    you will still hang on.*

Oh, Ryan, all I want you to know . . .

His breathing slowed and my tears dripped on his thin,
frail legs. I knew the time had come for me to face reality. I didn't
want to see it, but for the love of my son, I had to.

It was late when Ron came home from his trip. The house
was dark and the children were sleeping. I had kept the air con-
ditioners running; the July night was sweltering. Ron lay down
beside me and I felt his gentle kiss on my wet cheek. "Ron,"
I whispered in the darkness, "tomorrow we have to talk about
Ryan!"

Monday morning the summer heat wave continued. I went
about medicating and feeding Kari. I skipped over Ryan until I
had a chance to nurse and change the baby.

Jeremy kicked his little legs with delight when I entered
his room. "Good morning, baby." I tickled his little belly and
watched him smile in response. He was always so good and easy
to care for. He ate quickly and did not resist when I placed him in
the swing to wait his turn to be entertained.

I prepared Ryan's medications and entered his cool room.
He lay still, propped on his many pillows. I had left the feeding

pump turned off all night, and he had slept soundly without once needing my attention. I watched him closely as I injected the medicine slowly into his G-tube. He immediately arched his back and cried out in pain.

I picked him up and carried him to the kitchen where Ron was preparing our breakfast. It was his custom on his day away from the church to fix us a cooked breakfast. When he saw me enter, he started telling me of his trip to New England. I listened only halfheartedly as I continued to battle the pain within me. I pressed Ryan against me and rocked him gently.

"Ron . . ." He quieted when he saw I was no longer hearing him. "I don't believe Ryan can handle feeding anymore. He has lost another three pounds over the past two weeks. Look at him; he is nothing but bones! The weekend has been horrible! I've never seen him struggle for his breath like he has the past three days. He is terrified whenever I put anything in his stomach tube." My voice was barely a whisper. "Ron, I think Ryan is dying, but I haven't wanted to see it before."

Ron said nothing. The silence was oppressive. "What do we do, Joan?" He continued throwing out his desperate questions in my direction. "How much feeding did he take this weekend? What has the doctor said? Is there anything else we can try? How long can he live like this?" I answered each of his questions in detail, but paused on the final one. "Ron, his body is rejecting everything I put in him. He can't go on much longer like this. The doctor suggests we not force anything into him today and see how he does."

The rest of the day his little body was relaxed and happy. He smiled at everything. We hadn't witnessed a smile from Ryan in months, but today I could not enjoy it. His satisfaction in not taking nourishment was killing me. I wanted him to keep fighting, but he seemed too content with giving up. I cried all day. After dinner, I suggested we escape outside and enjoy the warm summer evening. The scorching midday heat had kept us trapped inside our air-conditioned home.

Ron and I worked silently in our little vegetable patch. We had not said much to each other all day. Nothing seemed important compared to the fact that our son was dying. Kari and Ryan both sat in their wheelchairs, and Jeremy watched contentedly from his stroller.

As the sun was setting, I laid down my hoe and unbuckled Ryan from his seat. His back was sweaty, but he continued to smile as I hugged him close to my hot body. His frail five-year-old body was light in my arms. I danced around the yard with him in my arms, singing a lullaby until my sobbing overtook my melody. "Oh, God," I cried as I collapsed on the freshly cut grass pulling Ryan on top of me, "please don't make him suffer long!"

The sun sank below the horizon as Ryan slept in my arms. As I carried him indoors, I had no idea this had been his last time outside.

"Someday I'll stop weeping and I'll find joy in the morning," I penned in my journal that evening after the children were sleeping. "But today my son is dying and my tears help me see even more clearly my incredible love for him."

Ryan slept through the night and continued his smiling and contented nature in the morning. I again called Ryan's physician, but he continued to encourage me not to force any feeding, only water. Throughout the day his breathing again became labored as water slowly dripped into his G-tube. By evening, fear had returned to his eyes again. I stopped the water drip and later he smiled at me when I placed him in his bed that evening. He lay awake quietly staring at the ceiling. By five in the morning, he still had not fallen asleep, so I crawled in bed beside him and cradled him in my arms. He trusted me and closed his eyes. His fear was gone.

A few hours later I awoke in a panic, "Ron, I just have to try to get him to take some fluid! I can't let my baby starve!" I slowly injected a teaspoon of water into his G-tube. Ryan instantly gasped for air and his bronchial tubes constricted, sending him into spasms of coughing. Blood sprayed from his lungs and he arched his back in pain. He cried out and his struggle did not stop for another hour. He gasped for air between sobs. He looked at me with eyes that screamed, "Mommy, don't you understand?" I left him in Ron's care after Ryan exhausted himself to sleep.

I slammed the door behind me as I left the house. I couldn't handle watching Ryan anymore. I had almost drowned my son with only a teaspoon of water—and I was drowning in fear.

I was so weary; I had not slept soundly in thirty-six hours. Loie was on vacation, but I was too afraid to call her to let her know that Ryan was not doing well. I continued to also care for Kari and Jeremy, but I was reaching my breaking point. I knew I had to call Loie; I would never forgive myself if Ryan died without her being here.

When I entered the house, Ron was still rocking Ryan. Jeremy was crying for food and it was already an hour past Kari's scheduled medication time. "Ron, I just have to help Ryan!" I collapsed in the chair to nurse Jeremy, avoiding the eyes of my husband. I didn't want him to see through me; I felt like a failure. Even my nursing degree was worthless to my son now.

"Joan, look at me." Ron spoke gently but firmly. "You are not starving your son! Ryan's body is shutting down. It is not accepting fluid anymore. You know what the doctor said, and you know what Ryan is trying to tell us. You must let him go!

"You are a good mother and you have done an incredible job caring for our son. But you must see that he can't go on much longer. God is giving you a chance to say good-bye to Ryan—please take advantage of this time. I want you to be here for him! Oh, honey, don't you see that the pain you're feeling is because you love Ryan so much, not because you are failing him? Don't leave him alone; I'll get us help for Kari and Jeremy."

Thursday, assistance did arrive. We opened our doors to caring individuals from our church. They provided food, hugs, tears, and encouragement. Loie came home from her vacation and stayed by our side throughout the day and night. Our parents helped with Kari, Jeremy, and the household responsibilities. Ron made arrangements with the funeral director and planned a memorial service. I gave all my energies to Ryan. I could not sleep and kept him cradled next to me day and night.

I played Michael Card's "Sleep Sound in Jesus" lullaby tape over and over for him. The corresponding book lay open on my bed and the meditations to parents eased my troubled spirit. When Ryan's pain was intense, I kept the page opened to a picture of a heavenly angel hovering over a sleeping boy. It reminded me that there were angels surrounding Ryan. They were just as concerned as I, but unable to do anything until their Commander-in-Chief gave orders to carry Ryan to heaven.

By early Saturday morning, seeing his suffering body was more than I could bear. As day was dawning, I silently slipped out of our house and walked down the deserted road. I raised my heart and eyes towards heaven. "How long, oh Lord, must I watch this child suffer? Why don't You take him? Do You take pleasure in seeing a five-year-old little boy in pain? Will You not accept him into Your presence? Haven't You promised You are preparing a room for him? He is so innocent he doesn't deserve to suffer. I am the one who is full of sin. What else do You want me to learn through this incredible suffering? Every time I look into my son's dying face, I see Yours, Jesus. I know You are identifying with him in his death. I can't bear this anymore. Please, Jesus, come for him!"

I entered the house and collapsed on Ryan's empty bed. He had been sleeping in ours for three days. I slept deeply for an hour and awoke feeling refreshed and strengthened. I shuddered when I remembered the questions I had thrown up into heaven's face. I knew my Lord was able to handle them and He was responding to me even now. The energy I felt after just an hour's sleep was reassurance to me that God was carrying me through this horribly painful journey.

Late that evening when my brother Joe arrived from Chicago, I knew the end of Ryan's life was coming soon. Joe was the only relative who had not had a chance to say good-bye and his presence was a comfort to all of us. Our son's battle for life was finally over the next morning. His soul had departed the shell of the little body that I cradled in my arms. Ron whispered tenderly into his ear, "Good-bye for now, little Ryan. We will see you later."

*   *   *

For days and months ahead, comfort to my grieving mother's heart came only through those final words, the confidence that I would see him again. When I saw the face of Christ in the face of my dying son, I was reassured that Ryan had taken part of the sufferings of Jesus. Now in his death he was beginning to partake of the blessings of the resurrection. (Philippians 3:10) He could walk and run and dance and sing and laugh! Most of all he could see his Savior face to face. He was free to worship Jesus without sin's devastating effects on his earthly body, and one day I would be reunited with my son and witness it all. This was the only hope that kept me sustained through the pit of my grief.

I chose to face the pain of being separated from my son head on. I did not deny it or run from it. He was gone and he had taken a part of my heart with him. The battery of emotions that revealed themselves when I was faced with the reality of his death overwhelmed me. I loved him deeply and his absence left a hole in my broken heart.

I had not withheld any love from Ryan while he lived. I had not turned my back on his disabilities or distanced myself from his suffering. Because I identified with him so fully, his death ripped my world apart. Even though I still had a newborn baby and a severely disabled seven-year-old, I felt as though I had nothing left to do in life. Ryan had consumed many of my energies in the last months and God had stretched my heart to provide the love that Ryan needed. No longer needed to provide his care, I felt strangely empty.

My mind became a roller coaster of emotions. I felt guilt for asking God to take my son during the depths of his suffering. Now only days after his death, I felt the time I had with Ryan had been too short. There were days that I felt relieved that I no longer had to care for him. Then I would plunge deep into guilt. I did not want life to be less complicated; I wanted my son. Life was not easier without him!

My desire to blame surprised me; my emotions were out of control. In my head, I knew I had committed my son to God, but my heart needed to cry out to someone whom I could hurt as I was hurting.

I received a card of condolence from Ryan's neurologist and his gastroenterologist on the same day. Both were genuinely compassionate in their sympathies, yet I treasured the one sent from the neurologist and rejected the other. The gastroenterologist was the one who could not nourish my dying son. He was the one who said no more could be done. I was ashamed at my need to find fault and too cowardly to lay my heart out before God. It meant that I would be brought face to face with His incredible compassion, His great love, and His everlasting justice. My feeble mind was no match for His available mercy.

Intense anger immobilized me. It exposed the ugliness of my heart and showed itself when I least expected. A comment that was comforting one day would send me into a frenzied battle of my mind on another. A routine trip to the pediatric dentist with Kari resulted in my body becoming a quivering mold of Jell-O. Panic ripped through me! "My son should also be with me!"

But the situation that sent me most into the grip of bitterness was seeing people who had never been able to reach out to Ryan during his brief lifetime. Now they were embracing my youngest son with open arms. Jeremy was easy to love, and he had much more potential to return that love. Jeremy's happy demeanor automatically drew people to him. Ryan had little success in life, and loving him required bearing his pain and self-sacrifice. It was easier to overlook his need for acceptance than to learn how to relate to him. I knew that if I dwelt on this bitter observation, it would consume and trap me.

"Oh, God, help me see beyond this. Let me see the pain in others that keeps them from reaching out in love to those who need it most—the weak in our world. Heal my wounded heart so that I may comfort others. Forgive my complaining, I don't want this root of bitterness to entangle me anymore!"

I was often fearful because I could no longer control the emotions within me. Sometimes I would run from people. Other times I longed to be with them. Often I felt panic before going to church, but once there, I felt comfort. God was there, and through my husband's sermons Jesus became more real to me than ever.

In my home, I sometimes felt closed in. I wanted to escape, for everything reminded me of Ryan. I missed him so much. Other times my house felt like strong comforting arms around me, and Ryan's belongings brought warm affection to my soul.

I fluctuated between wanting to talk and laugh and be silly and then longing to cry and be silent, dreaming about my son. These were all a part of the emotions that God had given me. Healing of my loss came as I trusted Him for each feeling, and He gave me joy in return. Eventually memories of Ryan became sweet to me, and the intense pain of grief diminished. Weeping had remained for the night, and it was a long night, but joy had come in my mourning.

*   *   *

The evening of Ryan's home going, I walked outside and looked up into the heavens. I knew he was there. The brightness of the day was dimming. A warm breeze gently brushed my face; the air was saturated with the aroma of fresh earth and cut grass. Mist rose from the neighboring swamp. Birds were singing their night song, crickets chirped in unison, and fireflies twinkled their fleeting light.

It was then that I noticed the brilliant sunset splashed across the sky. Bursts of color—orange, yellow, and red—were delicately layered on the canvas of the horizon. I called for Ron before the sun set and took with it the blazing display. "Come and see the picture that Ryan painted for us tonight!" Heaven had welcomed my son home. We imagined that this sunset was Ryan's way of saying, "Thank you, Mom and Dad. I'll see you soon!"

Ron's Reflections . . .

The day that Ryan died was to be the day in which Jeremy (along with several other children) was to be dedicated to the Lord in a special service at our church. We were going to publicly present our newborn son to the Lord. Instead, it was our five-year-old son that we privately presented that day. In place of the scheduled child dedication ceremony, the congregation held up our family in a special time of prayer as we kept watch by Ryan's bed. A few hours later he was with Jesus.

When Ryan was less than a year old, we had dedicated him to the Lord. It wasn't a typical dedication. The words were modified to acknowledge the fact that he wouldn't grow up to serve the Lord the way in which other children could. Even then, we had placed him in the Lord's care in a special way.

When we dedicate children to the Lord, it is a way of recognizing that they belong to God. They never really are our possession and they are with us for such a short period of time. The responsibility to raise them for the Lord is a big one and our ability to guide them and meet their needs is so limited. We do best when we remember that "little ones to him belong."

**A successful family
entrusts each member
into Jesus' loving care.**

CHAPTER TWENTY-ONE

When Ryan died, memories of experiences in surgical waiting rooms returned to me—the anxiety of sending Ryan through the operating room doors alone, the frustration of not being allowed beyond those doors, and the test of patience as I waited for my son's return, knowing he was in good hands all the while.

Again I felt those emotions. Ryan had gone somewhere that I could not go. Earth had become my waiting room, but I did not want to wait. I wanted to see my son again, but God whispered, "No, you wait here. And while you wait, though you are sad now, I want you to experience *My* joy."

How can I have joy in this place? Heaven is the new residence of my heart; flesh of my flesh is there in the presence of the Lord. The only joy I want to share in is with Ryan and what he is experiencing.

How can I have joy in my mourning? Will my family survive during this time of intense grief? What does joy mean to me anyway? I know joy is different than the happy feelings I have when I finally beat my husband in a tennis match, or the excitement I experience when packing for a camping getaway. I also know that I have experienced real joy during other times of difficulty.

Yes, I have experienced this emotion sent from God. If I hadn't, I would surely have become angry and bitter. I had tasted of these emotions when I had not allowed God to change me.

I do have a choice. Will I hold tightly to these emotions, or do I want to step out in faith and follow the path that God wants me to take? His path involves looking at the death of my son from His perspective and not from my own small view. I know God is good and allows only what is beneficial to my life—even perplexing things.

Truly, He has been faithful to our family, keeping us together through experiences that should have destroyed us. God has provided a way for His children to conquer this world of pain. The first step to experiencing His joy is placing my trust, hope, and faith in Jesus. At least that's the way it had worked in the past. Will it work that way now, now that death has visited our home?

I remember sitting in the kitchen of a mother whose six-month-old baby had died two days before. Kari was a year old at the time. I said little to this woman in her grief, for I had not lost a child and did not know what comfort to offer. I cradled her sobbing head on my shoulder, feeling the intensity of her misery.

When I finally spoke, I mentioned the sweet memories that little Billy had left behind. Her response startled me. She pushed herself away from me, cursing that she never wanted to hear his name said again. "The best thing I can hope for is to be able to forget that he ever lived. Then maybe my pain will go away and I can return to living a 'decent' life."

I now understand the pain of losing a child, but never do I want to feel the depth of hopelessness that Billy's mom had then. I don't want to forget Ryan for a moment. If anything, I fear that in the midst of my deep pain, I will misplace some of my treasured memories of him.

The day that we were told our children were severely disabled we had hope—hope that one day Jesus would return and make everything right. Our children would no longer suffer. That hope carried us and gave us the ability to enjoy our children each day. Will it also carry me now when I don't have Ryan with me at all?

The last time I visited Billy's mother, no pictures of Billy hung on the wall. She had done all she could to distance herself from him. She had also separated from her husband. She had kicked him out of their home and was filing for divorce. Her oldest son was on drugs and she had no idea where he was. She looked as if she had aged ten years.

Ron and I often reflected that during Ryan's life we were given a wonderful gift—the chance to love unconditionally. It has been a challenge to love in this way, but it has brought fulfillment—the fulfillment that comes as we give ourselves completely to a child committed to God.

Ryan taught us that. He couldn't say the words we wanted to hear. He couldn't do the "tricks" that make every parent proud. What he could do was need our love—our unconditional love—and in giving him that, we found great satisfaction.

Two years before Ryan's death, Ron and I had a "date night." Loie babysat while we went for dinner and a peaceful stroll around a nearby lake. It had been a stressful few weeks. Our child had come through another hospitalization and Ron was working long hours at the church. These few hours alone were cherished.

While watching the sunset from a resting place, Ron proposed a Bible verse for our family to consider as our "life message." It was Acts 20:35. "In everything I did, I showed you that by this kind of hard work we must help the weak, remembering the words the Lord Jesus himself said: 'It is more blessed to give than to receive.'"

Jesus had placed two of his weakest children in our family. His command to give rather than take connected with me. I could relate to the kind of hard work that verse was talking about, and I also have experienced the joy that comes from pouring my life into children who cannot give back. An amazing thing happened. As I would give, God not only provided the energy I needed to keep up with their care and endure their suffering, He also supplied me with enough joy and love to share with others.

Kari's surgery experience at New York's Presbyterian Hospital, when she was three, was an example of this. What was to be a simple surgical procedure became a nightmare. While on the operating table, her body began to seize. Eight hours later (and still in the recovery room) the seizure showed no signs of stopping. We feared we would lose her when finally an IV anticonvulsant took effect.

Later that evening, after the situation had stabilized, Kari was transferred to a semi-private room. When we arrived, I was introduced to her roommate. Vincent Edwards was an eight-year-old boy from New York City. Well-versed in street slang, but lacking in common courtesy, he had a tough exterior and a very annoying way with the nurses. He had used up their patience as he waited in the large city hospital for his mother to claim him again. After his arrival at the hospital, she abandoned him. Social Services were still trying to locate anyone who was even a distant relative of Vincent. So there he was, looking for trouble.

Fascinated with the arrival of his new roommate, Vincent insisted on knowing everything about Kari. He climbed on her intravenous pole to get a better look at her, crudely verbalizing his dislike at having to share a room with a girl. He searched through my bags for something to eat as the nurse asked me questions regarding Kari. I was exhausted; I didn't want to be bothered with an obnoxious eight-year-old on a day when Kari was so close to death.

I wanted to complain. Who could blame me if I demanded a room for the protection of my daughter and for my sanity? I hesitated. Something inside me said, "Joan, look beyond his tough skin. There is a scared little boy in there." During the next three days, I discovered the emotionally destitute child inside him and it was love that broke through.

Vincent ate all my cereal, crackers, juice, and fruit that I had hoped to survive on during that stay. He knocked over Kari's IV pole twice. He brought all the other bored kids in the hospital into our room to play games with me. At night, he would wake up with nightmares, screaming out for my presence. He was a nuisance. But in the midst of it all, I received supernatural joy, because God had placed in our room a little boy who had more needs than Kari or me. He needed to experience love and he needed to know Jesus.

Each night at bedtime, Vincent would crawl on my cot along with me as I read my Bible and told him about Jesus. He had never heard about Jesus and was eager to learn. What a privilege it was for me to be the first to introduce him to the God of the universe.

I still pray for Vincent. What kind of life could he possibly hope for? His family abandoned him after he was severely injured by a hit and run driver. And yet it seemed that God had hope for Vincent. Perhaps it was not by accident that Kari was assigned to his room.

Joy did not come to me in that New York City hospital because my daughter was healed, because she was not. It didn't come because God had sustained her life through a traumatic experience, though I was grateful that He had. It didn't come because I reached beyond my own needs to encourage Vincent, although that gave me a good feeling. But joy came through obedience to the desire of God, through trusting Him despite the frightening circumstances. It came by persevering through the long nights and anxiety-laden days. It was God's sweet reward to me. He took pride in giving me His best, in filling me with happiness and contentment. It was His power flowing through me that enabled me to find joy where I least expected to find it.

During each hospitalization, there were always opportunities to reach out beyond our own painful circumstances to share the love of Christ with a child or grieving parent who needed the same hope, joy, and love that we had found. It was never in my own strength. I felt weak and preferred to be selfish, focusing on my own concerns. But God gave me strength to reach out.

"It is more blessed to give than to receive." Yes, it was our family's desire to follow those words of Christ, even though there were many times when we weren't sure we could do it, not sure we even wanted to try, especially when we were hurting so badly.

So often Ron listened to others in their difficulties when he himself was filled with pain—even under the threat of losing one of his children. How often I sat by my child's hospital bed and prayed for the people in our church, sometimes sending notes of encouragement—trying desperately to look beyond my own painful circumstances and identify with theirs.

Sometimes it felt to us that pastoring a church and having two severely disabled children could not mix. Either one was difficult enough on its own.

I have no doubt that many would have understood if we had institutionalized our children so that we could be more effective in ministry. That was never an option we considered for even a moment. I'm also sure it would not have appeared abnormal if Ron had searched for a new job that didn't require the hours and emotional stress that pastoring a growing church demands.

There were times when I wanted to quit and leave the ministry, but God wasn't calling us to lay aside either the ministry or the daily care of our children to focus on just one of these areas. Our ministry was our family and our family was our ministry. We could not afford to have a breakdown of our family unit—the one God put together. We needed each other.

It has not been an easy life to balance; God hadn't promised us that. He did promise to give us the power to conquer the obstacles that come our way. He wanted us to trust and focus our attention on Him and not ourselves and our needs.

God had given us joy as we traveled through each of these experiences. But will I have joy in this new world of grief, without my precious son nearby?

Lamentations 3:32-33 says, "Though the Lord brings grief, he will show compassion, so great is His unfailing love. For He does not willingly bring affliction or grief to the children of men." I believe this promise. Without Ryan, life will be so different, but I do have the hope that I will see him again. If we continue to do the things that God is calling us to do, I am convinced that He will give us joy in this anxiety-laden waiting room—even in the midst of this new land of grieving.

Ron's Reflections . . .

In the telling of our story and the sharing of important principles, we would be remiss if we did not explain the most important of them. Of all the things that Joan and I have written, we would not want you to overlook this one. It explains, more than anything else, how we have been able to make it as a family. Before we can explain it, we must set the backdrop for why this principle is so critical.

The disappointments of our life, the pain we have experienced in watching our children suffer, the frustration of not being able to find a cure or therapy that will substantially help—all of these undeniably and vividly remind us that we live in a broken world. Fortunately, there is an explanation for our experience, one that also points to the solution. The Bible contains that explanation—the presence of evil in our world, which directly or indirectly causes the suffering we experience.

God's Word explains to us that the disobedience of the first man and woman was the entrance of evil into the world. It also says that, by nature and by choice, every individual fails to be the good person God asks him to be. If we are honest, we realize that we fail to live up to our own ideals of what it means to be a truly good person, let alone God's expectations for us. The result is that we feel guilt, are guilty of wrongdoing before God and directly or indirectly experience a multitude of other ways in which the world is less satisfying and beautiful than what God originally designed for us. The bad news is that we share in the responsibility for the presence of evil in our world.

Fortunately, God in His love for us provided a solution. The answer was His coming into our world in the person of Jesus—that historic figure who changed the world. Through his life, He modeled what it means to live a life of love for God and love for other people. He exhibited all the character that we, in our better moments, long to possess. Most importantly, what He accomplished was the cure each of us needs—forgiveness for sin and the undoing of the consequences of sin. He did this by laying down His life for us, taking the punishment for sin. This good news is for all who will receive it.

The best part of God's solution, and the purpose of His providing it, is that we are able to know Him. He is our joy!

In our youth, Joan and I had each responded to this good news from God, receiving His salvation. As we have grown older and and faced various situations in our lives, we have also grown in our realization of what a valuable gift we have received.

With Jesus come all kinds of wonderful promises for those who receive Him and His salvation. One of those promises is that one day our children will be healthy and whole in every way—physically and emotionally, as well as spiritually. For us, this is not wishful thinking; it is our hope, a certainty that allows us to keep moving forward with our lives. Jesus is the ultimate reason for the success of our family. We gratefully give the credit to Him.

A successful family
receives God's salvation
and has a full life
because of His promises.

An Update

It has been over seven years since Ryan died. Our family is still together, loving one another, enjoying God's goodness. Kari is fifteen years old and developmentally has made few advances. She has been through many trials, one of which was a six-month stretch in the hospital, during which time the majority of this book was written. There have been times when we almost lost her. Every birthday celebration is filled with rejoicing that God has allowed yet another year with her as part of our family. Jeremy is seven years old and continues to develop normally. He is precious to us.

Loie did get married and moved away five months after Ryan died and no longer needed her. God's timing is perfect. We were honored to play significant roles in Loie's wedding. She now lives in Reading, Pennsylvania, with her husband Ivan. They have three very beautiful children: Jonathan, Mikaela, and Elizabeth. They remain good friends and we'll always be grateful for Loie's love of our children.

After almost nine years of ministry in Red Hill, we resigned to take on yet another ministry assignment. Leaving Red Hill was very difficult for us, but we are thrilled the church at Red Hill is doing well. We enjoy every opportunity we have to visit with these dear people.

We presently serve as Minister to Field Staff with RHMA—a pastor-to-pastors position with this mission to small towns (mostly here in the United States). For most of the year we live in a thirty-foot travel trailer, which is our home. Life on the road with a severely disabled child, home schooling a second grader—each has its challenges. God continues to stretch us and teach us, and He gives us joy in the new lands into which He leads us.

THE PASSION BEHIND "RON'S REFLECTIONS"

There's more to the story...

As we have looked at this book that Joan has written, it seemed that we needed to do more than tell the story of God's grace in our lives. Aware of how many families come apart under stress, we also wanted to offer hope for other hurting families. We decided to highlight the things we learned. Rather than interrupt the flow of the story as Joan told it, we decided to relegate the "meaning behind it" to a reflection section at the end of the chapter. Each of those is concluded by a principle.

There are a multitude of principles (truths about life) that are important for families to succeed. We wouldn't claim to have identified them all, nor have we placed them in order of importance. In our book, we have focused specifically on principles that were helpful to us during times of crisis.

Every family experiences trials...

We're obviously not the only family who has experienced their world coming apart. We suspect every family either has faced or will face a time of trials in which it seems like their whole life is shaken. A family's world can be shattered in any number of ways. It could be the loss of a job or other significant financial setback. It might be in the discovery that a son is addicted to pornography, or a daughter is using drugs, or some other disappointing choices of a family member—choices that lead to devastating consequences. It could be a physical illness or injury leading to disability.

How principles can help...

We believe that God has given us everything that we need to allow us to live a full life, to be more than conquerors, even through disappointment and suffering. One of those resources is a group of principles for living successfully. In order for us to use this resource we must understand the nature of principles.

Principles should not be viewed as blanket promises. For example, it is not true that every "*risk taking family*" will succeed. It doesn't always work that way. This does not mean principles aren't always trustworthy or reliable. They can be counted on—everything else being equal, if other principles do not supercede them. We believe in the principle of "*holding on to God in times of trial*" as an important ingredient to family success; however, we don't believe a family is going to be very successful if they basically ignore God the rest of their life.

But what a difference it has made for us to apply, for example, the principle of holding on to God. He has been our comfort and our strength. What if we had chosen to ignore this principle? What if we decided that since God hadn't kept the good times rolling for us we therefore would do without him and somehow cope on our own? We believe we wouldn't have made it.

Principles are transferable...

In highlighting principles, we trust that we are providing some handles for others, a way to help them take our story and give it meaning for their own situation. Rather than this just being the story of one family who has stayed together, we trust it will result in helping many families succeed when their worlds are coming apart.

We've discovered something else along the way. The principles are transferable for us, too. As we face new challenges, we find that we ourselves are helped by our own story, by looking back and reviewing the principles that have benefited us in the past and applying them to the present situation.

Applying the principles...

If your family is in a time of crisis, our hearts go out to you. We encourage you to carefully review the principles that have helped us and ask yourself a few key questions:

- *Which principles might assist me in my situation?*
- *How would these principles work themselves out in my family?*
- *Are there other principles I need to consider for my family to succeed?*

Thanks for reading our book. If it has been a help and encouragement to you, please write and let us know.

We would love to pray for you. Our mailing address and Internet web site are found on the title page.

Ron and Joan Denlinger

A Parent's ^(Survival) Guide
How to Cope When Your Kid is Using Drugs

BAY
STREET

A Novel

PHILIP
SLAYTON

Oblonsky Editions

ISBN (Ebook) 978-0-9936389-1-6

ISBN (Hard Cover) 978-0-9936389-0-9

ABOUT THE AUTHOR

Philip Slayton is the best-selling author of
Lawyers Gone Bad (2007) and *Mighty Judgment* (2011).

He worked as a lawyer on Bay Street
for almost 20 years.
www.philipslayton.com

To H.N., with affection and gratitude

Bay Street

Chapter One
Piper

Piper Fantouche hated her name. She often apologized for it when she met someone new. "It's a strange name, I know," she would say, as she shook hands. "Not my choice," she'd add, blushing. "But easy to remember," she'd throw in, with a slight laugh.

Piper didn't like it when she blushed. Blushing revealed something about her, a raw nerve. Life had taught her that revealing something personal could be dangerous. But, try as she might, she couldn't stop herself turning red when she was embarrassed, and she embarrassed easily. "It's your capillaries," her friend Susan told her. "They're too close to the surface of your skin."

She sometimes reflected that maybe her Christian name wasn't all that bad. "Piper" suggested a woman who was peppy but mysterious, accessible yet formidable, someone who was fun to be with but had to be taken seriously – at least, that's what Peter, her boyfriend, told her one evening, although not as concisely, and it sounded flattering and right to Piper, although at that particular moment Peter mostly had her accessibility in mind, which is to say he wanted to fuck her.

Yes, she thought, maybe "Piper" struck the right note. She wanted to seem elusive and tough, someone who meant business and was not to be trifled with, a person who couldn't be pushed around, someone who had to be taken seriously. But she also wanted to suggest tenderness and a capacity for pleasure–to hint at a summer's day, was the way she put it to herself and close friends ("That's crap," Susan said). It was so difficult to balance everything. Thinking about how to balance everything sometimes made her feel as if she was going mad.

Piper had been teased about her name at school. Remembering how she had been bullied made her lip quiver even now. At recess in kindergarten the other kids had chanted, "Piper wears a diaper, Piper wears a diaper." That had got her wondering, at a very young age, why she had this nomenclatural burden, and she asked her mother for an explanation. Her mother told her that she had been named after an aeroplane manufacturing company because, at the time of her birth, her father, a man of passing but intense enthusiasms, was mad about learning to fly. Her dad never did take flying lessons– he couldn't afford it–which he regretted greatly until he moved on to collecting stamps and forgot all about civil aviation. Piper's younger sister, Penny Black Fantouche, was born during her father's numismatic period.

Okay, she could live with "Piper," but what sort of name was "Fantouche?" When Piper's father arrived in Canada from Latvia as a young man, his surname was Ozols. He quickly changed it. She asked him once, what was wrong with Ozols, and why Fantouche? "You can't get ahead in Canada with a name like Ozols," he told Piper, oblivious to the growing multiculturalism staring

him in the face, using what Piper called his "stern voice" which he employed only for serious subjects. "Ozols is not a good name for a bank manager, or a civil servant. It is not a good name for your typical Canadian job. It is a foreign name. It does not inspire confidence. In Canada, to have a future, you need a name that suggests the founding peoples. Where would I have got in life if I had kept the name Bendiks Ozols? But when I took the name Benjamin Fantouche, a Scottish name, opportunities opened up." When Piper's father had come to Canada he had been full of an immigrant's hope and ambition.

Piper hadn't the heart to point out to her father that opportunities hadn't opened up for him all that much. She loved him too much to say something that might hurt his feelings. Benjamin had worked for years as a security guard at an upscale downtown condominium where he was patronized by young apartment owners who worked in information technology and dressed in black. Also, she was not sure it was correct to describe the Scots as one of Canada's founding peoples. And was Fantouche really a Scottish name?

• • •

"Piper, may I have a word?"

She was walking by Jim Watt's office on her way to get lunch at the cafeteria. His door was open. It was almost always open. Watt had carefully placed his desk so that he could see everyone who went along the corridor. His head jerked up and down, as he went from studying a document on his desk, to regarding the person who happened to be passing by, and then back to reading the document. He summoned Piper into his office with a big wave, his arm pivoting awkwardly in its socket, his large

hand flailing strangely as it apparently sought to draw her towards him, his head bobbing like a pigeon's in what seemed like an uncontrollable reflex.

Jim Watt was managing partner of the law firm where Piper worked. He was in his mid forties although he looked older. He was lean and tall, almost cadaverous, with a concave chest, short black hair plastered on an unusually small head, an obvious toupée, angular facial features, and large old-fashioned bi-focal square glasses with plastic frames. He was not an attractive man. Slightly stooped, every day he wore a blue suit, highly-polished black shoes, a white button-down shirt, and a blue patternless silk tie. At home, he had a walk-in closet full of blue suits, black shoes, white shirts and blue patternless ties.

Piper didn't think much of the way Watt dressed. She liked a touch of flamboyance in her own appearance, although she was careful not to take it too far. It was the balance thing. A woman had to be on the demure side to be a successful junior partner in the top Toronto law firm of Dibbet & Dibbet, known to the legal and business world as Dibbets. Her clothes should not attract too much attention. She should not flaunt her assets. Funeral chic was the standard. But why not a little cleavage, or open-toe shoes?

Piper found the official demands of demureness hard to bear, and pushed back as much as she dared. Sometimes she wore Dsquared2 clothes to work. Dsquared2 was the label of Toronto designers Dean and Dan Caten, who designed clothes for Madonna. In the summer, she might be in a Lilly Pulitzer print. She had her hair styled by Sylvie Prud'Homme in her Queen Street West salon. Sylvie, a

beautiful bundle of youthful energy, was the best hair-dresser in the city. She was tattooed from head to foot. Sylvie had urged Piper to get a tattoo herself, and Piper had been interested, but it would have to be somewhere that was usually covered up and, anyway, what kind of tattoo would be suitable, the scales of justice? She knew that Dibbets wouldn't approve of tattoos, although she didn't think there was an official firm policy on the subject and, in any case, how would they ever know.

At home, every morning, just before she left for work, Piper would look at herself carefully, from all possible angles, in her full-length bedroom mirror. Did she look okay? Did she look attractive? Did she look too attractive? Her clothes seemed a bit tight. Was she putting on weight? Sometimes, at the last minute, on the point of going out the front door, she would suddenly tear off the clothes she was wearing and throw them on the bed to be put away later, pulling new things to wear off hangers and out of drawers. Sometimes, she would decide on the spur of the moment that she looked drab; it didn't have to be that way, she could spice things up a bit. Sometimes her judgment ran in the opposite direction; I look like a whore, she would think. Sometimes, she looked at herself in the full-length mirror, felt inexplicable anguish, burst into tears, decided nothing, and left for the office full of sadness.

Jim Watt thought Piper was beautiful. She was tall and slim, with a figure straight from the cover of a Harlequin Romance, long legs with toned calf muscles like those of a ballerina, auburn hair, large but oddly attractive ears (she often wore her hair up in a bun to show off her ears; she knew men liked her ears, fantasized about them),

brilliant big brown eyes, and a big smile. Older partners around the office sometimes remarked that she looked the way Susan Sarandon had looked in 1976. As for Watt, he tried to conceal his libidinous interest in Piper, ostentatiously looking the other way when she walked by, although even a casual observer would have noted that his eyes swivelled in one direction as he pretended to look in the other.

Many of the partners at Dibbets suspected how Watt felt about Piper and watched him closely when she was around. They hoped that he would do something stupid. If Watt behaved badly, then he would have a vulnerability that could be exploited in the constant jockeying for advantage in the firm. After all, Watt was a married man, married to Amanda, an accountant several years younger than he was; they had met when she had prepared his impressive income tax returns. Jim and Amanda had two children, Tory, fourteen, and her brother Blake, eleven. Tory attended Havergal, Toronto's best private girls' school. Blake was a problem; he had a learning disability and went to a remedial institution that Watt did not like to talk about.

• • •

"Piper," said Watt, speaking in a hushed tone and looking grave, "shut the door." When the door was closed, Watt lowered his voice even more, almost to a whisper. Piper strained to hear what he was saying.

"Piper, this is important," he said softly, and paused. The pause seemed to last for a long time. Eventually he spoke again, very slowly. "Piper, Canadian Unity Bank is planning a takeover of Liberty Insurance. I'd like to put you on the team that will lawyer the transaction. It's

a big, big deal. I'm not exaggerating in the slightest if I say, it's transformative. Transformative! The transaction is secret for the minute. You must not say anything to anybody. Piper, this is a great opportunity for you."

Watt leaned back in his chair with an air of great satisfaction. Piper tried to seem solemn. She concentrated on the words "big deal," wonderful words to a corporate lawyer, rolling the phrase around in her head, conscious that Watt was fixing her with what he would probably describe as a laser-like look.

"It'll be long hours, Piper, a lot of midnight oil. You and I will be working very closely together. It'll be a large team—tax people, intellectual property people, securities lawyers, banking experts, lots of junior folks, chimps to shuffle the papers, we always need chimps. Are you up for it?"

Watt tried to look serious and calm, but his excitement was obvious. By now, he had abandoned his whisper and was speaking in a normal, even loud, voice. His face was slightly flushed and his left arm twitched in a peculiar way. It occurred to Piper that he might have a neurological problem. She noticed that his old-fashioned plastic-framed glasses were askew on his face.

"Of course I am, Jim. As you say, a great opportunity!"

She gave Watt a big smile and did some quick mental arithmetic. There were two months to go before the end of the partnership's financial year, and so far she only had about twelve hundred billable hours. In the fall, every partner's share of the firm's profits would be reassessed by the compensation committee. Go before the committee with her billable hours hundreds short of what was considered acceptable? They'd cut her back by fifty, maybe

a hundred, thousand dollars a year. Warn her too. She could hear it now. "Couple of years to turn it around Piper, we're sure you can do it, but if not…"

"If not" meant out on your ass, fixed up with a poorly-paying general counsel position at one of the firm's smaller clients, expected to shovel work back to the mother ship, invited to an annual cocktail party for Dibbets so-called "alumni," or worse, taking refuge in a small law firm in the suburbs, a storefront operation, with boring work, a tiny income, and endless shame. But to be on the Canadian Unity Bank/Liberty Insurance takeover team, that had to be good for two hundred billables a month or more, all those long nights revising documents, shuffling papers, maybe two hundred and fifty billables a month, who's counting? Two months of that would get her into the safe zone. The compensation committee would treat her well. They wouldn't cut her back. They might even move her up to half-a-million a year. Piper, she said to herself, remember why you're here.

"When do we start, Jim?" asked Piper, giving Watt her Susan Sarandon circa 1976 smile.

"Let's have a meeting of the core team at eight tomorrow morning, main boardroom. We'll get it all sorted out, who's doing what. Remember, don't tell anyone about the deal, anyone at all. There's hasn't been an announcement and won't be for several days. Illegal trading in the target's stock would be a disaster. Be careful."

• • •

Piper ate an egg salad sandwich in the firm's cafeteria, sitting alone at a corner table, reading the Toronto Sun. She liked to eat lunch by herself and flourished the Sun to discourage anyone from joining her. When she'd

finished the sandwich, she threw the newspaper in a recycling bin, its job done, and went back to her office on the floor below.

Dibbets had ten floors in the fifty-storey Canadian Unity Bank building at the corner of Bay and Prince in downtown Toronto. The bank, called "CUB" by everybody, was Dibbets' biggest client as well as its landlord. The legal fees charged CUB by Dibbets each year were always almost exactly the amount of rent CUB charged Dibbets. Did that mean anything? No, said people in the know, of course not, it meant nothing at all, it was just a coincidence, a happy coincidence mind you, certainly a good thing for everyone concerned. For many years, as a sign of the special relationship between the bank and its lawyers, a senior partner of Dibbets had sat on the bank's board, occupying what had come to be known as the "Dibbets seat." These days, the Dibbets seat was occupied by Jim Watt.

Back in her office, Piper looked at her computer. Chart-the-Day was on the screen. All Dibbets lawyers used this software to keep meticulous track of how they spent their time. When they came into the office in the morning they turned Chart-the-Day on, and they didn't turn it off until they left. Between when they came in and when they left, every minute had to be accounted for, in six-minute segments, by a computer entry. Activity codes were used to describe what the lawyer had done in each six-minute segment; most important of all was entering the six-digit number assigned to the client who was going to pay for the work. Activity codes were things like "RL" for reading law, or "MT" for sending a memo to someone, or "AM" for attending a meeting, or "TF" for

taking an incoming telephone call. "RL" was a favourite; that was what lawyers put down when they couldn't think of anything else to put down; they often couldn't think of anything else; clients were frequently amazed by how much law was being read on their behalf.

Watt had once told Piper, when she was just an associate–he already had his eye on her and spent a lot of time giving her advice that he hoped people in the office regarded as strictly avuncular–"Piper, I bill portal-to-portal, and so should you. I come in at eight in the morning, and I leave at seven at night, that's if I'm lucky and get to go home and have dinner with Amanda and the little Watts. Eight to seven. That's eleven hours. Someone, Piper, someone, has to pay for that time, all of it, every last second. Portal-to-portal, Piper. That's the way to do it. That's what Dibbets expects from its lawyers. Bill portal-to-portal, Piper, and you'll do well here."

She looked at her computer screen. It was flashing "TWENTY MINUTES UNACCOUNTED FOR." She typed in "MRNF," the activity code for "meeting re new file." "CLIENT AND FILE NUMBER REQUIRED," demanded Chart-the-Day. The client number was easy: every Dibbets lawyer knew CUB's client number off by heart, 907855, that number was the ticket to riches, and Piper typed it in. But what was the file number? This was a new matter; no file had been opened up yet by Watt; there was no file number. "FILE NUMBER REQUIRED," said Chart-the-Day, "FILE NUMBER REQUIRED."

"Fuck!" said Piper. She turned the computer off, but she'd have to deal with Chart-the-Day when she turned it back on the next morning. Chart-the-Day didn't forget.

She looked at her watch. Ten-to-six. A bit early to go home. Watt liked to walk the floor about seven in the evening to see who was working. The rule for junior lawyers, even junior partners, was, don't leave before Watt. Be sure Watt sees you, the later the better. Watt would stick his head around a young lawyer's door and say, "Still here? Better go home to the wife and kids!"

"Can't do that quite yet, Jim. Need to get this contract finished up. Client wants it first thing in the morning. It's a tricky one. Hope to get out of here by midnight, if I'm lucky. It might be an all-nighter."

Watt would smile and move on, and the lawyer in question would go back to checking his Facebook page, RL for 907855, thinking what wife and kids would that be, asshole, I'm not married. But he had been seen by Watt, that was the important thing, and could leave at the first opportunity, which meant a few minutes after Watt had left. You had to wait just long enough for the managing partner to clear the underground parking lot in his Mercedes-Benz S Class sedan.

It was a bit different when Watt put his head round Piper's door in the early evening. "Piper, for someone working so hard you look fresh as a daisy! You should relax a bit. What say I take you to Mario's for a drink?" Sometimes Piper said yes and went to Mario's with Watt. She couldn't always say no; constant rebuff of the managing partner would be too dangerous; she had to think of her career. Piper hated the way Watt took her to a banquette in the corner of the sleazy restaurant across the street and squeezed in beside her, his leg pressing against hers.

"Dry martini?"

"That would be great, Jim. But not too dry."

"Now, tell me Piper, just how are you getting on and what can I do to help? You know, Piper, I think very highly of you and want to see you get ahead. With my help, you've got a great future at Dibbets!"

Chapter Two
Avalon

Piper lived in a Cabbagetown condominium, on the eastern edge of downtown Toronto, a part of the city that once was a hangout for prostitutes and drug dealers. Once, used condoms and discarded hypodermic needles covered Cabbagetown sidewalks in the morning. Today, there were still a few hookers and dealers around, but workers' cottages had become bijou residences, most of the whores and addicts had moved out, lawyers and investment bankers had moved in, and in the morning the sidewalks were pretty clean.

She had bought her place in February, when she turned thirty-two, just after she made partner at Dibbets, moving from a modest one-bedroom rented apartment in the West End where she'd lived for years. When Piper became a partner, things had started looking pretty good from a financial point of view. Her share of profits for her first year as a partner was projected to be $275,000. "Telephone numbers," said her father, amazed by the amount. He earned $42,000 as a security guard, which he had always thought was quite a bit of money. Penny Black, Piper's younger sister, was a free-lance writer and

part-time barista, and brought in $25,000 in a good year. "At least I'm doing what I want," Penny Black said. "At least I haven't sold out to the system, like some I could mention."

"Canada, what a country, you can do anything here," Benjamin said, visiting Piper in her new apartment, wearing his security guard uniform. He was proud of his uniform. The trousers had a knife-edge crease. His blue short-sleeved shirt with epaulettes was immaculately laundered. "Let's raise a glass and celebrate!" said Benjamin. Piper went and got a bottle of Aldaris Zelta, her father's favourite Latvian beer. She always kept some in the fridge in case he dropped by, which he often did; she was always delighted to see him. She poured herself a glass of pinot grigio.

"To Canada, the land of opportunity," said Benjamin, holding up his bottle of Zelta.

"To Canada," said Piper, sipping her glass of wine, and smiling at her father.

"If only your mother could have seen this day," said Benjamin sadly. He had been widowed early, eighteen years ago, when Piper and her sister were teenagers, and had not shown any interest in women since. Regina, his wife, had keeled over one day from a brain aneurysm, just after she had finished clearing away the supper dishes. It had been a shock. Benjamin didn't want to run the risk of another marital bereavement. And, although he missed Regina in a traditional way, he hadn't forgotten that he and his wife had fought a lot, sometimes bitterly. He hadn't forgotten the daily friction, sometimes almost intolerable, of living with someone else. On balance, he thought, it was better to be alone, although he worried

about what would happen when he got older and needed someone to take care of him. Anyway, it was his daughters that mattered to him now. "My girls," he called them. He lived a quiet life.

Benjamin was enormously proud of Piper. "My girl the lawyer," he would sometimes say to himself, in a ruminative moment. To Benjamin, the traditional professions were magnificent and mysterious. To have a child who belonged to something with the splendid name "The Law Society of Upper Canada" gave him ineffable joy. That had been one reason why Piper had pursued a legal career. She knew her father would feel this way and very much wanted to please him. The other reason was she had got excellent undergraduate marks and, when the time came, couldn't think of anything else to do. There didn't seem to be any good jobs out there. Studying dentistry wasn't appealing. She often wondered whether she'd made a mistake in going to law school. Her sister, Penny Black, thought she had. Penny Black thought Piper should live in someone's basement and write a novel. That's what Penny Black was doing.

• • •

Peter, Piper's boyfriend, had strongly encouraged her to buy real estate. His life was threadbare, and he had hoped to move into a nice place with Piper, on at least a semi-permanent basis, and that way get a little security and comfort. "Go for it," he kept telling her as she looked at condo listings. "You need a bigger place," he'd say when she showed him a listing for a one-bedroom that she thought looked promising but he considered too small for two.

His own place was a 600 square foot damp basement apartment in the West End. He'd been planning to move into something better, maybe a soft loft in Liberty Village, but a few months ago had lost his job as director of software development at a small hi-tech company that had fallen on hard times. Demoralized by having many job applications rejected, he had almost given up trying to find work. "Any leads?" Piper would ask regularly. "Nothing," he would reply. "Sent out any résumés lately?" she would inquire. "A few," he would say vaguely and then change the subject.

Unemployment was an unexpected and sad turn of events for Peter. He had enjoyed an almost-brilliant undergraduate career studying mathematics at the University of Toronto. Donald Coxeter, the greatest geometer since Euclid, had been his mathematical idol. Peter was fascinated by the now-dead University of Toronto professor's influential theories. "Coxeter groups!" he would sometimes spontaneously exclaim, referring to one of Coxeter's break-through theories. "Polytopes!" he would say without provocation, a grin spreading over his face (Professor Coxeter had been very interested in polytopes). But when he graduated, Peter figured that job opportunities for geometers were sparse, and decided to get into computers, something practical, rather than go to graduate school. And, it occurred to him, although he might one day be a good geometer, he would never be a great one. He would never be a Donald Coxeter. Later, he thought perhaps he'd made a mistake and was dogged by a sense of personal promise squandered.

Peter was the same age as Piper. He was good-looking in a traditional sort of way–tall, slim, regular features,

good head of brown hair, nice complexion. Piper particularly liked his green eyes. There was another thing about him that she liked: he played the piano beautifully. He had graduated from the Royal Conservatory of Music with the ARCT diploma, the highest level of achievement. He played classical music and show tunes, but liked jazz best of all. Once he had thought of being a piano teacher, but he knew from his own teachers what a disappointing career that could be. The only furniture Peter had in his west end apartment, apart from a bed, a chest of drawers, and a battered kitchenette set, was the upright Heintzman piano that he had inherited from his grandmother.

As his mathematical idol was Donald Coxeter, so his musical idol was the self-proclaimed genius Chilly Gonzalez. Chilly Gonzalez's real name was Jason Beck. He was from Montreal. After graduating in piano from McGill, Jason Beck changed his name to Chilly Gonzales and moved to Paris, where he enjoyed considerable success. Peter dreamed of a career like Chilly's. He thought of changing his name, the way Chilly had, and toyed with various possibilities. He liked "Umberto Eco," but that was taken.

Peter didn't just love geometry and music. He loved Piper, and thought that she was very beautiful. "You are beautiful," he would tell her, over and over again. She liked to hear it, even though she didn't believe him. "I love you," he would say. Sometimes, when he said that, she thought she loved him back.

• • •

Piper's condo was on the ground floor of a small building that had once been a munitions factory. "I love

the smell of cordite in the morning," Peter would say, as a standing joke, after he had slept over. "Yes, Colonel Kilgore," Piper, a movie buff, would reply. The apartment, fourteen hundred square feet, had ceiling beams and expensive kitchen appliances. It was well-furnished, with a few second-hand pieces left over from Piper's early days, but mostly with good stuff recently bought from the city's better furniture stores. And there was a piano for Peter, a Boston upright, bought from Remenyi's House of Music when she became a partner, bought so that Piper could always listen to Peter play. It had cost $12,000, but she could afford it.

Piper had painted the rooms interesting and vivid colours. They weren't rooms exactly; the apartment was one big space, with what you might call notional rooms; thanks to Piper, the notional rooms sang with colour. The condo had its own front door out to a picturesque Cabbagetown street. There was a little garden in front, with cosmos and other polychromatic flowers in the summer, and a wrought-iron gate to the sidewalk. Piper was happy in this place. It had a sentimental quality that suited her.

She always walked to work from her apartment, west down King Street. It took her twenty minutes, fifteen if she walked quickly. She could see the fifty-storey Canadian Unity Bank building the moment she stepped out of her front door. As she made her way westwards, it loomed larger and larger. She imagined Jim Watt, whose office was on the fortieth floor and faced east, watching her as she walked. She fantasized that he had high-powered binoculars within easy reach. She imagined Watt watching her go home on a summer's evening, heading

away from the CUB building when it was still light. This imagining was enough to keep Piper at the office until after Watt had left, or until after dark if he was still there. Anyway, as she often reminded herself, it was a good idea to stay late for other reasons. To be seen in the office in the evening would promote her career. It would show that she was serious about her work. And, to be sensible about it, it was ridiculous to fantasize about Watt watching her through high-powered binoculars. After all, he was a respectable senior lawyer in a firm that was more than 150 years old.

Piper often ruminated about her private life as she walked to and from the office. She worked too hard, that was the problem. There was never enough time to do what other people did, go to the Royal Ontario Museum, or see an exhibition at the Art Gallery, or go to the Toronto International Film Festival, the biggest film festival in the world after Cannes. Toronto was a hell of a town with a lot to offer, and she should take advantage of it. What was the point of living in the big city if all you saw of it was the view from your office window?

Piper liked movies and knew a lot about them, but she had only seen a film at TIFF once, that's how bad it was. Years ago, when she was a teenager, she had gone to the festival and had literally bumped into Brad Pitt, then an almost unknown actor, outside a movie theatre on Bloor Street. She'd just seen "Johnny Suede," a low-budget film about a rock-and-roll singer played by Pitt. Her friend Susan had taken a photo of Piper with Brad's arm around her. A few years ago, with Brad famous and Angelina Jolie waiting to give birth in Namibia and the newspapers full of it all, she had looked for that picture.

She wanted to enlarge it, make it poster-size, and hang it on her living room wall. She couldn't find it. Had she dreamed that whole thing with Brad Pitt? And why did Brad and Angelina go to Namibia for the birth of their child? As it happened, Susan, now a prosperous accountant, had been on holiday in Swakopmund, the most exotic and distant place she could think of, at the same time that Shiloh Nouvel Jolie-Pitt was born. "The place was crawling with paparazzi," she had reported. "Not a tribesman in sight."

When she first moved into her condominium, Piper stopped doing all her grocery shopping at Loblaw's supermarket and tried to get everything she wanted at little shops in Cabbagetown. On Saturday mornings she wandered along the pleasant streets with a large wicker basket that Peter had bought her at a craft fair, wearing a scarf over her head like a peasant woman, pretending she wasn't a corporate lawyer. She bought sausages at what was supposed to be a European butcher, and multi-grain bread at a little bakery. At the farmers' market, further east, she bought fresh vegetables and free-range eggs.

Shopping like this seemed interesting and right. Piper felt that she was being true to her roots. She began to affect a slight accent when she shopped, an accent that came quite spontaneously, popping up out of nowhere. She wondered, could she have a Latvian accent attached to a regressive gene? She had heard something on CBC Radio Two about foreign accent syndrome; maybe that explained it.

But after a while she began to think differently about her shopping habits. The Cabbagetown shopkeepers were rude. The stuff they sold was overpriced. The legacy

asparagus from the farmers' market was not good. The free-range eggs were seldom fresh. Going shop-to-shop took too long. She started going to Whole Foods in Yorkville. Expensive, environmentally sound, no plastic bags, and convenient parking. In Whole Foods, her slight foreign accent disappeared.

• • •

Shortly after she acquired her condominium, Piper decided she needed a new car to go with it. She was embarrassed to park her 2001 Honda Accord, with its dents and rust, outside her building. Her neighbours, junior investment bankers with new BMWs, would not be impressed, and they were, she had to remember, potential clients. According to the Wall Street Journal, derivatives were a big thing despite the global financial crises they periodically precipitated, and she suspected her investment banker neighbours were into derivatives. She was not exactly sure what derivatives were–the WSJ went on and on about them, but never gave a full explanation–but Piper had heard there was a lot of legal work involved. The way to move ahead at Dibbets was to get new clients, and new clients might literally be at her doorstep. She had to be sure they were suitably impressed with her way of life, including her car. She couldn't drive a car that suggested failure.

Jim Watt had said to her the other day, eying her breasts surreptitiously over a martini at Mario's, "Piper, what really counts is business development. What's really important as a partner, even a junior partner, is not the legal work you do, but the legal work you bring in for associates. It's all about new clients. And it's about leverage." Watt leant back against the banquette, gazed

29

at the ceiling, and smiled a big smile. "Leverage," he said again, softly, to himself. He rolled the word around in his mouth as if he were tasting a fine wine. "We pay a chimp one dollar to shuffle some papers, and charge the client two dollars. That's how it's done, Piper. New clients, plus leverage, equals success. Another martini?"

Her 2001 Honda Accord certainly wouldn't attract new clients who could be leveraged. What kind of car would help? She had to be careful: an automobile is always being interpreted. Her instincts were to buy a hybrid, or a smart car. Everyone had to be concerned about global warming and everyone needed to do her bit. If everybody did her bit, the world would be much better off. Also, hybrids, and smart cars, with their interesting designs, had sex appeal. But Dibbets had big clients in the oil and gas business, including companies working in the Alberta Tar Sands, and they were touchy and easily offended. Some of the investment bankers on her street were probably trying to get Initial Public Offerings organized for junior oil and drilling companies. A hybrid or smart car would send the wrong signal.

What about a Chevrolet, or a Ford? Dibbets had auto parts companies as clients, suppliers to General Motors and Ford. Waving that flag seemed like a good idea, but it was tough for Piper, a woman with a bit of a taste for the exotic, to get very interested in a Chevrolet or a Ford. Mercedes? Too expensive, and, anyway, Piper's maternal grandfather had been part-Jewish – very few people knew that – her father never admitted it–and before her grandfather died he had made everyone in his family swear on the Torah never to buy a German car. Piper hadn't particularly liked her grandfather, but an oath was an oath.

The same thing applied to Audi and BMW. Piper had been shocked when Peter told her that BMW stood for Bavarian Motor Works.

One day, while she was thinking all this over, walking down Bay Street, she saw the former governor-general, a classy lady by all accounts, drive by in a new Toyota Avalon. That's what I should get, thought Piper. That's the kind of car that a successful woman drives, solid and reassuring, but not in-your-face. Your car should tell the world who you want to be, not who you are. She was pleased when she went to the Toyota dealer to discover that there was a hybrid version of the Avalon. Two birds with one stone! A week later a gold-coloured Toyota Avalon Hybrid was parked outside Piper's condo. "Cool!" said Peter when he saw the car, although he would have preferred something sportier, and didn't really think Piper looked good in a boxy sedan. He'd been hoping for a Porsche. But it didn't really matter, because Piper refused to give him a key to her new car. She had already decided that Peter couldn't drive the Avalon, not ever.

• • •

My trouble, thought Piper as she walked to work, is that I just go along with events. I never figure out at the start what I want to do, and then try to do it. I became a lawyer because I couldn't think of anything else, and because I knew it would make my father proud. I went to work at Dibbets because they offered me a job and everyone said I'd be crazy to turn down an offer from a firm like Dibbets. I became a corporate lawyer because the partners at Dibbets told me that's what I should do. Peter is my boyfriend because I met him in the bar on the

corner when I lived in the West End, and he's charming and smart, and is impressed by what I do, and he plays the piano beautifully, and he chased after me and made me feel good, and he thinks I'm beautiful and says he loves me. And I bought an Avalon because the former governor-general has one. My life has been a series of choices presented to me by the world in which I happen to live, which is not the world I would have chosen.

Chapter Three
Operation Banking Freedom

The next morning, just before eight o'clock, Piper went into the main Dibbets boardroom on the thirty-eighth floor of the Canadian Unity Bank building. On one side of the boardroom a wall of windows faced Lake Ontario. It was late May; even this early, there were sailboats on the water. On the opposite wall hung a painting of birches by Tom Thomson. Two dozen high-backed grey leather chairs surrounded a huge oval table of exotic polished wood. A vase of multi-coloured fresh flowers sat in the middle of the table, cleverly cut low so as not to obscure anyone's view of the person opposite.

It was the first meeting of the Liberty Insurance takeover team. When Piper arrived, Jim Watt was sitting alone at the head of the table, hardly moving, waiting for the lawyers he had summoned. In front of him, carefully aligned with his chair, was a slim grey leather folder with his name embossed in gold on the cover. A gold pen, his name engraved on the barrel, sat on top of the folder. Each was a closing gift from a grateful client marking the conclusion of a successful transaction. Leather folders and expensive pens were often gifts on such occasions;

senior lawyers had drawers full of them. More prized were tombstones, miniature copies of newspaper advertisements, embedded in Lucite, giving details of a transaction with its dollar value in a large, bold font. "The Acme Corporation has issued $100,000,000 of Senior Notes. The Issue was underwritten by..." Tombstones were prized because they could be easily displayed. The more tombstones a lawyer displayed in his office, the more important, the more central to the world of law and commerce, he seemed.

"Piper, welcome," said Watt slowly, looking at her intently. He moved the leather folder slightly so it was exactly aligned with his chair. He glanced at his gold watch. Almost eight o'clock.

"Good morning, Jim," said Piper.

"Ready?" asked Watt, fiddling with his gold pen, suddenly squinting at his name on the barrel as if to make certain it was spelt correctly.

"You bet," said Piper enthusiastically.

"The others should be here any minute," said Watt, checking his watch again.

Most of the thirty-eighth floor was taken up by Dibbets boardrooms. The firm's main reception desk was on the same floor, in a large lobby steps from the elevator bank. Expensive Canadian art hung on the lobby's walls. The carpet was thick. The sofas were plush. Copies of the day's newspapers were arranged on a large coffee table, with the London Financial Times and the Wall Street Journal uppermost, the Toronto dailies underneath. Individually wrapped mints sat in a silver bowl on a small antique table. A pretty young woman behind

the reception desk answered the telephone which rang every few seconds.

"Dibbet & Dibbet, how may I direct your call? Just a moment please, I'll put you through..."

Even this early in the morning clients were coming to the reception desk, giving the name of the lawyer they had come to meet, speaking in the assured way of people who were accustomed to paying large legal bills and expected value for money.

"I'm here for a meeting with James Brown. My name is Ron Walker."

"Yes, Mr. Walker. I'll tell him you're here."

The receptionist pushed a button. "Mr. Brown, Mr. Walker is here to see you. Boardroom 38F, I'll have coffee and cookies sent in." The thirty-eighth floor had an elaborate kitchen, with a staff of three, providing snacks in the morning, sandwiches at lunch, hot meals for dinner, and alcohol anytime.

"No cookies," said Mr. Walker, who was worried about his waistline.

Other Dibbets lawyers came into the boardroom. Julia Anderson was the first to arrive after Piper. She was a tall, slim, expensively dressed woman in her late fifties, in three inch heels, her greying hair worn in an Anna Wintour bob, Japanese designer glasses perched on the end of her nose. Julia had been a partner at Dibbets for almost thirty years. She specialized in structured financing. Few Dibbets lawyers knew what structured financing was, exactly, but they all knew it was important. "Julia is the firm expert on structured financing," clients were told, and they seemed pleased to know that Dibbets had all the bases covered.

Once, quite some time ago, Julia Anderson had been married, but she had fallen in love with another Dibbets partner and her marriage had broken up. She and her lover had been indiscreet. The affair was passionate and had lasted two years; neither ever exactly understood why it came to an unhappy end. The man Julia loved, and who loved her, left Dibbets and went to live in Papua New Guinea to teach at a local law college. Later, he moved somewhere even more remote, no one seemed to know exactly where. Julia often thought about this man, and sometimes late at night would Google him hoping to find something out, but not even Google knew where he had gone.

Julia had never done as well at the firm as she should have. Perhaps her well-known affair was the reason, although there was a lot of sleeping around at Dibbets and nobody paid much attention to that sort of thing. Lots of sleeping around, but not much love; perhaps love had been the problem, her affair reminding people of something most of them didn't have; by falling in love, she had broken the rules of extramarital engagement. Now, Julia's relationship status on Facebook was "it's complicated," and she took her expensive foreign holidays alone. She regularly posted smiling pictures of herself on Facebook, and wondered if the man who went to Papua New Guinea, wherever he was now, ever looked at them. She posted them for him.

"Hello Julia, good to have you on board," said Watt, as she sat down at the other end of the big table.

Darrell Jones came in and sat next to Julia. Jones was a small and untidy man, about sixty, with an elongated bald head, thin at the base but expanding into a bulb at

its hairless top. He believed that he was cleverer than any other lawyer at Dibbets, indeed, cleverer than just about anyone. "He's got a brain size problem," Jones would often say, referring to one of his partners, or to someone he had just come across in a legal transaction, or had met at the grocery store, or in the elevator. Jones was not liked, but he was necessary. He was a skilled lawyer who specialized in the government regulation of financial institutions. The Liberty file needed one of those.

Agatha Hightower came into the boardroom and joined the little group sitting down at the end of the table, as far away from Jim Watt as possible. Agatha was a real estate lawyer. Almost every big corporate transaction involved real estate – title to office buildings might have to be transferred, or new mortgages arranged, or leases reviewed. Corporate lawyers like Watt thought that real estate lawyers were inferior, there to do intellectually undemanding fussy work and tidy up loose ends. Agatha, a short woman in her fifties, thin as a rail, habitually dressed in black, wearing flat shoes despite her short stature, accepted her second-class status, although she knew that she was smarter than Watt, smarter than Jones come to that. She made up for humiliation at the office by vigorous shopping at Toronto's most expensive stores. Sometimes her monthly Visa bill topped $30,000. That created problems between her and her husband, Wade Hightower. She paid the Visa bill, it was her money, God knows she suffered for what she was paid, but Wade, a labour lawyer who represented unions, was left wing and disapproved of extravagant spending on principle, except when it came to motorcycles. His Ducati Multistrada Granturismo had cost a lot.

Bill Seldom, a pudgy, pasty-faced securities lawyer in his late forties, came in right behind Agatha. Seldom often declaimed, "Dibbets is my life." Jim Watt said of him, "Seldom? A good number two. Not a leader." Seldom seemed grateful to be even number two, and was never unpleasantly competitive. But Seldom believed, he felt it in his bones, that one day he would be number one, that one day he would be in charge. When that day came, he would sit where Jim Watt now sat, at the head of the table. This belief, this sure knowledge of his destiny, sustained him.

"Hello, Agatha, good to see you, I'm sure you'll have a vital role in this file, we're really lucky to have you on the team," said Seldom unctuously, grinning at Agatha, showing slightly yellowed teeth, one of them, a lower molar near the back, broken and needing a cap.

"Thanks, Bill." Agatha knew that Seldom looked down on her. She tried to think of something else besides the people in this room. She wondered what her husband was up to. He'd been behaving strangely lately. He was distant, very distant. He spent a lot of time out on his motorcycle, much more than he used to, going God knows where. Was the marriage in trouble? Was he seeing someone else? Had she been spending too much on clothes? Her stomach was upset.

Junior lawyers straggled in. These were young associates, three or four years out of law school, desperately hoping to make partner, already preparing the speech for their parents and friends if they failed to do so. "Not a life style for me, God no," they would say if they had to. "No time to spend with family if you're on Bay Street. I'm much better off in a small town practice, people

buying houses, making wills, ordinary people need a good lawyer, access to justice, it's the human touch that counts, contributing to the local community, home by five o'clock, quiet walk down a leafy street with the dog." Hoping never to make that speech, they calculated how much they would earn if only they were admitted to the partnership. Millions. House in Rosedale. Cottage in Muskoka. Golf club. Porsche–a 911, not a crappy Boxster. Foreign holidays at luxury resorts, Maui, Fiji or the Seychelles.

The core CUB/Liberty takeover team was now together. Jim Watt cleared his throat. He moved his leather folder slightly to the right. He fiddled with his gold pen. He looked around the table portentously. He took his glasses off and then put then on again. The others regarded him expectantly, each one mentally estimating with a light heart his or her share of the huge number of billable hours that were about to begin. There was a hush. They waited for Watt to speak.

"This is a big transaction," said Watt. "A very big transaction. Yesterday the Canadian Unity Bank board approved a public takeover bid for Liberty Insurance. CUB has to expand beyond traditional banking to have a secure future in the modern world. And I needn't tell any of you, CUB is Dibbets' biggest client. A secure future for CUB is a secure future for Dibbets, and a secure future for Dibbets is a secure future for you. The lawyers in this room are the basic team for this deal, although I'll be adding folks from tax and intellectual property and others as needed. This is top secret for the moment. Top, top secret. Only refer to the transaction by its code name – Operation Banking Freedom."

"Is Liberty Insurance on board for this, or is it hostile?" asked Bill Seldom in a deferential tone. He had his hand up.

"For the moment, Liberty knows nothing about it. The Bank will be calling Brad Nemitz, Liberty's chief executive officer, this morning. He won't like what he hears. He'll be very upset. He'll come out swinging."

"Who's running the file for CUB?" asked Seldom, his hand still raised.

"Ron Tonks. Most of you know Ron. A great friend of Dibbets. He's put a lot of work our way. Ron is probably talking to Nemitz right now."

"Has someone worked out the regulatory side?" asked Darrell Jones. "A bank can't take over an insurance company just like that. What about the Bank Act?"

Watt was one of the few Dibbet's lawyers who didn't actively dislike Jones. Watt never paid much attention to someone's personality. What he cared about was an individual's ability and whether or not he, Watt, could benefit from it. And Jones, although obnoxious, was clever, and could be useful.

"That's why you're here Darrell," said Watt. "You're going to think it through for us. You're going to figure out the Bank Act."

"Okay, buddy," said Jones, brushing cigarillo ash off his lapel. "That's what I do for a living."

"Can you give us some idea who'll be doing what on the corporate side?" asked Julia. "How will we divide up the work?"

"We'll have to see things unfold," said Watt. "I look to you, Julia, for backup on just about everything. You've been here before. You know what can go wrong, and how

to fix it. And Piper will work closely with me as well, in a junior role of course. She and I have worked together a lot. We understand each other." Piper noticed one or two associates smirking at the end of the table. Were there rumours in the firm about her and Watt?

Piper looked around the room. The other night she'd watched "Ship of Fools" on the classic movie channel. She'd wondered about the title and had looked it up on Wikipedia. "The allegory depicts a vessel populated by human inhabitants who are deranged, frivolous, or oblivious passengers aboard a ship without a pilot, and seemingly ignorant of their own direction."

Piper had a bad feeling about Operation Banking Freedom.

Chapter Four
Ron Tonks

Ron Tonks was a no nonsense banker of the old school. He had worked his way up to Vice-President Special Projects from a teller job at a tiny Canadian Unity Bank branch in Wadena, Saskatchewan, the town where he had been born. He was fifty-five; his face was florid; his hair, slicked back. He had a paunch. He wore cheap suits bought in Chinatown, with a silk handkerchief spilling out of the breast pocket to add a little pizzazz. He walked with an odd flat-footed duck-like gait that some saw as a swagger. He'd never been to university. His stock in trade was cunning. His job was mergers and acquisitions, and sometimes capital restructuring. Capital restructuring meant bailing a corporate customer out of a financial mess it had itself created.

Tonks spent a lot of time with Dibbets lawyers. He preferred the older partners, who understood his importance and showed him appropriate deference. He liked Jim Watt, but was careful with him, because Watt was a CUB director and played a complicated game. He didn't like woman lawyers, and made that clear in lewd ways. He was anti-Semitic, given to offensive jokes about Jews.

He relied on the fact that lawyers working for him, even if offended, even if women, even if Jewish, would say nothing, because he had the power to throw them off a CUB file and ensure they never worked for the bank again, and in the legal world, particularly the world of Dibbets, that was a lot of power. His superiors at the bank didn't care for him, but they used him for a certain sort of dirty job and recognized his value.

"It's going to get nasty," Tonks' boss, a senior vice-president called Bert Hicks, would tell the bank president, Arthur Red. "The bank needs a real son-of-a-bitch on this file. That's Tonks."

"He's the man," Arthur Red, who had watched Tonks for years, would reply with a smile. "He's the man for a dirty job."

Hicks had told Tonks to call Brad Nemitz, the president of Liberty Insurance, at exactly ten that morning. Operation Banking Freedom was to be run with the precision of a military campaign. Bert Hicks was an officer in the army reserve. He enjoyed weekend military manoeuvres in rural Ontario, particularly riding around in a tank. He liked things to happen precisely as scheduled.

Sitting in his spacious office, Tonks dialled Nemitz's number. It was exactly ten o'clock. He leant back in his swivel chair and put his feet up on the desk.

"Mr. Nemitz's office," said a woman.

"May I speak with him?"

"Who's calling?"

"Tonks, Ron Tonks, vice-president, Canadian Unity Bank."

"A moment…"

"Brad Nemitz here," said a pleasant voice.

43

"Brad, it's Ron Tonks, vice-president, Canadian Unity Bank, how are you doing?" Tonks had been looking forward to this conversation. He felt powerful, at the centre of things, a mover and shaker. He'd come a long way since his days as a bank teller in rural Saskatchewan. "You might not remember me, Brad," said Tonks, leaning even further back in his chair, "but we've met two or three times, fundraisers, that sort of thing. Board of Trade golf tournament last year."

"Yes, sure, hi Ron, nice to hear from you." Nemitz was trying to think who Tonks was, and where he might have met him. Board of Trade golf tournament? Not there. Nemitz was one of the few Bay Street chief executives who didn't play golf. He had tried the game, but couldn't get the hang of it.

"Brad, there's something you and I need to discuss. Can we have a meeting today, maybe later this morning, or early afternoon?"

"That's not possible. I might be able to find some time next week. What's it about?" Nemitz was irritated. He didn't normally meet with bank vice-presidents—there were so many of them, hundreds, running all over Bay Street, it might be a big title but it wasn't a big job—and just at the minute he was preoccupied. Liberty Insurance's results hadn't been that good lately. Some of the bigger shareholders were dissatisfied and had let him know it over discreet lunches at the Toronto Club. There'd been a particularly unpleasant lunch yesterday; he'd woken up at three in the morning thinking about it and had only fallen asleep again after tossing and turning for an hour and taking a Sleep-Eze.

"Brad, it won't wait until next week. We have to meet as soon as possible, and this morning would be best. And I'll be bringing my lawyer, Jim Watt of Dibbets. I expect you know Jim. You might want to have your general counsel sit in on the meeting. Let's say eleven thirty, your office."

Brad Nemitz started to pay attention. Tonks seemed very self-assured. And he's bringing Jim Watt. He'd heard of Watt, nothing good. What was it that Grant Rubbers, an old business friend, had said to him at the Toronto Club the other day? "Watch your back, Brad. With results like last quarter's, someone is going to want to stick a knife in it."

"All right," said Nemitz. "It's not convenient, but I'll work it out. Come at eleven thirty. I can give you half an hour, no more. I'll see if I can find my general counsel. If you need a lawyer, I guess I need one too." He hung up.

Nemitz felt nervous. Something was going on. Tonks and Watt weren't coming over to ask for a contribution to the United Way. He rang his assistant. "I want Maura Hanson here at eleven thirty. It doesn't matter what else she's got going on, she'll have to drop it. I need her here." Maura Hanson was Liberty's general counsel. Before coming to Liberty, she had been an associate at Dibbets. Jim Watt had fired her. "I'm afraid you're not a team player," he'd told her.

• • •

Tonks called Watt. "We're on for eleven thirty, Jim. Come to my office a few minutes before, and we'll walk across the street together."

"Okay," said Watt. "I'll bring Piper Fantouche. You know Piper. She's a junior partner now. An excellent lawyer."

"I remember Piper," said Tonks. "Big tits. Bring her along."

Watt went to Piper's office. She was checking Chart-the-Day. Watt had opened a file for the takeover that morning, "Canadian Unity Bank re Special Project." It was listed in the daily new matter memo, an email sent each morning to everybody at the firm announcing new business. Now there was a file number in Chart-the-Day to bill against. Piper hadn't forgotten about the few minutes she had spent yesterday talking to Watt. She was entering the time when Watt came in to her office.

"Piper," said Watt, "we're meeting Nemitz at eleven thirty." He checked his watch. "That's in an hour and five minutes. I'll meet you downstairs in forty-five minutes. Don't say anything in the meeting. Just take notes. I think Liberty's general counsel, Maura Hanson, will be there. Keep an eye on her. I don't trust her. She used to work at Dibbets. It didn't work out. She wasn't a team player. I gave her the bad news. I don't think she likes me. There's bad blood. She might make trouble."

Watt left and Piper went back to Chart-the-Day to enter more time against "Canadian Unity Bank re Special Project." The words "special project" were magical at Dibbets. They meant something big. They meant something secret. Most important of all, they meant money. When it was a special project, the opportunity to rack up billable time, real and imagined, could be almost unlimited. With hundreds of millions of dollars at stake, maybe billions, what was a few million dollars here or

there for legal fees? No one would notice. Not if it was a special project.

• • •

Piper met Watt in the CUB building lobby on schedule at ten minutes past eleven. They crossed Bay Street, dashing through traffic ("careful, Piper, don't trip on those high heels!") to the Canada Bank Building where the Liberty Insurance head office took up the top few floors, except for the very top floor which was occupied by Flotsam, the city's most expensive restaurant. Piper and Watt took the elevator to fifty-three, one floor below Flotsam, and waited in an anteroom to be shown into Brad Nemitz's suite.

"Mr. Nemitz will see you now," said a secretary, and showed them into a large office. Nemitz came around from behind an oak desk and shook their hands. "Thanks for coming over," he said to Tonks with a smile that he hoped was clearly ironic.

"And thank you for seeing me at such short notice," said Tonks.

An attractive woman in her late thirties, with large brown eyes and auburn hair in a pageboy cut, dressed in a suit and blouse of muted colours, was sitting at the conference table by the windows. "Hello Maura!" said Watt jovially. "Good to see you. Always knew you would land on your feet. This is Piper Fantouche, who works with me. Sort of took your place, you could say. Hard shoes to fill, of course. Piper, meet Maura Hanson, Liberty's general counsel."

Nemitz sat down at the head of the conference table and waved his three visitors to chairs facing the window. The late morning sun shone into their eyes and made

them squint. Nemitz had found that sun in the eyes of unfriendly guests gave him a slight advantage. He had anticipated that these guests would be unfriendly. Before they arrived, he had raised the blinds. He was not above doing such a thing.

"Why did you want to see me?" he asked.

Tonks smiled, took a moment to feel important and enjoy the feeling, and began.

"Brad, Arthur Red, president of Canadian Unity Bank, sent me over."

"If Arthur Red has something to say to me," said Nemitz, "it would have been better if he had come himself."

"Arthur looks forward to meeting with you soon enough, but he thought it best if the first meeting was with me. Brad, I don't have to tell you that Liberty shares have not been doing well. The company has lost twenty-five per cent of its market capitalization in the last six months. Canadian Unity Bank owns about five per cent of your common shares. Canadian Unity Bank is not happy about what's happening."

Okay, thought Nemitz, I see what this is about. This is like those Toronto Club lunches I've been having, except there's no lunch. I've got to express concern, beat my breast, rend my clothes, describe big plans for the future, explain how I'm going to restore shareholder value, and then they'll go away and I can get on with my job.

"Ron, of course all of us at Liberty are concerned about the declining share price, but we're taking steps to fix the problem, to restore value, and I'd be happy to tell you in detail what those steps are. I think it would put

your mind at rest. And, more importantly, the mind of Arthur Red."

Tonks noticed the implied insult. He said nothing for a moment or two, and then spoke as gravely as he could manage. "The thing is, Brad, in the bank's mind the situation has gone beyond an easy fix. The bank thinks your board of directors has made a mess of things and should be replaced, some of them at least. And, I'm sorry to say, nothing personal, we believe new management is needed at Liberty as well. Including a new chief executive officer."

There was silence in the room. Nemitz stared at Tonks. He tried to stay calm. He wanted to leap out of his chair and throw Tonks to the ground and kick him in the head. He imagined doing it and the thought gave him pleasure.

"That overreaching a bit, don't you think?" Nemitz said eventually, in an even tone of voice. "Sure, the share price has faltered a bit, but that happens to every company. Sure, there are some things we need to fix and we're going to fix them. Other things, there's nothing that can be done. Markets go up, markets go down, sometimes because of events far away that we can't control and that have nothing to do with us. I seem to remember that CUB shares were doing poorly not so long ago. Whose fault was that? The bank's, or was it because of the financial situation in Europe?"

"That's irrelevant."

"Anyway," said Nemitz, "it's interesting to have your bank's point of view, but none of what you want, board and management replaced, is going to happen. You've got, what, four per cent of the shares? You may not like the way things are, but there's nothing you can do about

it. And I'm a busy man, I've got to worry about all the shareholders, not just Canadian Unity Bank, so I'd ask you to excuse me so I can get back to work running this company." Nemitz stood up. Tonks stayed sitting. Piper was trying to write everything down. Maura was watching her do it.

"It's not quite that simple Brad," said Tonks, lolling back in his chair. "True, CUB only has five per cent. It's five per cent, by the way, not four. But we've been talking to the pension funds, Professors Retirement, for example, which is your biggest shareholder. These funds together with CUB own close to thirty per cent of CUB's common shares. They're not happy with you, Brad. They're not happy at all. They're ready to work with us to change things."

Nemitz's stomach knotted up. This was big trouble. He had to be very careful what he said. He mustn't show emotion. He noticed that the woman with Tonks was writing everything down, scribbling away, and he didn't like it.

Jim Watt spoke. "The bank doesn't want an ugly confrontation with Liberty. That wouldn't help anyone. The lawyers on both sides should get together and see what can be worked out. We'd like smooth change, and I'm sure, Brad, that's what you'd like too. You'd get a pretty generous severance package."

"That's not what I'd like. The kind of change you seem to want, smooth or not smooth, is not what I'd like, and it's not a good idea for Liberty Insurance. And I'm not interested in a severance package. This meeting is over."

Nemitz stood up and walked carefully out of his office through a small side door. After he'd left, Tonks, Watt

and Piper headed for the big double doors on the other side of the room.

"Good to see you Maura," said Watt as he went out. "I expect we'll be seeing a lot of each other in the next little while. I'm glad you're getting along so well over here."

Maura remembered the lunches at Mario's with Watt, and was glad she didn't have to do that anymore.

• • •

"That worked out okay," said Watt in the elevator going down.

"I think so," said Tonks. "What do you think Nemitz will do now?"

"Nothing. What can he do?"

"I'll tell you what he'll do," said Tonks. "He'll call Arthur Red. He'll want to see him right away, and clear up this little misunderstanding."

'You're right," said Watt. "He's probably in the next elevator down, on his way over to Red's office."

"No he's not," said Tonks. "Red won't take his call. Red won't see him. We've talked about it. It's all been worked out. We've planned very carefully. It's time to move on to the next step."

Chapter Five
The Screaming Heebie-Jeebies

After the meeting, the three of them went back to Tonks' office. "Nemitz is a stupid bastard," Tonks crowed, red in the face, walking around his office excitedly, his large shoes flapping like a clown's. "He won't know what hit him. He'll be out on his ass before he realizes what's happened. He's completely out-classed. Did you see how he tried to patronize me, the way he treated me as if I was Arthur Red's errand boy? What an asshole!"

"We must be determined and vigilant on the legal side," Watt said in a measured voice, slightly uncomfortable with Tonks' excitement, anxious to add gravitas to the conversation. "It's fair to say that Canadian Unity Bank's legal team will completely surpass any group of lawyers that Liberty can field." He pulled an ironed and folded white handkerchief out of his pants pocket, cleaned the lenses of his glasses, and then held the spectacles up to the light to inspect his work. Satisfied, he put his glasses back on, carefully refolded the handkerchief and put it back in his pocket.

Piper asked, "Shouldn't we issue a press release about the takeover bid? There's a rule about it somewhere." She felt the need to be professional. They were lawyers, not blowhards and hucksters. The rules mattered. Their job was to make sure that clients obeyed the law.

"Not just now," said Watt. "Not just now."

"Hicks and I are meeting with Arthur Red tomorrow morning," said Tonks, still excited, still walking up and down. "He's going to be very pleased with our progress. Jim, you'd better come with us. Red likes to hear about the legal stuff. 'I'm almost a lawyer,' he says. Red loves the law. He says he should have gone to law school."

It had been Arthur Red who decided that CUB had to get into the insurance business. It was Arthur Red who wanted Liberty Insurance. It was Arthur Red whose reputation was at stake, who would be feted or ignored at the Toronto Club depending on how things worked out. Tonks looked forward to giving Arthur Red good news. He felt ebullient. Things were going well. Very well indeed.

• • •

Piper was in bed with Peter. It was minutes before midnight. They had just made love. Piper was in a dreamy state, but Peter was disgruntled. He had wanted to fuck Piper up the ass, but she wouldn't let him. She was passionate, but not adventurous. Peter felt resentful, although—as he languished between sheets with an exceptionally high thread count—he remembered that in many ways he had it pretty good. But he really did want to fuck her up the ass. Fucking someone up the ass was a commonplace thing, routine on Internet porn sites. It was

happening, right now, all over Toronto, women getting fucked up the ass, men too. It was probably happening right now, he thought, *in this apartment building.*

Soon he was snoring by Piper's side, farting occasionally. Piper lay awake. It wasn't thinking about the day's corporate scheming that kept her from sleeping; that was just business as usual. It wasn't the rebarbative noises coming from Peter; they were routine. It was what had happened after the meeting in Tonks' office that kept her brain going at top speed.

"I'm hungry," Watt had said, as he and Piper left Tonks' office about a quarter to two in the afternoon. "Let's go to Mario's and have a roast beef sandwich."

At Mario's, Watt slid into his favourite corner booth, and patted the banquette seat next to him. "Piper, you sit here." He was uncomfortably close. His leg pressed against hers. "Mario, two gin martinis, very dry" said Watt to the restaurant's proprietor who hovered nearby. Watt had been a good customer of Mario's for years. He got special treatment from the proprietor.

"Jim, I don't think I'll have a martini, thanks all the same," said Piper. "I have to do a lot of work this afternoon. I have to look at the securities law on the Liberty deal before I go home. That press release issue is bothering me. A martini will make me drowsy."

"Don't worry, Piper. It's up to me to decide what you do this afternoon. Don't forget, I'm a senior partner, and you're a junior partner. The senior partner decides. The junior partner obeys. The good news for you is that one day you'll be a senior partner and some junior partner will have to do what you tell him."

Mario brought the martinis. Watt ate the olive in his and took a gulp of gin and vermouth. Piper sipped her drink. Watt put his hand high on her thigh.

She didn't flinch. She showed no emotion. What she wanted to do was throw her drink in Watt's face and scream at him, tell him that he was repulsive. What she wanted to do was create a scene in Mario's that no one who was there would ever forget. What she did do, after three or four seconds, was gently remove his hand.

"Jim," she said quietly, "That's not a good idea."

"You're right, Piper," said Watt, without conviction. "I'm sorry. You're just so attractive, I forget that this is a public place, and that it's lunchtime."

This wasn't the first time Watt had done something like this. When it had happened before, she had tried to ignore the incident and forget the whole thing. After all, all he ever did was put his hand on her thigh for a little while and then take it away. Not such a big deal, she told herself. Many men had put a hand on her thigh. But he'd done it too many times, each time a little more insistent than the time before. She wanted it to stop.

If she created a scene in Mario's now, she supposed her career at Dibbets would be over. Not just at Dibbets: Bay Street disliked troublemakers, particularly if they were female. She would have to become a store front solo practitioner, in Guelph or Newmarket or some other small town, drafting divorce petitions and wills for people who walked in off the street. Although, sometimes it crossed Piper's mind that maybe she wasn't thinking about this problem in quite the right way. If she kicked up a big fuss, perhaps it would be Watt's career that would be ruined, not hers. These days, taking advantage of the weak

was considered a bad thing. In the past, of course, it had been the whole point of power.

The Human Resources Department at Dibbet & Dibbet employed a part-time sexual harassment officer, a single middle-aged Scottish woman called Janet Ground. As a courtesy, she was called Mrs. Ground, the way the unmarried cook in the television programme Upstairs Downstairs was known as Mrs. Bridges. Piper could always tell Mrs. Ground what had happened. If Mrs. Ground believed her, there would be an investigation; the Dibbet & Dibbet Harassment Policy, formally approved by the partnership, required it. Watt, even though he was the managing partner, would have to answer difficult questions. He might be fined and forced to take sensitivity training. The whole thing would get out–these things could never be kept confidential–and Watt's reputation would be damaged. Those who didn't like him would take advantage of the incident. "Competent," they'd say with feigned regret, "but with that weakness of his, can't keep his zipper closed, we shouldn't have him as managing partner. It just doesn't look good. And, by the way, it might be an idea to have someone else from Dibbets on the CUB board."

Peter farted again. Piper looked at him. His mouth was hanging open. His face was damp with sexual sweat. He hadn't shaved in two or three days. His potbelly seemed to have grown larger. What was he doing in her bed? With images of Jim Watt, Ron Tonks and Mrs. Ground in her head, and Peter snoring and farting by her side, Piper drifted into a troubled sleep.

• • •

Across town, in his large mock-Tudor Forest Hill house, Brad Nemitz was also having trouble getting to sleep. He rolled over in bed for what seemed like the hundredth time and thumped the pillow, hoping it would help. It had helped him get to sleep when he was a child.

The bedside clock said one thirty. Every weekday morning Nemitz got up at five o'clock so that he could spend an hour at the gym before going to the office. He'd be lucky if he got three hours sleep tonight, and to do that he'd have to fall asleep almost immediately. He'd be dog-tired at tomorrow's meeting, but would have to be at his best. He was going to talk to his senior and trusted executives about the possible take-over bid. The meeting would start early and might take all day. The bid, if it came, would be made by people who couldn't care less about Liberty Insurance. They'd rip the company apart to maximize "shareholder value," an odious expression. His stomach churned. Acid bubbled into his oesophagus. Why couldn't he be left alone to run his company? He'd done a good job so far. All the analysts said so. Perhaps he should take some Zantac.

Nemitz looked at Joanna, his wife, sleeping soundly in their king-sized bed. Joanna was still attractive in a well-bred sort of way. They still liked each other. They still enjoyed sex. They had three children. The eldest, John, was a Rhodes Scholar studying politics at Oxford University. Beatrice, the middle child, known as Middle Beatrice, wanted to be a writer, and was house sitting in Nova Scotia while she worked on a novel. Nemitz would have liked it better if she had gone to business or law school. "I'd prefer her unhappy in law school than happy in Nova Scotia," he'd tell friends, only half-joking.

Nathan, seventeen, loved the digital universe and wanted to study engineering at university when he left high school. Things were good at home. At the office, all of a sudden, it was a different story.

Nemitz decided he needed that Zantac. He got out of bed and walked softly on the thick Persian carpet across the large bedroom to the bathroom. He swallowed two pink pills. He went back into the bedroom, and stood in front of the picture window looking out at the pitch-black back garden. It was large garden for the city, half-an-acre, and, at this time of the year, the end of June, during the day, particularly in the early evening, it was beautiful, with a dazzling herbaceous border. Joanna loved the garden and worked hard in it, wearing a large straw hat with a ribbon, snipping away with secateurs.

Gazing into the darkness, Nemitz thought about Ron Tonks and Jim Watt. What awful people they were, the worst kind of Bay Street bullies, with no principles, caring only about themselves and money. Watt was even worse than Tonks. Tonks was an uneducated clown, hard to take seriously, but Watt was clever and dangerous. Tonks was pathetic, but Watt was evil. Nemitz became angry, standing in front of the window looking out into his backyard, there in the night and the darkness, in his pyjamas, overcome by what his mother used to call, when he was a child, the "three A.M. screaming heebie-jeebies." It's alright, Brad, calm down, his mother would say when he was very young, just a little boy, things always look worst in the middle of the night, go back to sleep, it'll be much better in the morning, I'll get you a glass of warm milk.

Nemitz looked out of the window into the blackness, and silently raged. He doubted that things would be much better in the morning. He wanted a glass of warm milk.

Chapter Six
Arthur Red

It was seven thirty in the morning on Day Two of Operation Banking Freedom. The takeover team sat around the huge table in the Dibbets main boardroom. It was the team's first daily briefing. Jim Watt, Piper Fantouche, Julia Anderson, Darrell Jones, Agatha Hightower and Bill Seldom were there. Ron Tonks and Bert Hicks were off to one side, chatting by themselves. Everyone was drinking Kick Ass coffee and eating fresh muffins, so fresh they crumbled in your hands when you picked them up. The continental breakfast was provided by the Dibbets catering department, on duty even at that early hour.

Watt spoke, in a clipped and authoritative tone. "There's a meeting this morning with Arthur Red. I'll brief you about it tomorrow morning. Meanwhile, there's a lot of work to do."

Heads nodded. Coffee cups clinked. "These are very good muffins," said Bill Seldom, brushing crumbs from his jacket, "and the coffee is wonderful, just what you need at this time in the morning."

• • •

Across Bay Street, in the Liberty Insurance executive offices, one floor below Flotsam, Brad Nemitz sat at his office conference table with Maura Hanson and Charles Kennedy, his executive vice-president. The three sipped Starbucks lattes that Nemitz had picked up after his workout at the gym. He'd hardly slept the night before. They were waiting for Ben Peck, senior partner of Smith and Peck, the law firm Liberty had used for years. Peck was one of the most highly regarded and experienced business lawyers in the country. Nemitz had called him after yesterday's meeting with Tonks.

"Could be a bit of trouble," Peck had said in his calm and reassuring way. "But it's nothing we can't deal with. I've seen this before, Brad. My legal advice for you today is go home early, have a stiff drink, spend a pleasant evening with Joanna, try and forget about Canadian Unity Bank, and sleep tight. I'll see you in the morning, first thing." Nemitz and Peck were old friends. The only part of Peck's advice that Nemitz had been able to follow was the bit about a stiff drink.

Peck walked into Nemitz's office. He was a large man, tall and heavy, known in the legal world as Big Ben. Peck never carried a briefcase, unusual on Bay Street where lawyers normally dragged around so many large bags that the uninformed thought they must be heading to the airport for a European vacation. "What I have to offer is in my head," Big Ben liked to say. "If you need anything else, somebody else can bring it." Some thought this arrogant, but Ben Peck was not an arrogant man. He was near the end of his career. He had made his share of

mistakes and knew what they were. He neither overestimated nor underestimated his place in the world.

"Well, well, this is a bit of fun," said Big Ben, squeezing his large body into a conference table chair, wheezing slightly as he did so.

"Ben, you know I love you dearly," said Nemitz, "and you're usually right about everything, but I wouldn't call this a bit of fun. We could be fighting for our life here."

"Maybe fun is not quite the right word," said Peck. "But let's not get too worked up. I've been thinking. Suppose Canadian Unity Bank does plan a takeover bid of Liberty Insurance. For starters, it's going to have to offer a hefty premium to have any chance at all. That could be a big problem for them. They've had their own difficulties lately. They're not as solid financially as they would like."

"But our shares have been trading way down, at much less than real value," said Nemitz. "It'll be easy for CUB to offer a big premium."

"Brad, everyone expects your shares will soon be back to where they were before. A takeover premium will have to be on the old price, let's call it the real price, and that will look pretty rich to the market. Arthur Red will have to be extremely careful, or he'll have his own shareholders baying for blood, his blood. He could be the victim, not you, if he's not careful."

"What should we do?" asked Charles Kennedy.

"Not panic, that's the first thing," said Peck. "We should think about possible defences to a bid. Is there a white knight out there, someone else who could take control of Liberty and that you prefer to CUB? Can you do something quickly to enhance shareholder value, so

shareholders become more confident and don't tender into a bid? You should get your board involved as soon as possible. And hire an investment banker, and a public relations firm."

• • •

On the other side of the street, in the big Dibbets boardroom, Watt was giving instructions to the team. "We need to divide up the work," he said. "Julia and Bill, start drafting the takeover bid circular. Bill, get an associate to prepare notifications for the stock exchanges and securities commissions. Piper, take a look at whether the bank has to file a material change report, and at that press release issue you mentioned yesterday. Darrell, any problems with competition law? I'm sure you're way ahead of us on that, Darrell. Agatha, start figuring out what real estate Liberty owns, and what we need to do about it."

"Time to go and see Arthur Red," said Bert Hicks, looking at his watch. It was a few minutes before nine. The meeting broke up. Hicks, Tonks and Watt took the elevator down to the lobby and changed elevator banks to go to Arthur Red's office on the twelfth floor. They rode up to the bank's executive offices in silence. They were nervous. The president of a Canadian bank was one of the most powerful people in the land, more powerful than the prime minister. The elevator stopped and the doors slid open. They stepped directly into a large, wood-panelled anteroom. The loudest noise in the room was the ticking of a grandfather clock. Thick carpets muffled even that sound. A burly man in a black business suit and with a discreet earpiece stood near the elevators and looked them over carefully. In the distance, a secretary sat at a large desk tapping on a keyboard in a methodical

PHILIP SLAYTON

way. The man in the black suit said nothing, but, apparently satisfied with their appearance and demeanour, waved them towards the secretary. They approached; it seemed to take a long time to get to her desk.

"Hello, Miss Dickson," said Hicks. Miss Dickson had been the CUB president's secretary for a long time. She had worked for many presidents. She knew more about the Canadian Unity Bank than anyone. She wore her grey hair in a chignon. She had a soothing exterior. She was ruthlessly efficient, and never forgot a face.

"Mr. Hicks, so nice to see you. Ah, and I see Mr. Tonks and Mr. Watt are keeping you company today. Mr. Red is expecting you all, but he's speaking to Hong Kong at the moment so if you wouldn't mind waiting. He won't be long." The bank's biggest shareholder, Lee Wong, lived in Hong Kong. He kept CUB on a short leash. He spoke to Arthur Red on the telephone two or three times a week, and often visited Toronto in his Gulfstream V jet.

The three sat silently side-by- side on a large leather sofa in the anteroom, waiting to be summoned by the president of the bank. The leather was slippery, and each man, as he leant back, found that his buttocks slowly slid forward, so that periodically he had to jerk upright, only to begin sliding forward again. Five minutes of sliding and jerking passed while Miss Dickson continued to type methodically without looking at them. Then her telephone rang.

"Yes sir, I'll show them in." She stood up and signalled Hicks, Tonks and Watt. "Mr. Red will see you now. Please follow me."

She knocked on a baronial door, opened it, and, followed respectfully by the three men, went into what was

probably the largest office in Toronto. "Mr. Red," she said, "you know these gentlemen. You have been expecting them, I believe." She withdrew and shut the door behind her.

"That Chinese cock-sucker!" said Red. He was a short, red-faced man with wire-rimmed glasses. His suit jacket was off, but he wore a vest. He paced angrily in front of his gigantic desk. He slammed his fist into the palm of his hand. "That little fucker Lee Wong! He rings me up from fucking Hong Kong and tells me, in that phony polite way of his, Mr. Red, we are worried about our investment in the bank, can you assure me steps are being taken to improve the situation? The slitty-eyed shit, he and his cronies own less than ten per cent of the bank and they behave as if it all belongs to them."

Red, still pacing angrily on his small well-shod feet, pointed a finger at Hicks who was standing with Tonks and Watt in the middle of the thick Aubusson carpet. "We've got to get Liberty Insurance. Our numbers must be better, our future has got to look brighter, more exciting. *We must look dynamic!* That's the only way I can get Lee Wong, the little Chinese fucker, off my back."

"Well, Arthur," Hicks began, "we've got good news on the Liberty front."

"Good news, that's want I want." Looking calmer, Red sat down behind his desk, and started stabbing at a yellow legal pad with a freshly-sharpened pencil.

"I met with Brad Nemitz yesterday," said Tonks, "the president of Liberty. He wasn't happy, but then we didn't think he would be. I don't think there's much fight in those guys."

"The legal team is moving fast," said Watt. "We're beginning to draft the bid circular. We're studying the regulatory issues."

"Good, good, keep things moving. What do you need from me?" asked Red, now doodling on the yellow pad. "Why don't you guys sit down? You're making me nervous, standing there like that."

"Three things," said Watt, sitting on the edge of a chair. "First, you must tell us how much you're prepared to offer for a Liberty share. How big is the premium? Second, are we going out in the market to buy shares before the formal takeover bid begins? Third, do we want a lockup agreement with Professors Retirement and some of the other big Liberty shareholders?"

Red said: "The bank board makes those decisions. But, needless to say, the board will follow my lead." Watt raised his eyebrows. He was a director of the bank. He liked to think that the board counted for something.

"Let's start with the premium," Red said. "It's got to be whatever it takes for the bid to be successful. Liberty is trading today at about twenty-five dollars. We should offer thirty-five." He drew a large "$35" on his pad, and held it up for everyone to see, as if he were a Sotheby's auctioneer displaying a valuable painting to an audience of potential buyers.

"We own five per cent already, we're going for fifty-one," said Tonks, who had also sat down. "There's eighty million outstanding shares, so we need about thirty-six million more than we've got today as a minimum. At thirty-five, that'll cost about a billion two. Depending on how many tender into the bid, whether we do a going-private later, the tab could easily be two billion."

"The money's not your problem," said Red. "I'll get the money. As for the other stuff, sure, let's go out in the market now, before the bid, and buy up what we can at twenty five, save a buck or two, and, sure, lock-up agreements with PR and the other pension funds and anybody else we can get on board. Why not?"

"You know, Arthur," said Tonks, "it could be over almost before it's begun."

Arthur Red was cheerful by now. He had forgotten about Lee Wong. Liberty Insurance was within his grasp. It would be the first major acquisition of his long banking career. The Globe and Mail would interview him, and Canadian Business Magazine might do a feature. Perhaps The Wall Street Journal would come calling. He'd be met by smiles and discreet congratulations when he lunched at the Toronto Club. He might even, at last, get the Order of Canada. If Conrad Black could get it, why not him? He'd like to get to know Conrad Black, he was quite a guy. People said he was a convicted felon, but that was just in the United States, which didn't count.

"Gentlemen, keep me informed of developments minute-by-minute." He spoke as if there were hundreds of people in the room. "Now, off you go. I have the business of the Bank to attend to."

Hicks, Tonks and Watt stood up. They started to leave. They began by backing away. Eventually, they turned around and, one by one left Arthur Red's office and went through into the anteroom

"Goodbye, Miss Dickson," said Hicks, as the three headed for the elevator.

"Goodbye, gentlemen," said Miss Dickson, without looking up from her keyboard.

• • •

Nemitz had his feet on his desk and the telephone on speaker. He was talking to the Liberty board's three-person executive committee. Marcia Simpson, chair of the committee, was a professional corporate director, smart and tough, chic and eccentric, arrogant and funny, seventy years old at least, a lawyer who had never practised but who knew more law than most, a woman who had never married but who was attractive to men despite her age. Simon Hall had once been a high government official and had then become an influential business advisor; he was well connected in many different worlds, insightful and excitable, fun to be with, spent money he didn't have, slept with women not his wife, and relied on others to get him out of the occasional bit of personal trouble brought on by his financial and sexual extravagance. David Rogers was an accountant, partner in one of the largest accounting firms, an expert in corporate finance, a man with a dry wit and bad teeth.

"This is a bit of a bombshell," said Hall happily. He bored easily, and liked trouble. "We'll fight it, of course." He felt good.

"We need to see the bid, if there is one, before deciding anything," said Rogers. "If it's rich, good for the shareholders, then maybe we should go along."

"That's right," said Ben Peck, who was on the call. "You all have a duty to maximize stakeholder value. Don't forget that. Let's wait and see what comes."

"We'll wait," said Marcia Simpson. "We'll wait and see."

• • •

Piper was in her office. She looked at her watch. It was almost seven o'clock. She was already late for her law school alumni reception and dinner at the Royal York Hotel down the street. She particularly wanted to be there. It would be good to get out of the office, away from Watt, away from Operation Banking Freedom. Piper turned off Chart-the-Day, grabbed her handbag and left the office.

Chapter Seven
The Alumni Dinner

Piper had graduated from the law faculty of the University of Southern Ontario. The university – known to everyone as USO–was in a small city two hundred miles from Toronto surrounded by monotonous farmland. It had a reputation as a party school, a place where rich kids from the big city went to have a good time. University officials considered the law faculty to be the jewel in USO's shining crown, but some others thought the crown was dented and tarnished, the jewel dull and occluded.

The law professors of USO were, for the most part, a lazy lot. The few vigorous ones were more interested in making money outside the faculty by consulting or labour arbitration than in pursuing scholarship and teaching within. And although the professors taught students who intended to practise law, in what was, after all, a trade school, all but one or two had never practised law themselves and therefore knew nothing about the trade in question. And so, with some reason, many of the students had little respect for those who taught them.

Tonight was the annual reception and dinner for the law faculty's Toronto alumni. The event was down the street from Canadian Unity Bank head office, in a ballroom at the Royal York Hotel, once the tallest building and the grandest hotel in the British Empire, now a place for evening gatherings of graduates and luncheon meetings of service clubs. In the ballroom, USO faculty members were busy ingratiating themselves with former students. Fellow alumni were sizing each other up, trying to pierce bonhomie and bluster and discover who was doing well and who wasn't. Two hundred lawyers milled about in the open space near the bar at the back, drinks in one hand, toothpicks that had been used to eat shrimp concealed in the other. Tables for ten, set for dinner, were waiting at the front of the room, each with a miniature University of Southern Ontario flag as centerpiece and a copy of the law faculty's latest newsletter at each place.

Piper had gone to USO's law faculty because her undergraduate marks were not quite good enough to get into one of the two Toronto law schools, and USO seemed the lesser of the out-of-town evils. She had enjoyed her time there. She liked studying law, although she felt no sense of vocation. She'd got good marks, good enough that she was recruited by Dibbets well before she graduated. The atmosphere in the faculty was relaxed. No one took anything very seriously, including the professors. She had a couple of love affairs that didn't end too badly. It was the memory of those love affairs that had brought her to the Royal York this evening, the first alumni event she had attended since graduating eight years ago. Perhaps one or two of her old boyfriends would show up. It would be interesting to see them. She was romantically restless.

An older man came up to her as soon as she arrived in the ballroom. "Piper Fantouche? So glad you could come," said Bill Argyle, shaking her hand. Argyle was the long-time dean of the USO law school. When he was a young man, he'd intended to be a serious scholar, but by accident he had ended up as a mid-level university administrator. He couldn't recall the exact nature of the accident. Maybe he just hadn't been good enough at scholarship or teaching. The universities were full of people who weren't good at scholarship or teaching and settled instead for committee work or idleness.

Argyle sometimes said that being dean of a faculty was like being manager of a Walmart, except that in his Walmart the clerks did whatever they liked, invoking academic freedom and, enjoying tenure, couldn't be fired no matter how they behaved. Occasionally late at night, in his study at home near the campus, a second large scotch in his hand, Bill Argyle mused that power without responsibility was bad, but responsibility without power was worse. Responsibility without power was servitude that leads to humiliation.

Argyle had spent much of the last two days studying student pictures in old law school yearbooks, refreshing his memory, and was now doing his best to match the faces of years ago to a later reality. In Piper's case, it was easy. She looked much the same as she had eight years before. She looked good. She looked the way Susan Sarandon had once looked. "It's good to see you again," said the dean, still shaking her hand. Susan Sarandon was his favourite actress.

"Dean Argyle, it's good to see you," said Piper. She had always liked Bill Argyle. "A great turnout," she said, looking around the ballroom.

"Yes, it's nice to see such enthusiasm. I hear you're doing very well at Dibbets. I have my ear to the ground, you know."

"Thank you, Dean."

"I think that's Fred West over there," said Argyle, looking over Piper's shoulder and recalling another year-book photograph. "He would have been at USO around your time. I must go and say hello." The dean went off towards a man he hoped was Fred West. Fred had been one of Piper's law school lovers. She looked at him across the room. Still slim, nice suit, boyish face, long brown hair. She caught his eye. He saw her and smiled. Dean Argyle went up to him and started shaking his hand. "Fred West? So glad you could come. I hear you're doing very well."

There was the sound of someone tapping on a live mike. John McTavish, the associate dean, portly and bearded, had moved to the head table microphone. He cleared his throat, and spoke slowly and solemnly, as if he were reporting a horrible disaster on the radio news. "Ladies and gentlemen, please take your seats. Dinner will be served soon."

There was no seating plan. People moved quickly to secure the best table, and then, table secured, the best seatmate possible–not the older man they didn't know, who would bore with tales of courtroom triumphs, but the young person of the opposite sex who might hang on their every word and be free for a drink afterwards.

73

Piper found a seat at a well-placed table. There was an empty chair on one side of her.

"May I sit beside you?" said a familiar voice. It was Fred West.

"Of course."

"I managed to pry myself loose from the dean. Not an easy thing to do." Fred sat down.

Sitting on the other side of Piper was an older man with close-cropped grey hair and a trim full beard. He wore a black t-shirt, black corduroy trousers, blue linen sports jacket and red Blundstone boots.

"I'm Sam Capponi, one of those solo criminal defence lawyers you're always reading about," he said, leaning towards Piper. "You're Bay Street, right?" She knew his name from the newspapers. Capponi was left leaning and rode a motorcycle, but had mysteriously become part of the establishment. He was a bencher of the law society, and had recently been awarded the Order of Canada.

"Yes, I'm with Dibbets. Nothing wrong with Bay Street, I hope. What gave it away?"

"Nothing wrong with Bay Street at all. We're in the same game, you and I. I just represent a better class of person than you do. What gave it away? Your style. Bay Street style. What's your name?"

"Piper Fantouche."

"A strange name."

"I didn't choose it." She began to blush, and hated herself for it. Bay Street lawyers were not supposed to blush.

Waiters were pouring wine and bringing appetizers. She turned from Capponi to Fred. "I haven't seen you for a long time."

"True enough."

"Life is good?"

"Not particularly. I don't much like practising law. I'm recently divorced and a bit lonely. But there are some good times. I muddle along."

Capponi spoke insistently at her other elbow. "So, you with the strange name, what kind of law do you practise in that Bay Street firm of yours?"

The table service was speeding up. Waiters whipped appetizers away, finished or not, and put plates of meat and two vegetables in their place. Dean Argyle went to the microphone. "Welcome University of Southern Ontario law graduates. As I look out into the room, I think to myself, what an accomplished group, and how proud the law faculty is of all of you. The USO law school may not be as glamorous as its big-city sisters, but it's the little law school that can."

"This is bullshit," said Capponi. "The USO law faculty has always been a junky sort of place." He turned to Piper and put his face close to hers. "You didn't answer my question. What do you do at Dibbets? Tax? Securities?"

The dean continued. "We may be a law faculty in a small town, but we are not a small town law faculty. As I look out into this room, I see some of Toronto's best and brightest lawyers. You are the people who lead the profession in this city. And you are all graduates of the law faculty of the University of Southern Ontario!"

"Does he think we believe this crap?" said Capponi.

"You won't be surprised to learn that your faculty needs your support. Part of what we need is money. We need money for the new library we hope to build, and for scholarships and other worthy projects. We offer naming

opportunities. But it's not just money we need. We need your advice and guidance as well."

Piper's mind drifted away. Fred seemed to be paying attention to the dean's speech. Capponi was looking around the room, demonstratively not paying attention to what was being said.

"Hey Piper," Capponi said. "Isn't that guy standing back there by the door what's-his-name who runs your firm?"

Piper looked around. Jim Watt was at the back of the room. He seemed agitated, standing on his toes, anxiously looking about. He spotted her and beckoned urgently.

"I smell trouble, " said Capponi. "You better hustle over there. Your boss wants you."

Dean Argyle was still talking. Trying to be discreet, Piper slid sideways out of her chair. Hunched over, attempting to be unobtrusive, she made her way to the side of the ballroom and then along the wall to the back until she reached Watt.

"Jim, I'm surprised to see you here."

"Piper, there's a problem." Watt was obviously disturbed. He was red in the face, and twitching more than usual. "Liberty shares have shot up. About an hour before the Exchange closed, there was suddenly huge trading volume, and the shares went up *almost twenty per cent*. Someone who knows what's going on – *an insider!*–is buying." His right arm was jerking up and down. "The trading will have triggered a computer alert at the Exchange. They'll be suspicious. First thing in the morning, someone from market surveillance will call Liberty Insurance and ask what's going on. There may be a trading halt. This is a big mess."

"Who's the insider? Who would do that?"

"I don't know," said Watt, "but I'm going to find out." He grabbed his right arm with his left hand to stop it jerking. Ah, thought Piper, it's Dr. Strangelove. "I just hope it's someone at Liberty and not at Dibbets," Watt continued. "Come back to the office and help me deal with this."

"Give me a minute to say a couple of goodbyes."

She went back to her table. Dean Argyle had finished his speech, and now was introducing the president of the law alumni association.

"Let me present Jean-Marc Caron, a distinguished member of the bar and a big booster of the law school," said the dean, sitting down as Caron stood up.

"Thank you so much, thank you so much Dean Argyle, what a pleasure, what a pleasure…" said Caron, peering over the podium. He was a short, stout man.

"I have to go," Piper whispered to Fred, "a problem's come up and I have to get back to the office."

"Can I call you sometime?" asked Fred.

"Yes."

"So, Bay Street lawyer, what's happening?" asked Capponi. "Fat cat client being hauled off for income tax evasion? Need the help of a good criminal lawyer?"

"Goodbye Sam."

Piper joined Watt at the back, and they left the ballroom. "Mario's?" asked Watt. "We could discuss strategy over a martini. A martini would help settle my nerves."

"Let's go to a conference room back at the office," said Piper. "That would be better."

Chapter Eight
Steiner

Piper and Jim Watt went to a small Dibbets conference room. Watt sat disconsolate, his elbows on the boardroom table, his head bowed, his hands pressed together in front of him, as if he were praying. Piper sat across the table, wondering what to say, wishing she were back in the Royal York ballroom talking to Fred West.

The situation was serious, Watt said in a monotone. If there had been insider trading, and it became public knowledge, the Canadian Unity Bank/Liberty deal would be dead. If the deal died, careers would be ruined, perhaps his career, although, needless to say, he said, suddenly becoming animated, he had done nothing wrong, absolutely nothing wrong. Enveloped in gloom, once more he suggested adjourning to Mario's for martinis.

"Why don't we both go home and get some rest instead?" Piper said. "Tomorrow will be a difficult day."

"Yes, it will. You're right. You know, Piper, it makes me feel better just talking to you. You're so sensible. Things will work out okay. We'll get through this. Together."

I don't think so, thought Piper. Not together.

• • •

Peter was waiting for her when she got home just before ten o'clock.

"How was the alumni dinner?"

"Forget the dinner. Have you heard of Liberty Insurance?"

"What?"

"Have you ever heard of Liberty Insurance?"

"What is it?"

"What do you mean, what is it? It's an insurance company."

"Never heard of it."

Piper believed him. She was relieved by his ignorance: she had let nothing slip; there'd been no indiscrete pillow talk, at least not about takeover bids. Although, the idea of Peter as a tippee trader was faintly ludicrous. He would have no idea what to do.

"Why are you asking me about this Liberty Insurance?"

"Never mind, Peter, it doesn't matter. I'm really tired. I'm going to bed."

"I'm coming. But I want to ask you something first."

"What?"

"You're always saying you want to go to Paris, you've never been there, your friend Susan has, everybody in the world has, it's supposed to be a wonderful place. And I'd like to go too. So, I had this idea. I was just sitting around thinking about it. Why don't we go to Paris? You and me?"

"Sure, why not. When would you like to leave? Tonight?" Sometimes it was impossible to take Peter seriously. He was a dreamer. His dreams were irritating when she was exhausted.

Peter ignored the sarcasm. "I walked past a Flight Centre this afternoon. They've got cheap flights early next week."

"Next week? That's ridiculous. Look, you're sweet, but I'm just beginning something new at work. There's no way I can leave just like that. That's not the kind of job I've got. You know that. Maybe sometime later this year. We'll talk later. Now I'm going to bed."

She glanced at Peter. He looked sad, almost on the point of tears. She felt tender towards him. Could she manage Paris next week? Of course not. It was tempting, but she was a lawyer, and she was working on a special project.

• • •

When Piper got in next morning at seven thirty, she went to see Jim Watt. There were angry voices on the other side of his closed door. She didn't knock. She went to her office, turned on Chart-the-Day and started entering billable hours from yesterday. There was pleasure in that. She'd try to see Watt later.

Watt had arrived at seven. Mark Steiner, chairman of Dibbets' executive committee, was waiting for him, sitting in Watt's client chair, pretending to read the morning newspaper. Steiner was head of the firm's tax department. He was known for his integrity, a quality everyone said they admired, although there were members of the tax department who complained that sometimes Steiner's integrity got in the way of creative tax planning and Dibbets' profits. The problem was, they said, he had *too much integrity*. Steiner thought Watt was sleazy and had tried to stop his appointment as managing partner,

but Watt, who considered Steiner a legal prude, had out-manoeuvred him. The two men despised each other.

"I had a call in the middle of the night about the Liberty deal," said Steiner as soon as Watt walked in. "From Ben Peck. Peck is not the kind of lawyer who makes calls in the middle of the night. He asked me if I knew anything about insider trading in Liberty shares. He said the shares had shot up, and there were rumours on the street about a takeover bid and that people at Dibbets were involved. I hope you're going to tell me that Peck doesn't know what he's talking about."

"There was some unusual trading in Liberty shares yesterday afternoon, Mark, it's true. High volume, the price jumped a lot. We're going to try and get to the bottom of it today. I'm sure that no one in the firm is involved."

"Who knows about the takeover bid?"

"Inside Dibbets? Maybe ten lawyers – including you– and a few paralegals and secretaries. Outside the firm, there are CUB executives, Arthur Red on down. There are people at Liberty, Liberty's lawyers. Including Ben Peck, by the way. Maybe fifty all together. I'm just guessing."

"Do you know what will happen if someone at Dibbets is insider trading and it comes out? The firm could be ruined. Some asshole could destroy this place *overnight*!"

Steiner had been slowly approaching Watt as he spoke, and by now the two men were toe-to-toe. Steiner, in late middle-age, the first Jew ever hired by Dibbets, hired some thirty years ago because of his extraordinary tax law acumen, a Jew who went to synagogue regularly, normally a peaceable person, wasn't peaceable now. Watt

backed away. "If it's someone on your takeover team," said Steiner, advancing some more, "I'm holding you responsible. You'll be finished."

"Don't talk to me like that," said Watt. "I'm the managing partner," he added. Steiner moved towards Watt again, and bumped up against him. "If you touch me," said Watt, suddenly frightened, "I'll call the police. I'll charge you with assault."

"Fuck you!" said Steiner. It was unusual for him to talk that way. Normally, he was a polite and gentle man.

• • •

It was nine o'clock. Piper wondered if it was safe to go and see Watt. She looked at Chart-the-Day again. Her billable hours were accumulating. Her position in the firm was becoming more secure. The telephone rang. It was Fred West.

"Did you hear what happened at the alumni dinner after you left?"

"No. What?"

"Caron, the alumni president, you remember him, the short fat guy, was droning on and on. I think you left just after he got going. He was incredibly boring, 'the faculty has a great future, fine graduates, outstanding professors,' all that stuff. Then this guy sitting at one of the tables near the front pulled something out of a tote bag and ran up to Caron and planted a cream pie right in his face."

"Jesus!"

"There was pandemonium! People leapt to their feet, shouting. A couple of guys grabbed the pie-thrower. Caron fell down moaning, covered with whipped cream.

Dean Argyle was yelling, 'call the police, someone call the police.'"

"Who was the guy who threw the pie?"

"Julius Pilzon. Remember him? He was a first-year student when we were in third year. He became an immigration lawyer and got mixed up in some racket. There was a police investigation but he was never charged with anything. It got into the newspapers and he became persona non grata at USO. He was always offering to give guest lectures on immigration law, but the law faculty made it pretty clear he wasn't welcome. I guess he got really pissed off, brooded about it, went nuts."

"I remember Pilzon. A fat guy with a moustache."

"That's him. Anyway, no one called the police. Hotel security booted Pilzon out. As they carted him off, he was yelling 'you're all a bunch of jerks.' Caron stopped moaning, wiped off the whipped cream, and picked up where he left off, 'distinguished graduates and professors,' I couldn't believe it."

"I'm sorry I missed it. And I'm glad you called."

"Why did you rush off last night? What's going on?"

"Just one of those office things. I can't talk about it."

• • •

Piper went into Watt's office. He showed the effects of a restless night and the early-morning argument with Steiner. His colour was bad. His patternless blue silk tie was awry. When he saw Piper, he made a visible effort to pull himself together, exhaling loudly and sitting up straight.

"Piper, good to see you. We have a lot on our plate. I need your help. Shut the door."

"Jim, what's happening?"

"Nothing new. I spent most of the night thinking. We don't know that anything illegal has happened, of course, but it might have. I thought first, maybe I should have a meeting of the takeover team, and invite the perpetrator – if he's one of us–to come forward."

"I don't think that'll work. Whoever did it isn't going to just step up and confess because you ask him to. And you'll offend a lot of honest people who will think you suspect them and won't like it."

Watt went over to the window and looked out at the city, his hands clasped behind his back. "Then, as I tossed and turned last night, I decided, as you say, that wouldn't work. No one will confess just because I ask them to and I'd offend a lot of people. So I decided, at about four in the morning, just couldn't sleep, unusual for me, Amanda was quite worried, that the best thing was to lie low and watch everyone very carefully. Wait in the weeds, so to speak. Watchful waiting. So that's what I'm going to do."

"I don't understand. Lie low and watch for what?"

"Suspicious behaviour. Someone acting furtively."

"Well, I suppose that's a sensible, cautious approach."

• • •

Across the street, in the executive offices of Liberty Insurance, Maura Hanson's telephone rang. She had been waiting for this call. Brad Nemitz had been waiting for it. Ever since Liberty's shares had shot up yesterday afternoon, they knew this call would be coming.

"Maura?" said a confident voice. "Do you mind if I call you Maura? It's Jim Baker of Market Surveillance at the Exchange. Do you have a minute?"

"Hi Jim. Your call's not a surprise. And please, call me Maura."

"I'm not surprised you're not surprised. Your shares had a pretty dramatic jump yesterday. Any idea why? Has there been a material change? Are you issuing a press release? What's going on?"

"Nothing definitive has happened. There's been no material change. But there are rumours of a possible takeover bid."

"Rumours? Is that all?"

"Not quite. There was a meeting yesterday. The potential bidder came to see us. At this point, it's all talk. We are not in agreement with what has been proposed."

"Who's the bidder?"

"I don't think I can tell you that, not without talking to outside counsel."

"Perhaps you had better talk to outside counsel and call me back. Has the Liberty board met?"

"There was a telephone meeting of the executive committee yesterday. I can't tell you anything more at this point."

"Okay, Maura, we'll see what happens this morning. If there's more unusual activity, we may have to suspend trading in the shares. That wouldn't surprise you either."

"I understand, Jim. Thanks for the call."

It occurred to Maura as she hung up that a suspension in trading might not be such a bad thing. It would distract everyone. It could derail a takeover bid. The dogs would be chasing a different scent. She went to tell Nemitz that the telephone call they had been expecting had come, and maybe, depending on how you looked at it, this development was not so terrible for Liberty Insurance, not so terrible at all.

• • •

"Jim, do you have a minute?"

Bill Seldom walked into Watt's office. Seldom looked pudgier than ever. He had expanded a great deal since his days as an eager articling student. He still often left the building in the evening clutching a gym bag and squash racket, but now their purpose was to suggest a physical vigour that he no longer possessed. He would carry the bag and racquet out of the building, toss them in the trunk of his Volvo, and go home for a big dinner – President's Choice shepherd's pie, with Sara Lee cherry cheesecake for dessert–and lots of wine. Seldom didn't realize that almost everybody knew of his pretence. Some younger partners, to amuse themselves, would occasionally invite Seldom to play squash, forcing him to invent an elaborate reason why he couldn't.

"Bill, what about a squash game tomorrow evening at the Racquet Club? Hear you're pretty good, you'll have to go easy on me!"

"Wow, Charlie, you know I'd love to, I always enjoy a good game, but tomorrow evening, as it happens, I've got a board meeting of a little charity I support that helps people with neurological disorders. Sorry about that."

Seldom sat down where Steiner had sat not long before. "Jim," he said, "where are we on Operation Banking Freedom? I've started drafting the takeover bid circular with Julia. It's going well, but I think I need direct contact with the client. I need to speak with Tonks, and maybe Arthur Red, to be sure I'm getting everything that needs to go into the circular. It's a question of due diligence."

"I hear you Bill. Leave it with me. It might be possible to arrange. I'll see what I can do." In a pig's eye, thought Watt. He wanted to be sure that the only thing Seldom

knew about the takeover was what he, Watt, chose to tell him.

"And how are things going with Julia?" asked Watt. He had always been interested in Julia. She was still an attractive woman. There was a time when Watt fantasized about her. Then Julia had that affair with the guy who disappeared into the Pacific. That had put Watt off. Julia was damaged goods, so far as he was concerned, and he thought of himself as an old-fashioned guy when it came to things like that. He didn't mess around with damaged goods.

"Oh fine," said Seldom. "Although, she can be difficult to deal with."

"I'm not surprised to hear that," said Watt.

• • •

Piper was back in her office, reading the Exchange's insider trading rules. She pretty much knew what they said, but it couldn't hurt to double check. Something might have changed recently. She might see something that she hadn't noticed before. Reading law for Canadian Unity Bank re Special Project–that was good billable time. Her hours were looking better, much better.

Sometimes, when Piper was bored, she looked at the Internet Toronto all-news channel. The stock market was up or down. Traffic was bad on Highway 401. Weather unusually hot for the time of year. Just now there was breaking news in a crawl across the bottom of the screen. "Local lawyer found dead in hotel room, suicide suspected." On the screen was a picture of Julius Pilzon.

Chapter Nine
The Way Out

Was someone at Dibbets engaged in insider trading? Mark Steiner knew that an insider trading scandal would destroy the firm. Clients would find other lawyers. The brightest law school graduates would look elsewhere for jobs. The best partners would cross the street and join other firms. The repercussions would last for years. And it would be doubly catastrophic if senior management of the firm—the managing partner, for example—had any direct involvement.

Steiner had been around long enough to remember the Lang Michener affair. That had happened more than twenty years ago. A rogue partner of Lang Michener, a major Toronto law firm, broke the law. The firm's executive committee found out about it, but did nothing until its hand was forced. The law society took disciplinary action against the do-nothing members of the committee. The newspapers were full of it for weeks. The story was retold years later in a best-selling book called *Lawyers Gone Bad*. A compelling account of Lang Michener's erstwhile disgrace survived in libraries across the land.

Steiner's personal reputation was bound up with Dibbets. The only job he'd ever had was as a lawyer in the firm. As chairman of the executive committee, he would be a target of any obloquy. Steiner was normally a gentle man. Sometimes he thought to himself that, in a world full of hate, he was unusual because he hated no one. But today that was not true. Today he hated Jim Watt.

Two years ago he'd tried to stop Watt's appointment as managing partner. Watt is not the person for the job, he'd told the executive committee. He has no intuitive sense of where the firm should be going. What he meant was, Watt is a sleazebag, someone who'll do anything if he thinks he can get away with it. And furthermore, Steiner told the committee, Watt presents poorly. He is without charm, and his so-called gravitas does not compensate for charm's absence. But the executive committee went ahead and appointed Watt anyway, by a large majority. To most of the committee's members, Watt seemed efficient, dedicated to the firm, polished, a good client man.

There was another thing that festered with Steiner, a nasty little incident that he wouldn't forget in a hurry. A few months ago, Watt had asked for tax advice on a CUB restructuring file. A real estate company, owned by a prominent family of orthodox Jews who wore yarmulkes and wouldn't meet on Saturdays, had a loan from CUB that it couldn't repay. Ron Tonks had the file; Bert Hicks thought Tonks was the only person tough enough to handle it. Tonks called Watt and Steiner to a meeting in his office.

"It's all the fault of those guys with the beanies," Tonks began, grinning. "By the way, shouldn't there be propellers on those beanies?" He laughed loudly. He looked at

Watt and Steiner for their reaction. Watt laughed with him. Steiner said nothing. "I know how to deal with this file," Tonks went on. "Let's get those guys with the beanies into a room and then *fill it with Zyklon B!*" He roared with laughter, his mouth open, spittle flying out.

Steiner stood up and headed for the door. "I'm Jewish," he said. "You both know that. I will not stay here and listen to this shit. Find somebody else for your tax advice."

Afterwards Watt came to Steiner's office. "Don't you think you over-reacted, Mark? Just a little bit? That's the way Tonks is. It's nothing to get excited about. He doesn't mean anything by it. He wasn't pleased, I can tell you. Touchy bastard, that Steiner, he said after you left. Can't take a joke. Find somebody else for the tax stuff, he told me, someone with a sense of humour. You know, Mark, you have to go along with client quirks, particularly when it comes to the bank. It's harmless."

"Tonks is an anti-Semite, and I want nothing to do with him," said Steiner. Or with you either, he thought, as Watt left.

Steiner sat at his desk, his head in his hands. He felt awful. His wife, Miriam, had died five years ago. There were no children. Since her death, until recently, all he did was work. But in the last few months, to his surprise, life had become enjoyable again. He had started dating, going out with Jewish women about his own age. He'd known some of them forty years before, back home in Winnipeg, at the University of Manitoba, or even before that, at Kelvin High School. He had wanted to go out with them then, but they had had no time for a bookworm with thick glasses and no car. They

had dated good-looking first year law students who had white Pontiac Parisienne convertibles, or fraternity boys in dentistry school who drove their dad's Oldsmobile. But it was different now. Many of these women from long ago, still attractive, were divorced or widowed. The law students and frat boys they had married were dead, or had come out of the closet, or had gone to jail, or had run off with their secretaries. Steiner was prosperous, well regarded and had aged well. Women who had once laughed at him were now ready to share his bed. But his new well-being was threatened, threatened by Watt.

• • •

Brad Nemitz was sitting on his office sofa with Maura Hanson, watching price feeds on a Bloomberg Terminal. Numbers flickered across two computer screens. Lines moved up and down on charts. Company press releases crawled across the bottom of the screens. It was ten in the morning. The Exchange had been open for thirty minutes. The trading in Liberty Insurance shares was light.

Maura had decided that a cease trade order would be good for Liberty. It would derail a takeover. She looked at the Bloomberg screen. Not much was happening. She was hoping for a new spike in the Liberty price, high volume, a replay of what had happened yesterday afternoon, a clear sign of insider trading. Her attention wandered. She looked out of the window. There were sailboats on the lake. Who could go sailing on a weekday morning?

"Look at this!" Nemitz said, intent on the screens. Suddenly, prices were plunging across the board. Volumes were soaring. The Dow Jones Industrial Average was losing one or two points every four or five seconds. Blue

chips registered bigger and bigger losses. But Liberty Insurance was an exception. Liberty was holding its own, even creeping up a little, a speck of green in a sea of red.

"What's happened?" said Maura.

"Maybe Hamas has shot a rocket into Israel. Or the president of the European Community Bank has made a pessimistic forecast. The market is nuts. It overreacts to everything."

"But look at Liberty. Everything is going down, but our stock is going up." Liberty shares were now trading at $31.50.

"Someone who knows about the takeover bid is in the market," said Nemitz. "Has to be. The Exchange will shut us down for sure."

• • •

Arthur Red, mouth agape, was looking at the business channel on his office television. The Bank's shares were sinking like a stone. They'd gone from $52 when the Exchange opened at nine thirty to $46 by eleven o'clock. A ten per cent drop in less than two hours! It was unprecedented. Even more upsetting was what was happening to Liberty Insurance shares. They were going up, just about the only thing that was, creeping towards $35. If this kept up, a Liberty share would soon be worth more than a CUB share. Everyone on Bay Street was phoning, emailing, texting and tweeting about what looked like a market collapse. Red called Bert Hicks.

"Hicks, what the hell is going on?"

"No idea, Arthur. It's just one of those weird things. I don't think it means anything. I'm guessing the

market will bounce right back this afternoon or tomorrow morning."

"If Liberty doesn't go back down, our takeover is fucked."

"It'll go back down. And I wonder why Liberty is going up when everything else is heading south. It's fishy."

"Fishy? Fishy? What does that mean?"

"It's suspicious. Maybe somebody is trading on inside information, somebody who knows about our takeover bid."

There was a knock on Red's door. Miss Dickson came in. "Mr. Red?"

"I'm on the phone with Hicks, you always interrupt."

"Lee Wong is calling from Hong Kong. I thought you would want to take the call."

"Fuck!" Red ran his right hand through his thin hair. "Bert, I'll call you later." He pressed a button on his telephone console. "Lee, good to hear from you. How are things in Hong Kong?"

"Not good, Arthur," said Lee Wong, in an upper-class English accent. "Not good."

Wong had been to Christ Church College at Oxford University, where he'd studied Latin and Greek and taken a First. Recently he'd given the University a large amount of money and had been made a member of the Oxford Court of Benefactors in a ceremony involving colourful robes, a ceremony that he'd enjoyed very much. He was an anglophile, a cultured man, who wore suits from Savile Row and Turnbull & Asser shirts, drove a Bentley and carried a Swaine Adeney Brigg umbrella even if rain was not forecast. Lee Wong sometimes regretted that Hong Kong was no longer a British colony.

"The Hang Seng index closed badly down," said Wong. "Everywhere seems to be the same including, I see from my screen, Toronto. Also, there are disquieting rumours in Hong Kong that a Canadian bank may be in serious difficulty. No one seems to know which bank it is, but there are unsettling rumours."

"That's ridiculous."

"I hope you're right. I see CUB shares are doing badly. Is this just part of today's worldwide madness? Or is there a particular reason? Should we keep a stiff upper lip?"

"Nothing to be done, Lee. It's nothing particular to this bank. Keep a stiff upper lip."

"Yes, Arthur. I'm sure you're right. But something must be done soon to enhance CUB shareholder value. We can talk about that another day."

"Lee, I look forward to it."

• • •

Bill Seldom was pleased. If the Liberty deal collapsed because of financial scandal, then Jim Watt, as CUB's lead lawyer, would be in big trouble. He would be tarred with sordid failure, forever identified with a huge transaction that cratered through chicanery, suspected by many of wrong-doing. His credibility and authority would be undermined. CUB would find another law firm. Other important clients would leave. Watt would have to resign as managing partner. Then, the partners of Dibbets would turn to Seldom for leadership. Or, so Seldom believed. That was the essence of his plan. And he had not left anything to chance. He had prepared for this opportunity, carefully and well in advance.

The idea had begun to develop more than two years ago, when he was in Grand Cayman on a beginner's one-week scuba diving holiday. He had thought scuba diving might be worth a try. It would be a chance to spend some time away from the vile Toronto winter, maybe meet a woman. It only took him two days on Grand Cayman to decide that he hated scuba diving. His mask kept filling with water. After a dive, there was pressure in his ears that took hours to go away and sometimes he had a nosebleed. There were no women in sight. He quickly stopped going to diving lessons. Now he had five empty days to kill before the charter flight back home. He wandered the streets of George Town. There were bank offices everywhere. He started thinking. He knew that the secrecy of Cayman Islands bank accounts were still protected by strict laws; some of his clients used these accounts for that reason. He wondered if he should have an account of his own. It might be useful, he wasn't sure why. He went into a branch and made inquiries. It was easy to open an account. It could be done by email. And an account could be opened in somebody else's name.

Back in Toronto, trying to forget his horrible holiday trip to Grand Cayman, Seldom began to develop a plan. He had to get rid of Jim Watt if he wanted to rise to the top in Dibbets, to be more than perennial number two on a file. Dibbets frequently acted for someone attempting the takeover of a public company. Jim Watt often led the legal team, and Seldom was usually a member of that team. Insider trading in shares of the target before the bid was announced, if it came became known or even suspected, would jeopardize or destroy the transaction and severely taint anyone connected with it. All Seldom had

to do, he decided, was arrange insider trading in a transaction led by Watt, arrange it in a way that couldn't be traced back to him, and then sit back and wait as everything collapsed and Watt was ruined. If the deal involved CUB, Dibbets flagship client, so much the better.

Mike Morton was part of the plan. Morton was a friend of Seldom's from high school. They had both been in Mrs. Newman's Grade Ten class at North Toronto Collegiate. Morton, now married with three small children, owned and ran a mid-town soup and sandwich shop called The Painted Duck. Seldom sometimes went into The Painted Duck for lunch on Saturday when he was shopping in the neighbourhood, and he and Morton would talk about the old days.

"That Mrs. Newman!"

"Bitter old maid…"

Morton worked very hard, but only scraped by. He worried about his mortgage and how much his kids cost ; their orthodontics were extremely expensive. Why wouldn't his wife get a job? Seldom commiserated with him. One Saturday, not so long ago, Seldom had gone into The Painted Duck before the lunch rush and taken Morton round the back for a quiet chat. "Mike," Seldom had said, in an avuncular way, "I know things are tough for you and your family. You and I, we're old pals. I'm doing pretty well, and I'd like to help. A business deal might come my way one of these days. You could be helpful and make quite a bit of money out of it. You wouldn't have to concern yourself with the details."

"Bill, I run a sandwich shop. How could I help in some fancy business deal?"

"Look, it's easy. Investors will open a bank account in your name in the Cayman Islands. We'll open a brokerage account in your name in the United States as well. Then we wait. When the time comes, when the right opportunity presents itself, we'll buy a stock and later sell it at a profit, using these accounts. You get to keep twenty per cent of the profit. All you have to do is sign some papers, give me a power of attorney over the accounts, ask no questions, and never mention my name or this arrangement."

"Why do you need me? I'm broke, but I don't want to be involved in anything shady."

"Mike, the transaction breaks some securities regulations, but they're pretty obscure and it's not a big deal. You'll be a nominee for principals who for technical reasons can't have their names on the documents. It happens all the time. If I were you, I wouldn't worry about how we do business on Bay Street. Stick to sandwiches."

Two days later, after reviewing sandwich sales for the past month (it had not been a good month), realizing the financial mess he was in was getting worse and worse, concerned that he might not be able to pay the end-of-month mortgage payment on his house, Morton called Seldom and agreed to help. This, he thought, might be his way out.

• • •

When Seldom found out about the CUB bid for Liberty, at that first morning meeting in the big boardroom on the thirty-eighth floor, he knew his moment had come. He went downstairs to the CUB Private Banking Centre, borrowed five million dollars and deposited it in

the Cayman Islands bank account he had opened up in Mike Morton's name. His youthful CUB financial advisor had been happy, even eager, to authorize a large loan for an up-and-coming Dibbets partner, particularly one who often worked on bank files and was known to senior bank executives. Using the power of attorney signed by Morton, and through an Atlanta brokerage house he knew about from a deal he had once done down in Georgia, Seldom bought thirty million dollars of Liberty shares on margin. He couldn't believe his luck when the entire market suddenly tanked, dramatically highlighting the curious rise in the price of Liberty Insurance and making a cease-trade order inevitable. The only problem was, when Liberty was cease-traded, Seldom owed a great deal of money, and it wasn't clear how and when he could pay it back. He was confident he would be able to deal with that problem in due course.

• • •

Julia Anderson had stayed at home today. She lived in a corner penthouse at the corner of Richmond and Spadina in downtown Toronto. It had spectacular views to the south and east. Julia, looking out of a floor-to-ceiling window at the traffic coming down Richmond Street, was thinking about her legal career. She didn't want to be a lawyer at Dibbets any more. She didn't want to go into the office, and sit down with Bill Seldom, and work on a takeover bid circular. They didn't tell you in law school how dull it all was. They didn't tell you how lawyers sat hushed in their offices, glued to computer screens, seldom talking to anyone. They didn't tell you in law school that if you went to Bay Street your sole purpose was to

make the rich a little bit richer. Where was the pleasure in that?

Julia picked up a weekly community newspaper she had come across the other day and looked again at an advertisement that had caught her eye. "Stationery and gift shop for sale in Orillia, Ontario." Julia had always liked paper products. This, she thought, might be her way out.

Chapter Ten
Panic Button

The Exchange halted trading in Liberty Insurance shares at noon. Jim Brady telephoned Maura Hanson mid-morning to warn her. She began writing a press release immediately. "Liberty Insurance does not know of any reason for the recent volatility in the trading of its shares…" Is that true, she wondered? Liberty did know about a threatened takeover bid. Did that explain the volatility? It seemed obvious. She sent the release to the newswire anyway. News of the Liberty Insurance trading halt quickly spread up and down Bay Street.

Arthur Red, told what had happened by Bert Hicks in a brief telephone conversation, paced his office in a rage. What should have been the brightest moment in his business career seemed about to turn into a humiliating disaster.

Brad Nemitz was torn in half. An urgent problem might have gone away, but he had been dragged into the muck. He remembered his anger when he had looked out of his bedroom window into the night after the meeting with Watt and Tonks. He felt it again.

Mark Steiner thought his worst fears were coming true. Dibbets was implicated in a scandal, and, as chairman of the executive committee, he was at the epicentre. People he cared about, not knowing the details, not understanding what had happened, would think the less of him.

Bill Seldom was excited. Things were going according to plan. He was in the ascendant.

Jim Watt knew he was in trouble.

As for Piper, she wasn't that concerned. She didn't believe that Dibbets was in serious danger. In its long history it had survived worse than this. But there was the matter of billable hours. If the takeover collapsed – and that was almost certain–all the billable hours it had promised, and that she needed, would come to nothing. The compensation committee would give her the "we know you can turn it around" speech.

Maybe she shouldn't have bought the Avalon.

• • •

There must have been insider trading, thought Jim Watt, sitting in his office with the door shut. But who? Somebody at Dibbets? Possibly. Someone on his takeover team? Maybe. It wouldn't have been a junior lawyer or a secretary. Chimps and secretaries wouldn't know how to trade illegally, and even if they did, they'd be too scared to try. Darrell Jones? Agatha Hightower? Not likely. Jones had too high an opinion of himself, and of what he considered his reputation, to do anything that might attract opprobrium. Agatha lacked the necessary initiative, although, come to think of it, he had heard rumours about her lavish spending. Where did she get the money?

That left Julia Anderson, Piper Fantouche and Bill Seldom. These days, Julia was too dreamy to concoct and implement an insider-trading scheme; once she had been as sharp and dangerous as a carving knife, capable of anything, but that had been long ago. Piper had too much to lose to try anything shady. With Watt, her trusted mentor and protector, to guide and look after her, Piper would go far at Dibbets, and, Watt felt confidently, she was aware of this potential and would do nothing to jeopardize it.

That left Seldom. "Always number two on a file…" as Watt liked to say. But, Watt had to admit, Seldom might not be cut out for leadership, but he could always be counted on to be calm and reliable, and was completely dedicated to Dibbets. He was a Dibbets man through and through, just like they were in the old days when a Dibbets partner stayed with the firm for life. Today a lawyer from Dibbets or anywhere else would walk across the street and join another firm for a few extra dollars. Sometimes, when the move didn't work out, he would be welcomed back, almost as a triumphant hero returning from battle overseas, instead of being shunned and derided as a deserter and traitor the way he deserved.

Watt had a high IQ – he had once considered joining Mensa, but abandoned the idea when he saw the silly test you had to take – but he was not astute in judging people. When he looked at Bill Seldom's pasty face, and his watery and opaque light blue eyes, Watt sensed something odd lurking behind what he saw, but he couldn't pin it down. "There's something there," he would think, but could never get beyond that point in his uncomfortable consideration, and didn't even know exactly what he

meant by "something there." Now, focusing on the possibility that Bill Seldom was trading illegally in Liberty shares, Watt wondered for the first time what the man was really like.

Should he confront Seldom? That wouldn't repair the damage that had been done. Seldom was hardly likely to confess if he'd done it. He could go to Steiner, as firm chairman, and demand that action be taken, an investigation be conducted, try and move the problem to someone else. But Steiner had made quite clear that he was holding Watt responsible for whatever had happened, and relations between the two men were poisonous.

• • •

Mark Steiner decided that he had to talk to Jim Watt. The firm was facing a crisis. He was chairman of the executive committee. It was up to him to do something. But he would have to stay calm. The argument with Watt earlier in the day had been unfortunate, but perhaps they could get over that. Harsh things had been said in the heat of the moment, but cooler heads might prevail. He would have to choke back his intense dislike of Watt, and the anger that burned inside him, but perhaps he could manage it.

Steiner took his suit jacket off the hook on the back of his office door and put it on. He smoothed his tie. He mustn't look too casual at this moment. He was visiting a partner on urgent business in his official capacity. He should take a legal pad and pencil as well. He might need to write something down. He looked around for a yellow pad. Once there were stacks of yellow legal pads everywhere, but the firm no longer supplied them. Dibbets, proud of its reputation as an early adopter of technology,

had given every partner an iPad with a note-taking app. Abandoning the search for a legal pad, he picked up his iPad instead and headed for Watt' office two floors down.

From the moment Steiner walked into his office, Watt was on the attack.

"Why are you here?"

"I think we should talk. We need to deal with this Liberty situation." Steiner stood just inside the doorway, holding his iPad in front of him as if it were a shield.

"There's no situation. There's been some odd trading in one of the hundreds of companies listed on the Exchange. That's all."

"Jim, you know it's more complicated than that. We've got to figure out what happened and how to respond."

"I'm not interested in anything you have to say, Mark, and I'm sick of your butting in all the time where you're not wanted and have nothing to contribute."

"You know," said Steiner, "we don't like each other, but maybe right now, for the time being, we should forget about that in the interests of the firm."

"What you should do right now, in the interests of the firm, is get out of my office."

Steiner turned on his heel and left. He walked to the elevator in carefully measured strides and took it two floors down. Back in his office, he shut the door quietly. He put the iPad on his desk, and hung his suit jacket back on the hook. He went over to his desk and stood in front of it for a moment or two, seemingly studying the neat surface. Then he made a fist of his right hand, slammed it on the desk as hard as he could, and burst into tears.

• • •

Shortly after Steiner left, Watt's telephone buzzed. Tonks was on the line. Tonks was not happy.

"Arthur Red's been on to me. Jesus, he was yelling some. He says the Liberty deal is on life support. The market's a mess, Liberty's up, we're down, but the big problem is the Liberty trading halt and the rumours spreading all over the Street that something bad is going on and we're involved. Red says more than likely we can't go ahead with the deal, and he is pissed! He wants to know who screwed up, and if it's anyone at Dibbets the bank is going to be looking for new lawyers. What the fuck do you know about this?"

"Nothing, Ron. There seems to be some sort of problem, but we can deal with it. No need to hit the panic button."

"Arthur Red has hit the panic button, and if Arthur Red hits the panic button, I hit the panic button, and if I hit the panic button, you should hit the fucking panic button."

"I think we should all keep calm. That's the best thing."

"You think we should keep calm? Arthur Red is CEO of this bank. Arthur Red sees his legacy going up in smoke. Arthur Red says if he finds who fucked this thing up he will kill him, and don't think he isn't capable of murder, and enjoying it. You don't get to be CEO of a bank unless you're capable of killing someone with your bare hands. If he decides it's your fault, he will come over to your office and kill you, I promise. How calm does that make you feel?"

"I'm looking into it all, Ron, that's all I can say. Let me call you back later."

Perhaps he should speak to Seldom. He picked up the telephone and dialled his number. "Oh Bill, it's Jim Watt, could you come up and see me for a couple of minutes?"

• • •

Seldom slid into Watt's office. He wore a poorly cut pale blue suit that accentuated his considerable girth. He had on a white shirt and a dark blue tie. His hair was short, half-frame glasses were perched on the end of his nose, his face was wan, his eyes liquid. He looked tentative, his manner seemed deferential as always, but he did not feel that way. He felt he was a slayer of giants, a field marshal come to accept the surrender of a defeated and humiliated opponent. His plan was unfolding gloriously. He was suffused with grandiosity. But he hid it well. It wasn't time yet to show his hand.

"You wanted to see me?"

Watt wasn't sure what tack to take. Accuse Seldom head on? He couldn't be certain that Seldom was the culprit. Skirt around the subject, waiting for the right moment? That wouldn't get him anywhere. He decided on something in between.

"Bill, you're a key member of the Operation Banking Freedom team, number two on the file. I want your take on what's going on. We're in a bit of trouble. You must know that."

"I know that CUB shares have gone down, Liberty shares have gone up, the acquisition could be quite a bit more costly. There's been a trading halt. I don't suppose the bank is too happy about any of it."

Seldom knew he had to be careful. The time would come when Watt would understand that Seldom was the author of his ruin—how sweet that would be—but that

time would be when Watt was powerless and discredited, not now.

"It's more complicated than that. The big question is, with the market sinking across the board, everything down, why have Liberty shares gone up?"

"I've no idea, Jim. Perhaps some investors see a good buying opportunity."

"People on the Street are saying there's been insider trading. Do you know anything about that?"

"I don't understand you, Jim, what do you mean, do I know anything about that? Why would I know anything about that? And why does anybody think there's insider trading?"

Seldom hadn't expected Watt to ask him questions like these. Had he become a suspect? Perhaps Watt wasn't suspicious of him, but just thought he might have picked up some information somewhere. No need to jump to conclusions.

"But Bill, *do* you know anything about it?"

"If I knew anything about insider trading, needless to say I'd report it right away. Are you implying that I'm involved in something illegal?"

"Not necessarily, Bill, not necessarily. But I think someone has used inside information to trade in Liberty shares, someone who knows that CUB intends a takeover bid, and that's creating big problems for CUB, and for Dibbets, and for me personally."

Seldom suddenly remembered that he'd once seen Jim Watt in The Painted Duck. He remembered that Watt had seemed to know Mike Morton and had chatted with him in a friendly way. Mind you, Watt lived in the neighbourhood. He was bound to have an occasional

sandwich at The Painted Duck, everybody around there did. Presumably Watt was just being friendly to Mike in a casual sort of way. It probably meant nothing.

"Not *necessarily*? Not *necessarily* involved in insider trading? That's offensive, Jim, very offensive." Seldom was abandoning his blandness. His nerves were on edge.

"I'm just trying to get at the truth," said Watt.

"Well, I resent the implication."

Seldom left Watt's office more decisively than he usually left a room; normally he departed with an apologetic air, but not this time. Watt sat at his desk thinking it was all going wrong – Steiner, Arthur Red, Tonks, Seldom, they were all becoming his enemies, and who knew what other enemies he had. Who could he turn to in this awful mess?

Back in his office, Bill Seldom, his eyes more watery than ever, resolved that something had to be done about Jim Watt and Mike Morton.

Chapter Eleven
Beleaguered

Jim Watt felt beleaguered. People everywhere were turning against him. Where could he find comfort? There was always Amanda. She was a good wife. She ran their home efficiently. She made sure that Tory and Blake were clothed and fed and got to school on time and took piano lessons. She dealt with tradesmen effectively. The grass was always cut, the chimneys were always swept, the windows were cleaned regularly (every six weeks – Amanda was fussy about windows). She ran a tight ship.

But did she offer what every man wanted, unqualified approval, better yet, admiration? She did not. What she did offer was regular, crisp and comprehensive criticism. And as for warmth and love, there wasn't much of that. Sex? The union wasn't quite a *marriage blanc*, but it came close. Sometimes Watt would count up the number of times he and Amanda had made love in, say, the last six months. The fingers of one hand were generally all he needed to keep track. And the lovemaking, when it happened, was efficient but hardly imaginative.

Watt thought about Piper. She didn't criticize him. She didn't contradict him. She never argued. She recognized

his intelligence. She realized what a good lawyer he was, and sometimes told him so. He particularly appreciated that. And she was sexy. Watt allowed himself a reverie for a few moments. He began to get an erection. He put his hands down the front of his pants and fondled his penis. Then he remembered the trouble in the office. His reverie ended. He took his hand away from his penis. His erection disappeared.

It was a few minutes past five o'clock in the afternoon. Watt looked out of the window. The streets below were filling up with secretaries from the big office towers, heading for Union Station, hurrying to catch a commuter train home. The sky was darkening; it looked as if it might rain. His telephone was ringing, but he ignored it. It was probably Arthur Red, calling to fire him from bank files and demand he leave the bank board, or Steiner requesting his resignation from the partnership. Watt wanted to talk to Piper. He went to his telephone, ignored the flashing lights of lines one and two, pushed the button for line three, and dialled her number.

Piper was thinking about going home. It was early to leave the office, but the corridors were empty, the telephone was quiet, the emails and texts had stopped, an abnormal silence gripped the office, and she was tired. She looked out of the window, saw the darkening sky, and went to the closet to get her umbrella.

The telephone buzzed. She picked up the receiver.

"Piper, it's Jim. What are you doing?"

She lied. "Working on the bid circular, the bit about risk factors. Bill asked me to take a crack at it. We should still be drafting the circular, right, despite what's going on?"

Watt answered with a lie of his own. "Yes, we should. There are some bumps in the road, but I'm certain the bid will go ahead. Listen, there are a couple of points I'd like to go over with you. Can you come up to my office?"

Piper did not want to go up to Watt's office. She wanted to go to the Vietnamese restaurant on the corner of her street for a bowl of chicken noodle soup. She wanted to drink a bottle of wine and go to bed and make love and fall asleep and forget all about Canadian Unity Bank, Liberty Insurance, Operation Banking Freedom, Dibbet & Dibbet, and Jim Watt. She wanted to listen to Peter play the piano. She wanted to go to Paris.

"I could come up for a little while, Jim, but I can't stay for long. I have a family commitment. A birthday party for my aunt."

"That's great, Piper. See you in a minute."

Piper put her umbrella back in the closet and headed with a heavy heart to Watt's office. Julia Anderson was in the elevator, elegant and self-possessed. "You're looking a little worse for wear," said Julia. "Why don't you go home?"

"Soon, I hope. I've got to see Jim Watt. How are you?"

"Ready for a career change. Practising law palls."

"I don't remember the professors warning me about that when I was an eager young law student at the University of Southern Ontario."

"They wouldn't have told you because they wouldn't have known anything about it. The closest most of them ever got to practising law was reading the law reports."

The elevator arrived at Watt's floor. Piper waved goodbye to Julia and went down to the managing partner's corner office. The door was open, but Watt was not at

his desk. He was slumped on the sofa by the window, his head on the armrest, apparently asleep.

"Jim? Are you all right?"

"I'm fine." He sat up. "Just resting for a moment or two. It's been a busy day." He pulled a white linen handkerchief out of the back pocket of his pants, took his glasses off, wiped his forehead and then ran the handkerchief over the rest of his face. He put his glasses back on and the handkerchief back in his pocket.

"What did you want to talk to me about?" asked Piper.

"There are some issues on that insider trading problem. Have you reviewed the Exchange rules?"

"I've looked them over, Jim. There's nothing we hadn't thought of. It's pretty straight forward."

Watt said nothing for a moment or two. Then he spoke. "Piper, let's go to Mario's. It's not been a great day for me, and I could do with a drink. We can talk about everything over a martini."

"It's not very convenient, Jim. I've got that family thing. My aunt's birthday…"

"Come on, Piper, just a drink and a chat. We must pull together. All of us on the team need each other just at the minute."

"Okay, Jim, but I can't take very long."

• • •

"Mr. Watt. Good to see you. And nice to see you again, Ms. Fantouche." Mario showed Watt and Piper to the corner banquette. Piper sat down, and Watt slid in beside her, his leg up against hers as usual. She was not pleased that Mario knew her name. Did he think of her as a regular?

"The usual, Mario," said Watt. The martinis came quickly. Watt gulped his. It was soon gone. Piper sipped hers. She glanced surreptitiously at her watch. Watt had drunk his martini in less than ten minutes. "I'll have another," said Watt to no one in particular, waving his empty glass in the air. A hovering waiter brought a fresh drink.

"Bottoms up, Piper," said Watt.

"What are those issues you wanted to talk to me about?"

"You know the kind of thing," Watt said, almost finished his second martini. "Legal problems, technical stuff. But you know what? I don't think it matters any more. The CUB/Liberty deal is dead." He tipped his glass up, stem pointing to the ceiling, finished the drink off, and put the empty glass heavily on the table. "Dead," he said again, emphatically. "Along with several careers, mine included."

"That's fatigue talking. You need a good night's sleep."

"I do. But first I need another drink, and so do you." He waved across the room to Mario. "Two more," he said in a loud voice.

"I don't think that's a very good idea."

"Piper, come along, another martini and then we can regroup. Maybe I am being a little defeatist. You know what, we should look at those issues. All is not lost. Drink up and we'll go back to the office." Watt was starting to slur his words. Two more martinis arrived.

Piper knew she should play along. The takeover might still go ahead, unlikely but still possible, with all those billable hours that she needed. Anyway, Watt was well on his way to being drunk. He wouldn't be able to keep his

eyes open much longer. Soon he'd be in a cab on his way home, and so would she.

"Cheers," said Watt, clinking his glass against hers, finishing his third martini in one long swallow.

"Cheers," said Piper, putting her drink discreetly aside.

"Let's go," said Watt, and started to slide out of the banquette. He got entangled with the tablecloth and fell to the floor. Mario rushed over.

"Mr. Watt, are you all right?"

"No problem, Mario, no problem," said Watt, his speech by now almost unintelligible. He stood up with difficulty. "Piper, let's go." He walked uncertainly to the exit, followed by Piper.

• • •

When they got to his office, Watt shut the door, took off his suit jacket and hung it up, undid his top shirt button, loosened his tie, and lay down on the couch. His eyelids fluttered and closed. He seemed to be asleep. Piper moved the client chair so it faced the couch, sat down and waited. Perhaps she should go home. Eventually Watt would wake up and go home himself.

"Oh God," Watt groaned. He stirred and half-sat up. "Piper, come here. Come and sit with me."

"I think we should call it a day," said Piper.

Watt was now sitting up completely. "No," he said. "Come over here."

Piper looked at her watch. "I didn't realize how late it was," she said. "I've got to go to my aunt's birthday party."

Watt stood up. He walked two or three unsteady paces towards Piper who was still sitting in the client chair.

He reached out and grabbed her arm. "You know how I feel about you," he said.

"No, Jim, I don't know, and I don't want to. Let go of my arm. I'm leaving." She stood up, Watt still hanging on to her arm.

"You're beautiful." He leaned forward to try and kiss her but Piper pushed him away. He stumbled backwards. "Don't push me," said Watt.

"I told you I have to go," said Piper, picking up her handbag from the floor.

Watt stood between her and the door. "I want you," he said. Piper tried to shove him aside. "I want you," he repeated, and pulled at the front of her blouse, ripping off the top two buttons. The blouse fell open showing her brassiere. He grabbed at the bra and pulled it down, exposing her breasts. "You're beautiful," Watt said again, putting his hands on her breasts before she could back away.

Piper slapped him hard. He reeled back and then righted himself, grabbed both her arms, pushed her down on the sofa, and threw himself on her as she struggled. Part of Piper's brain calmly considered what she should do. Scream? If she did, someone would probably hear her, a secretary staying late perhaps, or an articling student, and come to the rescue. Even if no one came, screaming might scare Watt and stop him trying to rape her. But screaming would also turn this absurd incident into a major scandal. As if he guessed what she was thinking, Watt put one hand over her mouth. With the other he tried to unzip her skirt. "I love you," he said, stinking of gin, his face an inch from hers. Piper managed to scratch his cheek with her left hand, and then hit him on the

side of his head with her right hand made into a fist. He looked surprised, took his hand away from her mouth and stopped fumbling with her clothes.

"Why did you do that?" said Watt. Suddenly the life seemed to go out of him. He closed his eyes. He lay still. A few moments passed. He started snoring.

Piper waited until she was certain he was asleep. He was still partly on top of her. She squirmed out from under him and got off the couch without waking him up. She put her bra back on, buttoned her blouse, straightened her skirt, and rearranged her hair. She stood quite still for a couple of moments trying to compose herself. Watt snored on the couch. She opened the door and walked out of Watt' office down to the elevator. It came quickly and was empty. She went to the ground floor and got a taxi from the stand in front of the building. She was trembling. The taxi driver eyed her curiously in the rear view mirror as he pulled away.

"Okay, miss?"

"Fine. Thank you."

• • •

When Piper got home, Peter was watching Sons of Anarchy on television. It was his favourite show, about a motorcycle gang in California. He barely looked up as she came in. She stood in the small entrance hall for a few seconds and burst into tears. Now she had Peter's attention. He turned off the television and came to her and wrapped her in his arms.

"What's wrong? What's happened?"

"Jim Watt tried to rape me." If Peter hadn't been holding her tight, she would have collapsed to the floor.

"Jim Watt tried to rape you? The managing partner?'

Piper told him what had happened.

"I'll kill the fucker," said Peter. "I'll kill him."

He went storming out of the apartment, slamming the door.

"Peter! Peter!" Piper called out after him, but he was gone.

Chapter Twelve
Dead

The next morning, when they awoke from troubled sleep, members of the Dibbets Operation Banking Freedom team felt nervous and confused. They lay in their beds, lacking the will to get up and go to work. They tossed and turned, thinking about recent events.

Things had fallen apart. Operation Banking Freedom seemed finished. Someone, perhaps someone from Dibbets, had been trading illegally in Liberty Insurance shares. A major scandal seemed inevitable. The relationship between Dibbets and Canadian Unity Bank was in serious jeopardy. There were bitter fights erupting within the firm. Maybe it would be better to stay home today and read a book, or just go back to sleep.

At Dibbets the corridors were quiet. Normally, by seven o'clock, there was a lot of activity. Young associates showed dedication to the firm and its work by moving about purposefully. Secretaries and paralegals, called in early by those young associates, bustled about to get mountains of documents ready for the imminent closing of some large transaction. Here and there a senior partner sat in his office determined to demonstrate he

was still important in the world of Big Law. Computer screens flickered, email and text message alerts binged and clanged, telephones rang. That is how it was, normally, early in the morning at Dibbets. But today it was not like that. Hardly anyone was about. There was an ominous quietude.

Jim Watt's assistant, Mary Johnston, arrived promptly at eight o'clock, as always. When she came in, the door to Jim Watt's office was closed. It was reckless to knock on Watt's door when it was shut, but by nine o'clock Mary was looking at it with concern. Was Watt working on a particularly demanding and important matter, requiring complete concentration? Or was something wrong?

At nine thirty Mary Johnston decided to act. She knocked on Watt's door. There was no reply. She knocked again and listened carefully. Nothing. She opened the door a crack, said, "excuse me" loudly, and peered in. There was no sign of Watt. Some of the cushions usually on the couch by the window were scattered on the floor. Papers had fallen off the desk and were mixed in with the cushions. The client chair, usually carefully positioned at an exact angle across from the desk, was off to one side. Watt's own high-backed leather chair was on the other side of the room, pushed against the wall.

A highly polished black brogue was sticking out from behind the desk. This was puzzling. Had Watt left a shoe in his office? Why would he do that? Where was the other one? Mary went into the office. She looked behind the desk, wondering about the shoe. It was attached to a leg. Jim Watt was lying motionless on the floor, his body twisted into an odd shape. He was not wearing his jacket and tie; Mary saw them crumpled in a corner. His white

shirt was caked with dried blood. His head was turned to one side, his left cheek resting on the floor. There was a bright red scratch on his right cheek. His hair was matted. His face was contorted. His eyes were open. Mary knew he was dead.

She felt calm. She looked down at the body for a few seconds. Then she left Watt's office quietly and closed the door behind her. She went and sat at her workstation, quite composed, her hands clasped in her lap. A series of disconnected thoughts flitted through her head. She thought of summer last year when she trekked through Gros Morne in Newfoundland with her niece Donna. She thought about the seagulls facing this way and that on a beach she had visited in Nova Scotia. For a moment she gave herself up to the pleasure of these memories. Then she wondered whether she should call Mark Steiner. He was the chairman of Dibbets. He should be told what had happened. No, that was the second call she had to make. She reached for her telephone and called 9-1-1. "I want to report a dead person," she told the operator who answered. She added, "I think he was murdered."

• • •

Two cruisers from 52 Division, sirens going, pulled up in front of the Canadian Unity Bank building and parked on the broad sidewalk in front. Four uniformed police officers, three men and a woman, got out of the cruisers and went into the building. An unmarked police car arrived less than a minute later and parked next to the cruisers. Two men in suits, detectives from the Homicide Squad on nearby College Street, got out and went into the bank tower.

• • •

The next call that Mary Johnston made was to Mark Steiner. "Mr. Steiner, it's Mary Johnston, Jim Watt's assistant. I think you should come down to Mr. Watt's office right away." Her voice trembled slightly.

"Mary, I'm in the middle of something."

"I think you had better come down here, Mr. Steiner. Something has happened."

"Mary, I've got to finish drafting a document. I'm on a plane to Calgary later this morning. I'll call Jim when I get to Calgary if it's important."

"Mr. Steiner, Mr. Watt is dead."

• • •

Detective Sergeant Sebastian Vitanza was looking around Watt's office in a casual sort of way. Mohan Singh, his partner, stood silently just inside the office door, watching him. Outside, four uniformed officers chatted with each other about last night's baseball game. The Blue Jays had lost badly to the Yankees. Most of the floor was already cordoned off with yellow crime scene tape. Down the corridor, beyond the tape, pressing up against it, peering towards the chatting police, was a small group of whispering Dibbets secretaries and paralegals.

Vitanza, fifty-two, was a good-looking man, despite his short stature and slight potbelly. He had a patrician face, a fine head of white hair, and a full white moustache hanging down over his upper lip. He wore a dark suit bought at Tom's Place in Kensington Market, a white shirt, a plain red tie and Rockport shoes. He appeared kind and gentle, but some would tell you that this was not the whole story. His ex-wife, Octavia, divorced some

fifteen years ago, had not found him to be kind and gentle. His psychiatrist, Saul Abramowitz, was concerned about his bad temper and growing sadness. Vitanza had been seeing Dr. Abramowitz once a week for the last three years, hoping that one of these days he would feel better. "You live on the precipice of sorrow," Saul had told him.

Sebastian Vitanza had come to Toronto with his parents and seven siblings from the small Sicilian farming community of Capri Leone when he was eight years old. His father, Gino, tired of selling vegetables in a Messina hill town, had immigrated to Toronto for a better life. Unable to escape completely from his past, Gino sold farm produce in a Little Italy corner store for thirty years. It was Gino's children, not Gino, who realized the Canadian dream. They all had good jobs. They had good marriages too, with the exception of Sebastian, and there were many grandchildren. Gino, now retired, widowed, and growing tomatoes in his backyard on Manning Street, was proud of them all. He was particularly proud of Sebastian. Olympia, his eldest daughter, was an emergency room doctor, but to Gino, being a homicide detective was a better job.

Mohan Singh, standing by the door, watched Vitanza staring at Watt's desk. Vitanza seemed more interested in the desk than the body behind it. What does he see, Singh wondered? There was nothing on the desk. Why is he staring at it so intently? Vitanza had the reputation of being clever; they said he saw things that others did not see. They also said that Sebastian Vitanza's air of kindly casualness sometimes led people to tell him things they later regretted.

"Interesting," said Vitanza. "His jacket and tie are in the corner. How did they get there? And why is there nothing on his desk?"

Singh was a Sikh and wore a turban. Most took him for an immigrant, but Singh had been born in a big house in Rosedale, Toronto's most exclusive neighbourhood. His father, Harpreet, had been a psychiatrist with affluent patients. Harpreet had come to Toronto from India to study medicine and had stayed on. He had met Mohan's mother, a Spanish ballet dancer named Abella, when he was on holiday in Barcelona. Abella had died not long after Mohan, an only child, was born.

When Mohan was fourteen, Harpreet had gone back to India for reasons that were never clear, at least not to Mohan, leaving the boy as a boarder in an exclusive boy's school. At school he was teased about his turban. In the summer months, unhappy and lonely, he stayed with distant relatives in Mississauga. Now, Mohan's only contact with his father, who suffered from late-onset schizophrenia, was the occasional incoherent and abusive letter he received from India. Mohan, in his mid-thirties, was single, and tried to forget about family. He had promised himself that he would never marry.

A uniformed police officer came into Watt's office. "Detective Vitanza, there's someone who says he's got to talk to you."

"Uh huh."

"He won't go away," said the officer. "Says he's the chairman of the firm. Says he has to talk to you. And the forensic officers have arrived."

"Okay, I'll see this guy. Send the forensic people in. And call the coroner."

• • •

Vitanza went up to Mark Steiner, who was waiting outside.

"I'm Detective Sergeant Sebastian Vitanza, officer in charge of this investigation."

"Steiner, Mark Steiner, chairman of Dibbets." They shook hands. "Can you tell me what's happened?"

"There's a dead man in that room. Maybe you could identify him for us." They went into the office. Vitanza pointed to the other side of the desk. Steiner went behind it and looked at the body.

"It's Jim Watt, the firm's managing partner. Excuse me, I have to sit down."

"Let's find a place where we can both sit down. I'd like a chat."

"There's the lunchroom down the corridor," said Steiner, trembling.

The lunchroom was empty. Vitanza and Steiner went in and sat down on two plastic chairs on opposite sides of a plastic table.

"Was he murdered?" asked Steiner, somewhat calmer, but still trembling slightly.

"I don't know yet. Tell me about Jim Watt. What was he like?"

"He was a good lawyer. Very meticulous. He'd been a successful partner of this firm for a long time. I can't believe he's dead. It's unbelievable. Why would someone kill him?"

"Did people like him?"

"Some did, some didn't. Same as everybody else. He could be a hard task master."

"Did you like him?"

"No."

"Why not?"

"We have – had–different management styles, let's put it like that. We had differences of opinion about how the firm should develop."

"What had Watt been working on lately?"

"That's confidential."

"Mr. Steiner, a man is dead. I'm a homicide detective. This may be a murder investigation."

"Okay. He'd been working on a bank takeover of an insurance company. It had run into difficulties."

"What kind of difficulties?"

"Legal difficulties, Detective Vitanza. It would take some time to explain it all."

"I want you to give me a list of everyone involved in this takeover, and not just people in the law firm, everyone, from everywhere, other law firms, the lot. If you're not sure whether someone should be on the list, put him on the list. And I'm going to want those 'legal difficulties' explained to me."

"I'll make the list as quickly as I can. We can talk about the difficulties whenever you like."

"What about Watt's private life?"

"Happily married, two children."

"Girlfriend?"

"What do you mean?"

"Did he have a girlfriend? Some married men do."

"Not that I'm aware of."

"Enemies?"

"You can't be a lawyer without making enemies."

"Who were they?"

"I've no idea. I was speaking in general terms."

"Were you one?"

"I was his partner. How could I be his enemy?"

"But you weren't his friend? You had differences of opinion."

"No, I wasn't his friend. I don't think Jim Watt had many friends. But I wasn't his enemy."

"Let me have that list as soon as you can."

"Detective Vitanza, I have to tell the partners and staff something. What can I say?"

"Say there's an ongoing police investigation into a suspicious death. Tell them this floor is a crime scene and off limits. Tell them they may be questioned. Tell them to carry on business as usual."

Chapter Thirteen
Nobody Died at Dewey

Word that Jim Watt was dead spread with astounding speed. Telephones rang all over Toronto and beyond. Text messages flew through radio networks. By eleven o'clock in the morning, most of the world – the world that counted, at any rate–knew that an important Bay Street lawyer had died in unusual circumstances. In the Dibbets office, lawyers gathered in small groups and talked in low voices, exchanging rumours. Operation Banking Freedom team members, at home in their pajamas, dressed quickly and headed in as soon as they heard what had happened, afraid of missing something.

Some Dibbets partners were already making quiet calculations of personal advantage. Watt had had good clients. Who would get them? Perhaps reassuring phone calls to those clients, promising continuity, stressing the depth of the firm's expertise, offering a good lunch at Flotsam… Other partners were nervous. Could they get mixed up in something nasty? They'd worked on deals with Watt, of course, but everyone had to realize that Watt had always been in charge; they'd just had a minor role. What did the suspicious death of Watt mean for the

firm? What did it portend for profit per partner? Would some clients leave? There was no grief. Watt had been widely disliked. He would not be missed. There would be no tearful tributes.

To the world outside Dibbets, the suspicious death of a senior and well-known Bay Street lawyer was a shocking event. Violent death was rare in Big Law, apart from suicide, which happened occasionally, and the odd accident. Old-timers still remembered the lawyer who fell to his death from a twenty-fourth floor boardroom window; he had thrown himself against the glass to demonstrate to articling students that it was unbreakable. Today, in downtown Toronto law firms, work, but not billing, was replaced by blather about Watt. "I heard someone split his head open with an axe. Watt was a bastard, for sure, but who would want to do a thing like that?" In the head offices of Dibbets' big clients, senior corporate officers pondered the implications of the developing scandal. "Perhaps we should look at some other law firms. The Dibbets people are competent enough, of course, but when the managing partner is beaten to a pulp with a hammer in his own office, I mean, you've got to ask…"

Arthur Red was told that Watt was dead by Bert Hicks, who burst into Red's office without asking Miss Dickson's permission. She stood up and tried to stop him as he sped by, but for once was left slack-jawed. Arthur Red was preternaturally composed at the news. "Murdered? That son-of-a-bitch. Fucked me over on the Liberty deal. He got what was coming to him. Bad news, though. Now I can't kill the fucker myself."

Two floors below, Ron Tonks sat nonplussed in his office, wondering who could have done it.

At palatial Osgoode Hall, Queen Street home of The Law Society of Upper Canada, officials and benchers took time out from regulating members of the bar in the public interest to fuss at the news over lunch in their private dining room. "Thank God we never gave Watt our annual gold medal for professional achievement," said the Treasurer. "We thought about it, remember? A narrow escape. We would have looked pretty stupid. I think I'll have another glass of this excellent Sancerre."

Brad Nemitz was not a religious man, but when he heard what had happened his first thought was that it was divine retribution. Jim Watt had been an evil man.

• • •

Julia Anderson was at home that morning. She was staying home more and more often. Joyce, her assistant, called with the news about Watt. After Julia hung up the telephone, after the intakes of breath and shocked exclamations appropriate in the circumstances, she sat thinking quite calmly. What had happened was appalling, but, in an odd way, not surprising. Watt had tried to live in the world free of the constraints accepted by almost everybody else. Once some boundaries were discarded, why should others remain?

According to Joyce, Watt didn't die a peaceful death. He didn't have a heart attack or a brain aneurysm, the kind of thing that killed other people who died suddenly. "Head split open like a ripe watermelon," Joyce had reported. "Happened sometime in the evening or maybe during the night," she had said, although who knew where she had got that information. "Probably a meat cleaver," she threw in as an afterthought. Who was the murderer, wondered Julia. There were a lot of people

who disliked Jim Watt. She was one of them. He'd always been more interested in her legs than her legal talent. She was sure that he'd badmouthed her over her affair with the man who had disappeared in the South Seas; this was likely one reason why her career at Dibbets had never prospered. Maybe the police would think she had a motive for Watt's murder and would put her on the list of suspects. Maybe they'd start wondering about the man who disappeared in the South Seas. Had he really disappeared, or had Julia killed him and stuffed the body in a suitcase and put the suitcase in her attic? There had been occasions when killing her lover had crossed her mind. Once when they were in the kitchen together, and she had been holding a carving knife, she had been shocked by a sudden strong urge to plunge it into his chest.

Julia remembered seeing Piper Fantouche in the elevator late yesterday afternoon, on her way to Watt's office. There was speculation in the firm that there was something between Piper and Watt. Julia didn't believe it. Piper was young, beautiful and smart: Watt, the opposite. That didn't mean, of course, that Watt hadn't tried to use his power to bamboozle Piper into bed. That, thought Julia, would be a good enough reason to kill him. She would have killed him if he tried something like that with her. She would have plunged a carving knife into his chest.

• • •

Someone in the elevator told Darrel Jones about the managing partner's death, as he went up to his office clutching his battered briefcase.

"Watt?" said Jones. "He wasn't that smart. He had a brain size problem. It's not much of a loss for the firm."

• • •

Agatha Hightower, who had planned to spend the day in bed with a book, arrived in the office about eleven o'clock. She had got a text message with the news from a junior real estate associate. She didn't know why she had bothered to come in to the office; somehow, it had seemed necessary; the gruesome event had a strong gravitational pull. As for Watt's death and how it had happened, she felt no emotions and had no opinions.

She managed to get into her office without seeing or speaking to anyone. There was a new Visa bill lying on her desk, delivered in the morning's mail. She put it in a drawer unopened, where it lay with several others. She looked at her watch. In forty-five minutes she could go and get lunch at Pangaea, probably the best restaurant in Toronto, run by her old friend Peter, and then drop into Holt Renfrew just around the corner. Her credit card hadn't been cancelled yet, and she would use it vigorously until it was.

• • •

Bill Seldom, in a state of high nerves, fidgeting incessantly, picking his nose compulsively, scratching at a scab on his right shoulder that he'd had for ever and that wouldn't go away, was sitting in his office trying to think clearly. He told himself over and over that the death of Jim Watt was a good thing. Isn't that what he'd wanted, Jim Watt out of the way? Well, Jim Watt was certainly out of the way now. The clever insider-trading plan had not been necessary. Events had overtaken it.

But the whole thing was messy, very messy. There was a dead body. The police were everywhere. A police

investigation might uncover the insider-trading scheme. He didn't think anyone knew about the horrible fight he'd had with Watt, or about Watt's suspicions of him, but he could be wrong about that. The police might decide he was a murder suspect. He suddenly remembered that Watt had some kind of relationship with Mike Morton. He'd seen them together at The Painted Duck. That was worrying.

The thing to do was keep calm. There were lots of people who were well known to have disliked the managing partner. There were lots of people who had had public fights with him, who – let's face it – wouldn't be exactly unhappy that he was dead. There was no particular reason the police or anybody else should single him out. The list of suspects must be long. Why would anyone be particularly interested in him?

• • •

Mark Steiner had called a meeting of the firm's executive committee for three o'clock that afternoon. All eleven committee members were present. The meeting was disorderly. Some didn't appear to realize how serious things were. Others were in a complete panic.

"It's not the first time a partner has been found dead in his office," said one complacently. "Remember old Henry Brown?"

Steiner reminded the committee that old Henry Brown was eighty-three when he died of a heart attack while having a nap.

"We mustn't get too excited over all this," said another. "These things happen from time-to-time."

"No they don't," said Steiner. "Managing partners do not get murdered from time-to-time."

Some committee members were almost in tears. "It's a disaster," one said. "We will all go to jail. The firm is finished." Another, the only woman on the committee, said she knew for a fact that many partners were planning to leave Dibbets and were approaching other law firms. "It's like Dewey LeBoeuf," she said, "only worse. Nobody died at Dewey."

Chapter Fourteen
A Tough Spot

Piper had been in tough spots with men before, but nothing like this had ever happened.

In the middle of the night, still trembling from her encounter with Jim Watt, unable to sleep, she desperately wondered what to do. There was no point in going to the police. She could imagine their cynical reaction if she did: drunken fumblings in the office, they would think; it happened all the time; she must have led him on; not a police matter. Report Watt to Mrs. Ground, Dibbets' sexual harassment officer? If a junior associate groped a secretary, Mrs. Ground might do something about it, but she wasn't going to touch the managing partner. "Best to move on," she'd say. "Put it behind you."

One thing was clear to Piper, with the clarity that comes only at three in the morning: her career at Dibbets was over. She couldn't survive this kind of run in with Jim Watt, however it played out. And it wasn't just Dibbets; her career in law was probably over too. Word would get round the legal community. Something bad had happened, involving Piper Fantouche, no one would be sure of the details. Piper Fantouche was trouble. Piper

Fantouche can't get along with people. Stay away from Piper Fantouche.

After Peter had rushed out yelling, "I'll kill him," she'd gone to bed but couldn't, of course, sleep. He had come back disheveled two hours later and slid in beside her, saying nothing. She was in no state to cross-question him. They made love but it was a desperate act. Then they lay awake side-by-side until dawn broke, speaking hardly at all.

They got up when light began filtering through the bedroom curtains. Piper made coffee. They sat at the tiny kitchen table in their bathrobes.

"Where did you go last night?"

"I just walked around," said Peter. His face flushed. "What are you going to do about that sick fuck?"

"I don't know. Leave Dibbets, for one thing. I'll have to."

"Dibbets is an awful place," said Peter. "Get out. Get away from Watt. Don't go back there for even one hour. You remember we were talking about Paris? We can get a flight today. We can be there in hours. Make the break. Change your life."

"That's running away. It wouldn't solve anything. I've still got a job. I'm working on a big file. I can't just get on a plane and leave. That's not professional. I'm a lawyer. That means something."

"Running away seems like a good idea to me. You told me that your big file had crashed and burned."

"Suppose we went to Paris. Where would we stay? How long would we go for?"

"We'll find a hotel on the Left Bank. We'll stay a week, two weeks, forever."

She refilled their coffee cups. The telephone rang. She picked up the extension on the bedside table and said hello. She listened and said nothing. Peter opened his eyes and looked at her. Her face was white. She gripped the receiver as if she were trying to crush it. She said, "Thank you for letting me know" and hung up. She sat without moving on the edge of the bed.

"Who was that? What's happened?" Peter was sitting up.

"It was Rachel, my assistant."

"What did she want?"

"She told me that Jim Watt was found dead in his office this morning."

"Holy shit! What happened? Did he have a heart attack?"

"No. It looks as if someone killed him. Rachel says the police are all over the place."

"Someone killed him?"

"Yes. Apparently."

"Holy fuck!"

• • •

Vitanza and Singh had set up what Vitanza liked to call a "command centre" in a small vacant boardroom on the thirty-eighth floor.

"So, Mohan, what do you think?" Vitanza asked, sitting at the boardroom table, his hands clasped in front of him. "Murder, but who did it? Client enraged by a huge bill for legal services? Angry girlfriend? Partner jealous of Watt's big files? A passing stranger who took an instant and violent dislike to the deceased?"

"Are we sure he was murdered?" Singh was a cautious man.

"You think that gash on his head was self-inflicted? By the way, any ideas on the murder weapon? It's a strange wound. I've never seen anything quite like it."

"Let's wait and see what the coroner says."

"Intuition is a big part of being a good detective," said Vitanza. "We shouldn't just wait for reports from experts. We should sleuth." Vitanza had learnt the word "sleuth" from watching Inspector Morse on television and liked it.

A woman came in and handed Vitanza a document. It said "Operation Banking Freedom Working List" in big print at the top. An elegant attached slip in copperplate said "compliments of Mark Steiner." It was a list of thirty-two names.

"We've got to talk to all of these people," said Vitanza, sighing. "I'll take the Dibbets lawyers and the Canadian Unity Bank executives. Mohan, you do the rest. You'd better start with the Dibbets support staff, the secretaries, paralegals. We want to know the relationship each person had with Watt, what they thought of him. We want to know what Operation Banking Freedom was all about and what went wrong."

"How about asking each person on the list whether they killed Watt?"

"We could try that."

"What about Watt's wife? Shouldn't we talk to her? Maybe she killed him."

"You and I will go and give Mrs. Watt our condolences. Meanwhile, you'd better go find a room for interviews. And don't be flippant, it doesn't suit you. This is serious business."

Vitanza looked at the names of the Dibbets law-yers who had worked on Operation Banking Freedom. Partners were listed alphabetically–Julia Anderson, Piper Fantouche (that's an odd name, he thought), Agatha Hightower, Darrell Jones, Bill Seldom. Other names were at the bottom in a smaller font. Those names had asterisks next to them; a note at the bottom of the page said asterisked names were associates. These law firms have a fierce hierarchy, thought Vitanza.

He might as well start with the first on the list, Julia Anderson. He called her office and got voice mail. He called her home and she answered. She agreed to meet him at Dibbets in an hour.

While I'm waiting for Julia Anderson, thought Vitanza, I'll try Piper Fantouche. She didn't answer at her office or at home; he didn't leave a message. He went to the next name, Agatha Hightower. He called her office. She answered on the second ring. Yes, she'd come and see him right away. She showed up minutes later.

"Ms. Hightower, thank you for coming. I'm Detective Sergeant Vitanza. I'm investigating the death of Jim Watt."

"Yes."

"Do you know anything about it?"

"No."

"What have you heard about what happened?"

"I've heard what everybody's heard. He was murdered."

"We don't know yet whether he was murdered. But let me ask you, did he have enemies? Was there anything unusual going on in the office? In his personal life?"

"I've no idea about any of that."

"What sort of person was Jim Watt?"

"Very good at certain things," she said. "Very good at drafting documents. Very good at structuring complicated business transactions. Very bad at dealing with people."

"Very bad at dealing with people. What does that mean?"

"Watt had no personal skills. Let me put it another way. He was a complete shit."

"The two of you didn't get along?"

"I wouldn't say that. He barely knew I existed. To him, I was just a drone who did real estate work. As for me, I hardly ever gave him a thought. When I did give him a thought, I thought he was a complete shit."

"Thank you," said Vitanza. "I may want to talk to you again."

Another woman appeared in the doorway as Agatha Hightower left. "Detective Vitanza?"

"You must be Julia Anderson."

"Yes." She sat down.

"Miss Anderson, I'm investigating the death of Jim Watt. I'd like to ask you a few questions. Did you know him well?"

"Fairly well. We often worked together. We were working on a big transaction when he died."

"That would be Operation Banking Freedom?"

"Yes."

"Tell me about it."

"Canadian Unity Bank was planning a takeover bid for Liberty Insurance. It would have been a major acquisition for the bank."

"You speak in the past tense. Is it not going ahead? Did something go wrong?"

"Yes, the leader of the bank's legal team was murdered."

Vitanza smiled slightly.

"And, anyway, the deal was in trouble already."

"Why?"

"Early on Liberty's stock price shot up. Insider trading was suspected, maybe insider trading by someone at Dibbets. That by itself would have derailed the whole thing."

"Was there insider trading?"

"I've no idea."

"When did you last see Watt?"

"Yesterday morning."

"Was he in the office all day, do you know?"

"I think he probably was. I didn't see him later, but I was in the elevator with Piper Fantouche, one of my partners, at about five thirty and she said she was going up to his office."

"Do you know why she was going to see him?"

"No, but Piper was working on Operation Banking Freedom. She often worked with Watt. They spent a lot of time together."

"A strictly working relationship?"

"I think so."

"What was your relationship with Jim Watt?"

"Very limited, no more than necessary. I stayed away from him as much as possible."

When Julia Anderson left, Vitanza called Piper Fantouche's office again. There was a new message on the tape. "This is Piper Fantouche. I will be out of the country for several days and will not be reachable while away. If you need immediate legal assistance, please press

zero and ask the operator to direct you to the appropriate Dibbets lawyer. Otherwise, leave a message."

Curious, thought Vitanza. A long-planned vacation or a sudden business trip? Fantouche must know that Watt is dead. She must realize that the police want to talk to her. He'd like to know when she left Toronto and where she'd gone. He'd like her to explain why she left the city so quickly.

A small man with an oddly shaped head came unannounced into the boardroom. "You'll want to speak to me about Jim Watt," said the man. "I'm Darrell Jones."

"Yes, Mr. Jones. I was going to call you. What do you have to tell me?"

"Jim Watt was not a smart man," said Jones. "That's important."

"A lot of your partners tell me different."

"Yeah, well they would. What you have to understand, detective, is that a lot of my partners aren't very smart either."

"Can you explain what that's got to do with my investigation?"

"Yes, I can. Don't look for a clever plot or a rational motive. You won't find them. Think stupid, and you'll figure it out."

"I'll bear that it in mind," said Vitanza.

Chapter Fifteen
Left Bank

Air Canada's overnight flight from Toronto arrived at Charles de Gaulle airport just after ten in the morning. They had travelled Executive Class. Peter had wanted to get cheap tickets from Flight Centre, but Piper said no. She liked to travel in comfort and could afford it, for the moment at least. They were first off the plane, tired–neither had slept much as the airplane flew across the night Atlantic–but buoyed up by anticipation. They were not thinking much about what had happened in Toronto. They were thinking about the next few days in Paris. They presented themselves to a woman immigration officer who was in the middle of a vigorous conversation with a fellow agent. She was speaking loudly, gesticulating extravagantly. She barely glanced at their passports. Their baggage, a suitcase each, arrived quickly. They were soon out of the terminal and into a taxi.

"The corner of Boulevard Saint-Germain and Boulevard Saint-Michel," Peter said to the driver, who nodded and set off at speed and in silence.

"Where's that?" asked Piper, who knew almost nothing about Paris. What she knew she had learnt from movies set in the city. Last Tango in Paris was her favourite.

"It's the heart of the Left Bank." Peter had been reading a guide to Paris on the plane. He'd bought it at Toronto airport.

"What are we doing about a hotel?" Piper had left the job of finding a hotel to Peter.

"There are all kinds of hotels on the Left Bank. It'll be easy."

Twenty minutes later, the taxi was going down the Champs-Élysées. The driver was taking the circuitous route he always used for tourists. He turned onto the Quai des Tuileries and took the Pont Neuf across the river. Soon he was at the intersection of Boulevard Saint-Germain and Boulevard Saint-Michel. The meter said eighty-five Euros. Peter gave the driver a hundred, and he and Piper were standing with their bags on the corner.

"There you go," said Peter, pointing to the building in front of them. A sign said "Hotel Saint Germain."

"What do you think?" said Piper. The hotel's façade was drab.

"It looks okay. I'm sure it's fine."

They went inside. The lobby attempted to be formal. Its walls were painted taupe. It was furnished with cheaply elegant grey and white furniture. A large flat screen television on the wall was tuned to a local all-news channel. An attractive young woman, dressed in black with red-framed glasses, was behind the reception desk.

They went up to the desk and Peter asked the woman for a room. He spoke English slowly, enunciating carefully. The woman looked them up and down and made

an appraisal. She was used to making quick and accurate judgments about couples.

"We only have one room left, the Romance Suite. Just right for you I think." She spoke excellent English.

"How much is it?"

"Two hundred and twenty Euros a night."

"That's fine, we'll take it.'

"How many nights?"

"We're not sure," said Peter. "Can we decide later?"

"Yes, of course. Here is your key. Room 405. The lift is over there, to your right."

They struggled to get into the tiny elevator with their bags. They closed the metal gate, which made a loud clanging sound. The cab rose slowly and noisily to the fourth floor. They got out of the elevator and followed an arrow on the wall down the corridor to the Romance Suite. The door had a small pink heart next to the room number. They went in and put their bags down.

"It's tiny," said Peter. "Too small for any kind of romance I can think of. And look at that awful mural."

The room was an attic with two skylights. A double bed, one chair and a chest of drawers took up most of the floor space. On the wall behind the bed was a huge painting, largely pink, of a woman with a parasol wearing a long dress and walking down a street while several men in frock coats doffed their top hats.

"We should see what else they've got," said Peter. "Maybe we should try another hotel."

But Piper liked the room. "It's small," she said, "but so what. The bed looks comfortable."

"Okay," said Peter, pleased.

"I'm hungry," said Piper. "Let's find somewhere for lunch."

They took the tiny elevator back down to the lobby and walked out onto the street. They walked west down Boulevard Saint-Michel. It was sunny and warm. Peter took his sweater off. The street was crowded. They went by the church of St.-Germain-des-Pres. They walked by the Café Les Deux Magots.

"What about this place?" said Piper. Couples were sitting outside Les Deux Magots in the sun, drinking wine. Two or three people sitting at tables by themselves were scribbling in notebooks.

"Keep going," said Peter. They went on for a few hundred feet and came to the Café de Flore.

"This is it," he said. They took a table outside. They ordered croque-monsieurs and a bottle of red wine.

"Why here?" said Piper.

"The travel guide says there are three famous cafés on this street. It says Café de Flore is the best."

"Three cafés? This one, the one we passed, where's the other? And why is Café de Flore the best?"

"The other one's across the street," said Peter, pointing. "Over there. Brasserie Lipp. Who knows why Café de Flore is the best. It just is."

The sun was hot. A beautiful woman of about fifty, in high heels and a broad-brimmed straw hat, strode by. An older man in wire-rimmed glasses, carrying books, crossed her path. There were children everywhere. They drank their wine.

By now they were exhausted and a little drunk. It was almost two o'clock. Peter paid the bill at the Café de Flore. They strolled back to Hotel Saint Germain. They

went to the Romance Suite. The bed was comfortable. The afternoon light came through the skylights and lit the pink mural. They made quiet, uncomplicated love. They slept. They awoke together, after half-an-hour or so, and lay side-by-side, saying nothing for a minute or two.

Then Peter said, "Do you think we should have a baby?"

Piper was astonished.

"What are you talking about?"

"It's sort of self-explanatory. Doesn't all this shit at Dibbets make you realize what matters? We love each other. We should be a family. We should have children."

After a few moments she said, not looking at Peter, but studying the skylight in the ceiling: "Are you asking me to marry you?"

"We don't have to get married. Lots of people who have babies aren't married. Marriage doesn't matter anymore."

"Marriage does matter."

Piper had never thought much about having children. She knew motherhood would be bad for her legal career. The men who ran law firms thought women with babies were not serious. Mothers didn't want to stay late at the office. Before long, they wanted to work part-time. They couldn't be counted on in a crisis.

There were several childless women in their late forties or fifties at Dibbets. They had made the sacrifice, but their careers had not been particularly successful. Why success had eluded them was hard to say. They had become brittle and aggressive. Perhaps they knew they had made a mistake. Perhaps they realized they had gambled and lost.

• • •

About an hour later they were walking hand-in-hand along Quai des Grands-Augustins, in the late afternoon sun, toward the Pont des Arts. They turned onto the pedestrian bridge and there, in front of them, on the other side of the Seine, was the Louvre.

"Is there anything more beautiful?" said Piper.

On the railings of the bridge, running its whole length on both sides, were thousands of padlocks of different sizes and designs, each with a romantic message and a date written or engraved on it. Some messages were simple–"Philip loves Cynthia." Others were more elaborate, with tiny writing meandering across the lock's surface.

"I've read about this," said Peter. "Love padlocks. You lock one on the railing and throw the key in the river. Then you are bound together forever."

"Or until city workers come with wire cutters and cut the padlocks off and take them to the municipal dump," said Piper.

"Just a minute,' Peter said, and went back to a street vendor's stall where the bridge met the Quai. A few minutes later he came back with a bronze padlock. Written on it in black felt pen was "Peter loves Piper" and the date. The stall-keeper had supplied a pen. He locked it to the railing and threw the key in the Seine. They walked across the bridge to the Louvre.

"We should find somewhere to eat," said Peter.

Piper's cell phone rang. It was in her purse. She fumbled for it.

"You should have turned that fucking thing off," said Peter. "Don't answer it."

"Lawyers answer the telephone when it rings." She pulled the phone from her purse. "Piper Fantouche speaking."

"Ms. Fantouche, it's Detective Sergeant Sebastian Vitanza of Toronto Homicide. I got this number from your secretary. You're in Paris, right, since this morning, with a friend?"

"Yes."

"I assume you know that your firm's managing partner, Jim Watt, was found dead yesterday morning."

"Yes."

"Ms. Fantouche, we'd like to talk to you. When are you back in Toronto?"

"I don't know. In a few days. Next week."

"I need to know when, Ms. Fantouche. And it should be sooner rather than later."

"I haven't booked a return flight yet."

"Perhaps you'd book one. I suggest Monday. Call me at 416-808-7400 to confirm your time of arrival. We can meet on Tuesday, at your office if that's convenient."

"Detective, is that really necessary? It's Friday. We've just arrived here. We're on holiday."

"I'm sorry, but this is a murder investigation, and we need to talk to you. Where are you staying in Paris?"

"It's called Hotel St. Germain." She added: "On the Left Bank."

That's a coincidence, thought Vitanza. He'd stayed at that hotel on his one trip to Paris, more than ten years ago. He had taken his girlfriend, Alessandra, his first real girlfriend after his divorce from Octavia, to Europe for ten days. It was a wonderful time, or so it seemed to him. But when they got back to Toronto, she said she didn't

want to see him anymore. She didn't explain why. She just said that their relationship was over. Vitanza never understood what had happened. But, he still remembered Paris, and particularly Hotel St. Germain, with considerable fondness.

"I know that hotel," said Vitanza. "A good choice. Call me when you've booked your flight. I'll see you on Tuesday. Goodbye, Ms. Fantouche."

Vitanza hung up. Piper put the phone back in her purse. Peter was staring at her.

"What's that all about? What's going on?"

"That was a detective investigating Jim Watt's death. He wants to talk to me. He wants me to go back to Toronto on Monday."

"We just got here!"

"I think I have to go back. I have to cooperate with the police. It was a mistake for me to come here."

"But we've just arrived."

"We've got the weekend. Let's make the most of it."

Chapter Sixteen
IQ84

It was Sunday morning. Vitanza and Singh were sitting in the small boardroom that Vitanza liked to call his command post. It was quiet on the thirty-eighth floor. The occasional associate wandered about holding a file folder, hoping to bump into a senior partner who would recognize him, but if you were a senior partner the chances are you were home in bed, or teeing off at the Rosedale Golf Club, or playing a game of doubles at the Toronto Lawn Tennis Club.

"This is a very bad idea," Bill Seldom had said to Mark Steiner, "letting the police onto the thirty-eighth floor, letting them take over a boardroom. Clients come in for meetings and see policemen. What will they think?"

"They'll think the police are investigating a murder that was reported on the front page of the Toronto Star, that's what they'll think." There's something wrong with Seldom, thought Steiner. He says the stupidest things.

Vitanza and Singh were dressed casually, Vitanza in ill-fitting dark blue jeans, a black T-shirt and an old brown sports jacket, and Singh, formally inclined and fastidious even on a Sunday morning, in slim-cut corduroy

pants, a white shirt and a smart grey jacket. The morning sun streamed in through the floor-to-ceiling windows. Vitanza sprawled in a grey leather office chair. Singh sat primly at the boardroom table, his hands folded in front of him.

"So, Mohan, what do we know?" Vitanza casually swivelled back and forth in his chair. "Who have you talked to? What have you learnt?"

"I've interviewed a lot of people–secretaries, paralegals, articling students. None of them seem to know anything. All of them say they're shocked, dumbfounded, can't imagine who could have done it, that sort of thing. None of them liked Jim Watt. That's about it. They're a dull lot, these people."

"What about Operation Banking Freedom? Has anyone said anything about that?"

"Most of them mentioned it, but no one seems to know much about it. Big deal, very important, they all knew that. Lots of billable hours. They all said that."

"Did they know that something had gone wrong with it?"

"No one mentioned it." Singh rubbed his eyes. He looked exhausted. "What about you?" he asked Vitanza. "Got anything?"

"Not much. I've talked to some of the lawyers who were working on the deal. Not all of them, yet. I'm trying to piece it together. Not easy. It's complicated." Vitanza pulled his notebook out and flipped through some pages. "Julia Anderson. I interviewed her first. Interesting woman. Smart. Good-looking. Not sure what to make of Julia." He flipped through more pages. "Agatha Hightower, same thing. These women don't seem to fit.

They're not the kind of people you'd expect to find in a place like this. Mind you, I don't really know what to expect. I don't understand these big law firms, who works here, how the people deal with each other, what they want. Anyhow, I didn't learn anything from Anderson and Hightower. But I may go back to them."

"We don't seem to be getting anywhere," said Singh gloomily, his eyes half shut. He hardly moved.

Vitanza peered at his notebook. "Then there's a funny little guy called Darrell Jones. Mostly he wanted me to know that he was the smartest guy in any room he happened to be in, smarter than me for sure. A useless jerk, in my opinion."

"No progress, no progress" said Singh, looking distractedly out of the window at the lake below dotted with white sails. He wished he were out there sailing, not that he knew how. Perhaps he should take lessons. He needed a hobby, a way of relaxing.

"Tomorrow I'm meeting with Mark Steiner, and somebody called Bill Seldom," said Vitanza. "Then there's a woman called Piper Fantouche, who went to Paris with her boyfriend right after Watt was killed, which I find interesting. She's coming back to Toronto tomorrow – I called her in Paris and told her to come back, which didn't make her happy. I'll interview her on Tuesday. You should be there. Something might come out of it."

They were both silent for a few moments. "I'd like to know why Piper Fantouche went to Paris," said Vitanza.

Singh stopped gazing out of the window and looked at him. "Piper Fantouche is a strange name," Singh said.

"Yes, it is."

They fell silent again.

"Do you have a theory about what happened?" asked Singh, after a few moments.

"Not yet," said Vitanza. "I need to understand the world of Dibbets first. What happened may have something to do with Operation Banking Freedom. I just don't know. But it's got to be about Dibbets and what they do here. The murder *came out* of Dibbets, if you see what I mean."

"When are we going to visit the grieving widow?"

"Tomorrow, after the Steiner meeting. We'll go together. Something to look forward to." Vitanza looked at his watch. "It's noon, Mohan. You seem kind of gloomy. Why don't I take you to lunch?"

"Thanks."

"There's a place across the street that looked open."

Vitanza and Singh went across the street to Mario's. Mario was there. He was there seven days a week, lunch and dinner, every day except Christmas Day, the only day the restaurant closed. Mario had been shocked by what had happened at Dibbets. For years Jim Watt had been his best customer. Now Watt was dead, possibly murdered. It was hard enough to lose a reliable patron in such circumstances, but it wasn't just about Watt. There were the attractive women he often brought in for lunch and dinner, adding a touch of glamour to what Cynthia Wine, once the Toronto Star restaurant reviewer, had described as a gloomy old-fashioned faux bistro serving lousy food to fat stockbrokers. Mario knew that those attractive women wouldn't be coming in by themselves for a martini and well-done rib eye steak.

Who were the two men who had just wandered into his restaurant, wondered Mario, and what were they

doing downtown on a Sunday? They didn't look like Bay Streeters. Too casually dressed, for one thing, even for a Sunday. Although, to Mario's regret, sartorial standards on the Street had lately slipped badly. Some lawyers and accountants – even investment bankers–almost never wore a tie, and sometimes could be seen in jeans. Mario was old school: three-piece pinstriped suit from Harry Rosen with a white handkerchief carefully arranged in his jacket's breast pocket, and highly-polished black shoes.

"This way gentlemen." Mario took Vitanza and Singh to a booth in the back and gave them each a menu. A waiter came a few minutes later to take their order. "Steak," said Vitanza, "with fries. And a nine-ounce glass of cabernet sauvignon." Sometimes Vitanza threw caution to the winds at lunch. "Chicken Caesar salad," said Singh. "And a glass of water."

"So, Mohan, what's bothering you?" asked Vitanza. They had worked together for two years, and liked each other, but were not friends. Neither confided in the other. It was the first time Vitanza had ever asked Mohan a question like this, and he didn't expect much of an answer.

"I'm tired. I haven't been sleeping well lately."

"The job?"

"No, no, nothing to do with the job. I love the job. It's what happens after the job that's the problem." He wanted to say that he felt bored and lonely in the evenings, but that would be telling Vitanza too much.

"You need a girlfriend," said Vitanza. He knew Mohan didn't date much. He was pretty sure that he wasn't gay. He had often wondered why Mohan didn't go out, why he stayed at home just about every evening, and, so far as

anybody knew, cooked himself a simple meal, and then spent hours reading a book. At the moment, Mohan was reading The Bird Artist by Howard Norman. He liked it very much. Before that he'd read The Cat's Table by Michael Ondaatje.

Mohan thought it ironic that Vitanza would tell him he needed a girlfriend. Everyone at the station said the same thing about Vitanza. Vitanza had dated from time-to-time, they all knew that. Some even remembered that woman he'd taken to Paris years ago; Vitanza had been very keen on her. But nothing seemed to work out, and Singh and the others suspected there were long periods when Vitanza stayed home at night and heated up convenience meals for himself and watched Dancing with the Stars. Mohan didn't have a television.

"Anyway," said Vitanza, "it's none of my business."

That's right, Mohan thought.

"But any time you want to talk..."

"Thanks, Sebastian, I appreciate it. Everything's okay, really."

Lunch came. Vitanza ate his steak with enjoyment, drank his wine quickly and ordered another glass. Singh picked at his Chicken Caesar, moving the croutons to the side of the plate and removing the skin from the pieces of chicken.

"I just don't get these big law firms," said Vitanza, shovelling French fries into his mouth. "How do they work? Who runs them? Jim Watt was the managing partner. Did that make him the boss? I don't know. What about Mark Steiner, who calls himself the chairman? What does 'chairman' mean?" He emptied his second

glass of wine, thought of ordering a third, but decided against it.

"I've no idea," said Singh. "But I can tell you this. The secretaries and paralegals and articling students are terrified of the partners, and do anything they say. There are about three hundred partners, so how the hell does that work? Three hundred people telling everyone what to do, issuing conflicting instructions. Not a recipe for success, I would have thought."

"It may be chaotic, but as far as I can tell they're making a shitload of money. Something is working right."

"Could the murder be about money?" said Singh. "Maybe we should find out who earns what, see if someone gets more money with Watt dead. Or does someone profit in some other way, maybe taking over one of Watt's big clients, or getting his seat on the bank board. Several of the people I talked said the board seat was pretty big stuff."

"By the way," said Vitanza. "The forensic report – I got it yesterday, I should have showed it to you–makes clear that it was murder. No surprise there. Struck on the head violently. His head was actually split open. But they're not sure about the murder weapon. It almost looks like an axe wound, but not exactly. Some kind of cleaver, the kind of thing you find in the kitchen. Dibbets has a kitchen, I think. Also, there was a bad scratch on his right cheek and a bruise on his forehead. And yes, you're right about looking into the money and clients and all that."

"My sense of it is that at Dibbets status is at least as important as money," said Singh. "It's not just money that matters. That's why that board seat might be important."

They ordered cappuccinos. "I don't feel much like going back to Dibbets this afternoon," said Vitanza. "There's a game on TV. I could do with a nap. I'd like to think things over. This is the worst cappuccino I've ever had." He remembered that he had an appointment with Dr. Abramowitz tomorrow and was glad of it. Maybe Abramowitz knew something about big law firms. He had to have a lot of clients who were lawyers.

"It's terrible," said Singh, pushing his coffee cup away. "I'd be happy to go home too." I could finish The Bird Artist, he was thinking, and start the new Murakami.

The waiter brought the bill. Vitanza threw cash on the table.

"Let's get out of here. I'll see you tomorrow. We're meeting Steiner at nine, and then you and I are going to call on Mrs. Watt." His appointment with Abramowitz was at three o'clock. He should be through with Steiner and Mrs. Watt by then, easily.

"Okay, boss."

"Don't call me 'boss.'"

They left the restaurant. Mario watched them go. Vitanza flagged a taxi. It was a nice day, and Singh decided to walk home.

• • •

On Sunday night, Piper and Peter went for dinner to Les Editeurs, a restaurant recommended by the young woman in black with the red glass frames at the hotel reception desk. The restaurant walls were lined with books. The chairs were upholstered in red leather. There was a large wall clock at one end of the room. The patrons were a mix of tourists and students, with a scattering of studious-looking middle-aged men and women sitting alone

and reading a book or newspaper. Peter ordered steak tartare and a bottle of wine. Piper ordered fried scallops.

"What time is our flight tomorrow morning?" asked Piper. "Eleven thirty. We should leave for the airport around eight."

"I don't even know why we're going back," said Piper.

"Yes you do. Some one has been murdered. The police want to talk to you. Maybe you did it."

"I have nothing to hide."

"Piper, the night he was killed Watt tried to rape you. You have to tell them that. They'll be pretty interested. You'll probably become a suspect." "What about you? You disappeared for two hours when I told you what happened. You ran out yelling, 'I'll kill him.' They'll be pretty interested in that too. You'll be a suspect as well."

"Neither of us killed Watt, said Peter. "We don't have to be afraid."

"Who did kill him?"

"How should I know? But the police will find out."

• • •

Mohan Singh was back in his apartment. He was sitting in his favourite chair by the window. He had just finished The Bird Artist, which he put down on the coffee table with a sigh. It was always sad to finish a very good book. Now he would start on the new Murakami, IQ84. That would be a different kettle of fish.

Chapter Seventeen
Self-Portrait #7

It was nine o'clock on Monday morning. Vitanza and Singh were sitting in Mark Steiner's corner office. Steiner was rocking back and forth in a high-backed chair at his big oak desk. It was a large desk and made Steiner, a small man, look as if he was hiding behind a piece of furniture. There wasn't much on the desk, just a pipe rack containing several battered pipes, an old-fashioned wooden in-tray that was empty, and a copy of the Income Tax Act bound in blinding red. Odd about the pipes, thought Vitanza. The city had prohibited smoking in offices years ago.

Steiner's office was decorated in a traditional way except for one startling thing. On the wall facing his desk hung a large oil painting of female buttocks, painted in garish orange against a red background. This was one of Fumiko Nakajima's famous series of self-portraits. All eighteen portraits in the series were of Nakajima's buttocks, painted from different angles, presumably using mirrors, and in different colours. A few years ago there had been an exhibition called "Nakajima: Self-Portraits" at the Pompidou Centre in Paris. Steiner had been in

Paris at the time, visited the Pompidou Centre, liked the paintings, and had gone out of his way to acquire one after the exhibition closed. It was "Self-Portrait #7" and had been very expensive. He hung it in his office. At first, it was on the wall behind his desk. If you went to see Steiner, sitting opposite him, you could not avoid looking at Self-Portrait #7. But, after hearing indirectly about complaints from young women associates, he moved the painting to the more discreet place where it now hung. Steiner didn't like to offend people if he could help it.

"I thought it was a good idea to have Julia here," Steiner said to Vitanza. Julia Anderson was sitting in one of Steiner's comfortable paisley-upholstered wing chairs. "She was part of the Operation Banking Freedom team and can give you first hand information, which I imagine is what you want. And she's a corporate lawyer, she knows all the ins and outs. I just do tax. Detective Vitanza, I think you've met Julia."

Vitanza was happy to see her. It had occurred to him that he might ask her out when the investigation was over. That is, if she wasn't the murderer. But asking her out might be a little tricky. There could be some kind of ethical issue. These days everyone watched the police and criticized them at the drop of a hat. You had to be careful if you didn't want some civil rights group, or the press, raking you over the coals.

"Nice to see you again," Vitanza said, smiling at her from behind his droopy moustache. "Have you met Detective Singh?" He waved in Singh's general direction.

"Hello, Detective Vitanza" said Julia. "A pleasure to meet you, Detective Singh." Singh inclined his turbaned head.

"So," said Vitanza to Steiner, "we're here for a primer on Operation Banking Freedom. I'm particularly interested in what went wrong."

"Can I ask first how the investigation is going?" said Steiner. "There are a lot of nervous people around here who want to know what happened to Jim Watt."

"I understand," said Vitanza. "But I have nothing to tell you right now. It's still early days in the investigation."

"When do you think there'll be progress?"

"Impossible to say. In the meantime, it would help if you explained OBF to us. Can I call it OBF? Operation Banking Freedom is a mouthful. Awkward to keep saying it."

"Okay," said Steiner. He took a pipe out of the rack on his desk and fiddled with it. "I'll do my best. Julia will tell me if I get anything wrong. But, you understand, Detective Vitanza, I have to be careful what I say. Solicitor-client privilege applies. There are things I can't tell you. And OBF is fine. I don't know why we didn't think of calling it that before. Much easier." Steiner put the empty pipe in his mouth and chewed on the stem, looking at Self-Portrait #7. Then, he carefully placed the pipe back in the rack. Vitanza decided not to argue about solicitor-client privilege, not just yet.

"Three months ago, Canadian Unity Bank decided to acquire Liberty Insurance," Steiner began. "It was a personal project of Arthur Red, the bank's chairman, who was very enthusiastic, you might almost say passionate, about it. There were regulatory problems – limits on a bank's involvement in the insurance industry, that sort of thing – but we thought they could be worked around. Liberty is a public company, so CUB had to make a

public takeover bid. That's a complicated thing. CUB asked Dibbets to take the project on, and Jim Watt, who sat on CUB's board, and was a banking lawyer, a very experienced one, put a working group together."

"How would Watt have chosen the members of the working group?" asked Vitanza.

"He would have picked partners with the right expertise, ones he trusted and had worked with before. People like Julia."

"The right expertise, you say. Like what?"

"A deal like that needs a wide range of skills. Corporate, securities, regulatory, real estate, competition, tax – the lot. It would have been a big and complicated transaction."

"Were you the tax member of the group?"

Steiner looked uncomfortable. He picked another pipe from the rack and examined it closely. "Watt asked me to look after that side, but the whole thing went off the rails before tax advice was seriously needed, so I wasn't really involved."

Vitanza pulled out his notebook and a battered plastic ballpoint pen and wrote something down.

"So, obviously the working group would know everything about OBF, but who else would know about it?"

"Other people in the office, junior lawyers, secretaries. People at Liberty; there was a meeting with senior executives of Liberty. People in the bank, of course. I've told you all this before. I gave you a list."

"I know you've told me before, but please tell me again. Who else would have known something?" Vitanza was writing in his notebook. The pen was leaking and there were spots of blue ink on his hand.

"In a deal like this we take a lot of trouble to preserve confidentiality. You can't control everything, and sometimes rumours get started, but we do everything we can to keep the whole thing under wraps."

"Did people working on the deal sign confidentiality agreements?" asked Singh. He'd read about confidentiality agreements.

"Everyone involved was a professional," replied Steiner. "We didn't need confidentiality agreements."

"What about investment bankers?" asked Vitanza. "Aren't they usually involved in these takeover bids?"

"That was true once upon a time," said Steiner. "But things have changed. Investment bankers used to charge millions. They'd get paid much more than lawyers for doing much less. It made a lot of people uncomfortable, but in a big deal, with hundreds of millions floating around, who's going to miss a million here, a million there. But when Lehman Brothers collapsed in 2008, a lot of people woke up and said, whoa, do we really need these guys? They don't care about their clients, they rip them off, they even secretly bet against them. Suddenly investment bankers became dispensable. That's fine with me."

"Okay," said Vitanza. "Let's go back a bit. CUB is going to launch a takeover bid for Liberty. Suddenly the whole thing collapses. Why?"

"Two reasons," said Steiner. "First, the Liberty share price suddenly shot through the roof, making it much more expensive to acquire the company than CUB had expected."

"How much more expensive?" asked Singh.

"A lot more expensive. Second, there was a suspicion that the sudden jump in price was because of insider

trading, which is illegal of course. The Exchange halted trading. The bid couldn't proceed, at least for the moment. Everybody involved got skittish and ran the other way."

"Was there insider trading?" asked Vitanza.

"Maybe. "

"Who did it?"

Steiner laughed. "Well, detective, I don't know, except for one thing. It wasn't me."

"So the deal collapsed?" asked Singh.

"It was in the process of collapsing," said Steiner. "Then Watt died. That finished it off."

"What are the consequences for Dibbets?" asked Vitanza.

"The firm lost a big transaction, probably the biggest it would have had this year. Several million dollars in legal fees went out the window. That sort of thing upsets the partners. Our relationship with Canadian Unity Bank, our biggest client, is in jeopardy. Relationships among some lawyers in the firm are frayed or worse. The consequences are bad. But Dibbets has been around for a long time and will survive."

"Tell me about the frayed relationships among lawyers."

"I can tell you about that," Julia interjected. "God knows, my relationships are frayed."

"I wasn't thinking of you," said Steiner.

"A law firm like this is a tough place to work," said Julia. "It's full of ambitious people who'll do just about anything for power and money. If everything is going well – if there's lots of high-profile work, lots of billable

hours – then partners will be nice to each other and look happy. But if anything goes wrong, the knives come out."

Vitanza looked at Steiner. "Do you agree? Is that what happens?"

Steiner knew he had to be careful. This was a murder investigation. He didn't want the police to think that Dibbets was full of people who would kill a colleague to get ahead. "Well," he said slowly, "I agree with Julia to some extent. Big Law is tough. It's competitive and can be uncomfortable. But, you're talking about smart grownups. The idea that they'll do anything at all for power and money is just plain silly. Although, Julia is right about one thing. As we say around here, the only happy partnership is the profitable partnership. If money becomes a problem, there's trouble."

"Let me tell you something, Detective Vitanza, that will help you understand what it's like," said Julia. "My neck's been bothering me lately. It's stiff, and its sore. Somebody says, try acupuncture. So I go to an acupuncturist, who asks what I do for a living. When I tell him I'm a lawyer on Bay Street, he says he's not surprised. He says, I've treated a lot of Bay Street lawyers with stiff necks. He calls it lawyer neck. You want to know what it's like being a lawyer in a firm like this? It makes your neck stiff and sore. It gives you lawyer neck."

"Something else," said Steiner, getting into the spirit of things. "When I joined Dibbets, thirty years ago, a partner was a partner, and a partner was loyal to the firm, and the firm was loyal to a partner. That's not true now, and more's the pity."

"Explain this to me," said Vitanza.

"Once, partners were more or less equal. Some made more money than others, but partners regarded each other as equally important and there was mutual respect. Now, we have stars, rainmakers, lawyers with big clients – they're important – and we have service partners who do the work and actually know some law – they're not important. Service partners are a commodity and no one cares about them. A star can make ten times what a service partner makes. Guess what effect that has on morale and relationships and ethics and loyalty."

"Ethics?"

"In the old days, you knew every partner. If someone was heading for trouble, you spotted it early on and tried to put him on the right track. And no one became a partner unless you were sure about him. Now, nobody knows who anybody is and nobody cares as long as the money rolls in."

"Loyalty?"

"When I came here," continued Steiner, "if you became a partner, you were a partner for life. No one was ever fired. And no one left to join the law firm across the street because they were offered more money. The only way to become a partner was to join as an articling student and work your way through the ranks, by which time everyone knew you very well and knew if they wanted you as a partner. Now the place is a revolving door. Partners come and go. Become unproductive, for whatever reason, even if you're ill – it doesn't matter why–and you're out. You work across the street, and want to become a partner of Dibbets? Just wave a big book of business in our face and we'll hire you and pay a lot for

the privilege. It doesn't matter that we don't really know who you are."

Vitanza made another note in his book. It occurred to him that Steiner's outburst might be the key to Watt's murder.

"Maybe just now I got a bit carried away," said Steiner. "But I remember the way things used to be, and I miss it."

"I understand," said Vitanza. "One more question. I'm almost embarrassed to ask it. It makes me sound like a detective in a bad movie. Who stands to benefit from Watt's death?"

"Whoever becomes managing partner," said Julia. "Whoever takes the Dibbets seat on the CUB board. Whoever becomes the relationship partner for the bank."

"That's about right," said Steiner. "Although, I have to say, none of those jobs is easy. And I don't know if we're going to need a relationship partner for the bank any more."

• • •

When the meeting with Steiner was over, Vitanza and Singh set off in Vitanza's Buick to visit Amanda Watt.

"What did you think of Steiner?" Singh asked Vitanza.

"First of all, my friend," said Vitanza, "what did you think of Steiner's picture? Pretty strange thing for a Bay Street lawyer to have a picture of a woman's ass hanging in his office, wouldn't you say?"

"Steiner may be more complicated than he seems," said Singh.

"As for Steiner's rant about how a Bay Street law firm used to be and what it's like now, I'm very interested in what he said. But I'm surprised that he let it rip like that.

I would have put Mark Steiner down as a pretty cool customer, and there was nothing cool about him this morning. Mohan, you're avoiding my question. Did you like the picture or not?"

Chapter Eighteen
#5 High Park Gardens

"Where the hell is number five High Park Gardens?" said Vitanza, peering over the steering wheel, first right and then left. He didn't know Toronto's west end very well. He was a downtown guy. Singh was looking at a crumpled map that he'd found in the Buick's glove compartment. Vitanza refused to use a GPS. He'd read too many stories about travelers sent down a disused logging road and found dead in their car the following spring. "It's got to be here somewhere," Vitanza said, turning on to a treed street lined with large houses. "What does the map say?"

"Over there," said Singh, pointing to a large red brick house on a corner lot. "There it is. Number five." Vitanza pulled the Buick over and parked behind a new BMW with personalized licence plates–IWKFRU. What the fuck does that mean, he wondered? Vitanza disliked vanity plates. His aversion was excessive, he realized that. He wondered if he should talk to Dr. Abramovitz about it.

Number five reminded Mohan Singh of his childhood home in Rosedale. It was a Georgian-style house with three stories and a lot of windows. There was a red

front door with a big brass knocker. A flagstone path leading to the entrance was flanked by a lawn of exactly the right shade of green. Large flowerbeds were carefully cultivated. The house signalled that its occupants were prosperous people who paid attention to detail. Vitanza ignored the ornate knocker and rapped on the front door with his bare knuckles. It hurt; why had he done that? A dog barked inside the house. There was no other sound. Vitanza knocked again, this time using the knocker. He heard steps. An attractive woman of about forty opened the door. She was dressed in sombre colours and wore no jewellery or makeup. A brown standard poodle standing at her side looked inquisitively at the two men. "Can I help you?" she said.

"I'm Detective Sebastian Vitanza of the Toronto Police Department, and this is Detective Mohan Singh."

"You're here about my husband," said the woman. "I'm Amanda Watt. Please come in."

She held the door open. Vitanza and Singh went into the spacious entrance hall. The walls were painted off white. The floor was of large Spanish-looking red tiles, slightly irregular in shape. On the left, as you faced the back of the house, was a closed door and, beyond it, at the foyer's far end, a wide staircase of dark oak. On the right, double doors opened into a spacious sitting room. The only furniture in the hallway was a side table with a vase of fresh flowers on it and a tall-backed chair with an embroidered red cushion. A large pile of unopened letters sat on the table, next to the vase. Flower petals had fallen on the envelopes.

Amanda Watt led Vitanza and Singh into the sitting room, her heels clicking loudly on the foyer's tiles. The

sitting room was large and full of light. The furniture and decorations suggested an expensive interior decorator had been there recently. The room seemed ready for a photo shoot. She waved to a sofa perpendicular to one side of a Georgian-style fireplace. Vitanza and Singh perched on it. She sat in a grey leather chair on the other side of the fireplace, facing them, separated from the sofa by a low glass coffee table. On the table was a paperback, Heart So White by Javier Marias. Next to the book was a green soapstone Eskimo sculpture of a whale coming up to spout. The poodle curled up on a rug in front of the fireplace and went to sleep.

Amanda looked at them. She sat very still. She waited.

"First," said Vitanza, "let me offer you condolences on the death of your husband. I'm sorry for your loss." Vitanza hated that phrase, although he'd used it many times.

She said nothing.

"We know it's a terrible time for you. The last thing you want to do is talk to us. But you appreciate that when someone dies the way your husband died, the police have to make enquiries."

"I understand," said Amanda. After a moment's hesitation, she continued: "You say, the way your husband died. How did he die? I know very little. Just a few facts from the uniformed policemen who came to give me the news. I haven't read the newspapers. I couldn't face it. I've heard gossip, of course. Friends have telephoned." She spoke very slowly.

"Trauma to the head," said Vitanza. "It's possible your husband fell and hit his head on the edge of his desk, but

we don't think so. It looks like someone hit him with a sharp object. The wound was a deep one."

"Murder," said Amanda.

"You have two children?" asked Singh.

"Yes. Tory is fourteen and Blake recently had his eleventh birthday. They're at school now. I thought it best to try and keep things as normal as possible. You can imagine what this is like for them. I won't let newspapers in the house, but their friends at school know all about what happened and ask them about it. They come home in tears. Particularly Blake. He is autistic. He goes to a special school."

"How long were you and your husband married?" asked Vitanza.

"We got married almost exactly twenty years ago, when he was a junior partner at Dibbets. We got married at St. John's Anglican Church. It was a big wedding. A lot of Jim's clients came. We went to Maui for our honeymoon."

"Was your marriage a happy one?"

Amanda looked at him for a moment before she spoke. "Are you married, Detective Vitanza?"

"No, regrettably not."

"If you get married, you will discover that marriage is a complicated business."

This was interesting, thought Vitanza. He'd like to know more about Amanda Watt's views on marriage. He agreed that marriage was a complicated business.

"If I may ask, Mrs. Watt, in what way was your marriage a complicated business?"

"Let me say, I don't understand what my marriage to Jim has got to do with your investigation."

"We need to know as much about your husband and his life as possible," said Vitanza. "Everything is relevant at this stage, including things that may appear irrelevant."

I like that, Singh thought. Everything is relevant including what may appear irrelevant. Vitanza is very smart.

"All right, Detective, what would you like to know about my marriage?" The poodle stirred and looked up at the two men on the couch.

"Was your husband faithful?" That was always the big question in a case like this. Vitanza thought it best to ask the question bluntly, not beat around the bush. He could tell a lot from the way a wife reacted to this inquiry. But from Amanda there was very little reaction. Perhaps a slight flushing of her neck and cheeks, a touch of rising red. She put her hands in her lap.

"You can never be sure," she said, "but I think the answer is yes. He looked at other women, of course, but all men do that."

"He looked at other women in general, or at one woman in particular?"

"In general. I would be surprised, Detective Vitanza, if you don't do the same thing, look at a pretty woman walking down the street."

"I think I can confess to that." Vitanza smiled. "Was there a woman at the office," he continued, "someone at Dibbets, that your husband might have been particularly interested in? Someone he worked with?"

"I think I've answered that. My husband was a highly regarded lawyer. He was the managing partner of his firm. He was a respectable member of society. He was a

caring husband and father. He went to church regularly. He was a decent and honest man."

"I'm sure all that is true," said Vitanza. Time, he thought, to take a different tack.

"Mrs. Watt, what sort of place is Dibbets, from your point of view?"

"What do you mean, what sort of place?"

"Detective Singh and I haven't had much experience with big law firms. We need to understand how they work. Perhaps you can explain it to us."

"How they work? What do you mean?"

"Well, for example, your husband was the managing partner. I'm assuming that means he was the chief executive officer. Or, to put it more simply, he was the boss."

Amanda smiled slightly. "You really don't understand big law firms, do you? A law firm like Dibbets doesn't have a boss. Jim wasn't the boss. No one is the boss at a place like Dibbets."

"But there's hundreds of people who work there. It has offices across the country. Outside the country as well, I believe. Somebody must run things."

"The partners run things."

"How many partners are there?"

"I'm not sure. About three hundred, I think."

"Mrs. Watt, I don't see how three hundred people can run anything."

"Detective, let me explain, although please remember that I only saw Dibbets through my husband's eyes. First of all, the firm is divided into partners and employees. Associate lawyers are employees. Paralegals are employees. Professional managers are employees. Secretaries are

employees. It goes without saying that the employees don't run the firm. They're employees."

"Okay, so that leaves the partners. All three hundred of them."

"A partner will tell you that he is the equal of any other partner, but that's not true. There are junior partners. They may impress their girlfriends or parents with big talk and business cards, but to all intents and purposes junior partners are employees as well. They don't get to decide anything that matters."

"How many of the three hundred are junior partners?"

"Maybe about a hundred, perhaps a bit more. Junior partnership is, shall we say, a fluid concept. There are more junior partners than will admit to it."

"So we're left with two hundred or so who, you say, run the show. It's still a lot of people. It doesn't take two hundred people to run anything, not even China."

"There are elected committees," Amanda said, "elected by the partners, an executive committee, a finance committee, the compensation committee, that sort of thing. The executive committee appoints the managing partner. But the important point is, when most partners vote on anything, including electing committees, most of them vote the way they're told."

"Who tells them how to vote?"

"Page one partners."

"What's a page one partner?"

"Some one on the first page of the compensation list. That's the list of who gets what percentage of the firm's profit. The bigger the percentage you get, the higher up the list you are. Those on page one get the most money. They have the most power. The compensation committee

reapportions profits every two years. The list changes. That's a tense time, as I'm sure you can imagine."

"How many pages does the compensation list have?"

"A lot."

"How do you get to be a page one partner?" asked Vitanza.

"Bring a lot of money into the firm. Control a big client. Better yet, control a big client that you brought to the firm; if you do that, you're king shit. It's about money, all about money."

"That's very helpful," said Vitanza. He was surprised to hear Amanda say "king shit."

"There's one other thing," said Amanda. "Occasionally there's a sort of throwback to the old days when it wasn't just money that mattered. Jim told me recently that he'd been to see a junior partner who'd stupidly got in a tricky situation. Jim told him that he'd behaved badly. The partner said, 'you think that, but I don't agree. You're a partner, but so am I. You're entitled to your opinion and I'm entitled to mine.' So, you see, sometimes, when it suits, there's a pretence of traditional partnership, but it's only a pretence."

"An interesting word to use," said Singh. "Pretence."

"A pretence of partnership," repeated Amanda.

"Mrs. Watt," Vitanza said, "just a couple of final, routine things. First, can you think of anyone who would want to kill your husband?"

"No."

"And, as I say, just routine, but can you tell us where you were last Wednesday night?"

Amanda smiled. "I was waiting for that question. I'm glad you didn't disappoint me, detective. I was here all

the time with the children. They would confirm that, if you care to ask them."

"I don't think that will be necessary," said Vitanza. He stood up. "Thank you for your time, Mrs. Watt. And, again, our sympathies on your loss." He hated that phrase.

"I hope to see you again, Detective Vitanza," said Amanda, and gave him a nice smile.

Chapter Nineteen
Trinacria

Vitanza went directly home after his session with Dr. Abramowitz. Why did Saul always want to talk about what happened with Octavia? That was more than fifteen years ago. He hadn't seen his ex-wife since the divorce. He didn't even know where she lived – out West, someone had told him, maybe Calgary. He was sick of talking about her. And Saul always asked why he didn't see more of his father and his brothers and sisters. There was no reason for it. He loved them, but he didn't have to visit all the time. Saul looked dubious when he heard this. Maybe he should stop seeing Abramowitz. But he should probably wait until he felt better.

Vitanza lived in a low-rise cooperative apartment building in south Rosedale near the ravine, just north of Bloor Street. It had been built in the 1950s and in those days had been the height of elegance. There was a broad undulating concrete canopy over the entrance, sheltering part of a sweeping drive, allowing taxis to pick up and discharge passengers comfortably in bad weather. Well-maintained gardens surrounded the building, giving it a refined and bucolic air. Once, Toronto socialites had

lived here, but that crowd had long since moved on to more glamorous and modern buildings, leaving only one or two aging dowagers behind. Now the inhabitants were retired radio producers and University of Toronto professors emeriti, although a distinguished psychiatrist lived and worked in a large first-floor suite; his well-known patients could be seen coming in and out of a back entrance, trying to be as discreet as possible, looking away if anybody recognized them. Vitanza had bought his place seven years ago for two hundred thousand dollars, which at the time had seemed like a lot of money. It was worth a good bit more than that today.

His one bedroom apartment on the third floor overlooked the ravine. Vitanza liked to sit on the balcony and look at the trees and imagine that he was in Sicily, although he only had the vaguest idea of what Sicily looked like; he had left the island as a young child and had never gone back. The apartment was neat, and well furnished, with good classical prints on the walls and books neatly arranged on long shelves. On the wall facing his favourite chair was a large carving of a trinacria, the symbol of Sicily, three bent legs, with the head of Medusa and three ears of wheat in the middle. The apartment ceilings were a bit low, and the bathroom and galley kitchen were antiquated, but Vitanza didn't mind. He was comfortable in this place. Maybe it was odd that a policeman from Italy had ended up in this building, among people who were very different from him—establishment intellectuals, retired professionals, ancient media celebrities who had faded from public view—but Vitanza thought of it as good fortune.

He parked the Buick in the underground garage and took the elevator up to the third floor. As soon as he was in his apartment, he checked for telephone messages, always the first thing he did when he got home. There were none today, which wasn't unusual. He went into the kitchen, took a bottle of Famous Grouse scotch from a cupboard, half-filled a small glass, put two ice cubes in the glass, and topped it up with water from the kitchen tap. He went to his favourite chair, a wingback by the door to the balcony, put his drink on the side table next to it, loosened his tie, and sat down. For a couple of minutes, he remained almost motionless, looking at the trinacria on the wall opposite. Then he took a sip of scotch, pulled out his notebook and looked at his recent scribblings.

Twenty minutes later he went and got another glass of Famous Grouse. He was getting a buzz from the liquor. He put a CD in the player, Oscar Peterson's "Live at the Blue Note." Vitanza liked jazz, particularly jazz piano. He went back to the wing chair and looked though his notes again, but half his brain was following Oscar's exquisite styling. Vitanza thought, through a haze of liquor and music, that the clue to the murder might be in what Mark Steiner and Amanda Watt had told him. There was a pathology of ambition and greed at Dibbets that could have extreme consequences. Or was that an over-simplification, just the drumming of the Famous Grouse? After all, if ambition and greed led to murder, Bay Street would be stacked with corpses ten feet deep. And it was all very well to say there was a pathology at Dibbets that made murder possible, but who was the murderer? He had to catch a person, not describe a disease.

He felt hungry. Normally Vitanza had pasta or fish for dinner. Although he paid no attention to what he had in restaurants, and never bothered much about breakfast, he was a careful eater when he ate at home in the evening. He rummaged in his kitchen cupboards and took out some De Cecco spaghetti, the only store-bought spaghetti that his mother and father would have in the house, a family preference he had adopted. He heated olive oil in a saucepan, sautéed some chopped onions, added chopped fresh garlic, emptied in a can of Marzano tomatoes, and added some salt and pepper, fresh oregano and a little bit of red wine left over from dinner the night before. He put the burner on simmer. The sauce would take about an hour to cook. He poured himself another scotch and went back to his favourite chair.

What about Piper Fantouche? Her flight from Paris must have landed at Pearson Airport by now. He would see her tomorrow. Perhaps he should call her now and make an appointment. No, it could wait until morning. It was odd how she had suddenly left for Paris right after Watt was killed. That wasn't normal behaviour. It wasn't exactly suspicious, not necessarily, but it wasn't normal. It wasn't the kind of thing you expected from a lawyer. Lawyers were such a cautious bunch.

Vitanza was having trouble thinking clearly. The scotch was taking its toll. The Grouse was drumming. He looked at his watch. The spaghetti sauce should be ready in another twenty minutes. He went to the cupboard where he kept his modest wine collection. He looked at what he had – not much was left, time to replenish – and picked a Nero D'Avola. He took his Italian waiter's

corkscrew out of the cutlery drawer and pulled the cork. He checked the sauce. It would be ready soon.

• • •

Piper and Peter were back in Piper's apartment. The flight from Paris had been uneventful. Peter disliked the pods in Executive Class. In the old days, in Executive Class, you and your companion sat side-by-side. You could put a blanket over your laps and easily fondle each other's private parts without upsetting anyone. The stewardesses knew what was going on, but looked the other way. But with these new isolated pods, that was impossible. Whoever had designed the expensive Star Alliance cabins just didn't understand a basic fact of flying across the Atlantic, which was that playing around made the whole travel experience much better. As it was, Peter and Piper sat in separate pods like chickens in battery cages, watching movies on a tiny screen, waving ruefully across the aisle at each other.

They got home about six o'clock. They slumped into chairs in the living room, leaving their luggage in the little hall.

"Want some tea?" Piper asked.

"Thanks. What are we going to do for dinner? When are we going to go to bed? I feel like shit."

"I'll make eggs and bacon later. We shouldn't go to bed too early, otherwise we'll be up in the middle of the night. I've got to see that detective tomorrow. I need to be fresh. He'll want to talk to you too."

"Why would he want to talk to me?"

"We've been over that. He'll want to ask you about me. And when I tell him you left for two hours that

night, yelling 'I'll kill him,' he'll want to know where you went and what you did."

"Why would you tell him all that? Why drag me into this mess?"

"I'm not dragging you into this mess. I'm just going to tell a policeman the truth about what happened, which seems like a good idea. And don't be so concerned about your own ass. I could be a murder suspect, and my legal career has gone up in smoke. A career that has been paying for this apartment that you like so much."

"Look," said Peter, "all we have to do is get through the next few days. The Watt business will soon be history. The police will go away. Everything will get back to normal."

Piper had a headache. Her nose was stuffed up and she was breathing through her mouth. She massaged her temples.

"I'll fix us some eggs and bacon," Piper said, "and then I think you should go and stay at your place. I need to collect my wits. I've got to get ready for the cops."

Peter still had his basement apartment in the west end, although he was seldom there. He often told Piper that it made no sense for him to keep a separate place. The rent was nine hundred dollars a month, not much for Toronto, even for a dump, but a lot for someone who was unemployed and whose modest savings were almost gone. But Piper made it clear that Peter wasn't moving in to her condominium, not yet anyway. "What do you mean, I can't move in?" Peter would say when they had this discussion. "Haven't you noticed, I *have* moved in. I'm here all the time. It's weeks since I slept in the west end. And you even bought me a piano."

"Moving in means your furniture is in the living room, your pictures are on the walls, your socks are in a dresser drawer, and you pay half the expenses. Right now, let's just stick to having your suitcase in the hall. And the piano, by the way, is *for me*."

"What are you talking about? I don't have any pictures and hardly any furniture. I do have socks. And you can't play the piano." Peter pulled out his cell phone and called a taxi. "Never mind about the eggs and bacon," he said. He picked up his suitcase and went out to the front steps to wait for the cab.

Piper ate the eggs and bacon she had cooked for two, reading yesterday's Le Monde that she had brought from Paris. She changed into her pyjamas. She went into the living room and sat in her favourite chair. What was she going to tell Vitanza? She would have to tell him about the attempted rape, even though that would make her a murder suspect. She would have to tell him about Peter's behaviour that night, although that would put him on the list of suspects too. Maybe she needed a lawyer, a criminal defence lawyer. There was that guy who sat next to her at the alumni dinner, Sam Capponi. He had a big reputation. She decided to call Capponi in the morning. It couldn't hurt.

Chapter Twenty
Extreme Fitness

The next morning Piper got to her office a few minutes before nine. Everything seemed normal. People bustled about, apparently intent on important tasks. Smart phones made electronic noises alerting their owners to critical text messages. Legal documents poured from laser printers. Nothing suggested that the firm's managing partner had died a violent death a few days before. The Dibbets landscape remained the same, or so it seemed. The firm's vast legal machine had apparently adjusted to events, and was functioning smoothly.

"Good morning Piper," said Rachel, her assistant. "I didn't expect you back so soon."

"I cut my trip short," said Piper. "The police want to interview me about Jim Watt. A detective called Sebastian Vitanza tracked me down in Paris."

"I gave him your cell number," said Rachel. "He was very insistent. And he just called. He wants to meet with you here at ten. He said there was no need to call him back unless you're not available. He's bringing someone called Mohan Singh with him. How was Paris?"

"I didn't see enough of it."

"It's been awful here," said Rachel. "As you can imagine."

Piper went into her office and shut the door. She sat down behind her desk and looked at a stack of paper mail. She turned on her computer and checked her email inbox. There were hundreds of new messages. When she began practising law, a senior partner told her that a serious lawyer should never take more than a week's holiday at a time. It was too dangerous, he said. You get out of touch. You lose control. You can even lose a client. Never go away for more than a week, he emphasized. It wasn't enough to be available electronically. Physical presence still counted for a lot. Sometimes a client just had to see you in the flesh. Or know that he could if he wanted to.

She turned on Chart-the-Day. There must be some billable time from somewhere to record. She couldn't think of any. That was depressing. She switched from Chart-the-Day to the Toronto online legal directory. She found Sam Capponi's phone number and called him. He answered the phone himself.

"Sam, it's Piper Fantouche at Dibbets. We sat next to each other at the alumni dinner the other day."

"We certainly did, I remember it well. How are things at Dibbets? I must say that you people have a strange way of thinning out the partnership ranks. I've been reading all about it on the front page. Who's next for the axe? And when I say axe, I mean axe!"

"I'm being interviewed by the police later this morning. I'm probably a suspect in the Watt murder. I think I need legal advice."

He hesitated for a moment, and then changed his tone and spoke in a measured way. "Okay, from this minute

on, you're my client, so we have solicitor-client privilege. You can tell me anything and it will be in confidence. Now, why would the police think you murdered Watt?"

"He tried to rape me the night he was killed. That's a good reason for murdering someone, don't you think?"

"Did you kill him?"

"Of course I didn't kill him. Should you be here when the police come? They'll be showing up any minute."

"Bad idea. If I'm there, they'll think you did it. Innocent people don't have a criminal lawyer at their elbow from the get-go. Handle it yourself. But don't do the 'I have the right to remain silent' thing. That drives the police crazy. And come and see me right afterwards so we can figure out what's going on and how to play it. By the way, I charge four hundred and fifty dollars an hour, but I'll knock fifty bucks off for you since we both went to the same law school."

• • •

Vitanza and Singh arrived at Dibbets at ten o'clock sharp. Vitanza had a headache. There was a patch of stubble under his chin where he hadn't shaved properly. He had drunk too much the night before, and had fallen asleep in his favourite chair. In the morning, with aches and pains from sleeping in an odd position, his head fuzzy, his neck and shoulders aching, he had found it difficult to follow his usual careful grooming process. Singh, by contrast, was wearing an immaculate grey Hugo Boss suit and a smart white shirt open at the collar. His shoes were shined. His turban was impeccably tied. He looked smart and felt rested.

Rachel showed them in to Piper's office.

"Miss Fantouche," said Vitanza, sitting down opposite her desk without waiting for an invitation, "I'm Detective Vitanza – we spoke on the phone, when you were in Paris–and this is Detective Mohan Singh. We're investigating the death of Jim Watt, as you know." He gave a small sigh. "Thank you for returning to Toronto early. We appreciate it. Sorry to spoil your holiday."

"I understand," said Piper. "That's okay. I'll help any way I can." She saw the bit of beard under his chin. She noticed that Singh, who was sitting in the other client chair across from her desk, was a good-looking man. She thought the turban, not an unusual sight in Toronto but still exotic to her, made him even more attractive.

"The first thing," said Vitanza, "the first thing is this, why did you go to Paris the day after Watt was found dead? You went with your boyfriend, I think. You must have realized that we would want to talk to you as part of our investigation. You knew the deceased, you worked closely with him. We've been told you visited him late afternoon or early evening on the night he died. Leaving Toronto when you did strikes me as curious. It doesn't necessarily make me suspicious, because I'm not the suspicious type, but if it did make me suspicious, I could be forgiven for it."

Piper was ready for this question. She had rehearsed her answer in the middle of the night. But how did Vitanza know that she had visited Watt the night he died?

"It was a mistake to leave, detective, I know that. I wasn't thinking clearly. I was very upset and had to get away to clear my head." Piper stopped and drew a deep breath. "Jim tried to rape me the night he died."

Vitanza and Singh stared at Piper. There was a long silence.

"He tried to rape you?" said Singh eventually. "What happened? You fought him off?"

"I didn't have to fight him off. He was drunk. He fell asleep. It was pathetic. He was on top of me, on his office couch, fumbling with my clothes, and then he fell asleep. I was still pretty much fully dressed. So was he."

"He fell asleep? And you did what?"

"I left as soon as I could. I went home. I took a taxi."

"What time was that?" asked Singh.

"I think it was about nine or nine thirty. Maybe later, I don't know, I was confused and upset. We'd had drinks at Mario's across the street. Jim had had two or three martinis. He always drank a lot, even at lunch. He said he needed to talk to me back at the office. He was drunk."

"Was this the first time he'd tried something like this?" asked Vitanza.

"It was the first time he had gone that far, but he'd made advances before, generally when he'd had too much to drink. Hand on my thigh, saying I was beautiful, that sort of thing."

You are beautiful, thought Mohan Singh.

"Did you ever report any of this?" asked Vitanza. "To some senior person in the firm? Human resources? To…" He paused, trying to remember the name. "To Mark Steiner?"

"The only person who knew about it was Peter. He's my boyfriend."

"He's the one you went to Paris with?" asked Singh.

"Yes, we've been together, sort of, for a while."

"Do you live together?"

"Some of the time. He still has his own place, in the west end."

Singh looked at Vitanza. He paused, giving Vitanza the chance to pick up the questioning. He noticed a framed photograph on Piper's credenza of a good-looking older man in what looked like a military uniform – her father, he guessed. It was the only photograph in her office. He thought its display showed an old-fashioned respect for family.

"Now," said Vitanza, "you say you told your boyfriend Peter about what was going on with Watt."

"I told him that night that Watt had tried to rape me," said Piper. "He was at my place when I got back. He was watching television. His favourite show, Sons of Anarchy. It's about a motorcycle gang. It starts at ten, I think, so it must have been after ten when I got home."

"What did he say?" Vitanza had never heard of Sons of Anarchy.

"He was very upset. He said Watt was a miserable shit, or something like that."

"And then what?"

"He went out."

"He went out."

"Yes."

"For how long?"

"I don't know. For a while. I was too upset to pay attention to the time."

"Where did he go? Did he say?"

"I don't know where he went. For a walk, I suppose, around the neighbourhood. He needed to cool down."

"We'd like to speak to Peter," said Vitanza. "Where can we reach him? What's his last name?"

"I suppose he's at his apartment. I'll give you the address and phone number. His last name is Gomes."

Vitanza didn't think that Piper Fantouche was the murdering type. It was intuition but, as Dr. Abramowitz often told him, he had very good intuition. The jealous boyfriend, rushing out of the house into the night, determined to avenge the honour of his girlfriend, might be a more promising line of inquiry, although there was something a bit trite about it.

"We'll go and see Peter Gomes," Vitanza said. Piper had written the address and phone number on a piece of paper. "But, Miss Fantouche, we'll want to speak to you again."

"One last thing," said Singh, as he stood up. "Why didn't you call the police about the attempted rape? Sexual assault is a serious crime."

"Not every crime is reported," said Piper. "If the police were called every time someone made an unwelcome sexual advance, you'd be very busy people."

"Even so, you should have reported it," said Singh.

• • •

Vitanza pulled the Buick up in front of the address Piper had given him. It was an old brick house on a quiet street running north off Bloor Street West. Paint peeled from window frames. A battered rain gutter had come loose and hung down from the roof's edge, held on by a single nail. The front garden was choked with weeds. Two rusty old bicycles, one without wheels, lay on their side among the dandelions. A large City of Toronto plastic garbage can, its lid open, was by the front steps.

"221B," said Vitanza, looking at Piper's bit of paper, and then at the house. "This is 221."

"It must be a basement apartment," said Singh. "There's probably a separate entrance at the side, or maybe around the back."

They followed a concrete path overgrown with weeds around to the side of the house. There were steps down to a battered wooden door with peeling red paint. The door had a black metal "B" nailed to it. Vitanza went down the steps and knocked. No one answered. He knocked again. Nothing. There was a small window in the door, and he peered into it but couldn't see much through the heavy coating of grime. He thought perhaps he saw a piano, an old upright.

"No one's home," said Vitanza. "Let's look around the back."

"What a dump," said Singh. He looked with irritation at concrete dust that had gathered on his highly polished shoes.

The back yard was even more chaotic than the front. Old tires were stacked in one corner, leaning up against a rusting chain link fence. A child's swing set, without swings, sat in waist-high weeds. An old shovel lay across the path. Bits of crumbling red brick had fallen away from the wall of the house.

"I wonder why Peter Gomes prefers living in Piper Fantouche's condominium," said Singh, brushing dust and burrs from his suit.

"Anyway, he's not here," said Vitanza.

"This is interesting," Singh said, pointing to a used hypodermic lying in the tall grass.

• • •

Vitanza dropped Singh off at his apartment at about five o'clock. Singh decided to go to the gym for a workout.

He belonged to an Extreme Fitness branch just down the street. He went there two or three times a week.

At the gym he changed into his workout clothes, being careful not to disturb his turban. He stood sideways in front of the locker room mirror and observed his flat stomach with satisfaction. He went into the exercise room. Singh normally started his workout with twenty minutes on an elliptical trainer, followed by weights and then stretching exercises. All the trainers were being used, and so he went to a treadmill, put it at a modest incline, set a speed of four miles per hour, and started walking. He thought about the Watt case. Sleuth, they had to sleuth, that's what Vitanza said. Sleuth – what an odd word. He considered the list of possible murderers. No one was an obvious candidate, although Piper Fantouche, and her boyfriend Peter Gomes, had behaved very oddly.

As he walked on the treadmill, he noticed a woman lifting weights on the other side of the room, facing a mirror on the wall, her back to him. She was wearing black leotards. She had the concave curve of a fit young woman, created by a line that extends from her shoulders down to her waist and out to the hips. The most beautiful line in the world, thought Mohan. No artist could draw a better one. The woman's auburn hair was piled on top of her head. She had large but attractive ears. From the back, she was beautiful. Mohan felt the beginnings of desire. He caught a glimpse of her face in the mirror as she lifted the weights above her head. He thought he recognized her. He had trouble placing her. Then he realized it was Piper Fantouche. He looked the other way. He didn't think she had seen him.

Chapter Twenty-One
Fingers Pointing

B rad Nemitz was sitting in the living room of his Forest Hill house. His wife Joanna was in the garden weeding the herbaceous border, enjoying the late afternoon sun. Nemitz could see her clearly through the large bay window that overlooked the back yard. She was wearing a broad-brimmed straw hat with a brightly coloured ribbon. He waved. She waved back, and gave him a big smile.

Nemitz had just got home. It had been another fraught day at the office. It was a good thing for him that the takeover bid for Liberty Insurance had collapsed – if it hadn't, he would have been out of a job–but past events continued to reverberate and he still felt threatened. Everyone on Bay Street knew that Canadian Unity Bank and other dissatisfied Liberty shareholders had planned to move against his company. Everyone knew that the takeover bid had collapsed because of an insider trading scandal, and there was much speculation about who was involved. Then, the unthinkable: the violent death, the probable murder, of the lawyer representing the bidders.

The affair had severely tainted Liberty Insurance. On Bay Street the company's management was now seen as weak, the company itself as vulnerable. Stock watchers expected Liberty Insurance shares to plunge once the Exchange lifted its trading suspension. Nemitz had received more invitations from big shareholders to have lunch at the Toronto Club, and he knew what they wanted to talk about as they drank vichyssoise, nibbled arugula salads, and sipped Chablis. One caller hadn't even bothered with a lunch invitation and had got right to the point: it was time for him to resign as chief executive officer. His board was agitated and not supportive. Simon Hall, who loved a crisis, phoned several times a day to offer exuberant and idiosyncratic advice. Marcia Simpson, the board chair, had sailed unannounced into his office the day before yesterday wearing a large red hat, her trademark, sat peremptorily on the sofa, and sourly demanded to be briefed. Ben Peck gave his usual balanced and comforting advice, to be sure, but even Peck seemed a little shaken and uncharacteristically cut short one telephone conversation with, "I've got an urgent call on the other line…"

Nemitz went over to the drinks table. He saw with modest pleasure that the ice bucket was full. Joanna always filled it before he got home. It was one of those little considerations that cemented his affection for her. Such small things, he was sure, were the stuff of a long and happy marriage. He put two ice cubes in a crystal tumbler and filled the glass with Macallan scotch. He took his drink back to the sofa, sat down, and put his feet up on a footstool. He sipped the scotch and reflected

once more on what had happened. He thought, as he had thought many times before, about the death of Jim Watt.

Although Nemitz was president of a large insurance company, he didn't consider himself a Bay Street type. He was a kid from Sault Ste. Marie who had worked hard and been lucky. He prided himself on not having the values of the Street—extreme ambition, thirst for wealth, ruthlessness, absence of compassion, arrogance, lack of social conscience, a philosophy of winner-take-all. Watt had had these characteristics. Watt had been the quintessential Bay Streeter. That was why Nemitz had abhorred him. That, and the fact that Watt and his client, Canadian Unity Bank, had directly threatened Nemitz's well-being and that of his family. Joanna would have been devastated if he'd lost his job. His children, smart as they were, would not have understood if he'd been thrown out of Liberty Insurance.

The police were coming to see him tomorrow morning, a Detective Sebastian Vitanza and somebody else whose name he forgot. He had better be careful what he said to them. He had better not tell them that he was glad Watt was dead.

"Hello darling," said Joanna, coming into the living room. She went over to the sofa and kissed her husband on his forehead. "It's a beautiful evening. Why don't we sit outside?"

• • •

Arthur Red was in his office, at his vast desk, staring at Ron Tonks sitting on the edge of a chair on the other side. Red had decided to blame Tonks for the Liberty Insurance debacle. It was official: Tonks was to blame.

Somebody had to take the fall. Why not Tonks? He was a nasty little man.

Wong Lee had been very insistent on the telephone from Hong Kong that someone be held responsible for what had happened. Ron Tonks was the culprit, Red had said on the spur of the moment. Ron Tonks is to blame. "I beg your pardon," Wong had asked, "but who is Ron Tonks?" "Tonks is nobody," Red had replied. "How could someone who is nobody do such damage?" asked Wong.

"You've fucked me over, Tonks," said Red, breaking the tense silence that had lasted since Miss Dickson had showed Tonks in. "You've ruined what would have been the highlight of my career. I should have known that there was no way someone from Saskatchewan could handle high finance. You're fired."

Tonks stared at Red. Fired? This was terribly unfair. Why was he being blamed? He'd had nothing to do with the insider trading that had doomed the deal. Someone at Dibbets had done that, he was sure of it. He hadn't killed Watt. But it was his career that was about to be ruined. His wife would sneer at him. "You and your big talk about the bank," she would say. "You were always nothing at home. Now it turns out that you were nothing at the bank as well." Worst of all, he'd have to resign from the golf club, just as he was beginning to get somewhere with his game, a handicap of only twenty. His humiliation would be complete. Maybe he could still make Arthur Red see that this was unjust, a huge mistake. Maybe there was still a chance.

"Mr. Red," he said. "I'd like to say…"

"Shut the fuck up, Tonks. You're fired. Do you hear me? You're fired! By the way, you're not just fired. You're

also about to be disgraced. Your picture will be on the front page of the Report on Business. The headline will say, 'Incompetent banker from Saskatchewan ruins major transaction.' They'll interview me. I'll say: 'I promoted Mr. Tonks because I wanted bankers from Western Canada to have important positions in our organization. But, I made a mistake.' Brian Borzykowski – you ever heard of him? He's Canada's best financial journalist–will write an article in Moneysense, or maybe even The New York Times, about how people from the West don't cut it, and you'll be Borzykowski's prime example."

"Mr. Red," said Tonks, "Can I say something…"

"No, Tonks, you can't fucking say something. What you can do is get the fuck out of my office."

"Can I ask about my severance package?"

"Severance package?" Arthur Red laughed. While Red was laughing, apparently completely absorbed in his mirth, Tonks got up, crossed the thick carpet to the door, and left. As soon as the door shut, Red fell silent, as if a switch had been flipped. He picked up a Dibbet & Dibbet promotional brochure that was sitting on his desk. On the cover was a photograph of a smiling Jim Watt. Red took a felt pen out of his desk drawer. He looked at the picture. Slowly, with great deliberation and satisfaction, he drew a heavy black X over Watt face.

• • •

Amanda Watt was worried about Tory and Blake. They had come home from school in tears once again. That had happened every day this week. They were brave children, and tried their best to be strong. At the funeral, at St. John's Anglican Church, where she had married Jim, their stoicism had been remarkable. Afterwards, at

the graveside, in Mount Pleasant Cemetery, they had set an example for the adults, standing there calmly as the coffin was lowered into the ground. But every day they came home in tears.

It was not because they missed their father, or thought that they would miss him in the future. Jim had not been warm and loving towards his children. He had been like his own father, cold and remote. He had believed in the old ways and the old adages – "children should be seen and not heard," that sort of thing. He inspected their fingernails for cleanliness before he let them sit down for a meal and turned them away, to go to their room hungry, if he found dirt. He wanted to be respected rather than loved.

No, they would not miss their father. That was not why they cried. They cried because they no longer felt part of a respectable and reliable family. Fathers left home, parents got divorced, families broke up, but no one else's father had been murdered. The other school children were respectful – they didn't tease Tory and Blake about what had happened–but they whispered to each other in the schoolyard and in the school corridors, and Tory and Blake knew what they were whispering about. Perhaps they would have to move to another part of town, or even another city, where nobody knew who they were, where no one knew their father had been savagely killed in his office. They hoped so. Meanwhile, they came home in tears.

Amanda did not cry. She hadn't liked her husband. She wouldn't miss him. She had often thought of leaving him, but held back, partly because of the children, but also because she enjoyed the luxuries his big income

made possible. She liked having a full-time Scottish housekeeper, Barbara, who kept the place spotless and was deferential. And if she left Jim, what, exactly, would she do, and where would she go?

She had realized not long after marrying Jim that she'd made a mistake. He was polite and efficient, reliable in a tedious sort of way, but remote and dictatorial. He had a lot of rules, big and small, about how things should be done, about how a good and dutiful wife should behave, about what time the children should go to bed and how much time they could spend playing video games, about what was a satisfactory dinner and what time it should be on the table. Her girlfriends, with the exception of Gail, who was smarter than the rest of them, always said what a wonderful husband Jim was, and in a certain sort of traditional way he was indeed a good husband. But he didn't have a sense of humour, and he wasn't sexy, and she had hated the marriage. Gail understood that.

Surprisingly, more to her than anyone else, she had remained faithful to him. (Gail thought that was ridiculous.) Not that she hadn't come close to infidelity. Amanda had a couple of men friends that she saw frequently for lunch or coffee. Each, she was pretty sure, wanted to go to bed with her and would seize any opportunity she might offer. She flirted with both, but always stepped back when she sensed things might go too far. Then, when she got home and the danger was passed, she would think, why not? It was just a matter of logistics. Where would they go? A hotel? What about some contrived out-of-town trip? How could they be sure they wouldn't be seen by someone who knew them? It could be done. *She wanted to be fucked!*

• • •

Had he got away with it? Bill Seldom thought he had. The Liberty deal had collapsed. The bank had egg on its face. Fingers were pointing at Dibbets. Best of all, Watt was dead. What a wonderful extra advantage that was, a real bonus! Now Dibbets had to find someone new to get it out of the mess, someone who could placate the bank, reassure other clients, restore law firm morale, put things back on an even keel, get everybody settled down, start things moving ahead again. Who would that be? Some might see Mark Steiner as a possibility, but as chairman he was really only a figurehead, not a hands-on kind of guy. Also he was a Jewish tax lawyer, all right in his place, good at his job, but not a suitable person to lead an establishment law firm like Dibbet & Dibbet, rooted in the country's history and traditions, over 150 years old, founded by Scottish Presbyterians. Who else could step into the breach? Nobody really sprang to mind – except him!

Seldom was sitting in his apartment on the forty-eighth floor of the Manulife Centre at the corner of Bay and Bloor, about three kilometers north of the Canadian Unity Bank building. He had rented a three bedroom apartment, not because he needed a place that big, but because he wanted to face south, so he could see the CUB building from every window, and only the three bedroom units faced south. His father had asked him why he rented an apartment, why he didn't buy a condominium, even a house. God knows you can afford it, his father said, the kind of money you make, and real estate is always a good long-term investment.

Seldom was from the small town of Wawa in north-eastern Ontario. His father and mother still lived there, although his father, Patrick, had lost his job when the pulp mill closed in 2007. When that happened, they had moved into a very small bungalow, and now lived hand-to-mouth off modest savings. Sometimes Seldom considered giving money to his parents, to help them out, but he always thought better of the idea. It would be unwise to encourage dependency.

His apartment was sparsely furnished. The two spare bedrooms each contained only a single metal bed with a thin mattress, the kind of bed that you can fold up and put away in a cupboard. Very occasionally Seldom's parents would visit from Wawa, and then he would put the fold-up beds together in one of the bedrooms, trying to make them look like an ordinary double bed. Patrick would say to Emma, his wife and Bill's mother: Why does the boy live like this? Our little house is much more comfortable than this place, and he can afford ten times what we can. Why doesn't he buy proper furniture? At night, Patrick and Emma would toss and turn, the metal frames of the beds biting into their bodies.

Seldom was sitting in his La-Z-Boy recliner, looking out of the window, south to the Canadian Unity Bank building. He could see the windows of his thirty-ninth floor office. Sometimes he sat in his office looking at the windows of his apartment. The symmetry of the relationship between where he lived and where he worked comforted him. What was his next move? Would they come to him and ask him to be the new managing partner? Would Mark Steiner, as chairman, make the approach? He was worried about Steiner. He didn't think

Steiner liked him. But that didn't matter much. The real problem was Mike Morton, the sandwich shop owner. Mike Morton knew all about the insider-trading scheme. Morton was where the danger lay, now that Watt was dead. Morton could ruin his career with one or two careless remarks. Seldom remembered the World War Two poster hanging in his parents' house in Wawa: "Loose Lips Sink Ships."

Seldom pulled the handle on the side of the La-Z-Boy and tilted the recliner back until he was almost horizontal. He lay there, studying the chandelier. It was a cheap, gold-plated fixture, the kind you get in rental buildings. Seldom didn't care much about his surroundings. He could live in – even own – a much nicer place, as his parents often pointed out. But that, he believed, would distract him from the things that had to be done.

• • •

Julia wondered about Piper Fantouche. Could she be a murderer? Piper had certainly been with Watt the night he had been killed. Julia had seen her in the elevator, on her way up to his office. She remembered that Piper had looked pale, perhaps a bit distressed. She'd had to tell the police all this, of course. Julia presumed that Watt had been hitting on Piper, who was, after all, a beautiful woman, but so what? Extreme sexual tension was commonplace on Bay Street.

Julia picked up the legal file on her desk. It was a personal matter. Her offer for the paper store in Orillia had been accepted. The closing was next week. On the top of the file was her draft letter of resignation from Dibbets, addressed to the chairman, Mark Steiner.

Chapter Twenty-Two
Phantom

Vitanza sensed that he was getting somewhere in the Jim Watt case. He couldn't quite put his finger on it–there was nothing precise, he had no theory of the crime yet, he hadn't even got a prime suspect–but he felt an idea forming somewhere in the back of his head independently of his conscious thinking, an idea that would reveal itself when it was good and ready. He hoped it would be good and ready soon. He'd solved several crimes in this curious way, sometimes waking up in the middle of the night with sudden clear knowledge of who had done it.

It was early morning and he was at home, sitting in his favourite chair, eating a couple of spicy German sausages that he'd found in the fridge, not a great way to start the day, but Vitanza never bothered much about breakfast. Dinner was the only meal he paid attention to. He had already flipped through the newspaper; there was nothing in it of much interest; another Euro zone crisis; more trouble in the Middle East; another overnight shooting on Richmond Street in downtown Toronto (he didn't want to be assigned that case – drug deals gone wrong

were never interesting). He looked out over the ravine. It was the beginning of a beautiful summer's day, bright sun but the air still cool, the trees susurrating, birdsong as counterpoint to the rustling of leaves. He finished the sausages, put the plate aside, drank a glass of water, leant back in his chair, looked at the trinacria on the wall opposite, closed his eyes and thought about the case.

Who had killed Jim Watt? Peter Gomes was an obvious suspect, but after being initially interested in the possibility, Vitanza had pretty much ruled him out, precisely because he was so obvious. An angry man rushing out into the night to avenge the attempted rape of his girlfriend? A cliché, and, in Vitanza's experience, clichés rarely explained crimes. Piper Fantouche was a more interesting prospect. There was that sudden trip to Paris. It wasn't the sort of thing you'd expect a smart lawyer to do in the circumstances. He tried to imagine Fantouche, in a flash of anger after a drunken Watt tried to rape her, bashing him over the head. Bashing him over the head with what? They still hadn't found the murder weapon, or even figured out what it was. But, at the end of the day, he couldn't get very interested in Fantouche either. Not the murdering type – that had been his intuition, and history showed that his intuition was almost always right, as Dr. Abramowitz liked to point out. "Trust your intuition," Abramowitz often told him.

Who else might have done it? It was clear that a lot of people on Bay Street had seriously disliked Watt. He was going to see two of them today. Brad Nemitz, the boss of Liberty Insurance, had been on the receiving end of the unwelcome takeover bid partly orchestrated by Watt, a bid that would have put Nemitz out of a job. Arthur

Red, Canadian Unity Bank president, had been on the delivering end of the bid and by all accounts was very upset when it collapsed. But it was hard to imagine these businessmen killing Watt. Capitalists don't kill, thought Vitanza, except, of course, indirectly.

The widow? Amanda Watt hadn't loved her husband, that was clear enough, and probably considered herself better off with him dead. He wouldn't mind betting that, sitting in that elegant house with the poodle at her feet and fresh flowers on the table, turning the pages of a Javier Marias novel, she was already fully imagining her new life, and saw that it would be good. For one thing, her husband had probably left her quite a bit of money. At the very least, there would be a big payout from a group life insurance policy. He'd get Singh to check that out. He shouldn't forget about Amanda, not just yet, but he didn't think of her as a serious suspect. Wives in loveless marriages don't kill their husbands, with the occasional exception – there had been one or two of those exceptions in his career.

That brought him back to Dibbets. He'd interviewed most of the partners who had worked closely with Watt. Vitanza didn't think Julia Anderson had the particular kind of passion that serious violence required. Agatha Hightower couldn't care less about anything connected with Dibbets, husbanding her energy for shopping expeditions. Darrell Jones was self-obsessed and ineffectual; a murderer, in Vitanza's experience, might be self-obsessed, but was never ineffectual. Mark Steiner gave him pause. There had been serious conflict between Steiner and Watt. It was, of course, implausible that the chairman of a major law firm, a man with an excellent reputation,

known for his probity, would murder one of his partners. But Vitanza sensed passion behind Steiner's tax technician façade; there seemed something out of kilter with him; there was that strange picture of buttocks in his office; perhaps Steiner was capable of the unexpected, the implausible. He shouldn't rule out Steiner. Vitanza's thoughts drifted back to Julia Anderson. She was a good-looking woman.

He looked for the list of names that Steiner had given him, the people who had been part of Operation Banking Freedom. He found it on the side table, partly hidden under the latest Canadian Automobile Association magazine. There was a check mark against every name on the list except one, Bill Seldom. No one had interviewed Seldom yet. I'd better go and see this guy, thought Vitanza. Several of the Dibbets lawyers he had talked to had mentioned Seldom. Apparently he had been Jim Watts' right hand man. Vitanza looked at his notebook. Oh yes, Julia Anderson had said something interesting about Seldom. He'd made a note of it. "There's more to Bill Seldom than most people think," Julia had said. "What do you mean?" Vitanza had asked. "Everyone thinks he's so polite and passive and harmless. I don't think he's like that at all. He frightens me."

What sort of place was Dibbets anyway? Vitanza felt he was beginning to understand it a little. The frankness of Mark Steiner and Amanda Watt had helped. Dibbets lawyers didn't care about each other, that was clear. Good personal relationships were not part of the firm's architecture. Money was what mattered. Greed drove the firm. A partner's worth was measured by his ability to increase profits. A client's value depended on the size of the bills it

paid. Unfettered pursuit of money produced brutal competition. In such a setting, thought Vitanza, murder was indeed possible.

Another thing occurred to him, as he studied the trinacria on the wall opposite for the umpteenth time. The firm had no physical substance. It was just people in rented space, sending out bills. There was no building, no heavy machinery, no physical inventory, no minerals in the ground, no plan of exploration, no processing, no manufacturing, no distribution system, no patents, no trucks, nothing except ambitious people reading law and exchanging memoranda with each other. In the middle of the night, when everyone had gone home, except perhaps the odd articling student or very junior lawyer pulling an all-nighter and feeling the thrill of it, the firm was little more than a phantom.

He opened his notebook and picked up a cheap plastic pen, given to him by his plumber, from the side table. A list of suspects might help focus his thinking. "Fantouche," he wrote at the top. Underneath "Fantouche" he wrote "Gomes," and underneath that "Amanda Watt." He added "Steiner." He hesitated, and then wrote "Seldom" and put an asterisk next to it. At the bottom of the paper, he put a question mark. He took the list into the kitchen and attached it to the refrigerator door with animal magnets that he'd bought years ago at the Toronto Zoo. He looked at his watch. His appointment with Arthur Red was in forty-five minutes. He should leave, pick up Mohan, and go to Bay Street.

• • •

"What did you say your names were?" asked Arthur Red, who knew the identity of his visitors perfectly well.

Vitanza and Singh were in his enormous office. Red was sitting behind his desk, his high-backed leather chair tilted so far back that he was almost horizontal. "You're policemen?" he said, apparently addressing the ceiling. "Why are you here?"

"Detective Sergeant Sebastian Vitanza and Detective Constable Mohan Singh," said Vitanza. "We're investigating the death of Jim Watt."

"Watt," said Red. He struggled to sit upright in his chair. He fiddled with a lever at its side. Suddenly the back of the chair shot forward, almost catapulting him across his desk. "Whoa!" said Red, struggling to regain his composure, settling back into the now vertical chair, exhaling noisily. "Watt," he said again. "I won't miss him."

"Could you tell us about the bank's relationship with Watt?" asked Vitanza.

"He sat on our board. Dibbets used to be our main lawyers. They aren't any more. He ran most of the files we had with Dibbets."

"You knew him well?"

"No, of course I didn't know him well. He wasn't my friend. He worked for me. Lawyers are hired help, like the guy who cuts my lawn. The guy who cuts my lawn works for me and Watt worked for me just like the lawn guy. I don't have the lawn guy in for tea and crumpets, and I didn't have that cocksucker Watt to my house for cocktails and dinner."

"Do you know of any reason why someone would want to harm him?"

"How much time have you got? Everyone who knew Watt wanted to harm him. He was a bastard. There are a

lot of people on Bay Street who've been on the opposite side of a deal with him, and lost bad, and hated his guts."

"Enough to kill him?"

"You may want to kill someone, but that doesn't mean that you actually go out and kill him. I would have liked to kill Watt myself, but I didn't do it." How extraordinary, thought Vitanza, for someone to tell the police that he would have liked to kill a person who was found dead just a few days earlier. Bankers think they can say anything and get away with it.

"Why did you feel that way about Jim Watt?" asked Singh.

"Because Watt screwed up what should have been the deal of my career. Thanks to him, my takeover of Liberty Insurance never got off the ground. Fuck him in hell."

"Why was it his fault?"

"He did two stupid things. He didn't make sure that insider trading couldn't happen. For all I know he was trading himself. And then the fucker got himself killed. After that, no one would come within a hundred miles of the deal."

"When did you last see him?" asked Vitanza.

"At a meeting in this office a few days ago."

"The two of you were working together?"

"No, we were not working together. The chief executive officer of a bank does not work with a lawyer for the bank. He tells someone what to do, who tells someone else what to do, and that person tells the lawyer what to do. I told you, he was hired help."

"Who was the person who told Watt what to do?"

"A vice-president, somebody called Ron Tonks."

"Where can we find Ron Tonks?" asked Vitanza.

"How should I know?" said Red. "Selling pencils on the street most likely. He's been fired."

"Why was he fired?

"He was the bank's man on the Liberty Insurance file. Someone had to pay for what happened. He paid."

• • •

"What do you think?" Vitanza asked Singh a few minutes later, as they took the elevator down from Arthur Red's suite to the lobby of the Canadian Unity Bank building. They were on their way to see Brad Nemitz in the Canada Bank Building across the street. It was a quarter to eleven.

"Think about what?"

"Arthur Red. Don't play coy."

"An unpleasant man," said Singh.

"That's putting it mildly." Vitanza had been hoping for a rant about Red. A terse three-word comment was disappointing, but he was used to Singh's brevity.

"Do you suspect Red?" asked Vitanza.

"No."

"I agree. He may be president of a bank, and a total asshole, but he's not a killer."

They left the CUB building, walked half a block to Prince Street, and waited for the light to change. The sidewalks were full of well-dressed men and women moving between bank towers that sat on the four corners of the intersection, as if in a ballet.

"What do we know about Nemitz?" asked Singh.

"Not much. Low profile. Worked his way up through the ranks, that sort of thing. Good reputation." The light changed. They crossed the street and went into the

Canada Bank Building. Vitanza approached a security guard sitting at a desk, staring at a television monitor.

"What floor for Brad Nemitz of Liberty Insurance?"

"Fifty three," said the guard, without looking up from the screen. "Floor before Flotsam."

They squeezed into an elevator full of people watching a television set mounted above the doors. It flashed current stock quotations, a new one every few seconds. The watchers were subdued. The market had not been doing well. There was a collective sigh when the monitor reported one company's dramatic drop in value, more than three percent, since the market's opening that morning. The company was Canadian Unity Bank. "That stock's a dog," someone said.

The elevator reached fifty-three. Vitanza and Singh got off. Liberty Insurance's executive offices occupied the whole floor. They went to the reception desk. "Detectives Vitanza and Singh for Mr. Nemitz," said Singh to a woman in horn-rimmed glasses. "He's expecting you," she said. "Come with me." She took them down a quiet corridor, knocked on a door at the end, opened it without waiting, and led the two men in. Nemitz, sitting at his desk in shirtsleeves, looked up, smiled, came around his desk to shake their hands, and gestured to easy chairs placed around a low table. He had thoughtfully lowered the blinds so that the sunlight streaming through the windows didn't make his visitors squint.

"Would you like some coffee? Muffins?" A change from Arthur Red, thought Vitanza. Red had offered them nothing; he'd made a silent point of it. "You're here to talk about Jim Watt," said Nemitz. "He was not a man

I liked or respected, but I regret his passing and the manner of it."

Vitanza waited two or three seconds. "You say you didn't like or respect Mr. Watt. Why?"

"Well, Detective Vitanza, when it comes to liking, you like some people and you dislike others. It can be hard to explain why. A lot of it is just instinctive, or chemistry. I didn't like Watt' suits, the kind of glasses he wore, for example – stupid, really – but that's how liking or not liking works in my experience."

"And when it comes to respect?"

"Respect is objective. I didn't respect Jim Watt because he only cared about himself. Nothing else mattered: Just his own advancement, how much money he made, whether he won or lost. It didn't matter who he hurt along the way, what damage he caused."

"He almost hurt you, didn't he, along the way? I'm thinking of the Canadian Unity Bank takeover bid."

"I don't think anyone took that bid seriously. It was a nuisance, no more than that. There never was a bid, just talk. And now it's ancient history."

• • •

Twenty minutes later, finished with Nemitz, Vitanza and Singh were on the fifty-third floor waiting for an elevator. Vitanza looked at his watch. "Flotsam is one floor up. It's noon. Let me buy you lunch, Mohan."

"Thank you. I've never been to Flotsam. I hear it's pretty good. You've got to stop buying me lunch."

When they got to the fifty-fourth floor a man in a dark suit asked if they had a reservation. No, said Vitanza. The man frowned over a reservations book, flipping pages. Finally, he said he could fit them in. He seated them by a

window. One other table was occupied, on the other side of the room.

"That's a coincidence," said Singh. "You see who's over there?" It was Arthur Red and a Chinese man. The Chinese man was very well dressed. Arthur Red looked unhappy.

"By the way," said Singh. "Nemitz didn't tell us the truth. A lot of people took that takeover bid very seriously."

"I know," said Vitanza.

Chapter Twenty-Three
Fat Boy

Piper was sure she must be a serious suspect in the Jim Watt murder. Maybe the police would focus on Peter to begin with – the cops must be pretty interested in the dramatic way he had rushed out that night – but she knew Peter hadn't killed Watt and the police would discover that sooner or later. That would leave her at the top of the list.

It was after lunch. She was in the office, working on a new file, trying to overcome her nervousness and get on with the job, trying to have a normal day. Hans Grabber, a man from the tennis club where she played occasionally, had a decent-sized business cleaning downtown offices at night. Grabber was a bad tennis player, physically clumsy and emotionally volatile, swore a lot, a racket-smasher, easy to beat. He was also a dreamer and wanted to expand his business. Cleaning coast-to-coast-to-coast was his ambition, that's the way he put it, with a distant look in his eye as he spoke, the distant look of a visionary. He had offered to buy his main competitor, and the owner, who was sick of emptying wastebaskets in the small hours and wanted to go to the Alberta tar

sands where he thought he could make a fortune out of bitumen, seized the opportunity to get out of night-time cleaning. Grabber had come to Piper, the only lawyer he knew, to do what he knowingly called "the legals."

The management of Dibbets frowned on files like this. The fees wouldn't amount to more than ten thousand dollars, a trivial sum for a Bay Street law firm. "That's not the kind of work we do," the late Jim Watt often said about such matters, and many senior partners agreed with him. "We do major transactions," said Watt, "and if there isn't a major transaction, we wait until one comes along." Of course, there was a lot of posturing in this. Senior partners might be able to sit in their corner offices doing nothing while they waited for major transactions to come along, passing the time making pompous pronouncements about the practice of law, but small fry had to take what they could get. It still rankled with Bill Seldom that Watt had once said when Seldom was quite junior (the comment had been eagerly reported to him by several of his colleagues), "Oh yes, Seldom, he specializes in whatever he can get his hands on." There had always been little files like the Grabber file, and many lawyers, even at Dibbets, were glad to get them. There were always those who specialized in whatever they could get their hands on, even in the best of times.

This was not the best of times. There were rumours on the Street that large corporate clients of Dibbets, spooked by the Watt business, had moved big files to other law firms. It was thought that Dibbets, blamed for the Liberty Insurance fiasco, had lost the Canadian Unity Bank work, which, if true, was a catastrophe. There were worrying omens. It had suddenly become harder for the

firm to collect accounts receivable. The usual daily avalanche of cheques and electronic transfers had slowed considerably, as clients cared less and less about the state of their relationship with Dibbets and lost interest in paying their bills promptly. The phones didn't seem to be ringing as much; there were fewer visitors arriving at the thirty-eighth floor reception; conference rooms, normally hard to book, were easily available; the in-house caterers were idle; the corridors were quiet; some partners seemed to be staying away from the office altogether.

Could there be a revenue crisis in the offing? Dibbets had a large bank loan from CUB, payable on demand. Not long before the Watt affair it had hired twenty senior lawyers from other big firms, giving each a substantial multi-year income guarantee, presuming what had seemed reasonable before someone bashed in Watt's head, that good times could only get better. Monthly draws paid to all of the partners were made against rosy predictions of income that had not yet been earned. The capital contribution of partners to the partnership was trivial, and almost every partner had borrowed his contribution, also from CUB, also payable on demand. Debt was everywhere. The system worked if Dibbets remained the money machine it had always been, but would collapse under pressure. The best partners, particularly the lateral hires with no loyalty to Dibbets, would leave if they had the slightest suspicion that things were going wrong. Remaining clients would go to other law firms. Loans would be called; no indulgence could be expected from a vengeful CUB. Dibbets could disappear. Other law firms had. It was easy to imagine.

The Grabber file was dull. It was a routine asset acquisition. Piper planned to use a computer precedent. All she had to do was fill in the blanks. It was clerical work, but highly paid. She plodded through it, her mind elsewhere, the nervousness creeping up on her. She looked at her watch . She had a three o'clock appointment with Sam Capponi.

• • •

Capponi's office was in an old house off the Danforth, across the Bloor Street Viaduct. He shared the premises with three other criminal defence lawyers, each younger and less well known than he was. Once the house had been the elegant home of a prosperous merchant, a place where dinner parties were held in a wood-panelled dining room and a nanny put the children to bed after taking them into the drawing room to bid a polite good night to their parents. Now it resembled a fraternity house, carpets stained, paint peeling, wallpaper drooping, loud voices and boisterous laughter coming from another room or floor. Every day Capponi parked his Harley-Davidson Softail Fat Boy just inside the front door, taking up almost the entire entrance hallway, making it difficult to get into the building. Piper supposed the motorcycle to be a sort of advertisement for Capponi, emphasizing his anti-establishment persona, underlining his bad boy attitude, intended to reassure the thieves and drug dealers and accused murderers who came to see him.

She struggled sideways past the Fat Boy to the receptionist, a young woman sitting behind an old desk, wearing few clothes, showing much cleavage, absorbed on the telephone. She waited for the receptionist to look up. As she waited, Capponi came down the stairs. He wore

black chinos, a black T-shirt and cowboy boots. When he saw her he said, "Hey Fantouche, killed anyone lately?" and laughed. The receptionist, suddenly interested, put the telephone down and paid attention. "Come up to my office," said Capponi.

His ordered office was reassuring. Perhaps the room had been the original owner's study. There was oak wainscoting. Law reports were carefully organized by year in an old-fashioned bookcase with glass doors. Cartoons by Spy of 19th century English judges and lawyers hung on the wall behind a battered partner's desk. Two wing-back chairs for clients were on the other side of the desk. An ornate, ticking grandmother clock stood in a corner. There was a calmness to the room. Capponi sat down and waved Piper into one of the wing chairs.

"I'm presuming you didn't kill him," he said without ceremony, putting his feet up on the desk. "You say you didn't, and that's the end of that discussion. We don't need to talk about it anymore. But we do need to talk about your relationship with Watt."

"My relationship? He was the managing partner at Dibbets. I'm a newish and very junior partner. I was part of the Watt Group, that's what they called it, and worked with him a lot, mostly on Canadian Unity Bank files. That was the extent of my relationship with Watt."

"Did you sleep with him?"

"No."

"You told me that he tried to rape you the night he was murdered. Was that the first time he tried something like that?"

"He was always coming on to me, buying me drinks, making suggestive comments, but that kind of stuff is

219

pretty standard at Dibbets. You get used to it. You learn to ignore it."

"Have you had sex lately with any of the senior partners?"

"No, I haven't. Not lately or ever. What kind of question is that?"

"I'm just trying to get a general idea of what goes on at your law firm. The context. How did you deal with it, when Watt came on to you?"

"I just made it clear I wasn't interested. He seemed to get it. I didn't like the situation but thought I could manage it. Until that last time."

"You've told all this to the police?"

"Yes, pretty much as I've told it to you."

"Who do you think killed Watt?"

"I've no idea."

"Who, besides you of course, had a reason to kill him?"

"I don't know of anybody who had a reason. What kind of reason do you need to kill someone? He wasn't a popular person, he could be aggressive and unpleasant and there was no charm in him, but so what. There are a lot of people like that on Bay Street."

"So I believe."

"What should I do?"

"Nothing."

"Nothing?"

"What can you do? I'm presuming you've told the police the truth. If you have, there won't be forensic evidence pointing in your direction. The police may come back to see you, just because they can't think of anything else to do, and if they do come back, tell them again what

you've already told them. But don't mention that you've seen me. The police think that exercising your constitutional right to talk to a lawyer is a sure sign of guilt. But make certain I know what's going on. Just in case."

"Are we through?"

"For the moment." There was a brief silence. "You know, Piper, Jim Watt was no fool. You're an attractive woman."

He's going to make a pass, thought Piper. Does it never end?

"I've had sex with several of my clients," said Capponi.

"Isn't that against Law Society rules?" said Piper. "You could get thrown out of the Bar. And these clients you had sex with, were they all women, or did you fuck the Hell's Angels as well?"

• • •

Arthur Red was in his office, sitting at his desk, looking at a piece of paper he was holding, his mouth hanging open, sweat sparkling on his forehead. "I don't fucking believe it," he said.

In his trembling hands was a letter from Helman Joseph, Q.C., senior partner of the law firm of Joseph & Bald. It announced that the firm had been appointed independent counsel to the management resources committee of Canadian Unity Bank's board of directors. It informed Arthur Red that the board was replacing him as the bank's chief executive officer. It said the severance terms would be generous. It invited Arthur Red to contact the undersigned. It concluded, "Yours sincerely..."

"Miss Dickson, get Lee Wong on the phone!" Red yelled at the door that separated him from his secretary, but the door was padded and she couldn't hear him. He

suddenly remembered the padding, picked up the telephone, pushed a button and shouted into the receiver. "Get me Lee Wong! He's got to be back in Hong Kong by now."

"Yes, Mr. Red," said Miss Dickson softly. "I'll try and get him."

Arthur Red crumpled the letter from Helman Joseph, Q.C., and threw it in the wastebasket. He paced up and down. He smacked the closed fist of his right hand into the palm of his left. "They're crazy!" he said. "Whose fucking idea was this? Lee Wong didn't say anything at lunch. He wasn't happy, but he didn't say they were going to fire me." He went back to the padded door, wrenched it open, stood in front of Miss Dickson's desk, and shouted, "Where is Lee Wong?"

"I'm having trouble getting hold of him," she said. "His office in Hong Kong say he's not available."

"He always takes my calls!"

"They keep saying he's not available."

"Have you tried his private line? He always picks that up. If he's not in the office they forward the call to his plane or limo or wherever he is."

"He's not picking up on that number."

"Fuck!" said Arthur Red, and went back into his office. He tried to slam the padded door behind him, but a pneumatic device closed it with a gentle swoosh.

• • •

Mohan Singh was at Extreme Fitness. He was working on muscle tone. He did weight resistance at the gym three days a week. He was eating a lot of fish and chicken, and drinking ten glasses of water a day. He felt better and thought he looked better. Often, when he was at

Extreme Fitness, Piper Fantouche was there as well. She was there today. They had exchanged glances in the past, but hadn't talked. Today Mohan went up to her.

"Miss Fantouche, it's Mohan Singh."

"I remember you, detective."

"I've noticed you here before. I just wanted to say hello. No point in pretending we don't know each other."

"You're a policeman and I'm a suspect in a murder you happen to be investigating. Maybe that's a good reason to pretend we don't know each other."

"'Suspect' is not the right word, but I see what you mean. Sorry to have interrupted your workout." He turned to go.

"I don't mean to be rude, Detective Singh."

He turned back. "Call me Mohan. May I call you Piper?"

"If you like."

"I think you come here the same days and time as me, more or less."

"It looks like it."

"So I'll see you Friday." Mohan went back to lifting weights on the other side of the room.

Chapter Twenty-Four
Brisket

It was two-thirty in the afternoon, a quiet time at The Painted Duck. The last of the late lunch crowd–office workers delayed by meetings, kids playing hooky from the high school up the road, moms who had had to wait until baby finished a long nap–had come in to get their beef brisket sandwiches with Dijon mustard and caramelized onions, or pulled pork sandwiches with barbecue sauce, or chicken sandwiches with chipotle mayo, all prepared with great care by Mike Morton, who loved his job, and took great pride in his sandwiches (seven dollars each), but wished he could make more money than he did, because he had three children all of whom needed dental work and Diane, his wife, refused to get a job.

The Painted Duck closed at five-thirty. Neighbourhood wives, most of them stay-at-home moms with spouses who had well-paying jobs on Bay Street, started coming in about an hour before that to get sandwiches for their husbands' dinners because, although they knew it would be better if they cooked hot meals for their spouses when they came home from the office exhausted and hungry, that was a lot of work, and anyway every man loved

The Painted Duck's beef brisket sandwich and was quite prepared to settle for one, in many cases preferring it to what his wife would otherwise whip up. So there was a four-thirty rush, and Mike Morton was getting ready for it, preparing a big pile of beef brisket sandwiches.

Money was a big problem for Morton, a problem that was getting bigger all the time. You had to sell a lot of sandwiches at seven dollars each to make even a modest living. Lately he had started worrying at the end of every month about the mortgage payment on his Bedford Park Avenue house. He'd hoped the deal with Bill Seldom, his old friend from North Toronto Collegiate, would improve things, although he didn't really understand how it worked and felt uneasy with the arrangements. Cayman Islands? U.S. brokerage account? He'd said nothing about it to anyone, not even to Diane, and had been waiting for the promised share of profits, which he needed badly. So far he hadn't got a penny, and Seldom hadn't returned the two calls he'd made. He'd telephoned with trepidation, and had been easily brushed off by a secretary. Morton had read in the Toronto Star about the suspicious death of one of Seldom's partners, and supposed that these days, what with one thing and another, people at the law firm were pretty busy.

The month was almost over. Could he make the mortgage payment? How much was in his chequing account? He looked at his watch. He had enough time to go across the road to his bank's automatic teller machine and check his account balance. He already had a stack of brisket sandwiches wrapped and ready to go, and it would be an hour before customers started showing up. Morton took off his apron, hung it up, washed his hands in the sink at

the back, put a sign in the window that said "back in 5 minutes," went outside and locked the sandwich shop's door, and stood on the sidewalk looking both ways, waiting for a break in traffic. There was a light at the corner half-a-block away, but he never bothered to go down to the intersection, always dashing across Yonge Street when it looked safe, just like everybody else.

A blue Volvo was coming north on Yonge. There was a momentary gap in traffic, and the Volvo accelerated into it just as Morton, seeing the same gap, stepped off the curb. The car hit him head-on with a thud. Morton was flung into the air and sailed over the Volvo, hitting the pavement behind it head first, skidding across the road. People who saw what happened, or heard the muffled noise of the impact, cried out and rushed forward. Morton lay on his back, on the street, quite still, his face covered in blood, staring unseeing up at the sky. A woman was already on her cell phone calling 911. Cars going in both directions stopped and the drivers got out. People gathered around Morton and looked at him. A man took off his suit jacket and laid it over Morton's chest. A woman with two small children took them by the hand and walked away quickly, saying, "It's nothing to worry about. Let's go home." After a minute or two, sirens could be heard coming down the street.

A fire engine was the first to arrive, bulldozing its way to the scene of the accident, its siren very loud, the driver honking the horn repeatedly. Firemen jumped out and went to Morton. One examined him and started thumping his chest rhythmically. Another asked the crowd to move back. A third briefed his dispatcher on a two-way radio. Three police cars and an ambulance pulled up,

weaving with difficulty through the stalled traffic. Some of the police told onlookers to move on. Others started closing the street and diverting traffic. Some started questioning people standing on the sidewalk about what had happened.

The blue Volvo, its bumper crumpled, its hood bent, was parked diagonally, part on the street and part on the sidewalk, about fifty feet up Yonge Street from where Morton had been hit. The driver, a middle-aged pudgy man with a pale face and watery eyes, wearing a grey pin-striped suit with a white shirt and red tie, was standing by its side. He seemed calm, except that he was wringing his hands gently. He was talking to a policeman wearing dark glasses. "He just stepped out of nowhere," the man said, shaking slightly, still wringing his hands, but in control of himself. "Right in front of my car. There was nothing I could do. Is he going to be all right? Who is he?"

"Your driving licence and vehicle registration," said the policeman, holding out his hand. His nametag said "Constable Kazimierz Kwiatkowski." The man went to the passenger side of his car, took documents out of the glove compartment and handed them to the policeman who studied them for what seemed like a long time. Eventually, the policeman looked up.

"Your name is William J. Seldom?"

"Yes."

"You live at 55 Bloor Street West?"

"Yes. It's an apartment building. The ManuLife Centre."

"Wait here," said the policeman. He went to his cruiser to check Seldom's credentials on its mobile data terminal.

While the policeman was using the terminal, Mike Morton was loaded into the ambulance on a stretcher. The door was slammed shut, and the ambulance took off, siren blaring, lights flashing. Policemen were making measurements with a long yellow tape and marking the road. The crowd started to lose interest. People wandered away. A woman rattled the door of The Painted Duck. "It's locked," she said, looking around. "What's happened? Where are my brisket sandwiches? I need two brisket sandwiches, or I'm going to have to make dinner myself." A tow truck pulled up and started to put the Volvo on the hoist.

The policeman in dark glasses came back to the driver and pulled out a notebook and pen. "You'd better tell me what happened," he said.

"I told you, he stepped out of nowhere. It's almost as if he wanted me to hit him. Maybe he was trying to commit suicide." The policeman wrote something in his notebook.

"Sir, are you employed?"

"Where are they taking my car?" The tow truck was pulling away with the Volvo.

"It's being taken to the police pound. Are you employed?"

"Yes, I'm employed. I'm a lawyer. I'm a partner at Dibbet & Dibbet. It's a big law firm. You must have heard of it. How do I get my car back?" Seldom took a business card out of his wallet and handed it to Kwiatkowski.

"I need to know where you were coming from this afternoon, where you were going, and why."

"I was coming from my office on Bay Street. I was going to a furniture store. I'm looking for a new couch."

"Did you have lunch before you left your office?"

"Just a sandwich at my desk. I always have a sandwich at my desk for lunch. Tuna salad. Sometimes egg salad. Every day. Except when I go to Mario's, which is not often. Do you know Mario's, officer?"

"Did you have wine at lunch?"

"With a tuna salad sandwich? Of course not."

Kwiatkowski leant forward and smelled Seldom's breath.

"Did you know the person you hit?"

"How do I know if I knew him? I don't know who he was."

"How fast were you going when the accident happened?"

"I don't know exactly. Not fast. You can't go fast on Yonge Street. Look, how do I get my car back?"

"An officer will be in touch with you." The policeman looked at Seldom's business card and put it in his pocket. He turned away and went back to his cruiser. The ambulance had left. The Volvo had been towed away to the police pound. The fire truck was gone. The crowd had dissolved. Bill Seldom hailed a taxi and headed downtown. A few policemen remained, measuring and marking on Yonge Street.

• • •

The ambulance pulled into Emergency at Sunnybrook Hospital on Bayview Avenue. Mike Morton was put on a gurney and rushed inside. A trauma team, alerted earlier by radio, began to work. The emergency physician put a tube in Morton's trachea. A nurse shocked him with a defibrillator. Intravenous lines were started. The team worked for fifteen minutes. "He's gone," said the doctor,

at the end of it. "Time?" he asked. "Three forty-seven," said the head nurse. The doctor wrote it down. The team drifted away. Someone in the office called the police to tell them Morton was dead.

• • •

Bill Seldom got back to the Canadian Unity Bank building at four o'clock. He went directly to his office, shut the door and sat behind his desk. He thought about what had just happened. Everyone would think it had been an accident. A foolish man coming out of his sandwich shop, wanting to cross the street, hadn't the patience to go to the light on the corner. He'd stepped off the curb into busy afternoon traffic. What happened was the man's fault. He – Bill Seldom – hadn't done anything wrong. The police would quickly lose interest in the case. They might issue a statement warning people to be more careful, telling them to cross only at the traffic light on busy streets. This is the sort of tragic accident that can happen, they'd say, if you don't take all reasonable precautions. Too many pedestrians are killed by cars. The police liked to issue statements like that.

Seldom wondered: Was Morton dead? How could he find out? Maybe he'd have to wait until tomorrow morning's newspaper. Or perhaps it would be on the radio news or on the CP24 television station. He didn't want to call the police and ask, although that would be quite a natural thing to do, no one would think twice about it. He was going to go home soon, and he'd listen to his car radio on the way. No, he couldn't do that; his car was in the police pound. He'd have to wait until he got to his apartment. Then he'd find out. On the whole, Bill Seldom felt okay, maybe even pretty good, considering

he'd just been in a nasty accident, considering that he might have killed a man.

• • •

"Here's something strange," said Mohan Singh, bringing a piece of paper over to Sebastian Vitanza's desk in 52 Division. "Look at this."

"What is it?" said Vitanza.

"An accident report. I just happened to notice it."

"Have we been moved to traffic duty or something? Why are you showing me an accident report?"

"Look at it."

Vitanza glanced at the piece of paper. "A fatal accident on Yonge Street yesterday afternoon. That doesn't seem very interesting."

"Read who was driving the car."

Vitanza looked at the paper again and sat up in his chair. "William J. Seldom. I know who that is. He's a lawyer at Dibbets who worked with Jim Watt. I was thinking about him last night. No one's interviewed him yet about the murder, and I was wondering why. This is a hell of a coincidence."

"We have an appointment with him for tomorrow. Any possible connection between the murder of Watt and this accident?"

"It's hard to see what it could be," said Vitanza. "Maybe Seldom and death just go together. A natural pairing, as they say at the wine store."

" It'll be interesting to see Seldom," said Singh. "He must be pretty shaken up. You're right, it's a hell of a coincidence."

• • •

A woman happened to glance out of her living room window on Bedford Park Avenue. She saw a police cruiser pull up and park in front of the house across the street. Two officers got out of the cruiser and walked up to the front door, rang the bell, and waited for a few moments. Someone came to the door; the woman looking out of her window recognized Diane Morton, her neighbour. There was a brief conversation between Diane and the policemen. The policemen went inside. It was only the next day, when the woman across the street read the newspaper, that she knew why the police had been visiting Diane.

Chapter Twenty-Five
Lonely

Sweat was pouring off Mohan Singh. It was dripping onto the gym floor. His T-shirt was stained with it. He had just finished a vigorous session of weights. He'd bench-pressed a hundred and eighty-five pounds, the most he had ever done. Before the weights, Karen, his personal trainer, a hard taskmaster, known to her clients as "Call Me God," had put him through a demanding workout. He was feeling very strong.

Mohan leant over Piper Fantouche, who was pedaling energetically on a stationary bike. She looked up at him.

"Can I take you for a drink?" he asked.

"Okay," said Piper, after a slight hesitation. "But I haven't finished on the bike, and then I have to shower. I'll meet you at the front door in half-an-hour."

"Front door, half-an-hour." Mohan gave Piper a half-wave, and went to the men's locker room.

He thought it highly unlikely that Piper had anything to do with the Watt murder. There was no evidence that implicated her. Sebastian Vitanza might not agree with him, at least not yet, not completely, he knew that. Sebastian had his suspicions. But, so far as he was

concerned, it was fine to take Piper Fantouche out for a drink. He couldn't be expected not to take a personal interest in every woman who had been fleetingly involved in a police investigation. That would be a lot of women. And he and Piper were just going out for a drink.

Piper thought about Mohan as she showered. She liked policemen – not that she knew a lot about them. Police work seemed romantic, all that solving of puzzles, grilling of suspects. And the police were powerful. They carried guns. Mohan must carry a gun. She wondered where he kept it. In the small of his back, tucked into his waistband? Did he carry it always?

She met him at the front door. He wore jeans, a T-shirt and brown penny loafers. The front of his T-shirt had a picture of Babe Ruth with a line through it and "Babe, you're history" written underneath. His turban was neatly tied.

"Milestones?" said Mohan. "It's a bar and restaurant around the corner. Not a fancy place."

"I know it."

They went to Milestones. A sign at the entrance said it was Date Night. "Dinner for two, only $50," it said. "$5 off any bottle of wine."

"Shall we have dinner?" asked Mohan. "Fifty bucks for two is a good deal."

"Okay," said Piper, again.

• • •

Diane Morton was grief-stricken and desperate. She could hardly sleep at night. She could barely move by day. She had tried to explain everything to the three children. "But what happened to Daddy?" they asked, over and over again. She couldn't fully grasp what had happened

herself, let alone explain it to the children. And what was she supposed to do now? There was no money. She couldn't run The Painted Duck; she'd never had much to do with it, and didn't understand the business. The store had been shut since the accident, and soon its customers, even the most loyal, would find another place to buy brisket sandwiches. She knew that there had been a problem meeting mortgage payments on the house. Could she get a job? She wasn't qualified for anything, except perhaps to be a sales clerk in a department store. And, worst of all, she had loved Mike. How was she going to live without him? And the poor, poor children. How were they going to live without their father?

She had to figure out what to do about money; that couldn't wait. Mike had run the family finances single-handedly. "That's my job," he often said. "Not something I want you to worry about." She knew that he had tried to protect her from their precarious situation. He kept financial records–receipts, bank records, chequebooks, insurance policies – in his desk in the basement family room. They called it the family room, but it wasn't much of a room. There was industrial carpet on a concrete floor, a couple of unsteady standing lamps, pictures bought at garage sales hanging on nails pounded into bare concrete walls, an old barcalounger sitting in a corner. Mike's large wooden desk, that had belonged to her now dead father, dominated the room. Sitting behind it was a battered office chair that Mike had picked up from a boulevard in Rosedale where someone had put it hoping a scavenger would take it away. The top of the desk was scattered with papers, and plastic pens from

hotels. There was an old-fashioned calculator with a paper roll, and a family portrait in a cheap frame.

Diane went into the basement and stared at the desk. She pulled at a drawer and it flew open. It was stuffed with old bank statements. She opened another. It had sandwich shop documents – invoices from suppliers, sales tax returns, a lease. She tried a third. There were a few bits of paper at the bottom. She pulled something out at random. It was a letter, dated two months ago, from the First National Bank of the Grand Cayman in George Town. It confirmed that Michael W. Morton had opened a chequing account at the bank by email, and that William Seldom of the Toronto law firm of Dibbet & Dibbet held power of attorney over the account. She pulled a second letter from the drawer. It was also dated two months ago; this one confirmed that Michael W. Morton had opened a brokerage account at J.P. Smith Investment Banking of Atlanta, Georgia, and that correspondence concerning the account was to be sent to Mr. W. Seldom of Dibbets. J.P. Smith Investment Banking, the letter said, looked forward to being of service to Mr. Morton.

Diane held the two letters in her hand. She stood quite still in the dimly lit basement. What did they mean? Mike had run a sandwich shop. Why would he have a bank account in the Cayman Islands and a brokerage account in Atlanta? Who was William Seldom? The name seemed familiar. She thought she'd heard it recently. Then she remembered. The policemen who came to the house to tell her about the accident mentioned the name. William Seldom was the driver of the car that had killed her husband.

• • •

It was only four o'clock, but Sebastian Vitanza was already at home. He was sitting in his favourite chair with a glass of scotch. It was a bit early to start drinking – he generally tried to wait until at least six – but he was bored and had to pass the time somehow. Dr. Abramowitz had talked to him about his drinking. It doesn't help you, Saul said, it hurts you. Vitanza knew Saul was right, and was trying, not very successfully, to cut back. He could, he supposed, go for a walk through the ravine instead of having a drink, it would be much better for him, but he didn't feel like it. He swirled the scotch around in his glass and listened with pleasure to the tinkle of ice cubes. He considered putting on a CD, Ella Fitzgerald perhaps, or Peggy Lee, or Chilly Gonzales.

It had been a dull day at the office. The Watt investigation had stalled. He had spent hours in what seemed like a pointless review of his interview notes. The weather was good, and he had decided he might as well leave 52 Division early. The original idea had been to go for that healthy walk, but once he got to his apartment the lure of his chair and his desire for scotch prevailed. Lately, he had often made that kind of decision, and supposed that was why he was gaining weight. He'd developed a potbelly and was self-conscious about it. He weighed himself every morning on a digital scale, and the readout was invariably depressing. Maybe, he thought, the solution was to just stop weighing himself. He didn't like to look at himself naked in the mirror. He had taken to wearing looser clothing that made him look less rotund. He used to think women found him attractive, but he wasn't so sure anymore. Women, he was pretty certain, preferred

slim men. It wasn't a good idea to be naked in front of a woman if you had a potbelly. But, why should he worry? He wasn't expecting to be naked in front of a woman anytime in the near future.

He was tired of spending evening after evening alone. He missed having a woman in his bed. He missed aimless and pleasurable conversation and gossip. There was no one to enjoy his competent cooking and share a bottle of wine. His last girlfriend, Marie, had said he drank too much. She had said, at the end, when she was walking out, that he was a morose and self-pitying drunk. He was prepared to cut down on the drinking if it would help his dating life, he was sure he could do it, Dr. Abramowitz encouraged him in that direction, but now it was time for another scotch. After Marie left, he'd asked Saul, am I morose and self-pitying? Saul said, what do you think? That wasn't very helpful, but Saul always did that, answered a question with a question.

Sipping on his drink, he made a mental list of attractive women he knew. He often did this. It amused him to put a woman on the list and later, on a whim, take her off. There was Christine, a secretary at 52 Division who had recently caught his eye; she was on the list. She was young, had red hair–Vitanza liked red hair–and was slim with nice breasts. Julia Anderson at Dibbets had been on the list since he met her. Sometimes he ranked the women on the list, and recently when he did that Julia Anderson came first. He wondered again if he could ask her out. Not yet. He had to wait until the Watt investigation was over.

Sebastian Vitanza turned his neck, stiff these days with a touch of arthritis, and looked out of the window

into the ravine. It was turning into a beautiful evening. Couples walked along the trail. Laughter came through the trees. He looked away. What should he cook for dinner? He peered into his glass. It was empty, except for remnants of ice cubes. He got up, went to the kitchen, opened the liquor cupboard, got the bottle of scotch and poured himself a generous measure. He opened the freezer and took some fresh ice cubes out of the ice tray and put them in his glass. He went back to his favourite chair. He reviewed his list of attractive women. He wondered what he should have for dinner. He ate junk for breakfast and lunch, but Sebastian cared about dinner.

• • •

That morning, Julia Anderson had gone to Mark Steiner's office and handed him, without a word, her letter of resignation from Dibbets. He read the letter and then reread it. He was amazed. Eventually, he put the letter down on his desk and stared at her.

"How well have you thought this through?"

"Very well."

There was more silence. Steiner fiddled with an empty pipe.

"Why do you want to leave? You've had a pretty good career here."

"I'm fifty-nine, almost sixty. It's time. And my career here hasn't been all that good. You know why."

"What do you mean, it's time? Time for what? And I think you're career has been fine, despite that business with what's-his-name. Nobody really cared about that, except Jim Watt."

"It's time for me to go. Time for me to do something else."

"Like what?"

"I've bought a paper shop in Orillia. I love paper. Orillia is a nice town."

"A paper shop? Don't we live in a digital age? Who uses paper? How good a business can a small-town paper shop be?"

"I've done my due diligence. It's not a great business. It doesn't have to be. I've saved a fair bit, and my real estate agent says I can get a million dollars for my condo. I'll live carefully. There's not a lot to spend your money on in Orillia. And, by the way, there are still people who like to see words on paper rather than on screens."

Steiner fell silent again. He looked at her. Then he spoke, slowly.

"Julia, I'm putting your letter in a drawer. Come back in a week and tell me again if you still want to resign. Otherwise, I'll throw the letter away and forget we had this conversation."

"Thank you, Mark. It's kind of you to do that. I'll see you in a week."

• • •

Later, starting to get her apartment ready for sale, reducing the clutter, positioning the furniture, deciding where to put flowers, Julia thought about her conversation with Steiner. It was decent of him to give her a week to reconsider, but she had no doubts. She would leave Dibbet & Dibbet, where she had worked for over thirty years. She would leave her beautiful apartment, a light box in the sky. She would leave Toronto, and go and live in a small town, and sell paper in a shop on the main street. She would buy an arts-and-crafts cottage with a

garden. She would leave Toronto, and go and live alone in the cottage in Orillia. Where was the man she had loved, who had gone to Papua New Guinea, and then had gone further yet and disappeared?

Chapter Twenty-Six
Loose Ends

Vitanza had a bad headache. He had taken two Tylenol with breakfast, but they hadn't helped. His temples throbbed as he steered the Buick out of the apartment parking lot. It was that last scotch that had done it, his third or maybe it had been his fourth, the one he had drunk just before going to bed. And, of course, he hadn't slept well. He had woken up at three o'clock, desperate for a piss. He'd staggered to the bathroom in the dark, on the way stubbing his toe on a chair. When he got to the bathroom, he hadn't been able to pee properly. Oh god, he thought, maybe I've got prostate cancer. His prostate-specific antigen number had been high at his last annual check up. We better keep an eye on that, the doctor had said; if it goes up any more, you'll need a biopsy. A detective at the Division had died from prostate cancer last year and Vitanza was always reading about the disease in the newspaper. He hadn't slept properly after the visit to the bathroom in the middle of the night. He was worried he had cancer.

He arrived at 52 Division a few minutes before nine. It was a short drive from his apartment. People often

told him how lucky he was to live near where he worked. Many people with jobs in Toronto had a long commute. There were people at the Division who lived in Barrie and had a two-hour drive each way, and that was if the weather was good. Yes, he was lucky, people said. But sometimes Vitanza didn't think he was so lucky. Sometimes he envied people who spent hours on the road every day, alone, enclosed in their car, with nothing but the radio and their thoughts. Perhaps they were the lucky ones.

As he walked into the station, the secretary with red hair, Christine, the one on his list of attractive women, waved at him. "Detective Vitanza, Detective Singh is looking for you. He's in an interview room. He said you should go and see him as soon as you came in. Before Starbucks."

Vitanza felt even more depressed. His headache was pounding. He needed strong coffee. The Division coffee was no good. The carafes sat on the burners for hours. The coffee always had a burnt taste. That was why everyone went to the Starbucks across the street. It was the first thing everyone did in the morning. Mohan Singh was in interview room C, sitting across from a woman in her late thirties. She was wearing jeans and a sweatshirt that said "Athabaska U." She was crying. Vitanza knocked and went in.

"Ah," said Singh, in a curious formal manner, as if he were introducing someone at an embassy reception, "Mrs. Morton, this is Detective Sergeant Sebastian Vitanza. Sebastian, this is Diane Morton. She is the widow of the man killed by a car on Yonge Street two days ago. The driver of the car, you may remember, is a partner at the law firm of Dibbet & Dibbet."

"I remember," said Vitanza.

"And that is why Traffic sent Mrs. Morton over to see us, they know we are interested in Dibbet & Dibbet. Mrs. Morton, would you tell Detective Vitanza what you told me? I want him to hear it directly from you."

Diane Morton squeezed the handkerchief she was holding into a tight ball, as if she were exercising the muscles in her hand. Then she carefully unfolded the handkerchief, smoothed it out, and used it to wipe her eyes.

She said, "My husband knew the man who killed him."

Vitanza forgot about his headache. Suddenly he felt alert.

"How did he know him?" he asked.

"I don't know exactly. I found these letters in my husband's desk drawer." She picked up papers that were sitting on the table and handed them to Vitanza. She watched him as he put on his glasses and read them.

"Mrs. Morton, can you explain any of this?" said Vitanza, putting the letters back on the table, folding his glasses carefully and tucking them back in the breast pocket of his jacket. "About the Cayman Islands bank account, and the brokerage account in the United States?"

"Nothing. I don't understand any of it. My husband didn't have much money. We've had trouble paying the mortgage. He used to worry terribly about it. How could he have foreign accounts? And what does this man Seldom have to do with all this?"

"I don't know," said Vitanza. "But we'll find out. Thank you for coming to see us." He stood up.

Diane Morton clenched her handkerchief again. "Will you tell me if you discover anything?"

"We will," said Vitanza gently. "Of course we will. Now, let me take you to your car."

"Thank you," said Diane Morton, "but I came by bus."

• • •

"I'm in trouble," said Bill Seldom to himself. He was sitting in his office with the door shut. "I'm in trouble," he said again, staring in front of him, looking at nothing in particular, red in the face, sweat on his brow. It was four o'clock.

He had planned the murder of Mike Morton very carefully. It was brilliant, he thought, how he had run Morton down in his car, and then stopped and got out to answer questions from the police. No killer would do that, put himself at the scene of the crime, then deliver himself up to the police the way he had done. He had put himself above suspicion. It was a pity about Morton – they had been at high school together, in the same class– but Morton had been unreliable. It had been a mistake to bring him into the insider trading plan.

It had been easy to figure out how to kill him. Seldom had noticed on his visits to The Painted Duck that, after the lunch rush, Morton would often dash across Yonge Street to do banking business at an automatic teller machine. It was dangerous to cross Yonge Street the way Morton did, with all that traffic. An accident could easily happen. Seldom had figured that if he started waiting in his car down the street, between about three and four o'clock in the afternoon, the time when Seldom did his Yonge Street dash if he was going to do it, sooner or

later he'd have his chance. By good luck, the opportunity came the very first time he waited. He saw Morton lock the shop door and teeter on the sidewalk, looking for a break in the traffic. He took off in his Volvo and hit him square on. The whole thing had been surprisingly easy. His legs were a little wobbly when he got out of the car, his stomach was gurgling, but that was all, and he felt better pretty quickly.

But now, two days later, things looked a little different. He had started worrying that there might still be loose ends. Had Morton talked to his wife? He'd told him not to say anything to anyone, but Morton had been erratic and couldn't be trusted. Then there were those phone messages Morton had left. They could connect him to the dead man. He'd shredded the paper messages, but Mary, his assistant, might remember the calls. Morton's wife and Mary – they were the ones he needed to worry about now. What was he going to do about them?

The main point of his plan had been to get Jim Watt out of the way, and that had certainly happened, no doubt about it, although not as he had originally envisaged. With Watt gone, he had expected that the firm would turn to him for a steady hand in its moment of crisis. But there was no sign of this happening. Mind you, there was a reason for that, the firm was paralyzed, first by the shock of the managing partner's violent death, and then by the flight of clients that threatened its existence. The firm wasn't turning to anyone just at the moment. It was in a complete dither. And Seldom had begun to think that his partners were looking at him strangely when they passed him in the corridors. They were barely civil. No one had come into his office to discuss what was going

on, to ask his opinion or advice. He was being shunned. But why? Did they suspect something? Did they blame him for the loss of Canadian Unity Bank as a client? Why would they do that? That was Watt's fault.

"I'm in trouble," Seldom said again, to himself. His phone buzzed. He picked it up. "Yes?" he said. "Two policemen here to see you," Mary said, "Detectives Vitanza and Singh."

He felt panic. "Ask them to wait," he said, his voice trembling slightly. "There's something I have to finish. I'll be out in a minute or two." He tried to think quickly. Why were these policemen here? He reassured himself. Just further routine inquiries about Watt, that must be it. Or maybe it was about Mike Morton, although policemen from another department, Traffic Services, had interviewed him about the accident. He had to appear calm and cooperative. He took a couple of deep breaths. He'd read in a magazine that deep breathing had a calming effect. Maybe he should take Yoga lessons. The magazine article had said that Yoga was the road to inner peace. He must look into that as soon as things calmed down.

Seldom went to the door of his office, opened it and peered out. Vitanza and Singh were sitting on the chairs against the wall, just outside. They stood up when they saw him.

"Detectives, come in," said Seldom, trying to sound hearty. He waved them into his office. "Sit down, please." He pointed to the chairs facing his desk. He went and sat up straight on his office swivel chair on the other side of the desk. "How can I help you?"

"Thanks for seeing us," said Vitanza. "We wanted to follow up on the Yonge Street accident that killed Mr. Morton."

"That was a horrible thing. I'm so terribly sorry about it. I plan to go and see his widow as soon as I can. I haven't been sleeping well since it happened. He just stepped in front of my car. There was nothing I could do. It's terrible, terrible."

"Did you know Morton?"

"That's the strange thing, yes, I did know him, only slightly, but I did know him. He ran a sandwich shop that I went into occasionally, mostly on Saturdays when I was shopping in the neighbourhood. It's called The Painted Duck. And, as it turns out, we both realized this when we were chatting one day, we were in the same Grade Ten Class, Mrs. Newman's class, at North Toronto Collegiate, although we weren't particular friends there or anything. So I did know him, but not well, he was just a sort-of passing acquaintance. I was horrified when I heard that it was Mike who was killed." Seldom realized that he was talking too much.

"You didn't have any business dealings with him?" asked Vitanza.

"Business dealings? No, of course not. I'm a corporate lawyer. He ran a sandwich shop. What sort of business dealings would I have with him?" Seldom thought he was going to vomit.

This time is was Mohan Singh who spoke. "Mike Morton's widow found papers in his desk that suggest you had a business relationship with her husband."

"Papers? What kind of papers?"

"A letter that said Morton had opened a chequing account at a bank in Grand Cayman and that you held power of attorney over the account. Another letter confirming that Morton had opened a brokerage account in Atlanta, Georgia and saying that correspondence concerning the account was to be sent to you." It was over, thought Seldom. If the police went down this road, they would find out everything. He was ruined. He would go to prison forever. That fool Morton.

"That's most peculiar. I just don't understand it." Seldom's voice quavered. "It must have been something that Morton was trying to set up. Maybe he was going to try and get me involved in some project with him. Of course, I wouldn't have done that. He did mention once or twice that he had money troubles and I might have said, let me know if I can help, you know, old school friends and all that. Maybe the papers had something to do with that." The inside of Seldom's right leg felt warm and clammy. He wondered if he was pissing himself.

"Would it be possible for someone to have power of attorney over a bank account without knowing about it?" asked Singh.

"No, no, not in this country, but maybe it's different in the Cayman Islands, I don't know. I don't know anything about the law there. I guess it's possible. After all, it looks like it happened. Apparently I was given a power of attorney without anyone asking me or telling me. That's what seems to have happened. I've never been to the Cayman Islands. Except once, but that was a vacation, years ago. Scuba diving." I'm babbling, thought Seldom.

"The Atlanta letter says correspondence about the brokerage account is to be sent to you. Have you received any correspondence from them?"

"No, I don't think so. I get a lot of mail. My assistant throws out the junk. I never see it. If anything came from Atlanta, she would probably think it was junk–some kind of promotional thing–and toss it. I don't have any clients who do business in Atlanta."

"Mr. Seldom," said Vitanza, "doesn't it seem a remarkable coincidence that the man you killed with your car had business papers with your name on them in his desk?"

"Yes, yes, for sure, it's strange, bizarre. But, as they say, coincidences do happen."

"We certainly see a lot of coincidences in police work," said Vitanza. "Do you think Mike Morton knew Jim Watt?"

"Do I think Mike Morton knew Jim Watt?"

"Yes, do you think he did?"

"I've no idea. I wouldn't think so. How would he? Maybe Jim used to go into The Painted Duck. Come to think of it, I've seen him there. I don't understand why you would ask that question. What's Jim Watt got to do with Mike Morton?"

"This law firm is a common denominator in two recent violent deaths. But, probably just another coincidence."

"I don't know what to say. How can there have been a connection between Morton and Watt? The only possible connection would be sandwiches." They've figured it out, thought Seldom. They've figured it out. It's over.

"It does seem unlikely," said Vitanza. "It was just a thought. Anyway, we'll look into these Cayman and

Atlanta accounts. Morton probably had some scheme to try and put his finances in shape, and thought that using the Dibbets name would help. We'll let you know what we find out."

"I'd be most interested to know. Thank you so much."

• • •

Seldom left shortly after Vitanza and Singh. "I'm going home to work on some documents," he told his assistant as he walked out, carrying the large briefcase he took with him everywhere. Sometimes the briefcase was empty except for a banana and the National Post newspaper.

When he got to his apartment, he sat for a while in the chair by the south-facing windows. He could see the Canadian Unity Bank building about two miles away. There were construction cranes beginning to interfere with the view. Large condominiums were popping up all over the place. In a year or two, you wouldn't be able to see his office from his apartment. Crazy, he thought: who's going to live in all those condos? He was upset that his view would be spoilt.

Seldom got up and went to the hall closet. He reached onto the top shelf, behind his hats, and took out something wrapped in a bright orange scarf. His mother had given him that scarf. He never wore it. He sat in his chair again, unwound the orange scarf and threw it on the floor. He held an iPad in his hands. He looked at it carefully, as if it were a museum exhibit. One edge was discoloured where he'd scoured it with a copper pad. What did this thing weigh? Not much more than a pound. Made of aluminum, he thought. Who would have believed it could be used as a weapon? It had cleaved Watt's head like a knife through butter.

Chapter Twenty-Seven
Contender

He slept very little. In the darkest part of the night, he was half-sleeping, half-awake, rehashing events of the last few days in a dream-like way, reviewing his failed plan to replace Jim Watt and become the leader on big files rather than always the second-in-command, reliving his murder of Watt in anger and fear after being confronted by Watt with his suspicions about insider trading, seeing in phantasmagorical Technicolor the body of Mike Morton flying past the windshield of his Volvo, hearing the crunch as the body hit the pavement behind his car. He had no regrets. It hadn't worked out, but it could have. Before going to bed, he'd turned on the television, the classic movie channel. It was playing "On the Waterfront." He heard Marlon Brando say his famous line: "I coulda been a contender, I could've been somebody..." He could have been a contender too, Seldom thought, just like Terry Malloy, the character in the movie. He could have been somebody. The line went through his head over and over again, as he tossed and turned, as night dragged into morning. He could have been a contender.

He got up about seven o'clock. No point in staying in bed: he couldn't sleep, and, anyway, he had things to do. He had a stale muffin and some coffee and got dressed. He didn't bother to shave or brush his teeth. He went on the Internet to find out what time the Canadian Tire store near him opened: eight o'clock. He searched for where he could buy handcuffs: an army surplus store downtown, not far from his apartment, which also opened at eight. He went down to the underground parking garage and got into his car, still dented and battered from hitting Mike Morton, only released from the police pound yesterday afternoon, and drove to the Canadian Tire, arriving just as the staff unlocked the doors. He went to the automotive section and bought ten twenty-litre heavy-duty plastic gas containers. A young male clerk helped him take them out to his car. He put five of the gas cans in the trunk, and the other five in the back seat. He drove to the army surplus store and bought a pair of Smith and Wesson stainless steel handcuffs, the most expensive the store had. He went to the Esso station near his apartment and filled up the gas containers with premium gasoline, paying at the pump with his Esso credit card, putting in his Aeroplan card to get travel points.

An attendant looked at him curiously. "You should be careful with those," he said, pointing at the containers. "That's a lot of gasoline. It's dangerous carrying gasoline around like that. It's against the law."

"For the tractor at the farm," Seldom told him.

"Tractors don't need premium," said the attendant, and went into the cashier's office.

Seldom put the containers full of gasoline in the Volvo's passenger compartment, four in the front, and six

in the back. He drove to the Canadian Unity Bank building – it only took about fifteen minutes to get there – and into the underground parking lot, to the third and lowest level. The third level was never more than half-full. They had overbuilt the garage to begin with, or maybe the operator charged too much to park there and people used the municipal parking lot across the street instead. He drove to the far end of the floor, backed his car into an empty spot at the end of a lane that crossed the floor to the other side, and turned off the engine.

He sat motionless, at the steering wheel. He tried to empty his head. He took some deep breaths. Someone had told him about mindfulness and meditation. Maybe it had been his assistant at Dibbets, Mary Johnston, who was always into something new. Before mindfulness, it had been The Secret. "Be in the moment," Mary had told him once, when he was obviously stressed. Sitting behind the steering wheel, he tried to be in the moment. He sat quietly for a while, breathing deeply, trying to think of nothing at all. Then he picked up the handcuffs, which were sitting on the passenger seat. He put one of the cuffs on his left hand and attached the other to the steering wheel. He made sure they clicked shut. He picked up the key to the handcuffs with his right hand and threw it in the back of the car. He started the engine. He took another deep breath, a very deep breath, and pushed the accelerator to the floor. The Volvo was going almost forty-five miles an hour when it hit the wall at the other end of the lane. There was an explosion and the car burst into flames. He struggled to get free, but was held by the cuffs.

• • •

Upstairs in her office, thirty-six stories above the burning car, Piper Fantouche had heard a slight thud. She had paid no attention, and continued to pick listlessly at papers on her desk. Julia Anderson, cleaning out her office, and Mark Steiner, sitting in the chair behind his desk, sucking on an empty pipe and looking at Self-Portrait #7, had heard the same thud, but neither had thought anything of it. A few minutes later, loud sirens approached the building from all directions. Piper looked out of her window and saw fire trucks and police cars below. Julia Anderson looked out of her window and noticed smoke in the street; it seemed to be coming out of the parking garage entrance. Mark Steiner looked out of his window and saw the police closing the street with barricades, and firemen putting on breathing apparatus. There was the beginning of a buzz in the corridors of Dibbet & Dibbet. Something had happened.

• • •

Hours later a few facts were known, dribbled out by the police, teased out by the press, reported by the radio and television. Someone had burned to death in the underground parking garage. It seemed a suicide, although the police would not confirm that; they were still investigating. A car, perhaps laden with gasoline–what appeared to be melted plastic gas containers had been found in the wreckage–had been driven into the wall; the driver was handcuffed to the steering wheel; there was no evidence that anyone else was involved; the car was registered to a William J. Seldom; the presumption was that he was the driver, although formal identification from dental records would take several days; no one, other than the dead driver, had been hurt.

Bill Seldom has killed himself, that was the word passed around in the corridors and offices of Dibbets. Almost everyone went home when they heard the news, too shocked even to gather and gossip. Julia Anderson, back in her apartment, knew that she would never go back inside the Canadian Unity Bank Building. The few personal possessions still in her office could stay there. Piper Fantouche decided to leave Bay Street soon and forever. Only Mark Steiner took events in his stride. He was back in his office, after talking to the police. He appeared calm. He sat quietly behind his desk. He looked at the Income Tax Act sitting on the desk, a large book bound in red, and found it reassuring. He picked up an empty pipe. He had the sense that things had come full circle. In a while, Dibbets would again be what Dibbets had once been. He was sure of it.

Chapter Twenty-Eight
Billy Bishop

"Can I take you to dinner?"

Julia Anderson was packing up a few last things – she was down to cutlery and underwear–when Sebastian Vitanza telephoned.

She'd sold the penthouse easily. These days everyone wanted to live in downtown Toronto. She'd bought a cottage on Lake Couchiching, not far from Orillia. She already called it "my lake house." Julia was moving the middle of next week. Meanwhile, she was staying in the Hilton Garden Inn on Peter Street.

"Are you still there?" asked Vitanza. He was nervous. Julia hadn't answered his question. "Dinner sometime?" went on Vitanza, speaking quickly, trying to fill dead air. "Whenever you're free. Maybe next week…" Saul Abramowitz had encouraged him to ask Julia out. "I think you're ready," Saul had said.

When she had answered the telephone, and he had announced, in a rather formal tone, "It's Sebastian Vitanza," she'd assumed he was calling on police business. What now, she had wondered; isn't it over? She'd thought – the

newspapers had said – the cases were closed. The police were satisfied. Bill Seldom had murdered Jim Watt and Mike Morton and had then committed suicide. They'd found the Watt murder weapon, an iPad, in Seldom's apartment. They'd discovered that Seldom was involved in an illegal insider-trading scheme with Morton, that Watt had figured it out and confronted Seldom, that Seldom feared Morton's indiscretion. Seldom's answer to everything had been death, including, finally, his own.

So why was Vitanza calling? "Detective, I've told you everything I know," she said.

"This is a personal call," he replied.

It was then he asked, "Can I take you to dinner?" and added "Please call me Sebastian."

"Take me to dinner?" she said. "Last time we talked you were a policeman investigating a murder and I was a suspect or a person of interest. Now you're asking me out to dinner. That's a bit of a switch."

"There's no conflict, Julia. The cases are over. And you were never a suspect."

"Well, Detective Vitanza, Sebastian, where shall we go for dinner?

"There's a new Sicilian restaurant in Parkdale. We could give it a try."

"Sebastian, before we go any further, you should know I'm leaving Toronto. I'm moving to Orillia. I've quit Dibbets, and I've bought a paper store in Orillia. On the main street."

"That's bad news," said Vitanza, after a pause. "For me, anyway. How far is Orillia from Toronto?"

"Two hours on the highway. But, I'm not leaving until the middle of next week, so if you like we could have dinner on Monday or Tuesday."

"Monday," said Vitanza. "I'll pick you up at seven."

"At the Hilton Garden Inn on Peter Street," said Julia. "I've moved out of my apartment."

"I know that hotel. The one with a huge red sign. By the way, if you ask me, you're well out of Dibbets. Although it's a pity about Orillia."

• • •

At the Milestones dinner, Mohan had told Piper about his unhappy childhood, but he hadn't been tedious or self-pitying about it. When he had finished, she changed the subject.

"Why do you wear a turban?"

"A Sikh's hair must be kept intact," he said. "The hair is sacred, that is what they say. But for me it is about identity, not religion."

"Do you ever take it off?"

"Not often."

"When?"

"I take it off when I go to bed. "

"When you go to bed?"

"Yes."

"How long is your hair?"

"Long."

"Does it cover the pillow?"

Mohan wanted to change the subject. "It's my turn to ask you a personal question," he said.

"That's fair."

"Something that I've wondered about since we first met."

"Okay."

"What sort of a name is Piper Fantouche?"

"Everyone asks that."

"I'm sorry."

"It's a simple story. My father was crazy about airplanes when I was born. There is a famous manufacturer of small airplanes called Piper."

"And Fantouche?"

"When he came to Canada from Latvia, my dad thought he needed a Canadian surname and somehow came up with Fantouche. I've no idea where he got it."

"Do you see your father a lot?" Mohan asked.

"As much as I can. I love him. He is a good man."

"Is he happy?"

"Yes, he is. My mother died a long time ago, and he has been alone ever since. He has an ordinary job and not much money. But he is full of enthusiasm and that makes him happy."

"Enthusiasm for what?"

"Lots of things. He's the concierge in an apartment building. He loves the building and everyone in it. He drives an old Pontiac. He loves that car. He lives in a one-bedroom apartment in Little Italy. He loves his apartment."

"And he loves you."

"Yes," said Piper.

Afterwards Mohan offered to drive her home, but she said no. She did agree to see him on the weekend. I know a nice Indian restaurant, he said. And perhaps they would see each other at the gym before that.

Perhaps, said Piper.

• • •

Sitting in her office, looking out of the window, Piper was thinking about Mohan when the phone rang.

"Piper Fantouche, it's Sam Capponi. Have you survived all that shit over there at Dibbets?"

"I've survived. You haven't sent me a bill."

"I'm not going to. And there's something else you owe me for. Have you checked your mail?"

There was a stack of unopened letters on the corner of Piper's desk. She'd ignored it for days.

"Not recently."

"You should. You might find something interesting. I've got to go. The Hell's Angels have just walked in the door."

Piper flipped through the pile of envelopes. The return address on one was "Supreme Court of Canada, Ottawa." She opened it. It was a letter from the Chief Justice. It invited her to apply for the job of Executive Legal Officer to the Court. The position had unexpectedly become vacant and the Chief wanted to fill it quickly. Piper was asked to send her résumé by email. There was a handwritten note at the bottom of the typed letter. "You may wonder why I am writing to you out of the blue. We need to fill this position as soon as possible, and last week I was talking to my friend Sam Capponi and he told me about you and said you might be interested. It sounded like a good fit. I trust Sam's judgment."

Piper looked out of the window. Her office faced south. She could see Billy Bishop Airport on the Toronto Islands. If you used Billy Bishop, Ottawa and Toronto

were only an hour apart. If she moved to Ottawa, she could easily see Mohan – if that seemed like a good idea.

On a sudden impulse, she phoned Sylvie Prud'Homme. She wanted a tattoo, a discreet one, perhaps a tattoo of a single-engine aeroplane, somewhere on her body that was normally covered by clothing. Sylvie would know the best place to get a tattoo like that.

ACKNOWLEDGMENTS

Several people read drafts of Bay Street and gave me very useful comments and criticisms. You know who you are. Thank you. I am grateful to Avrum Fenson for excellent cover photography, and Brian Halley for fine cover design. Most of all, thanks to Gabrielle Domingues who shepherded the book from the beginning to the end with her usual extreme competence.